ANDALON PARADOX

ANDALON ORIGINS – BOOK TWO

T. B. PHILLIPS

ANDALON
PRESS

Andalon Paradox
Andalon Origins, Book Two

Published by Andalon Press
Copyright © 2023 by T.B. Phillips

Cover design by Lynnette Bonner of Indie Cover Design, images ©
  AdobeStock# 128268136
  AdobeStock# 567365701
  AdobeStock# 573520916
Book interior design by Stewart Design, https://StewartDesign.studio

ISBN 979-8-9872191-3-3

This is a work of fiction. Names, characters, places, and incidents are a product of the author's imagination. Locales and public names are sometimes used for atmospheric purposes. Any resemblance to actual people, living or dead, or to businesses, companies, events, institutions, or locales is completely coincidental.

Books by T. B. Phillips

Chilling Tales
Ferryman (October 2022)

Corrupted Realms
Wailing Tempest (April 2021)
Howling Shadow (September 2021)

Andalon Saga

Andalon Origins
Andalon Project (May 2022)
Andalon Paradox (April 2023)
Andalon Prophecies (expected Fall 2023)

Dreamers of Andalon
Andalon Awakens (June 2019)
Andalon Arises (July 2020)
Andalon Attacks (December 2020)

Children of Andalon
Andalon Legacy (September 2022)

Signed copies can be purchased by visiting:
andalonstudios.com

"One need not think to be considered alive,
only to feel and, in regard to this government, to obey.
That's the paradox Astia faces, a coexistence with those whose very existence
threatens our own."

—Chancellor Michael Esterling

Address to the Astian Council in the year 20 A.D. (After Destruction)

PART I
THE PARADOX

PROLOGUE

Ludlow Falls, Ohio
Five Hours Before Destruction

Rusty defiantly helped with dinner, going against his wife's strict orders to stay out of the kitchen. That was her rule whenever she was away from home, and he tried his best to follow her orders. Unfortunately, boredom and hunger had crept in and wreaked havoc upon his better judgement.

The main course was nearly ready, a slow-cooked pot roast bubbling with mushrooms and carrots. Susan had placed it in the warmer earlier that morning. Rusty had tried to behave, broken by the torturous smells that filled the house all day. They tempted him several times to lift the lid and steal a taste. He needed to do something to pass the time until she returned home and had barely placed a small pot of instant mashed potatoes on the stove when the front door opened and she arrived, catching him mid-act of setting the table.

"What's this?" Susan asked, her forehead wrinkled with surprise. By the slow and deliberate way she walked, it was obvious her day had been harder than it should have been. At their ages, each day proved more tiresome than the last.

"I wanted to surprise you," he said with the half of his face that could still grin. The left side, a product of Bell's palsy leftover by a stroke more than a year before, drooped. His left arm curled into his body, muscles tight while clutching silverware and napkins to his chest. The concern in his wife's eyes dampened his helpful mood, and Rusty suddenly felt silly standing there acting like anything but a crippled old man.

Susan took the items and finished laying them out. "You shouldn't be cooking and could've burned the house down," she said, not angrily, but with voice filled with exhaustion. Both husband and wife turned

1

eyes toward the kitchen. The dark soot above the range had never washed away from his last attempt to surprise her with a meal. "You promised you wouldn't again, unless I'm home," she added gently.

"It was only instant potatoes," Rusty argued, slumping into his chair, defeated. "I'm trying to keep relevant. Sitting around all day is killing me slowly, and I feel bad when you spend all day at the clinic while I'm home doing nothing."

Susan finished setting the table, still wearing scrubs and a nametag reading, *Montgomery County ASPCA*. "You *are* relevant, just a retired form of it now," she insisted.

"How many surgeries today?" he asked, changing the subject.

"An entire day's full. I swear we're seeing more and more designer dogs. Doctor Paul worked on a Shih Tzu crossed with pit bull today. The younger folk kept calling it a *bullshit*."

Rusty chuckled at the name. "At least the responsible owners are getting them fixed. Not like in the old days." Before the stroke it had been *him* spaying and neutering the animals, but that was when both hands worked with surgical precision.

The table began to shake, slowly at first but intensifying with each rumble. Rusty and Susan tried to hold it down, but the bouncing forced them both to stand and take a step back. A sudden crash of glass startled them both as the crock pot lid leapt from the counter. Soon, pictures fell from the walls and Susan's collection of souvenir spoons fell one by one to the floor. *Yellowstone National Park* skidded to a halt at their feet. That had been a memorable vacation.

"What was that?" Susan demanded after the earth had finished its tantrum.

"Earthquake," Rusty answered immediately, "but the first I've ever felt in Ohio!"

It took them several minutes to put the kitchen back in order, deciding the sweeping of glass could wait until after their dinner. The pot roast did, after all, smell delicious.

Several hours later, a vintage episode of *Friends* flickered across their television, that one with the holiday armadillo. It was Rusty's favorite, second only to the holiday when Monica put the turkey on her head. Chandler had just barged in dressed as Santa Claus, stealing the show from Ross, when the signal snapped off into darkness.

Rusty tried the remote several times without success. "What is *with* tonight?" he demanded. The lamp beside him also refused to click on.

"Honey?" Susan called from the bedroom. "Are you okay?"

The entire house had plunged into darkness. Rusty looked around, even the time on the microwave refused to flash. "Just a power outage!" He pulled a flashlight from the drawer while peering out the sliding glass door into the valley below.

They had a great view from their retirement home, perched above the Stillwater River and backed against the Brukner Nature Center. Though it often felt like too much upkeep for the pair after his stroke, Rusty always felt energized after looking out at this view. But this time he trembled. Off in the distance, the western horizon brightly flashed then sent a shimmering glow eastward across the sky. The pulse reflected eerily off the clouds above.

"What is it?" Susan asked, joining her husband. She had also seen the flash of lights.

"I don't know, but it seemed far, much too far away to affect us." He frowned, slapping the flashlight against his leg before giving it a shake. It refused to turn on. "These batteries were new," he muttered, unable to take his eyes off the horizon.

The moonlight played tricks on his eyes, as if the entire valley now crawled toward their hillside. Another flash off to the southwest revealed a massive body of water filling it in. The last time the area had flooded was after several days of rain and, even then, the water had gathered gradually. This reminded him more of that time when he was in the service and laid over in Guam during a tsunami warning. That rush of water had crawled like this did now, a massive wall devouring everything in its path. It crashed violently against his barn.

Panicked barking and terrified whimpering sent Susan racing out the door, chasing after three large shapes paddling for their lives.

"Stop!" Rusty cried after his wife, but the current swept three dogs into the unexpected lake. These were Bear, Cliffa, and Maggie Mae, the neighbor's Great Pyrenees. *She'll drown herself to save them,* he realized, hurrying outside to help.

Susan had already waded out, pushing and pulling the animals against the current. Had she not reached them, they would surely have gone under. She caught Cliffa just as she dipped, grabbing the huge dog by its collar and heaving it toward Rusty waiting in the shallows. The thankless animal bowled him over in the process. All three had made it to shore, but now Susan had to rescue her husband.

He felt the undertow as it dragged a useless old man toward deeper water. Unable to use his left hand, his right dug into the mud with desperate fingers. He coughed and sputtered as he scrambled, finally feeling Susan grab ahold of his shirt and belt. She righted him just as water rushed into Rusty's nose. Both relieved to be alive, the couple staggered onto the shoreline and fell into each other's arms.

"That was stupid, risking your neck," he whispered to his wife, "but I understand why you did."

Neither of them could bear to witness such innocent loss of life as an animal. Humans, they both knew, were of a differently deserving fate.

Shaken but mostly unharmed, the older pair laughed and giggled at their ordeal, each now standing and embracing the love of their lives.

Several yards away, Bear growled.

It was out of character for the large animal, usually calm and gentle unless running off a fox from the valley. The deep rumble of his anger now drew Rusty's attention. The body of a man lay face down and still, unmoving at the dog's feet. The others whined, sniffed, and nudged it while their alpha gave warning.

"Turn him onto his back!" Rusty yelled to his wife, shooing away the dogs.

"I think he's alive!" a panicked Susan exclaimed.

"Barely," Rusty muttered, looking the poor man over. He was drenched from head to toe, washed ashore from some unknown place. *God knows how far away,* he thought.

The man's clothing was simple, only work boots, blue jeans, and a union shirt emblazoned with the words, *Unfair Wages Grind my Gears*. What worried Rusty most were the two bullet holes in his shoulder and upper chest. They were serious but not life threatening, but he also had no idea to know how much blood this man had already lost. Luckily for him the water was ice cold and would have slowed his heart rate.

"Let's get him inside," the retired surgical vet told his wife, and they went to work dragging him up the hillside.

Far away, on every horizon, several more lights lit the night sky. *Explosions*, Rusty could tell, and the worst kind of them. The mushroom clouds billowing high toward the stars sent a surge of fear unlike any he'd ever experienced. This night was not a normal one, and he may never finish that episode of *Friends*.

He wished to God he had never had that stupid stroke.

Ludlow Falls, Ohio
Six Months After Destruction

1960s music drifted through the night, breaking the silence and caus-ing Clint Fletcher to sway back and forth while greedily loading his bag with valuables.

Welcome to my world, the music sauntered, *won't you come on in?*

It was past time to go and he could feel the moss threatening to sprout beneath his feet if he stayed. The geezers, Rusty and Susan, had been good to him—saved his life, actually, with their surgical expertise.

Thank God they only removed the bullets instead of neutering me like their other patients.

He laughed at the thought. He already had one brat, what would he ever want with another?

The rhythm of the music swayed, one of Clint's favorites. This partic-ular rendition was by Dean Martin, who sang while the blue hairs danced. Their giggling sounded like a pair of lovebirds without any care, no matter to them the world had ended six months before. He glanced down the hall, watching them dance cheek to cheek, giddily circling the living room. It was good to see the pair up and about after all this time.

Into his satchel he shoved the old bat's jewelry, the cripple's cash, and everything else he found in their safe. It had taken him forever to learn the combination, a long wait that had frustrated his impatient urge to leave much earlier. But patience proved worthwhile as he pulled out a gun, a small Ruger 9mm and a box of ammunition totaling one hundred rounds. More of those could be easily found along the way. He tucked the pistol in his belt and tossed the ammo atop the cans of food, jugs of water, and everything else he'd found useful. In all there wasn't much. The bulk of the geezers' rations had barely lasted this far.

With the song still crooning in his head, Clint danced from the bedroom with an invisible partner. As he spun her around, he realized she was Cathy, his ex-wife, the reason for the bullet-sized scars in his chest and shoulder. He lovingly grasped her tightly by the throat and squeezed while phantom eyes stared up large and wanton. She was a whore, one who stripped off her clothing for other men, and had a habit of running away with his son. Her favorite cruelness had been keeping little Josh from his father.

Clint tossed the apparition angrily aside then danced into the hall, cackling loudly as he entered the living room.

He cut off that laughter as the music abruptly stopped, finding himself standing in a room without electricity. Dark and full of ghosts it ushered in a brief moment of reality. In their overstuffed recliners rested the geezers with skin long ago greyed from death. Gaunt faces stared with eyes wide open, laying as they had for several months. Clint broke the silence by pointing and laughing wildly at their expressions, each full of surprise by the taking of their life.

Killing them had proven the perfect way to deal with stress, something he had looked forward to since awakening in their spare bedroom six months before. After putting up with their mothball-smelling oldness for several weeks, he had finally stumbled upon the chance to put them out of his misery. Finding them both asleep, he had stepped between their rockers and choked them slowly, one throat in each hand. The weak creatures were too pathetic to fight back.

Post-mortem bruises now covered their skin, delightfully placed on their bodies any time Clint had a fit of rage or patch of cabin fever during his frustrated months of sitting still. There had been a lot of those lately. Suddenly tired of Susan's condemning stare, he slapped the old bat across the head, flinging a necrotic ear across the room.

The thrill of his rage restarted the music and Dean Martin once more sang into his mind, sending Clint into a delighted pirouette down the hallway. As he danced out the front door and into the night, he heard the crooner say, *Welcome to* my *world!*

CHAPTER ONE

The Shelter, Evansville, Indiana
Six Months After Destruction

Society had ended, but the world trudged ever onward, ignoring the tribulations of those clinging to life upon its back. Six months earlier apocalyptic events shook the planet, covering most of it with a thick layer of ashy snow. Though falling slower, it still came relentlessly. First it had dropped as radioactive fallout but then transitioned to nuclear winter, rendering the ground useless to humans. Now it fell less as ash and mostly snow, a good sign despite this was June. All across the world, packed ice remained on the ground and survivors starved.

Only the most prepared or better organized had survived and, among these, fate favored Max Rankin. The soldier stood in his office, staring out over the city ignoring the grey clouds hovering overhead. They completely filtered out the sun. According to the notes he had found in this room, the sky would eventually return to normal, possibly within the year, but showed no signs of clearing any time soon.

Max trusted these notes, left behind by a man once known as the Colonel. He had long planned for this disaster and mostly had it right. Or, he at least had it right, *so far*. What he hadn't planned for was the city itself and the problems his followers would face while defending it.

Their home, called simply the Shelter, was a perfectly placed colosseum, structurally sound and packed full of long-term storage and survival amenities. But it was also surrounded by narrow streets and high windows that served as potential sniper nests and ambush points. Those other buildings closed in around Max, adding to the stifling anxiety that came with leadership.

He yearned to get away, to return to his life driving his rig and coming home to his wife, Betty, and their son, Tom. But that life he enjoyed after returning from war had ended with society, forcing him back into the role of Marine.

Max was not an ambitious man. He never wanted leadership of the Regiment but could not allow the militia to fracture. It would have, had he not stepped into the position. Someone had murdered the Colonel and all his officers.

Chaos followed. Opportunists had grabbed resources and deserted the Regiment. The panicked had tried to leave as well, but cooler heads prevailed and talked them into trusting Max Rankin and Shayde Walters to solve their problems. They, unlike the Colonel's officers who had only played at being soldiers, had survived countless hours of combat experience.

If anyone in Evansville knew how to survive, it was this pair of Marines.

Now, Max faced too many problems to count. From prolonged harassment by the gangs in the west to the threat of attack by a militia from the south, he had much more to worry about than solving the murder of the Colonel and his officers. But that mystery would not let go of his mind. Poison had claimed thirty people in their sleep, and he could not rest without figuring out how and by whom.

I have other problems too, he realized. The foremost being his son, Tom. A great chasm stood between him and the boy, black men with different views of the white-dominated world around them. While Max had driven his rig, enjoying the comforts of a quiet cab, Betty had struggled with the teen's drug use and choice of friends. That distance had grown wider since the bombs fell, and now Tom fought alongside those gangs plaguing Max's supply lines.

You're a sellout and Mom's dead because you weren't home, the teen had said when they had finally met up. The words hurt more than the rifle muzzle pressed against his father's forehead. *You were never there for us, always choosing the road!*

I'm not a sellout, Son. You're fighting the wrong war, was his reply, hoping to reason with the boy.

Mom's dead, the words echoed, and Max fought against tears over his wife. *Betty...* Max mourned her memory once more.

He also mourned the loss of his boy, alive but ideologically different from his father. While Max hoped for peace and loving cooperation between mankind, Tom chose a more modern, aggressively militant approach, viewing society simply as black versus white.

"Get out of your head, Devil Dog," Shayde Walter's voice called from the doorway. The tall man's hair had grown out, and he no longer resembled the Marine he once was.

Max turned with a sigh, so lost in his thoughts he never heard the door open. "We're in *over* our heads, you know."

"Yeah," his partner replied, "I do." He moved beside him to look out the window. "What're you doing? Trying to lure a sniper out of hiding? There's better ways than to risk your own life, General."

"Don't call me that. You know damned well I'm only a Gunnery Sergeant."

Shayde shrugged. "What do we call you, then, now that you're in charge? We can't call you Gunny, you need some sort of officer title. Sergeants ain't gonna be enough for these people, but especially not to our enemies. You need mystique. Have to be a king or even godlike to them."

"I'm neither king nor god, but especially not an officer," Max grumbled. "What are we really playing at, Shayde? Restarting the United States of Nothing?"

"We're staying alive. Now, with that in mind, can you please move away from the window?"

Max sighed. Those other windows overlooking his were a potential problem, the one he had been pondering before thoughts of Tom and Betty pulled him under. He pointed. "We need to collapse all those surrounding buildings and make a kill zone around the Shelter. I feel claustrophobic and, though the gangs are a nuisance, it'll be worse if and when the Nature Boys arrive."

The gangs were exactly that—an organized assortment of street gangs fighting their own war for resources. Their looting had driven out most of the city's survivors, scattering law-abiding families in all directions or forcing them to seek safety inside the Shelter. Early on, they had competed with the Regiment for food and medicine, neither side taking each other on directly unless looting the same home or business. That had changed when the hard drugs and opioids disappeared and the gangs realized they also had to eat and treat infections.

Now they were the biggest problem to the Regiment on this side of the Ohio River, attacking supply lines between the Shelter and the airport sixteen miles north. Max was responsible for a second population gathering there as well. But the gangs weren't the only threat. Another group known only as the Nature Boys were a problem further south. All the scouts knew about this new threat was they roamed northward, and Max hoped they would take their time getting to Evansville.

Time enough to recon and learn more, he mused.

"Speaking of the gangs, have you heard from *him* again?" Shayde meant Tom, Max's son.

"No. Not since the day we found the airport." *And the dead officers. Don't forget* that *happened as well. Not everything is about* you, *Max!* he reminded himself. "He left a message for me, though." Max again pointed. Across the parking lot a single word had been painted on the tire shop. *Sellout.*

Shayde sucked air through his teeth. "Yikes. Kids will be kids, won't they? Want me to scrub it off?"

"No, leave it. He and I will eventually meet up again, and hopefully he'll listen. If he thinks I sold out my race for another, he's wrong. I fight for everyone, even him. But if he means I sold out him and his mom, then he's right. I was an absent father, even when I was present. My mind never left Fallujah."

"A lot of us didn't."

"I'm still there right now, except with snow instead of sand blanketing the same but different crumbling buildings. That's why I became a trucker after the war. I didn't have to deal directly with people and could free my mind with solitude. If it weren't for that escape, I'd have been as unemployable as the VA claimed."

"Tell *him* exactly that. Tell your son what you went through over there."

"He won't understand even if he listens. He hasn't seen real combat yet. Just this harassing hit and run nonsense."

"He will soon. Chad Pescari said the Nature Boys' scouts have been crossing the river, creeping around the perimeter of the city, and testing both our flanks."

Pescari had also reported the Nature Boys, unlike the gangs, appeared to be a fully trained militia. The worst kind in Max's mind. Racist to the core, they sought to use this new era as a chance to purge the land of everyone darker than them. So far, they had not clashed with the Regiment, but that would eventually change as food ran out. There were even rumors they had been taking slaves as far south as Tennessee.

"Have you thought about how we're going to deal with that threat?" Shayde asked his friend and commander.

"Why do *I* have to come up with all the answers?"

"It's your job, General."

"Stop calling me that."

"Your Highness, then?"

Max was about to tell his friend to shove off when a woman knocked and entered. Both men looked up, moving away from the window.

Cathy Fletcher was a young mother in her early twenties. Athletic, she could have been a dancer or a gymnast before the bombs. Rumors circulated among the men, most of these suggesting she had been the former. Max didn't care either way. A skilled nurse, she had taken over the hospital duties after the real doctor died alongside the other officers. Her primary task was to quarantine, screen, and treat newcomers to the Shelter.

"What is it, Cathy?"

"Radiation sickness," she replied, matter-of-factly. "It's getting worse with each batch we bring in. We're getting to a point we'll have to start turning refugees away soon. They'll be too sick to be anything but a burden."

Max opened his mouth to speak but was interrupted by Shayde. "You should turn them *all* away, in my opinion. What if the Nature Boys are trying to infiltrate our group? Even if they don't, how will we feed all these people? We're nearly busting at the seams and have that lot in the airport to deal with too."

That was it. The point where Max and Shayde disagreed over how to run the Shelter. Max had been the one to open its doors to all—distributed flyers by sending scouts in every direction. In these he gave directions to Evansville and a list of precautions and supplies to bring. He urged all patriots to unify in one place, hopeful they could rebuild what was left of the United States. It was the core belief he had shared with the Colonel.

"If our nation is to survive, Shayde, we need to bring them now, before the famine really hits hard. We've got enough food stores to feed everyone we have and more for a year."

"And after it runs out? If this nuclear winter grips us longer?"

"The Colonel planned for that too." Max pulled out a sketch of make-shift greenhouses, complete with raised beds. "Everything in this design can be found in hardware or home and garden stores. All we have to do is build enclosures and fill the beds with compost and bagged dirt. The plastic bags contain polyethylene and would have shielded the dirt within from radiation. Using his plans, we can get a jumpstart on farming until the ground fully thaws and recovers."

Cathy leaned in, examined the design, then nodded dismissively. "That's great, but I have *immediate* problems. I need a bigger hospital than the stage downstairs. It's too crowded."

Max nodded, turning his attention once more out the window. "How do we do it?" he asked. "How do we secure those buildings, clear a safety perimeter by knocking most of them down, build our farms, *and* provide for a hospital and housing? We've got no heavy machinery, little to no explosives, and come under constant harassment while in the open. How the hell do we do it all?"

Neither member of his counsel replied. Those were questions to which no one had answers. Cathy, having so much work to do after saying her piece, turned to leave.

"Wait," Max commanded, and she paused. "I need to ask you something."

She turned and shrugged. "Ask away."

"I haven't come any closer to finding who was responsible for the deaths of the Colonel and the other officers. The morning they were found, you told me it was poison. I need you to elaborate. All signs pointed to illness, food poisoning, or flu, but no one else has fallen ill since. Why did you say poison?"

Cathy's stalwart confidence faltered then faded. "I said it *might* be."

"No, your first guess was that it was poison, not any of the more obvious assumptions. That night before, it was your wedding night, wasn't it?"

All color drained from Cathy's face. Max hoped she wasn't the killer, but the woman had been forced by the Colonel to marry one of his officers. That had occurred following an incident in which she had blinded the groom's brother. She had medical knowledge and know-how enough to kill and could have also had access to poisons.

"If *you* did it, why did you kill them all? Why not just Hank and Steve?"

"I didn't," Cathy protested.

He held up a book from the Colonel's library and opened up to a dog-eared page. "Ricin seems the most likely culprit. Its symptoms mimic flu."

"I swear I didn't kill anyone!"

"Relax. At this point, I need your services as a doctor more than I need Hank, Steve, and the others." He pointed at the stacks of notebooks and ledgers all around. "I still have the Colonel, or at least his recorded notes and plans. What I don't have is full trust in *you*. I need to know exactly what happened or I can't protect you. The other soldiers, those who were loyal to those officers, will figure it out sooner or later, and I need to protect you if I can. Please tell me the truth."

She wavered as if considering her words then finally answered. "It wasn't me. I did own the ricin and planned to use it on Hank and Steve, but not so soon after my wedding night. I was smarter than that and intended to wait several weeks."

"Then who? Who else had access to the officer's mess and could have delivered the poison? Who knew about it?"

Cathy never glanced at Shayde—that was a good thing. If he had been part of the cover-up, Max would have been furious. He must, at the very least, be able to trust one close advisor.

"Linda Johnson and James Parker," she finally admitted. "I told them both my plan and where to find the poison. I had a false stitch in my bag, and kept it there."

"Why would anyone carry around ricin?" Shayde asked, dumbfounded.

"It was intended for my ex-husband. He was a violent man—murdered my sister and also tried to kill me. I had run away with Josh and started over several times, but he always found us and dragged us back. The last time was the night of the missiles. He tried to kill me, but I killed him. The poison was my exit plan if things had gone differently than they did, and I still had it hidden in my things."

Max nodded. This woman had an angry streak—could be a loose cannon like when she had blinded that man when she thought he would rape Linda. But she was a hell of a nurse. There had to be a source for that much rage, and her history with her ex provided more than enough.

"Which of those two, James or Linda, would have had motive to kill the entire officer's mess?" he demanded.

"I don't..." she stammered, then her eyes fell to view the floor. "Linda had access, she worked in the kitchens. But James had motive. He was courting me and I was growing sweet on him before the Colonel forced me to marry Hank."

"Which of the two had access to the poison, Linda or James?"

"Both of them, I guess. Linda carried my things to Hank's shack, but James was with her. Either one of them could have done it."

"Or both," Shayde suggested.

Max nodded his agreement. "Or both." He paused, watching the woman's face closely. "Are you and James Parker still a thing? You said he was fond of you and you sweet on him. Are you a couple?"

"No. I've felt so... violated after that night with Hank. I wouldn't... I never even let James near me after that. Please, I don't know which of them fed the officers the poison."

"Understandable," Max agreed. "Go on your way, Cathy. If I have any more questions I'll call you back. In the meantime, I'll look for a different clinic for you to use other than the stage."

She nodded and fled as quickly as she could, closing the door behind her.

"Which do you think it was?" Shayde asked after she had gone.

"I don't know. I lived with Linda for a time and it's certainly in her demeanor, but I doubt she has the guts to carry murder out on her own."

"But with help and an accomplice?"

Recalling their journey to Evansville when crossing a certain bridge, he added, "I think she'd kill them on the spot. I've *seen* her kill without batting an eye." Changing the subject, he asked, "You said Sergeant Pescari had encountered some Nature Boys? Where is *he* today?"

"South of the river, trading with Mike Donelson's compound."

"Mike Donelson? Who's that?"

"Just a crazy prepper the Colonel had an arrangement with. He reloads our ammo and gives a monthly donation to the cause, and we give him protection by keeping an eye on his compound."

Max felt his blood chill. "We're not mobsters, Shayde. We don't sell protection!"

"Actually, we do, and have been doing so this entire time. The Colonel said that's how we'll assert our authority until we establish the new USA."

"Stop doing that at once. Not just with him, but with others as well. We provide services, but for *free* from now on? Do you understand?"

"What's the difference? If they're paying us for services rendered, they feel more invested. That's what the Colonel always said."

"The Colonel's dead!" Max snapped at his friend, the anger too much to contain. After he shouted he breathed deeply, trying to find his usual calm. "I'm sorry. This is all too much. I'm not a warlord, and I won't act like those we struggled against in Afghanistan and Iraq."

"I hate to break this to you, buddy, but you *are* a warlord, whether you like it or not. You own Evansville and everything surrounding it."

"Just make sure our services are free from now on. We need to build trust, not fear."

"Okay, General." Getting down to business, Shayde reached down and pointed at a map on the table. "If the Nature Boys are moving closer, we need to shore up our defenses now, not later." He dragged his finger in a triangular pattern down the riverbank, up to the freeway, and westward to where it crossed a creek. "We can't dig a trench, but we can build a barrier. Let's move vehicles and whatever else we can find to form a perimeter around downtown. We can figure out a way to remove the unnecessary buildings later."

"That's a good idea. Thanks, Shayde."

Sergeant Walters nodded and left him alone.

Max moved once more to the window, more careful this time not to stand in its center, and read the words across the street. *Sellout.* He sure felt like one.

CHAPTER TWO

Deep snow muffled the sound of hoof beats, each step crunching beneath the lumbering beasts. Other than the horses, no other animal made a sound and only the wind whistling through barren branches met the cavalrymen's ears. The eeriness of it all felt off, even this far south of the city. It was as if everything living in the world had died with civilization.

Atop the back of each horse rode a member of *Pescari's Outrider Squad.* Chosen for their ability to ride as well as trustworthiness, there were twenty Outriders in all. Each squad member carried a blade for hand to hand combat, a shotgun for clearing a building or for close engagement, and had a long-range rifle resting in a quiver on their saddle. Sergeant Chad Pescari hoped none of those weapons would be needed on this mission, but he kept an eye peeled for both street gangs and Nature Boys.

"This is the compound Cathy told me about, Sergeant," one of the Outriders said, breaking the silence. It was James Parker who had spoken. He was young and eager, but a good soldier.

Pescari jumped a bit in the saddle, startled by the interruption and thankful for it at the same time. "This is who rescued and gave our nurse over to the Shelter?"

"That's not *her* side of the story, Sarge. She claims this guy kidnapped her, took everything of value, and handed her over to the Colonel as a slave," Parker explained. He would know, he spent a lot of time with Nurse Fletcher.

The sergeant frowned. As far as he knew all the newcomers had come along willingly, though whispers among the ranks suggested the officers had done otherwise before their deaths. The single among them wanted wives to restart civilization with, and may have found the nurse very pretty. Besides, the Colonel *had* forced her to marry one of his officers. "Well," Chad replied, "we're not here for *that*, now are we?"

"No, Sarge."

Pescari patted a bag hanging from his saddle. The brass inside rattled. "We drop off these spent shells and pick up the reloads and whatever else he offers. Then we check perimeters and get back to the Shelter."

Parker nodded, then eased his mare, dropping back a bit.

The young man had a lot on his mind lately, distracted all the time, and Pescari knew why. His friend, Cathy, had solidly pushed Parker into the friend zone after her wedding. Of course, it hadn't helped that her husband and all the other officers died that very night. Talk all around the Shelter was that either she had killed them out of spite or Max Rankin had done so to seize control.

They topped the ridge and looked out over the valley. This place should have been green and lush under a June sun but was instead painted a dull grey under ashen snow. Without leaves, the sergeant shivered as a gust of wind suggested winter would last into August and beyond. The compound was easy to pick out against this landscape, with a recently constructed wall standing high around its perimeter. Hewn from fence boards and tree trunks, the place stood more like a fort than a group of homes.

Pescari frowned, it had grown since he last saw it.

Parker rejoined his side. "What's wrong, Sarge?"

"I don't like it. Something's off." Chad gently spurred his stallion forward, allowing him to choose his own path into the valley. The horse snorted irritation at all the snow, but soon led the Outriders where Pescari intended. Vulnerable the entire approach, Chad felt the rifles that no doubt followed them all the way in.

Despite his fears, the gates opened, offering refuge inside. A smiling Mike Donelson stood in front of three teenage boys while two armed men stood overhead on the makeshift parapet. The scruffy man wore an air of amusement, but his hard eyes dared the Outriders to step out of line.

It really is *a fort now*, Chad Pescari observed. The walls were better reinforced than he expected, with hulking shells of trucks and automobiles standing on edge against the outer fence line. An interior row of sturdy posts held these upright, and a sturdy breezeway allowed the defenders to move easily over them. *But built by only three grown men and a handful of teens?* he thought. *There's no way they could've build this on their own.*

"You've been busy, Donelson," was all he said when the man caught his appraising stare.

"Well, I can't be *too* careful with those street gangs around. We're still expecting those cartel types to show up as well."

Ten more men rounded one of the houses, each holding a rifle with muzzles pointed downwards. They posed no threat for now.

"You've been recruiting friends," Pescari said, tying Chief off outside the wall. He quietly signaled the others to do the same. If something went wrong they needed a swift escape, and that would not be possible with the horses trapped inside. He looped the reins with a special knot that could be pulled free by a human but not by the beast.

He leaned in close to Parker and whispered. "I'll do the talking but you do the scouting. Look for weaknesses, strengths, and things out of the usual. Report them all to me."

"Aye, Sarge," the younger man grinned.

"What is it? What's so funny?"

"Out of the usual? What's more unusual than a post-apocalyptic fort?"

"Out of the usual *for* an apocalypse, Parker!" Pescari growled quietly. If he had not felt so tense he, too, would have laughed, but this was certainly not the time. He drew a deep breath, then put on his best poker face and approached Mike Donelson.

"Sergeant," the man offered, pointing at a meager pile of offerings. "This is all we have."

The last time Pescari made this visit, the pile had been larger and richer. This paltry gift suggested hard times, something the elaborate walls disagreed with. "That's it?" Chad demanded, handing over several bags of empty brass to the teens.

"That's all we can spare," Crazy Mike said with a shrug. "Things are dwindling out here with no chance for crops or anything else." Though the man spoke doom and gloom, he smiled at Pescari, showing several missing teeth on one side.

"Radiation troubling you and your boys? How are you set on potassium iodide tablets?"

"Well-stocked," Mike said, suddenly losing his smile. He pointed at the bags of spent shell casings. "I'm running out of primers, though, for reloads."

"I can get you some. We came across a few boxes last month, but Sergeant Rankin will have to approve it."

"Sergeant Rankin?" Donelson's smile returned, but this time more cautious and less revealing. "Who's he and why would he approve or disapprove? What's wrong with the Colonel?"

Chad held back a grimace, keeping his poker face and hoping not to reveal anything too telling. He chose to lie. "Rankin's his armorer, that's all. He approves what comes in and out of the stockpile."

"So it's a stockpile you have now?" Mike asked slyly. "So the Regiment *is* doing well for itself, *isn't* it?"

"Why wouldn't it?"

"Oh, not that it would or anything, but maybe because one of your defectors came by recently and said the Colonel was dead. Claimed *all* the officers were, and that some upstart took over the reins. He also claimed the stockpile was raided. Is there any truth to that?"

Chad felt his insides drop, but held his face and hoped his voice wouldn't betray him. "That a defector would lie? Sure, I'd expect that. Point him out, and I'll take care of him for you."

"Oh, no need. We sent him on further south."

Chad nodded but knew what Donelson meant. He had sent whoever it had been to join the Nature Boys. They probably also had the loyalty of this entire compound, by the looks of the scant tribute. "Well, good for that, but next time hang our defectors on sight. That's what *we* do with those who so easily shift loyalties."

Mike's face briefly changed at that, less adept at this game of cat and mouse.

"Well, we best be going. Night's falling soon." Chad pointed at the pile and Parker and the other Outriders scooped them up eagerly. "Before we go, though, tell me what's been out this way? Any street gangs roaming? Or worse?"

"Just the usual sightings. They've been scouting our perimeter."

"A mighty fine one it is," Chad pointed out the structure. "Must've been a lot of effort moving those vehicles and cutting those logs, but you've done well. I hope it holds against a Nature Boys attack."

"Oh, we haven't been seeing any of *them* this far north, Sergeant."

"That's good. We'll be off, then." Chad motioned for Parker and the others to load the horses, then turned to buy a few more precious minutes. "The Colonel's curious, Donelson, about a certain woman you rescued."

"I've rescued a few."

"Yes, but he picked this one up himself."

Donelson frowned. "I don't recall them all."

"She claimed to be taken against her will—that she didn't need saving."

"They *all* need saving, Sergeant, or don't you have eyes in your smart head? Civilization has ended, and it ain't gonna be put back right any time soon. A woman's place ain't no longer next to a man, it's under or beneath him!"

"That's all I needed to know."

"What'dya mean?"

"I mean, sir, that you doubt the Regiment will restore both civilization *and* the United States."

"United States died with the pandemics," Crazy Mike spat. "It wasn't even the bombs that killed it! It was greedy politicians that couldn't string two sentences together without a teleprompter and a dozen handlers."

"The Colonel insists our nation's alive and well," Chad said as he turned to leave, "in the hearts and minds of people like you and me. That is, as long as we remember what the USA was all about."

Parker, like a good lad, held his sergeant's reins, handing them over as the sergeant approached.

As they rode away, the younger man gave his report. "The wall isn't finished. There's a weaker section on the western side that needs reinforcing. The men we saw on the ramparts and the ten behind the main house weren't the only people living there, either. I counted them and the bunk houses and this compound can easily hold sixty."

"You think there's that many soldiers?"

"No, Sarge. By the tracks in the snow, I'd say there're easily fifty or sixty men here, but not all soldiers."

Chad sat taller in the saddle, stealing a glance at the eyes watching them ride away. "What did you see, Parker? Why don't you think they're soldiers?"

"Drag marks in between their legs, Sarge. Our friend back there has slaves dragging chains between their ankles. That's how they're moving the timbers and the vehicles."

"Rankin and Walters will need to hear about this," Pescari said, letting out a held breath. The world had changed so much in only a few months.

CHAPTER THREE

David Andalon stared out over a wide valley—a place he had passed through many times but never given a second thought. That was until seeing it this way, broken, twisted, and demolished. The sight compelled the doctor to take notice of the carnage, the change, and the hopelessness. The world he knew had departed, and in its place he found total destruction.

This had once been the steel belt and the birth of the American Steel Revolution. A place he knew as Pittsburgh. The city had stood in the perfect location, with navigable waterways, coal, timber, natural gas, iron, and limestone. It rose to prominence as a place where the future was more than a possibility.

That future had ended abruptly.

All that remained formed a black scar on an even darker swath of earth. As for the waterways, those had rerouted and chosen their own paths. This epicenter of civilization would no longer draw mankind. It had collapsed, half-covered with snow and ash, and soon would disappear entirely. The airborne radiation had mostly dissipated, but nuclear winter would persist and the ground would be contaminated far longer.

Eventually the ice would melt, leaving the ash which would eventually harden, turning to sludge or soil, but unable to bear fruit for another five years more. Further south, maybe near the equator, things would grow. But this was the Ohio River valley. He sighed. It *was* the Ohio River valley. Now all the tributaries blended together, just like the Great Lakes had to the north. They were only one now, and he had seen it—a lake as grand as a sea.

"Dr. Andalon," Stephanie Yurik called. "They're *Dreaming*."

"What?" David demanded, turning to find the military woman kneeling over the children, each deep into their trancelike sleep. Irritation crept into his mood at their timing. "Here and now? We only set camp briefly to rest. We're not in a good place to bed down."

But Adam and Eve weren't going to sleep. What they called *Dreaming* was more than subconscious visions. To these special children it was prophetic, a journey into the now and what might eventually be. He had no choice but to wait; they searched the valley for the remaining survivors of civilization.

Civilization, he mused, *more likely to resemble lawlessness.*

NASA had once issued an article declaring humanity had come and gone thirty-two times as advanced civilizations. A professor of genetics and student of mankind, David Andalon had paid attention. Since discovering farming, humans had banded together to survive wherever and whenever possible. They failed in deserts and on mountaintops; life there was too hard. They flourished in tropical paradises, but failed to create arts or written language and refused to progress because there lacked the need. True human civilization thrived in the river valleys, the Goldilocks zone—not too easy nor too difficult.

He felt a bit of anger find its way into his heart. This event—the nuclear attack, the seismic catastrophe at Yellowstone, and the electromagnetic pulse that knocked out electricity—all marked a turning point for humanity, not just America, and Goldilocks rules no longer meant a damned thing. These children about to dream represented the future, and, though Dr. Andalon cursed those who destroyed the world, he stood intrigued by what might develop in time. He hoped it would be better but knew a different threat existed across the ocean.

Astia, he thought, *is what they'll call it, Esterling's launch pad for further destruction.*

His friend Michael, his wife Brooke, and her brother Jake had all turned their backs on this, their former home, intent on creating Michael Esterling's utopia overseas. They would return to the old Americas eventually, but would find a utopia of *David's* making, crafted by the children, and full of people like them. Mankind and humanity *must* endure, and Adam and Eve were flawless humans. With a little help, their offspring would flourish.

David watched them *Dream,* seemingly asleep except for their lucid conversation. Adam had sworn they would find people here soon, needing the help only David could provide. His eyes flicked to his bags and boxes, neatly stacked and waiting for the children to provide another boat or even a sled.

Their last vessel had been a three-masted ship crafted entirely by aerokinesis—with decks of air a person could stand on and sails that caught the wind the children provided. A marvel of their abilities, it only scratched the surface of what they could do. David flinched at the thought of their full power, and they were only ten years old.

"We're vulnerable here," he abruptly told Stephanie, looking around for shelter.

"Like we have a choice over what these children do or when?" she grumbled. Stephanie Yurik was a doctor too, the scientist who cloned and nurtured these children. But irritation and lack of sleep had affected her mood as well as David's. She was right, of course. Adam and Eve had dictated every move they had made since departing Germany, heedless of their surroundings and without a care for the worries of their adult escorts.

The children act as if they're in charge, David realized, but not for the first time.

Benjamin Roark, always present and nearby his wife, sensed Stephanie's frustration. The soldier stood. A strong man, dangerously quiet and quite able in any fight, he picked up his rifle and placed a supportive hand on her shoulder. "I'll watch our perimeter," he promised, nodding to David before departing to watch their backs.

Andalon sighed. "I'm sorry. I thought this would be easier, that they'd lead us to the community without any trouble. I hadn't expected this much uncertainty."

"We're not perfect, Father," the girl muttered from her trance. Eve was the most outspoken of the two, and her mature voice and vocabulary clashed with her young face. "There are several civilizations, and we're trying to locate the exact position of the larger, more stable one we glimpsed before. If you would kindly stop interrupting, we'll narrow it down for you."

"I'm sorry," David muttered, climbing atop a box of rations to get comfortable during the wait. He looked around. They had brought over plenty of supplies from Europe and never worried about hauling it all till now. It had stowed easily aboard the shimmering vessel of woven air that carried them across the ocean, but now they chose to travel on foot. The children refused to re-manifest *Estowen.*

"We're close," Adam finally revealed. "Evansville, Indiana, about five hundred miles upriver."

"Close?" David stood, barely able to contain his frustration. "That's at least a week by foot! Can't we sail *halfway,* at least?"

"There are pockets of survivors here, Father," Eve explained to the adult as if he were a child. "Revealing our craft won't do. That's not how we win over these people. We must earn their trust and gift them the strength they will need when Esterling changes his mind."

Changes his mind, Andalon's thoughts wandered, feeling like a modern day Moses who just learned Pharaoh's heart had hardened, choosing to pursue his slaves across the Red Sea. That *was* essentially the same thing that happened here, but thankfully, they were deep into North America and Michael still had no way to cross the Atlantic.

"They're right," Stephanie agreed. She had been mostly quiet during the voyage and even less help on dry land. She and Benjamin Roark mostly kept to themselves or attended the children. "Losing our cool won't help."

"I'm sorry," he finally admitted, letting his true emotions flow. "I've been irritable and not myself. I'm so angry with Brooke for choosing to stay behind. It all happened so fast, and it's only just now hitting me what we gave up... What *I* gave up." He sighed. "I love her, still."

"You've given nothing up, Father," Eve explained, using the moniker he hated. David was father to no one, his previous efforts abandoned by Brooke's selfish impatience. "She betrayed you, pregnant with another man's child."

David had tried so hard to forget her betrayal—the artificial insemination by Michael Esterling. Brooke had given up too soon on her husband's efforts to correct his own infertility, desperate for a child. "We need a game plan, even if only to calm my anxiety. What do we do once we make it to Evansville?"

"Anxiety is all in your mind, Dr. Andalon," Eve snapped, breaking both her and Adam from their *Dreaming*. "Human emotion must be controlled, and we are not responsible for *your* inability to do so."

David felt anger brim, the first time he had come close to losing his cool with the children... his experiments... Maybe he should regard them as such now, especially when acting so obstinate. Seeking that control she mentioned, he swallowed, took a deep breath, and calmed himself the best he could.

"Human emotion is unpredictable," he told the child, "not only in others, but also within our own perception of ourselves. You two are young with limited experience in the world, and I don't expect you to understand."

"We know much about the world," Eve stated flatly.

"Nonsense!" David snapped. "You were born in a lab with no concept of the outside world. You lack experience to make decisions about *anything*, much less what behavior is appropriate or normal!"

"We understand..." Adam began, but was quickly cut off.

"You understand nothing!" David shouted, his voice echoing through the valley. "You're children! *Lab rats* with intelligence! Trust the adults with experience!"

Eve, to everyone's surprise, was unfazed by his anger. She smiled slyly and said, "I now fully understand why monkeys burned your lab and all your work to the ground, Dr. Andalon."

David opened his mouth to speak, ready to send a slew of angry retorts, but was cut off by Stephanie Yurik.

"Everyone get a grip!" she said in a low voice. "There's no telling what dangers you'll attract!"

David immediately felt like an ass. He stared at the children, the *experiments*, and studied their faces. Adam watched expectantly, while Eve sat smug and overconfident.

"I'm sorry," he said again, meaning it wholeheartedly.

"Hello," a pleasant voice called from the barren trees behind them.

The group looked up to find a man, ruggedly handsome and fit, smiling disarmingly and standing as if to appear non-threatening. His right hand was held in plain sight, and his satchel hung loosely from his left.

"Hold it right there," Benjamin Roark commanded from behind the newcomer. He had watched the man approach and managed a flanking move with rifle pointed forward.

"I mean no harm, sir," the man promised. "I heard shouting and wanted to make sure you folks were okay."

"We're fine," Roark insisted. "You can be on your way now."

"Wait," David insisted, stepping forward. Something was odd about this man. Something he couldn't quite place. "What are you doing out here, in the radiation, this *nuclear* winter, so far from civilization?"

"The radiation isn't so bad now," the man explained nonchalantly.

He had all his teeth and no sores the doctor could see, so it may be so. David couldn't feel any ill effects himself, not since he had inoculated himself and the others, altering their DNA with his vaccine.

"I *was* in a shelter with other people," the man explained.

"Where are they now?" David demanded.

"They were old and couldn't handle the changes."

"I'm sorry," Stephanie Yurik told the man. "Did they pass?"

"Yes," the man said without emotion, "and now I'm quite alone."

David watched him closely, noticing how the children, *the experiments*, also eyed him with deep interest. "Where were you?" he asked.

"Ohio, several days west of here. I was hoping to find people further east."

"You won't find anything alive east of here," David assured him. "It's total devastation all the way to the coast."

"Oh," the man said thoughtfully. "Where are *you* headed, then?"

"Evansville," Adam blurted out. "Indiana. That's where the survivors are."

"I see," the man replied curiously. "How many?"

"Enough," Eve said smugly, "to restart civilization."

"Can I join you, then?" the man asked immediately, suddenly appearing very eager for their help. He eyed the box of rations under David as if eager for a taste. He must be very hungry.

"That depends," David replied, again aware of how much they had to carry. "Do you have a boat?"

29

The man lit up immediately. "I do, actually! I came across one yesterday. It can carry all of this *and* us!"

"Well then," David said, standing and reaching out his hand. "I'm David Andalon, this is Benjamin Roark, Stephanie Yurik, and Adam and Eve."

The man grinned widely at the introductions. "I'm Clint," he said. "Clint Fletcher. I'm so glad to have found you."

CHAPTER FOUR

Michael Esterling purveyed his empire, flipping through maps and reading scribbled notes neatly paper clipped to each. On the outside he appeared calm and in control, the Chancellor of a new empire. But looks are often deceiving and, in the case of this man, a complete and total lie. Inside he grasped for control, locked in a perpetual balancing act of spinning plates. As one steadied another wobbled and threatened to fall. If he could not set everything on a straight path soon it could all fall apart.

Thankfully, some of the bigger nations had aligned quickly, strengthening his grasp. Germany had fallen firmly under his control when he had defeated a Russian invasion. Following that battle in Waghäusel he had sent scouts in every direction, offering a message of hope to the starving people of Europe. All fledgling pockets of survivors accepted aid under his banner, eager for normalcy and no longer caring about borders.

He had been surprised by their willingness to follow this American Senator so far from home, certain he would have met resistance. But they had been controlled by the European Union far too long, and nationalistic ideologies no longer mattered except in Britain and the far eastern nations like Ukraine and Belarus. The only concern left to matter in Europe was over food, shelter, and protection—all things his new Astian Nation could easily deliver.

But not all nations had fared so well as Germany, kept mostly intact by its furthest proximity to a chain of electromagnetic pulses (EMPs). Those devices had actually been released by his own doing, a damning secret that would bring his dream of Astia to a crashing halt if the truth got out. His brief, back-channel dealings with a terrorist for hire had provided the information needed to hack USA's nuclear defense system, arming the warheads and making the telemetry data appear to go where it wasn't.

He should regret his role in killing millions, of feeding just the right information to the right people, but felt odd satisfaction knowing the fate of the world now followed prophecy.

Astia, he thought. *It was all for Astia.*

Besides, the destruction was inevitable, a certain and unstoppable end of society, and all he did was give a gentle nudge. The children born in his lab had predicted the explosions and he merely provided the fuse-lighting catalyst.

Naturally occurring seismic events had done the rest, launching the missiles that earned retaliatory response.

He felt better knowing the worst had passed, fueled by a renewed mission to right society. Though he had crossed a line, setting the stage for nuclear war and total destruction of western nations, Michael Esterling slept soundly each night. His only concern was over who may use that information against him. Not even his best friend, General Jake Braston, knew of his role in that part of the apocalypse, but Stephanie Yurik did. He regretted letting her in on his secret, now realizing that had been the main reason she left him.

Good riddance, he thought, refocusing attention on his maps.

These charts reflected a world now fully in the past. All his attention aimed at redrawing the future—a new world after a great reset.

He frowned at the task ahead. Britain had been leveled under the missiles, and the situation there remained dire. Those living, if *any* had survived, would hardly be worth saving once he could reach them. That would take time since most of Astia's soldiers were tied up securing trade routes.

Herr General Richter, the leader of German forces before assimilation into Astia, currently marched Astian troops westward into France, having first arced northward through Belgium and Denmark, liberating the people there. The last report put the general somewhere south of Paris, though he would hopefully return soon. Other columns marched southward, bringing the message of survival to what was once Italy and the Balkans.

For securing the eastern nations, Michael sent Russian General Ivan Petrov. The military leader had been the first Astian captive in the war, his mind stolen by the power of emotancy. It felt strange controlling another man's thoughts and movements, the gift given to him by David Andalon when he betrayed the Astian dream and fled to North America with Adam and Eve.

But not only with them...

Stephanie... The thought of her betrayal crept once more into his thoughts. She had fled with David and an enlisted soldier she claimed was the father of her unborn child. Until that moment he had believed that child to be his. The Chancellor of Astia suddenly found himself unsure which betrayal hurt the most, his friend's or his former lover's.

There was plenty of time to deal with David and Stephanie later. Besides, his true child would be born to Brooke. In the meantime, he had to remain focused on his primary goal, the expansion of Astia.

Once General Petrov rose high enough in ranks, Russia would also be his. It would be a gradual process but, once it could be achieved, China would remain Astia's only threat. Elsewhere, no other nation was left of any consequence. India and Pakistan had presumably nuked one another into oblivion. Africa, South America, and Australia would prove tough conquests, but were thankfully isolated. Without electrical power or hope for it anytime soon, they would have fallen into dark ages. Warlords would have emerged to challenge their governments, and Michael would easily dominate them as a modern day Charlemagne.

Thus Chancellor Esterling stood, an emperor of a new nation under a unified banner, bringer of hope to a dying world. Astia was the *vessel of normalcy*, as Adam had called it, unified under Michael, the real Astia, the bringer of normalcy.

The door opened and Michael lifted his eyes from his maps, resting them on General Jake Braston and his sister Brooke. Her stomach had fully rounded and dropped, sitting low with child. She was due within a month, but pregnancy never slowed her task of picking up the pieces of her ex-husband's work. That mission seemed to drive the woman, also a doctor, giving her renewed purpose.

Michael's eyes fell to her belly. The woman he could not have, but the child *was* and *would be* his.

An Esterling will always sit the throne in Andalon, Adam had promised during one of his prophecies, but Michael knew he meant Astia instead of Andalon, the new name he had given to North America in honor of his friend.

Let David have that place, for now, he decided. Ignoring Brooke, the chancellor addressed Jake. "What do you have for me?"

"No news from outside, but some issues in the lab."

Issues, always issues. Since David abandoned Astia, his team struggled to succeed in creating another Adam and Eve. The last two embryo attempts failed to produce the correct theta waves, predominately surging in unwanted delta patterns. Both were destroyed as useless in their artificial wombs.

Michael had blamed the old team.

Brooke was too careful and so were her assistants Sam and Mi-Jung Nakala. They disregarded timelines, refusing to take the risks Stephanie had when creating the children. Her daring attempts were the opposite approach of David and his team.

"What *kind* of issues?" the chancellor demanded.

"Not *issues,* per se," Brooke explained, "but roadblocks. I've been all over the notes David didn't purge from the system. What he left is not even the same experiment. That's why we thought it failed on the last pair."

"What do you mean, *thought it failed.* You told me it was an utter failure." Anxiety rose within Michael as he envisioned his old friend gumming up the works and deleting files before he departed. "Did he sabotage our efforts? Can we duplicate Adam and Eve or not?" They *had* to create more emotants.

"I'm afraid he did. The key DNA process is missing, altered completely, and we'll never achieve the same results, not in the same form as Adam and Eve."

Michael felt his anxiety turn to anger, welling up inside like a pressure cooker. He was ready to burst with it, *needed* to burst with it, if only to relieve his nerves. Trapped in this bunker, he suddenly yearned for freedom and to scream at the night sky overhead. After swallowing down the worst of it, he calmly asked, "What form did he leave, then? What about his promise when he left?"

"Unbroken," Jake said, breaking in, "just misunderstood by all of us. Adam said that your child would be the only emotant left in Astia, and that means we won't achieve full emotancy, but something usably similar."

Brooke touched her belly while her brother spoke, her eyes betraying deep worry. Michael, on the other hand, felt a rush at this. His child, the one she carried... his *son*, the heir to Astia, would be special after all. "Go on," Esterling urged.

"David ensured that what we would have are not emotants, but drones capable of producing a serum we can farm and consume."

"I don't follow."

"He duped us, Michael." Jake replied. "He added something to our radiation vaccine that enabled some of us to utilize serums derived from the original batches. Before leaving, he instructed Sam and Mi-Jung to put it into a pill form. His plan was that we would never have emotants, only access to their powers on a temporary basis as needed. He didn't trust us not to create an army of super humans."

"That's *exactly* what we need—an army of super humans," Michael lamented. "But this may be better. Adam and Eve proved we can't control emotants, but if we *feed* the pills to our army and achieve the same effect, those with the abilities still depend on us like addicts."

"I don't think you understand our real problem," Brooke cut in. "He also limited our supply to the embryos we have in storage. After the last destruction, we only have about seventy to bring to term. Even farming them for the pills, that's scarcely enough to feed an army with."

"So keep the units small, like special forces. Jake, get to planning it out at once. I want those you choose to test be vetted, trusted, and led by you."

"Me?" Braston laughed, his go-to deflection when worried. "I would have to take the pills too, and that's not something I'm comfortable with. I don't want or need those kind of powers."

Michael narrowed his eyes, looking deep into his friend's eyes. They had been as close as brothers since college and, though the saying was that no one ever said *no* to Jake Braston, it was time to flip their position. "You *will* have them, because I *need* you to have them, Jake. I want my general to lead this cadre with complete control."

"We have another problem," Brooke added with a frown. "David left behind four sets of serum, each different, and only labeled *Alpha, Bravo, Charlie,* and *Delta.* We know the original batch Alpha was the formula I sent to Stephanie and what she used to create Adam and Eve. But we only ever tested the other batches on monkeys in his Mendel Lab. Batch Bravo produced Felicima, the monkey who burned down that lab. We don't want to use it for obvious reasons, and we only have a limited idea of what to expect from batches Charlie and Delta."

"Why not?"

"Why not what?"

"Why *not* use batch Bravo? We're humans, not lab monkeys so it could work differently. Use it. Use all four. I want to know what our full capabilities are. Test them on the entire cadre, even me."

"No!" Brooke protested too aggressively. She quickly calmed and added, you're too important to lose in case something goes wrong."

"Which one did David take?"

"I don't know for certain, but we think it was Charlie."

"Figure it out. I want what *he* has. The power over life itself."

Brooke and Jake stood waiting for more, but Michael was done talking. He returned his eyes to his maps and notes, frowning at a scribble about a warlord in Spain. Irritated they were still waiting, he snapped, "Dismissed!"

"He's changed." Brooke blurted out in the hallway.

Jake let out a laugh, always shrugging off danger. "Since when? College? We've all changed since then. You, me, even David."

"No, since this entire *end-of-times* scenario. I swear, Jake! Stephanie warned me about this before she left, how quickly absolute power had changed him. He thinks he's a god among men now!"

Jake grabbed his sister's arm, spinning her around to face him. The look he shot her sent chills down her spine, his jovial nature gone and replaced by intensity and concern. "He's not a god," he hissed just above a whisper, "but he *is* the most powerful man in this messed up world! So keep your voice quiet before he or one of my soldiers hear and accuse you of sedition!"

Brooke blanched. He had only ever spoken to her like that once in her life, and that was when she had ventured onto thin ice to play as a child. He was fifteen at the time and she was ten, petulant and self-assured she could do as she please. He had grabbed her then as now and spun her around the same way. Then he took a branch that weighed about as much as she, and slid it out onto the ice to prove his point. It cracked and swallowed the meal at once, leaving him to hold a startled and bawling little girl version of Brooke.

For him to speak to her now, with that same caution, silenced her inner fool.

"I..." she stammered, then regained control. "I'm sorry, Jake. You're right, of course." Touching her belly, she added, "It must be the hormones." But it wasn't. In her gut, she knew Michael Esterling had changed for the worse and knew the real reasons Stephanie had left him to follow David to North America—she still refused to call it Andalon.

David, she thought, *you shouldn't have left me here.* But that wasn't right, was it?

He had also seen the same storm brewing in Michael and offered her to join him in the last minute. His eyes, when she refused, were more betrayed by her decision to stay than they were when learning she had been artificially inseminated with Michael's sperm.

I sent you off, David. You didn't go, she admitted. Thinking next of the experiments, of what Stephanie had warned and what Michael wanted Jake to do, she added, *Oh David, I should have gone with you!*

"You're right, though," Jake suddenly whispered, snapping her from those horrible thoughts.

She stiffened. Of what part had she been correct?

"He *has* changed," Jake admitted, "but I'm not yet sure if it's for the worse or better. The world *needs* hard men now. Men, like him, with the knowledge to lead and build a government."

"You," Brooke suddenly insisted, "you're a hard man, and *you're* a leader. Take Astia from him and set things right!"

"No, I'm not the same kind of leader as him. I'm a good tactician and even better at planning strategy, but I'm first and foremost a pilot, one who will never fly again. True, as an officer I've been a leader in times of war or peace, but I don't know the first thing about reforming society and never built from scratch the right system of government this world needs."

"Power hungry or not," Braston continued, "Michael's correct about one thing, neither democracy nor republics will work here, not in this fractured state. He has a dream of this Astia, and that's more than I have, so I'll defer to my friend. You should as well."

"Okay," she promised, her thoughts returning to mountains of work waiting in the lab.

She had lied to Michael, that the only saboteur had been David. Before leaving, Stephanie Yurik had tried to convince Brooke that Esterling was a problem, growing into a tyrant who would stop at nothing to achieve his goals—including putting his own children in danger.

But Brooke had to see it for herself, to come to the same conclusions as Stephanie, and that's why she had stayed behind—refusing to go with her husband.

Now certain her friend's fears were real, she had to ensure Michael never succeeded in building his army. No matter what, the chancellor could only ever have drones and not emotants.

Would Sam and Mi-Jung try and interfere, she wondered about the lab assistants, *if they knew they were helping hinder Michael's plans?* Probably not but, in this new world, everyone was a potential wild card. *Even me?* she wondered. *Was Stephanie right that he would take away my child?* Adam had foreseen it, at least that's what Yurik had feared for her own and why she fled.

She wanted to say all this to her brother, to clue him to the danger his friend posed, but he was right, this wasn't the time or place. Michael's soldiers always loomed, watching and listening for betrayal.

"Today would have been Dad's birthday," Jake suddenly reminded her. "Let's honor his and Mom's deaths by getting along, Sis."

She blanched, shocked she hadn't thought about it first. Partly from the hormones of pregnancy, she was an emotional wreck after keeping everything inside. *I haven't even* mourned *Mom and Dad, much less dealt with David's leaving. I've poured everything into my work,* she knew. *What's wrong with me?*

Then she understood. Jake had not mourned, either. He was a soldier, and soldiers wait until after the fighting is over. In this bunker, within this new world, *she* was a soldier also. There was not time, not with so many uncertainties ahead. Mourning would only happen after her mind and body found a semblance of home.

CHAPTER FIVE

Cathy Fletcher leaned over the woman, a mother of two teen boys. All three were affected by radiation, but the boys were spared the debilitating affects their mother endured. Though most of the burns had already healed, they would live with the discoloration and scars for the rest of their shortened lives. Both boys stared at their mother, the lumps on her neck swollen to the size of two ripe apples. She could no longer talk, so her older son did so for her.

"She's not been in pain till recently," he said, "but has been tired all this time. She can barely eat and stopped talking a week ago."

The nurse nodded. She had seen this often over the past few months. The radiation had affected the woman's thyroid—no doubt an underactive gland in this case. Hypothyroidism was to be expected without introducing iodine into your diet soon after a thermonuclear event.

"Can you help her?" the younger boy asked with eager eyes begging for a miracle.

"I have some medicine that might," is all Cathy found to reply. She knew the methimazole would reduce the goiters, but supplies were limited and the woman would need it for the rest of her life—however long that may be. This would probably progress to thyroid cancer in her case, and these drugs would run out soon. An entire population would need them to stave off chronic fatigue and weight gain, followed by heart disease and probably an eventual myxedema coma and death.

"Thank you, ma'am," the older boy said, smiling up with several missing teeth.

Cathy impulsively reached up and felt both his and his brother's necks for swelling. They were clear.

She would admit them all into the Shelter but not without a lengthy quarantine.

Movement caught her eye, a pregnant woman with long dark hair crossing the stage, and she lifted her head to a welcome sight. Linda Johnson, with her fully rounded stomach, was due within the month. Despite her condition she carried a pot of stew into the isolation area. She appeared haggard and tired but overall showed good health. Cathy had been meaning to have a hard discussion with her friend for a few days, but their schedules never matched up. She washed her hands with an alcohol mix and waved her friend to another table away from the family of newcomers.

"What do you want?" Linda grumbled. "Can't you see I'm busy?"

Cathy smiled and casually ignored her friend's rudeness. She always put up walls when most nervous—it was her way of coping. She wasn't a mean or nasty woman, though she did have an awful temper that usually burned hot but was short-lived.

"I want to check on the baby. Isn't that reason enough to speak with my best friend?"

Linda placed her hand over her stomach defensively, diverting her eyes as if looking for an exit. She had never hidden her biggest fear from Cathy—that her child would be born with monstrous deformities or as something out of a bad science fiction movie.

Cathy slid a blood pressure cuff on her arm and manually pumped the bulb slowly and deliberately. She would get the most minutes out of this conversation that she could.

Linda saw right through her stalling and accused, "I thought *James Parker* was your best friend. Yet it seems you don't even talk to *him* anymore."

"You know why that is and why it *has* to be. He wants more of me than I'm ready to give right now." It was getting easier, but she really doubted she would ever get over that wedding night. But three years of marriage to Clint had been monstrous compared to a single night with a drunk man's sloppiness, and so she knew she eventually would.

"James is in love with you," Linda said, meeting her friend's eyes.

This woman had lost everything *she* loved just before and during the nuclear attack, so this sudden compassion caught Cathy off guard. First, Linda lost both her teenagers to a horrible accident on vacation. Then, her husband died in a car wreck or to the missiles themselves. She had been plagued with bad luck, this woman, and her occasional crassness was forgivable.

"But I'm not in love with *him*, Linda. He's a nice young man but too eager, and I'm not ready. After both my marriages, I've realized I need a different kind of man altogether. I want one with brains and who is emotionally stable. One who doesn't overwhelm me with affection the way James does." She paused then added, "Or beat the crap out of me like Clint did."

"Understandable, but look around, sweetie. There ain't much to choose from in this world. You're young and have a better chance at love than me, but you are being too choosy while the rest of us suffer from neglect. Look at me. I'm nearly thirty-five and most of the guys here are mid-twenties like you, or younger."

"Chad Pescari seems interested in you."

Linda groaned. "He's barely over twenty-five, keeps calling me 'ma'am,' and blushing when I serve him food. I know I'm too old for him. Besides, I'm about to have a monster child."

"You're about to have a *normal* child," Cathy corrected. "We need to choose names, by the way. What do you like if he's a boy?"

"Grendel. Like the monster from literature. Or Frankenstein."

"Frankenstein was the doctor."

"Fine. Grendel it is."

"And if it's a girl?"

"In this world?" Linda's eyes met Cathy's with true sorrow. "If there ever was and still *is* a god, I pray that fate never befalls this little monster."

They both fell silent. Despite the closest thing the Shelter had to a doctor, Cathy knew all too well that a woman's voice was no longer as strong as it had once been. Crazy Mike Donelson had made that clear—*very* clear.

"You and little Grendel seem healthy," Cathy announced. "You're almost due, so maybe let someone else carry the stew pots and heavier things."

Linda shrugged. They both knew she was due in a matter of weeks, not months, and she worked hard to distract from the dread of actually seeing the child.

Cathy changed the subject. "Linda, I have something very important to ask. I've been meaning to but had avoided it because I didn't care at the time. But now I *have* to ask because others are wondering and will be asking you about it very soon."

The older woman frowned. "What are you talking about? Stop beating around the bush and just ask me what you want to know." Her fierce eyes met Cathy's, locking them into a nonverbal challenge and daring her to say what she surely knew she would ask. "We don't have time for bullshit."

"On the night I married Hank," Cathy continued, matching her friend's look with one of determination, "I showed you and James my packet of ricin—only to you two. Then you walked upstairs together, carried my bags to Hank's hovel, and you went on to serve dinner."

As she spoke, Linda's eyes grew darker, angry and full of... full of something. Whether it was guilt, vengeance, or fury, Cathy couldn't tell.

"Are you asking me if I killed them? If I put your precious *packet* into the stew?"

"Yes. Did you kill the officers, Linda? And all their wives and families? There were a *lot* of bodies that next day, and all of them ate *your* stew."

"*You* didn't die," Cathy pointed out.

"I didn't eat the stew. Some kind friend brought me a dish of crackers knowing full well I wouldn't have an appetite."

Linda broke away her stare, diverting it upward toward the gallery overlooking the stage. That's where it had happened, where the officers and their families had lived and died. "I won't answer your questions, Cathy, because I don't have to. But if you want to find someone to throw under the bus why don't you ask your little boyfriend about that night and what part *he* played with your little packet of ricin." She ripped off the blood pressure cuff and stood, storming from the stage and toward the kitchens.

Cathy didn't follow after her friend, only watched her angry departure and considered her final words. *James?* she wondered. *Surely not. He's too kind, too sweet, not angry like... Not at all capable of vengeance like Linda.* But he was a man, and even quiet and sweet men could be dangerous when jealousy got involved.

She checked the clock, wondering suddenly at the time. Her shift was nearly over and she would be needing to gather her son Josh from the nursery. She and he both missed their special time, and those precious moments grew fewer and farther apart with each busy day. Now, more than ever, he needed her, but so did all these refugees coming into the Shelter.

There it was—the real reason she needn't fill her time with romances or to be tied down to men like James Parker. She had a man already, or at least a little boy she had a job to turn into one.

Max Rankin and Shayde Walters met Pescari's Outriders Squadron outside the stables. The riders approached carefully with eyes on the windows overhead of their approach. Max's snipers had already set up their nests overlooking those, and rangers had swept the rooms twice already that morning. Until they could level the buildings, entry and egress was a continued problem for the Shelter.

"There they are," Shayde pointed out, "our P.O.S. regiment," he said with a chuckle. The acronym meant something else to military men. "Good to have them around though. Feels like Uncle Sam's Army finally arrived to take over for the Marines... yep, just like the good ol' days."

Max smiled at the joke. It felt good to smile—he had almost forgotten he could. "I wonder how it went?"

"We'll know soon enough," Shayde promised.

He was right. Chad Pescari and his Outriders made it to the stables where they immediately dismounted. They carried few new supplies, and it almost appeared as if the venture had given away more than it brought back. They wore worried faces that told a dire story. Max knew at once they were losing a vital alliance with Mike Donelson.

"Well?" he asked Chad.

"What used to be a prepper commune is a full-fledged Fort Knox, General," Pescari reported.

"I'm not a General, Pescari."

"Sure you're not. Would you prefer Captain? As in *oh my god, Captain Obvious,* you're a General now?"

Shayde let out a laugh, an uncontrollable one that made the horses snort uncomfortably. Max, irritated at the interruption, gave his friend a backhanded tap to the nuts that shut him up. The laughter ended with a gasp of air and every Outrider let out their tension with a laugh. Max had missed this kind of camaraderie. It felt like the *good ol' days* of Fallujah, if there really were any of those.

"Tell me about this *Fort Knox*," he commanded.

"James? You saw it best," Chad asked Corporal Parker to relay his observations.

"The outer construction is made of timbers, rows of them like something you'd find on the Plains Frontier in the 1800s. They lashed them with braided hemp or, more readily available, vines. I couldn't tell which. But they've moved in heavy steel somehow, lining the inner walls with cars and trucks tipped over on their sides and pressed against the outer layer. Then they lined that with another layer of timbers and built parapets and gangways over the top."

"Geez," Shayde let out a whistle, his air having returned. "That *is* a Fort Knox."

"But there's a vulnerability," Pescari threw in. "They aren't finished with one of the walls, and we didn't see any more vehicles around with which they could reinforce. If you want to take this compound, we'll need to hit it soon."

Max felt his body stiffen at the suggestion. "Take it? Why would we do that?"

"Sir, the position is prime and would secure our supply line to the south. With a garrison facing the Nature Boys, you could focus on reinforcing the airport and all lines north, east, and west."

"Dammit Pescari, why aren't *you* a friggin' General?" Walters wanted to know. Turning to Max he asked, "Did you know he was this smart?"

"I knew he was smarter than you."

James Parker added to his report. "There's still more, General, *much* more, and the reason Pescari thinks we should take it over. The fighting force is still small, only a couple of families, but they've built additional bunkhouses and now single men have joined them."

"You think they're recruiting their own army?"

"Possibly. We saw ten more than last time but nothing full-fledged. I think they've given their loyalty to the Nature Boys and aren't worried about our protection anymore." Chad suggested.

"Then why the extra bunkhouses, and who's building the heavy defenses?"

Pescari said it bluntly. "They've taken slaves, General Rankin. There's between thirty and fifty noncombatants in that compound, wearing shackles and doing all the work."

Max's hair bristled at the thought of slaves. That was one institution he and the Colonel had agreed should never be allowed to exist in New America. Those Nature Boys and men like Mike Donelson were a hindrance to rebuilding society, and this backward step would incite the street gangs into more violence if they thought the Regiment supported it. Worse, they wouldn't attack the problem, they would end up attacking those opposed to it.

"You're certain of it?"

"Highest probability, sir," Pescari assured him. "Without seeing the slaves with our own eyes I can't be certain, but I'll send more scouts to set up observation if you order it."

"Make it so. I need certainty and facts, not probability to make decisions like this."

"Aye, sir."

The Outriders had stowed their mounts and began moving the satchels toward the building. Max met eyes with James Parker, singling him out. "Corporal, I want you to stay behind. Can you spare him, Sergeant Pescari?"

"I can."

"Good." Max waited till everyone had left but him, Shayde, and James.

"What can I do for you, General?" Parker asked, standing taller.

"Stop calling me that."

"Stop telling the men to stop calling you that," Shayde suddenly corrected his leader.

Rankin flashed caution.

"Oh, get over it. If the men see you as their general and call you that, it's because they don't want another *Colonel*. They want and respect *you* and are placing you higher than him in their respect. Just friggin' go with it, *General* Rankin."

Max let out a reluctant sigh then turned back to Parker. "Well, you may respect me as such now, Parker, but you may not soon. I need to ask you some questions about the night the officers died."

"Anything, sir!" The young man's eyes clouded with worry but he stood taller, clenching his teeth. There was true anxiety here.

"Cathy Fletcher... Doc... said she only showed two people the location of her hidden poison. She admitted that you were one of those two people. Who was the other?"

"Linda Johnson, sir!"

"Did you know Ms. Johnson, Corporal?" Max watched the young man's face closely for a response.

"I do. She works in the kitchen." Though appearing thoughtful, he gave nothing away.

"So, you *knew* she worked in the kitchen and had access to ricin, but you never reported that to Walters or me after the event?"

"Well, no, sir! I was the one who reported it happened, but you had just been attacked on the street and people inside were panicking. It was a crazy time, sir! After that, I just kind of didn't think about it." His eyes flickered. There was a lie hidden somewhere in that statement.

"Do you think Ms. Johnson killed the officers?"

"I don't know, sir, but I don't think she's capable of it. Nice lady, her."

"Was it you?" Shayde asked casually. "Did you do it?"

"Sarge? No, of course not. I just carried the satchel upstairs, I thought..." He cut off abruptly, about to say something damning for somebody.

"Thought *what*, exactly, Parker? Tell us," Max insisted, watching the young man, barely more than a boy, carefully.

Parker turned crestfallen, sad even. "I think Cathy did it herself. She said she planned to in a couple of weeks, after things quieted, but only Hank and Steve. She never intended to kill them all. I think she panicked and did it to avoid her wedding night. Or, she meant to put Linda up to it. I think killing them *all* was an accident."

"You're in love with Cathy Fletcher?"

The corporal nodded. "Yes, sir. Very much. She has a boy too. He can't be without his mom. Can't you just let this go? The Colonel and the others are gone and you're in charge. Leave it a mystery. No one has to be found out or punished. Please, sir."

"I can't and I won't," Max said shaking his head. "We're about law and order in New America, and someone *will* have to be held accountable. I, like you, hope it wasn't Cathy. But the likely killer *will* be found and held accountable unless someone else steps forward and confesses." The corporal said nothing, only stared at the ground. "Do you understand, son?"

"Yes, sir."

"Then go get showered and cleaned up. You did well today and your intel is valuable. We just need to corroborate it before taking action. Good job, son."

"Thank you, General." James did not waste any time scurrying toward the building, leaving Max and Shayde alone.

"You think he did it?" Shayde asked.

"I *think* Linda Johnson did it, not him or Cathy, but there's no way to know."

"I think it was Cathy, but we need her. We *could* do as he suggested— just leave it alone and unsolved."

"No, Shayde. If we do that we'll have bigger problems later. We need to find the killer and hold him or her responsible, then make a public display of their punishment."

"There *is* one way to speed things up," Walters suggested.

Max flinched at the memory of his own arrival to the Shelter. Yes, there was a way. "Come on, let's get inside. All these windows make me nervous."

CHAPTER SIX

Clint Fletcher was a nice man. At least he seemed to be. Stephanie Yurik, Benjamin Roark, and the children all thought so.

David found him offsetting, too confident, and somewhat boastful. Full of stories about his army time, he talked openly about his battles and held nothing back. It was almost as if he enjoyed the rush and thrill of it all, especially the bloodiness, and that bothered David the most.

Benjamin Roark listened intently, taking it all in and nodding along. The children listened just as closely, but with wide eyes that seemed to regard this man as a battle-hardened warrior. That worried David just as much but, as long as he sailed the boat upriver, the braggart could chatter about whatever he wanted.

The boat turned out to be perfect. A river craft with a single mast and oars. It easily carried their supplies and, while much slower than *Estowen*, made good time. David realized, of course, the children had kept a steady stream of soft wind in the sail, making the journey easier for the pilot even if he never noticed.

After a day on the water they came across something unexpected, so much so it silenced Clint immediately. He changed at once, suddenly serious and less talkative, jumping into action alongside Roark.

"What is it?" Stephanie asked.

"Movement in those trees," Roark had seen it too, ever watchful and an expert scout. "Seems civilian, but I advise pushing forward."

"I agree," David said without hesitation. He wanted to get to Evansville quickly and without delay.

"No," Eve suddenly dissented. All eyes turned to her. "They *are* civilians—and friendlies. They need our help and we have room for them all."

"Absolutely not!" Clint argued quietly. "We know nothing about them, not their motives, whether they're armed, nothing! They will probably kill us and rob your supplies. These things are precious commodities."

"Like you once planned to do to *us*?" Eve asked casually with a raised eyebrow.

Clint paused at this, turning red in the face. "I never!"

"You did when you first approached. Your original plan was to feel us out and then kill on the spot, but Sergeant Roark showed himself and you released your gun. I had seen it several times. In some visions you drew it but in others you didn't. Each time you tried, the attempt failed because he gunned you down first."

"What *is* this crazy shit?" Clint demanded, turning to Roark instead of David. The sergeant only shrugged and deferred to Dr. Andalon.

"There are children, Mr. Fletcher, and then there are *these* children. They are special, and that's why we travel with them. That's all you need to know."

"That's crazy talk, not *special*. What did she mean by she had *seen* it? What's this talk about *visions*?"

"You keep a gun in the appendix of your waistband, Mr. Fletcher," Adam explained. "It's a Ruger 9mm, nothing special, but easy to carry concealed. You don't have a lot of rounds for it, though. Only one hundred total, so you really don't want to use those up in a firefight. That's why you waited."

Clint's eyes had grown wide with shock, but watched and listened, waiting to learn more. "Where did I get it, then?"

"Not where you found the boat. You told the truth that you walked from Ohio—Ludlow Falls, to be exact, but you are originally from Michigan. I overheard you tell that to Rusty and Susan in one of my dreams," Eve explained.

David had no idea who Rusty and Susan were and could tell Eve was leaving out details. So did Clint, apparently. Whatever it was seemed to put him off balance. *How much evil has he done that she won't mention it aloud to him?* he wondered. *She's manipulating the man, getting inside of his head and making him wonder.*

"That's all?" Clint asked. "You had a dream?" He laughed it off dismissively. "That still ain't enough to make me pull this boat over to *parlay* with potential hostiles."

"They aren't hostiles, Mr. Fletcher," Adam insisted. "It's a man, his wife, and his sister. His sister is pregnant and needs medical attention that only Dr. Andalon can provide. If we stop and help them, they will help us much more later—more than you could ever imagine."

Clint stared blankly, considering his options, then abruptly sprang into action. In a single motion he closed the sail and moved the rudder to port. In a few moments they had drifted near shore. Without getting out of the boat he dropped anchor and pointed to the five feet of water between the vessel and land. "Go on, this is as far as I go. I ain't gettin' my feet wet on this one."

Roark held out his left hand. "After you give me the Ruger," he said with a dangerous tone, pointing at the man's waistband. His right-hand held his own sidearm, a much beefier Kimber 1911 .45 caliber.

David watched the exchange, two men no longer sizing each other up but now squaring off in a contest of will.

After the briefest of moments, Clint shrugged off his reluctance and smiled. "You guys are in charge," he said, carefully drawing out and handing over his pistol.

Benjamin eased his posture, keeping both eyes on Clint to ensure he didn't run off with the boat after they disembarked.

That left it to David to climb over the side and wade to the shoreline, pulling on a long rope to bring it ashore. After tying it off, he helped Stephanie and Eve to step down. He hoped the presence of another woman and child would prove to the family they were harmless—if you could consider Eve harmless.

The girl looked up and winked as if reading his thoughts. He really hated when she did stuff like that.

Get out of my head, he told her.

No, I like it in there, she giggled.

It didn't take long for the man to approach.

David noticed the women held back, hiding in the trees. One of them was seated with her back to a tree. He waved with a smile and hoped the man was exactly what Eve insisted he was.

He is, she said into his mind. *He's harmless, not like Clint. You're going to have to deal with* him *later, by the way. Prepare yourself for that.*

"What?" David asked the girl, shocked.

"Hello!" the man called out. He had a deep accent from West Virginia, David guessed. "Please help us," he called again. He held a wad of cash in front of him. All American dollars which caused David to frown.

Doesn't he know that's worthless? he wondered. But then again, the man was desperate.

"My sister's pregnant," the man added, "about to give birth any day!"

"Put your money away, sir," David said calmly. "We don't need it and won't take it. We'll help. Just tell us your story. Where are we? What part of West Virginia?"

"Huntington," the man said, cramming the bills back into his pocket. "We've been holed up for months, but once Sally started contractions, we tried to go into town."

"How far away is it?" David asked.

The man stared blankly and pointed at the river. "Washed away, all of it. The entire town is gone from that flood a few months ago. We didn't know, or we wouldn't have come!"

That's not good, David thought. "How far apart are her contractions?"

The man looked to one of the women who held up two hands.

Ten minutes. She's in active labor. "Come on," he said. "Get her on the boat. I'm a doctor and I have supplies."

"Wait, what kind of doctor?" the man demanded.

Really? Now you care what kind of help you get? "I'm a doctor!" David snapped. "Get her aboard! Your wife, too!" He nodded to Stephanie and Eve who hurried forward to help the woman get up off the ground. As they moved her to the water, David paused to reach his hand out to shake the man's. "I'm Dr. David Andalon," he said.

"Elijah Miller," the man replied in an Appalachian accent. "My sister's Sally, and my wife's Emma."

David nodded and together they handed first Sally, then the other women and Eve up to Clint and Benjamin. They hauled them on board then armed up David and Elijah. As he stepped onboard, the doctor said to Clint. "We only moved about ninety miles upriver, today, which means we're more than four days out of Evansville. We have to move faster." Turning to Adam and Eve, he said, "More wind, don't hold back. Get us there safely in two."

Clint looked to Roark and asked, "What does he mean by more wind?" Then stared at the children with wide eyes as the sergeant explained.

David rushed downstairs, uncaring that secrets were revealed to Clint. *How bad could he be,* he wondered, *if the children trust him?*

There was one bunk room in the boat, not large but big enough for a delivery. Stephanie settled Sally while David scrubbed with alcohol and readied his medical kit. He had never delivered a baby before, but knew the basics well enough. His first order of business was to check the child's position. Placing both hands on Sally's belly he felt for the head.

The baby was breech.

At least, he thought it was. Careful not to appear panicked to the others, he slightly moved his hands to the side.

Is it alive? Eve's voice asked in his mind.

I think so, he replied.

Don't think so, she urged, *know so.*

Andalon tried again, this time like before on the battlefield in Germany, and let a trickle of his own lifeforce cross through his palms. It felt odd probing a living human, feeling both the mother's and child's forces move aside to admit his own. That had been a surprise, at how easily he gained entrance.

He first examined the child. *It lives,* he told Eve.

Good. Go on.

It was indeed breech, and David thought of ways to turn it. Without experience in obstetrics, he couldn't just start pushing and poking at it. He urged it tenderly with his own lifeforce, convincing it to turn, that it *wanted* to turn. Then he poured forth more, that it *needed* to turn and soon. To his shock it worked, as the fetus slowly wriggled away to find the correct position.

I'm a healer, he marveled.

Exactly, Eve agreed. *Now heal* her.

Her? He knew who the girl meant, but did not grasp the urgency. *What's wrong with her?*

I don't know. I can't do what you do, Father, but she is gravely ill.

David finished moving the infant and probed Sally. As she moaned with contractions, he felt them too, rippling through his body and fully sharing with him the experience. He regretted any time he had joked with a woman by downplaying the pain of childbirth. There was no way he could endure as much more of it as she would.

At first all he could feel were the birthing pangs. But then a part of his mind opened and he knew the extent of her damage. Her radiation poisoning had destroyed her thyroid. Though not yet showing goiters, she would and very soon. This young woman, deep in her prime, would never experience life the same way. He immediately went to work finding a way to heal the damage he found.

Exhausted, he pulled away his hands. The final vision he glimpsed of her lifeforce was the organ glowing with renewed vigor. As if the woman could tell, she immediately grew more energy, pushing into the next contraction with vigor.

"No, dear, not yet. The baby just got into position and I haven't checked your cervix." This was the part he dreaded, reaching down without properly cleaned hands or a sterile setting. Any sort of infection could result and…

Just do it, Eve urged, and he did.

Ten centimeters. The child could come soon.

He looked Sally in the eye and waited till she showed signs of the next contraction then nodded. It was time. "Push," he told her.

After several more of those, the infant emerged, a tiny girl. David Andalon, the man incapable of making life, had delivered it. He took a cloth and wiped the child before swaddling and handing her off to Sally. He thought they would have a few minutes before dealing with the afterbirth.

Cut the cord, Eve reminded.

Oh, yes.

"Thank you, Doctor," Sally managed, smiling up through her exhaustion.

"Not a problem at all, ma'am," he smiled back. "Also, I think you'll find you will have a lot more energy, now that you've delivered."

What else did you do to her? Eve asked.

I'll tell you later, he replied.

But she's better?

Yes. I think we all *will be soon.*

Good job today, Father. I knew you could do it. I love you.

David had not heard those first words ever and the second words in such a long time. He fought tears as he clipped and cut the umbilical cord, but somehow managed. He finally felt like a father and, much more, finally felt appreciated for his efforts.

If only Brooke could have seen him as a father too, instead of just as a husband.

"I'll take care of the afterbirth," Stephanie Yurik told him.

David nodded and grabbed a bag from his supplies. Taking these topside, he emerged to greet Elijah Miller sitting with Benjamin Roark and Clint Fletcher. The man watched him with expectant eyes.

"Healthy," Andalon assured him, "both mother and child."

"Thank you," the man wrapped the doctor in an eager embrace, thrilled by the news.

"She's fine, but had some damage caused by the radiation," David explained. "I patched her up a bit during the delivery, but you need to consider treatment for yourself too."

"What can I do? We've all been exposed," Miller asked.

"I have a vaccine that can stave off further affects and even repair damage already done. I think you should be dosed."

Miller rolled up his sleeve eagerly and allowed David to draw a needle and plunge it into his shoulder.

"You too?" David asked Clint.

"Nope. Not a chance in hell I'm getting a vaccine, certainly not after that bullshit they gave me in 2021."

"This is different," Roark insisted, backing up the doctor. "I've had it myself and can walk freely in the worst of it." He smiled and showed his teeth to the man, proving they were all intact.

"I said, no!" Clint insisted.

David shrugged and put away his vials. "Not a problem," he said, "It's a free country." He looked around, noticing how much faster the boat moved with both children filling the sail with wind. *There will be others to treat in Evansville.* "But radiation poisoning is a different kind of threat, and you're already exposed. You could bleed internally, lose bone mass and density, or even lose your ability for an erection," he added for measure. "But, this will stop the effect and reverse any adverse symptoms you may already have."

That bit about an erectile dysfunction seemed to have caused worry. "Just one dose? None of those *boosters*?"

"That's right."

Clint rolled up his sleeve. "Fine. Can't be worse than those Anthrax shots they gave me before deployment."

David pulled out three vials, pausing for a brief moment while weighing his choice.

Batch Bravo in this man might prove helpful later, Eve's voice suggested.

That's dangerous. We know nothing about this man!

Adam and I have both seen his destiny and agree it's best, she insisted.

David replaced one of the vials, drawing a bit of the two remaining into a syringe.

"You've made a good choice," David told Clint, then wondered and hoped he had too. With only a brief hesitation he plunged the mixture into the man's upper arm.

CHAPTER SEVEN

Max lit the candle wicks while Cathy Fletcher watched curiously. When his soldiers had come, forcibly taking the nurse in the night, she had expected interrogation or worse, but certainly not dinner by candlelight. If this was a line of questioning, this man had a strange way of setting up the fear and anxiety, skipping straight to the romantic dinner and gentlemanly behavior.

"What the hell *is* this?" she asked.

"What's what?" he replied, shrugging off her question.

She pointed at the spread, a wealthy meal given their circumstances, something she had not seen in six months. Though comprised mostly of rations, there were luxuries like honey and butter to spread on fresh cornbread. A very nice bottle of wine sat nearby with two glasses—expensive crystal waiting to be filled. "Either you've decided now to wine, dine, and *bed* me, or you're about to interrogate me. You can't have it both ways, Mr. Rankin."

"I assure you my intentions are purely proper, Cathy." His voice was as calm as it always was. A soldier through and through, despite his recent elevation to general or king, or whatever Max Rankin had become to the Regiment. "I *do* wish to wine and dine you, but not to take you to bed. Rest easy on that worry. I simply want to talk."

"Talk? You have a funny way of sending an invitation. Soldiers came and grabbed James, Linda, and me from our hovels by force, in the middle of the night of all times!" She felt anger rise at that memory, having just put Josh down for sleep when the arrest was made. "Where's my son? They took him an opposite way from me!"

She thought of Josh's eyes in that moment and how the school teacher had led him away, promising, "Mommy needs to talk to these men, so you get to hang out with *me* tonight." Though they both trusted Mr. Starlings, the way the man's eyes had met hers held a sinister look, almost judgmental, like he knew *why* they took the boy's mother away.

"That was uncalled for," she insisted, "taking my child by force. I would have left him with Mr. Starlings myself if you had given me notice. I would have willingly met with you."

"I needed to do it this way, but my actions were not against *you*." Max picked up the bottle of wine and began to pour, then offered a glass to Cathy.

There was no way she was missing out on a glass of fine Cabernet and took it eagerly.

"In fact, I'm very sorry for how tonight went down, but every action we took served a purpose. Trust me when I say it *isn't* about you at all. You already gave us your statement."

"Surely you don't think I'm stupid. I know this is a ruse to get more out of me—to *ease* it out with wine and put me off guard. Well, I gave you the *entire* truth the other day. Yes, I had the ricin in my bag. Yes, I was going to use it, just not that night. I don't know who did!"

"That's what tonight's for, Cathy." Max took a sip from his own glass and sat back with a sigh. "I don't have time for a full investigation. I need answers *now*. I'm about to make a decision that will bring either war or peace, or possibly both at the same time. But I *can't* and *won't* make that lightly. Not without facts. The death of the Colonel and the other officers, not to mention their wives and families, was a mass *murder*. I won't be a fit ruler until I've solved the mystery and held someone accountable. Until I do, I can't win over the street gangs and especially not men like Mike Donelson."

She laughed angrily at the name. "Crazy Mike. I'd *love* to have some words with *that* man."

"I know you would," Max agreed.

"So, if you're looking for the killer, what's your plan? Sequester me away to luxury just to keep me away from the others? Then you tell them lies like *I said it was Linda or James* to get them to fess up? That won't work. They won't talk. I already tried, and Linda wouldn't confess."

"Then it was James Parker."

"No, I don't think so. I mean, he *did* want Hank and Steve dead, even said that night they deserved it, but... No, I don't think he did it."

"So you think it's Linda?"

"She's my best bet. I saved her from Steve, remember?" The memory of gouging the man's eyes passed nausea through her stomach, almost ruining her appetite. She had overreacted, Cathy knew that now. "But she's about to give birth," she added. "What good would punishing a new mother do? What kind of statement would that make?"

He merely nodded, lifting a set of silver cutlery and began to carve a piece of ham. Cathy nearly salivated. Actual meat had been absent from the menu for months. "Is that real?" she asked.

He nodded. "Salt-cured and kept in the cellar. It's part of what the Colonel had planned to serve for the first Christmas feast after the event. I pulled out the smallest, thought it would make this conversation go easier."

"It's working," Cathy admitted.

"So, tell me *why* you think it's Linda," he said gently, "and don't forget I spent several days on the road with her. I know all about her attitude, have seen her temper first hand, and even witnessed her kill others to save herself. But even so, after all that, I'm not convinced it's her. Please tell me why *you* think she did this."

"Well for one, in her mind, she's lost everything to live for."

"That's no reason to kill. So have I. Besides, she's expecting a child—a happy development and something to look forward to. Why would a mother risk not being there to raise her child?"

"That's just it, Max. Deep down she wants it but doubts her worth as a mother after losing her husband and teenagers. She also fears it will be a mutant monster. She's afraid, terrified actually, of living alone or with that *thing* if it's not human."

"Still not a reason to kill thirty people in a single night."

"No, but enough to weaken your mind enough to do something that leads to murder, even on that scale."

Max nodded, thoughtfully considering her words.

Linda Johnson entered the room blindfolded and dignified. After all she had been through, it would take more than intimidation and isolation to break her. She was a mother—a wife who had lost everything, with grit and determination to make it through whatever interrogation they brought down.

Her anger fumed, but mostly at the way they had come in the night and taken James Parker, Cathy Fletcher, separating them to interrogate each alone. Linda was a smart woman and knew that meant they had nothing concrete—no evidence to support their hunches. Max Rankin grasped at straws, willing to rush his investigation into the killing of the officers. *They can ask questions all they want,* she thought. Max had nothing on any of them—no proof at all.

Linda removed the blindfold. The room was nothing out of the ordinary and wasn't nearly worth the pomp and circumstance of her arrest. She had nothing to fear. Even in the dark of night it was an ordinary jail cell. Glancing upward she noticed high windows, uncovered to let light in during the day. That eased her nerves—light would be good. She decided to rest here, to sleep deeply and gather her thoughts before answering whatever questions they asked in the morning.

Linda Johnson had nothing to fear from interrogation.

"Let's talk about James Parker, then." Max changed the topic from Linda. "He loves you, but do you think he loves you enough to *kill* for you?"

"I don't know," Cathy admitted. "Look, the truth is that whichever of them did it, I'm glad it was done. True, innocent people died, but can you truly say it wasn't for the best? None of those *officers* were even real military men. They knew nothing about war or about forming or running a nation. They were wealthy men of convenience who played soldier with the Colonel and shot guns on the weekends. They were only his officers because they donated money for him to set this place up."

"That's true," Max agreed, "and I'll agree to all of that. Most of them *were* nothing more than donors to his cause, but they were still people, most of whom never harmed anyone. None of them deserved to die, not even Hank and Steve. Especially not the Colonel and the other men and their wives." He rested his elbows on the table and looked deeply into her eyes. "Tell me about James Parker. Was he angry enough that night to risk killing so many to get to Hank and Steve?"

Cathy thought again about that awful night and the words James said to her and Linda. He was plenty angry and, most of all, highly protective of *her*. He could have been feeling useless, unable to stop the unwanted wedding night she was about to endure, and that may have been enough to push him into killing without thinking about the consequences.

"How did *he* feel about the officers?" Max asked, breaking the nurse from her thoughts.

"He didn't respect them at all, thinking them frauds. He respected the sergeants though, fawning first over Shayde Walters and later you, in awe over your combat experience and true military bearing. He wanted to be like you and resented those lording down from their perch high above the gym floor. They were aristocrats, and he saw himself stuck at ground level."

"So it's possible he would have taken the chance of killing them all to hide the murder of two."

"I guess so," she agreed.

Rough hands heaved James Parker into the air, tossing him around like a ragdoll before folding the beaten man and depositing him into a cramped barrel. He wasn't afraid, knowing these men were on his own team and wouldn't have orders to kill. They would only ask questions, using the barrel as a tool to gain answers. It was cramped, a tight fit, but not impossible to breathe inside of. That's what they were doing, forcing him to breathe with his legs pulled tightly to his chest to only make him *feel* like he would suffocate. The proof they meant him no harm was the drilled holes along the top edge. Like a pet in a shoebox, he at least had air to breathe in his tiny prison. He had nothing to worry about, even after the lid closed tightly overhead.

A few minutes later, water poured in from one of those holes along the top.

At first it was only a sensation of cold dripping on his face and taking away what little breath he could muster against the pressure. He learned to conserve his air by looking away and breathing in only through his nose. It worked to relax him as well, reminding the young prisoner it wasn't actually torture, only a test of his resolve against their words. He would give up nothing more than he had already, focusing on what he had already said.

But then the water poured faster and panic set in.

"Well then," Max said suddenly, standing and swigging the last of his wine, "that's all I really wanted to ask you, so I bid you goodnight, Cathy."

"Am I free to go get Josh and return to my hovel?"

"No, I'm afraid you're still in custody. At least for tonight and tomorrow. In the next room you will find more luxuries, a soft gown to sleep in, and a queen-sized bed with a real mattress. It belonged to the Colonel, but I needed something firmer, so I had it brought here. It's yours for the next night or so, and I hope you enjoy a full night of rest."

The general turned to leave.

"Wait!" Cathy pleaded.

He paused.

"That's it? You really only wanted to share polite conversation in a nice atmosphere, then grant me a full night's sleep?"

"Yep. That was it."

"You're strange, Max Rankin, but not a bad man. I think I could really trust and like you if you hadn't split me from my son."

Max paused by the door and knocked, alerting the guard outside he was ready to be let out. Before he departed, he turned his head and said without looking her in the eye, "Thank you for the kind words, but when you figure out what I *really* did tonight, you're going to hate me forever. You deserved this evening of pleasantry because it's the last you'll ever want from me."

Cathy watched him leave, blinking and wondering at his final words.

Linda Johnson awoke, covering her eyes from blinding light and wincing at the pain it brought. After months of living indoors and rarely even venturing out, it was too much to bear. As she blinked them open, she realized the room itself was the problem—painted entirely white, the brightest shade possible, light flooded in and amplified the brilliance. As her orbs adjusted she realized *everything* in this room glowed just as stark. Her pillow, the sheets, the mattress, the bunk, even the table beside all those, all were brightly reflecting a radiant scene.

How odd, she thought, that a room could retain such an immaculate purity after civilization itself had crumbled into darkness and decay.

After a few minutes of staring at the walls and ceiling, the door, also white, opened to reveal a white hallway. Two men emerged dressed from head to toe in white scrubs, placed a white tray with a white dish and white plastic utensil on the white table, and departed. They locked the white lock behind them.

Linda stared at the food in her white bowl. White rice.

She began to laugh hysterically at Max's joke. Soon that laughter turned to tears which fell into sobs, and she sent the bowl of rice flying across the white room in a fit of red rage.

CHAPTER EIGHT

The stress of leadership always wearies the man or woman bearing it—a crushing weight with invisible and unfathomable pressure, especially those who never intended to carry the burden. After three days of keeping Cathy and the others in captivity, Max Rankin was losing more and more respect for himself. He was no better than the Colonel now, having stooped to the lowest level possible—and not only for the torture, but for the *other* part of it all. True, he was closer to revealing the killer, but then what? What would he actually do with the knowledge, no matter *who* the culprit had been?

That was only part of his weariness, and the decision to expand his territory southward also loomed. In order to claim the city, he needed to secure all four directions and hold them equally. Chad Pescari had been right to suggest expansion, but at what cost? To do that he would have to crush the street gangs, bringing what remained under his banner. But before *they* could be dealt with, he needed to figure out what Mike Donelson was up to in his compound.

Pescari had been right about that too. It stood in a prime location that would protect the main city and its flanks. But what rationale would the Regiment use to take a man's property? *Is* Crazy Mike *using slaves to build his fortress?* the general wondered, considering the man's end goal of playing both parties while stuck firmly between the Nature Boys and the Regiment. *Is he simply thinking survival?* Donelson couldn't keep two masters long and surely had already betrayed one to the other.

Max *needed* answers.

A knock on the door suggested some may have arrived. Lifting weary eyes, he focused on Chad Pescari.

"Well?" he asked. "What've you found out, Sergeant?"

"More than we thought we would, General."

Enough with that General crap! Max was ready to scream and would have if he wasn't so damned tired. "Go on," he urged.

"I'll start with the far south. My Outriders pushed deeper than ever, and we've got a bigger problem than we thought. The Nature Boys hold a triangle from Hopkinsville to Bowling Green and up to Beaver Dam. Their base of operations is the old Fort Campbell. They must have had members in place on the base for it to have fallen to them so quickly."

"There had better be good news as well."

"There is. Everything west of that territory is flooded to Madisonville, so they moved east and haven't completely settled. That's why we never ran into them. Their main force is nomadic."

"How many fighting men?"

"I counted at least six hundred, sir, but I fear they may have a thousand. They're much stronger and better outfitted than we. They even wear matching uniforms."

Max felt a lump in his throat. Most of his population were civilians, old or too young, sick or lame, but all certainly untrained. At best he could only muster two hundred men to fight, despite how well stocked the Shelter was. *Our resources will make us their target very soon.* "Then we don't have a choice at all," he finally said aloud. "We only hold downtown, everything between the river and the freeway. We'll defend against an invasion like Lee held against Burnside at Fredericksburg."

Pescari shook his head. "With all due respect, sir, I need to finish giving my report. I told you they reach as far north as Beaver Dam, but now I'm certain they also claim Mike Donelson as an ally. With his compound south of Owensboro available to them, they'll be on our doorstep in no time. They don't have any troops there yet, but his fort will give them a firm position to own everything south of the Ohio river once it's finished. We're running out of time."

Max considered this. *If* Donelson has already chosen the Nature Boys, then the battle to claim Evansville would be easier by far. His fort would serve as the tip of the arrow to feed the invasion northward from there, then west along the river bank. The Shelter would easily fall in a manner of weeks—sooner if they bring artillery.

"I don't know," he mused. "I need proof he's connected himself to them. What about the slave situation? Did you get a visual?"

"Not yet. We can't see inside while they're working, but there's certainly activity to suggest there's a lot of people inside those walls," Pescari agreed. "Worse, we saw tracks in the snow to suggest they moved more vehicles inside while we roamed south for a peek at the Nature Boys."

Slaves. Max thought of his son, Tom. *He called me a sellout to my people. What if he's right? The street gangs predicted groups like the Nature Boys would take slaves, and this would be proof to him and others they had a bigger war to fight.* But that wasn't right, was it? There was no guarantee the slaves would be of African descent. For all Max knew they could all be white farmers taken in their time of weakness, just like when Crazy Mike kidnapped and sold Cathy Fletcher to the Colonel.

"I have to see their skin color," Max muttered, then had another thought. Perhaps the threat of the problem would be enough to *gain* allies in the fight against the south. *I have to move first. To get to them before the Nature Boys spin a different tale.* "Chad? Can you get me a meeting with the street gangs?"

The sergeant's face blanched as if all blood had left him. "I can... I can try, General. What do I tell them you want?"

"Tell them I want a parlay. Tell them I took over the Regiment, and that the Colonel is dead..."

"Sir! If you tell them that, then Donelson will know as well. With that knowledge, the Nature Boys will see us as week and surely attack!"

"True, but I think they already know, so there's no more use hiding it from anybody. Tell them I'm ready to talk. They wouldn't meet with the Colonel, but they may give my face ten minutes of their time."

Pescari nodded then turned to leave, pausing as the door opened to admit Sergeant Walters.

Shayde noticed immediately the man was bothered, eyeing Max for answers while anxious to give his own news. He waited until Pescari left and for the door to shut in their privacy.

"What was that all about?" Shayde asked.

"I ordered him to get me a meeting with the street gangs. I need to negotiate an end to that part of the war."

"Ouch. That goal's gonna be tough. What will you offer?"

"I don't know. The airport, maybe?"

"Too critical. Give them the university and let *them* be our western flank."

"Southern Indiana?" Max considered. It *was* still mostly intact, but was close to the Shelter. It also housed a small group of refugees who never chose a side. "They might accept it as a way of balancing central power," the general agreed.

"That balance won't matter if we take Donelson's fort on the south side of the river. With that, downtown, and the airport we'll retain the upper hand."

"I'll think on it." Max leaned back, took in a deep breath, then asked the question he dreaded the most. "What did you find out? I'm assuming you're here because you know who killed the officers."

Shayde sat down across from his friend and put his feet up on the desk, smiling broadly as he did. "It was three days of dirty business, but they all finally broke."

"You have the entire story?" Max sat up, eager to hear.

"I do. Cathy Fletcher was telling the truth. She had nothing to do with that night and truly intended to kill only Hank and Steve a few weeks later."

"Was it Linda?"

"Hold your horses, this is *my* story and *I* get to tell it."

Max smiled. It felt good to let someone else be in charge for a bit, even if only one moment. "Go on," he urged, grinning away.

"James Parker isn't weak, by the way. He handled that barrel almost as good as you. But he *did* crack and admitted he *was* going to kill them all. He had thought about it, talked it over with Linda, and even took the ricin packet out of Cathy's bag. They discussed a plan to the simplest detail which involved spiking the stew. But he claims to have changed his mind and chickened out at the last moment."

"So how about Linda then? How'd she handle the White Room?"

"It broke her the first day. She's a mess right now, sniveling and crumbled in the corner of it and crying about her lost family. She admitted to pocketing the ricin pouch when Parker left the kitchen to put Cathy's bags in Hank's bedroom. Linda admitted to going as far as opening the packet and holding it over the pot but then set it back down again." Shayde frowned a bit and added, "Cathy was right about Linda. She's not as strong as she gives off, and that bitch act is all a front. She's terrified of her own shadow and every kind of uncertainty. She didn't do it, Max. She hid the packet in a cabinet."

"And Parker and Fletcher never knew where she put it, so neither of them did it?"

"Exactly."

"Damn it, I hate I was right."

"I do too, for *his* sake. It didn't turn out as cut and dry as we'd hoped. So now we need a scapegoat."

"I think I have one. Let Linda out of the white room, but dry off Parker and bring him to me. I need to make him an offer that puts it all back together."

"Like duct tape," Shayde pointed out. "That shit fixed everything on the battlefield."

"Like duct tape," Max agreed. "And Shayde, make sure Fletcher doesn't get out until Parker makes his choice."

Shayde exaggerated a salute and then left to carry out his orders.

To Max's surprise the meeting with the street gangs actually happened, and he found himself standing face to face with Tom. It was a low blow, sending his own son to meet with him, an emotional power move for sure. The venue was neutral and wide open—Garvin Park near the lake. With all the green space, both sides felt more comfortable, and they met at the ballpark to avoid snipers from either side hiding in trees.

"You look healthy, Son."

"Not your son," his boy replied, not meeting his eyes.

"Whether you like it or not, you'll always be my son. I love you and I always will."

"You chose your side when you joined these slave masters! You're part of the colonial aristocracy!"

"The aristocracy's dead, Tom. All of them. The Colonel, all of his financial backers, and even their wives. It was a total wipe."

Tom laughed. "Ain't no way *you* did that. Sellout."

"No, I didn't. It wasn't my intent to kill anyone or take over anything, but they *are* gone and I'm now completely in charge. I've got the power to negotiate, and I want this war between us to end. I'm coming with a proposition that will benefit all of us. Your faction is dying—starving out. I also think you lost a lot of fighters when the drugs ran out."

"Most got dry."

"For now," Max shrugged. "Either way, you need what only we can offer. We have supplies enough to feed and *arm* all of us if we work together."

"Or we can *take* those supplies from you," Tom threatened. "We don't need you, just what you've got."

"No, Son, your side isn't powerful enough to take what I have, and you *need* me to share it with you. There's an entire army moving up from the south. It's the Nature Boys, our *real* enemy. Word is they're taking slaves and building a kingdom."

"Slaves don't mean nothin' to us, unless they're black."

"Black or white doesn't matter anymore."

"Yes it does! You're just too whitewashed to see it! You're blind, just like Mom and I never mattered to you!"

"How *did* she die, Son? You never told me."

Tom paused, as if reliving the memory. "Gunshot by one of your *Regiment*. We were trying to get to one of the city's shelters, but they thought we were looters. A shot rang out and Mom dropped her bags and fell over. I couldn't save her."

"How did you know the shooter was with the Regiment?"

"He was white."

Max groaned with irritation. Talking to Tom when he was like this felt like talking to a wall. "The color of the shooter doesn't mean they were Regiment. It could have been a homeowner who panicked."

Tom shrugged but didn't press, so that was progress.

"Like I was saying, the Nature Boys have big numbers and are moving north. We have to work together or they'll fracture us into starvation. Either way, you'll have no say in the matter and end up with either us or them and will be forced to settle down as a new society."

"Miko's gonna want guarantees the slaves they're taking are black. He won't care about them taking whites."

"I don't have that proof yet but will give it to you as soon as I do."

Tom laughed. "You ain't got shit, do you?"

"I've got proof they're using slaves south of the river, just not what they look like."

"Get us that, and I'll get Miko to talk to you."

"Tom... Son, please. You know me, and although I wasn't the best dad, you know I'm not a sellout to my people. I love my country, *everyone* in it!"

"Yeah, you love ninety percent of it more than your own kind." Tom turned to leave. He was finished talking.

"Tell Miko I'm offering him to hold the University of Southern Indiana and enough supplies for all your people for one year."

Tom paused, asking over his shoulder, "In exchange for what?"

"Stop the attacks on our convoys and cease sniping near the Shelter. The University's yours as long as we get a cease fire. If he won't help, then I want Miko's promise he'll stop attacking long enough for us to face off the Nature Boys."

Tom grunted then casually strolled away, joining his friends across the park.

Did I offer too much? Max wondered, watching his son walk away from him a second time since the fall of civilization. *And did I offer it all because of him?*

CHAPTER NINE

Sam Nakala used a pipette to draw a bit of the serum. It was cloudy, deeply opaque with a greyish appearance, but otherwise indistinguishable from the other three samples. He allowed three drops to drip and stepped back. Everything they had done since Doctor Andalon had departed felt strange, but this added a bit of wrongness—this business of taking fluid from unborn fetuses. He exchanged a glance with Mi-Jung, belly now round with her own child, and accepted her warm smile as reassurance. Only his wife understood how awful he felt doing this, and he loved her very much.

"Good, Sam," Brooke Andalon praised from across the table, "now all we have to do is feed it to the mice."

Sam knew that wasn't right, though. There was more they had to do like adding the catalyst. Every experiment needed one to force change, even these dark ones. He merely nodded and carried each tray of food, placed them one by one to the designated cage, and stepped back once more. At least *he* wouldn't have to initiate the catalyst. All he had to do was feed the mice.

Four cages with five critters in each gave them twenty subjects total. It wasn't much to work with but seemed a miraculous bounty considering what few embryos they had to produce the serums. Brooke had chosen twenty of those fetuses, five each dedicated to David's batches, and every single one locked in their odd, drone-like states. They had no movement, no higher brain function, and no purpose above this one—to produce the serum.

Whatever Dr. Andalon had done to the formula before leaving, he had severely limited the development of the entire program. There would never be another Adam and Eve, only these non-sentient husks floating in their artificial wombs. It was safer, sure, than playing god with cloned humans—infinitely dangerous ones at that. Adam and Eve had proven far superior to the entire human race and not just for their powers. Their intellect had also been part of the success of the Andalon Project, the piece these drones completely lacked.

Sam watched as Brooke approached the first cage. Labeled *Batch Alpha,* it contained the serum drawn from the drones similar to Adam and Eve. *Emotants capable of manipulating air and possessing telepathy.* If this process worked, Esterling and his advisors would be able to harness those powers for themselves. The mice trapped inside the cage would determine if that outrageous hypothesis was even possible.

The tiny lifeforms had finished eating and settled down as if exhausted.

"That's odd," Brooke had noticed their state. There seemed to be a near instant effect of the serum. She pointed at each one of the cages, all twenty mice in a similar state of near sleep. "Let's begin," she hurriedly suggested. Time was essential.

The first cage was equipped with tiny tubing pumping in a steady stream of fresh air. She needed the mice to somehow work this like potter's clay, like the children had worked their own craft before. She applied the first catalyst, an injection of adrenaline into each.

At first nothing happened. Though their tiny heartbeats raced, the animals lay slumped with wide eyes staring off into the distance. One by one they began to convulse slightly, a ripple of muscle movement twitching beneath their skin.

"That's new," Sam observed, "but not at all how Adam and Eve described *their* powers coming on." Whatever David had done, the experiment had changed completely.

Brooke said nothing, only readied the next catalyst. She carefully placed the box within the cage, removing a tiny wire keeping it shut.

Sam watched with bated breath. The mice chosen for this part of the experiment had been specially altered to infuriate the others. He and Mi-Jung had called them hwanan, the Korean word for angry. Each had been modified by blocking certain brain receptors in their pre-frontal cortex, and this had severely lowered monoamine oxidase A in their bodies.

Without that enzyme all animals, including humans, would become prone to extreme aggression. These tiny hwanan mice had been bred to attack any others they came into contact with.

The door on the little box burst open and the first emerged, growling and hissing at the others lying quietly in their corner. It lunged and the others recoiled in fear. Unabated, the hwanan mouse attacked the closest, biting and ripping at its neck as if eagerly devouring a meal. Sam knew it would not stop until its victim lay dead.

"The others are watching but doing nothing," Brooke said with disappointment. This sickened Sam more deeply, to hear such hope for violence from a doctor he so well respected.

We've all changed, he realized, *since coming to this lab.*

"Wait!" Mi-Jung said with awe, squeezing a tiny bulb. Her action pumped a puff of blue baby powder into the cage that caught the air swirling inside. It traced the patterns as tiny wisps began to form, crudely weaving together invisible ropes. These wrapped like tendrils around the hwanan, catching its arms, legs, and snout while slowly constricting like boas killing their meal.

All at once the drugged mice stood and faced the newcomer, staring him down from across the cage. Mi-Jung squeezed another puff of blue powder into their cage and the humans watched in shocked excitement as the hwanan raised up as if dangling by a thread. The tiny tendrils of air continued to wrap around him, winding a tightly formed cocoon that seemed to shrink upon itself. One by one his tiny bones began to break, twisting and contorting his body until it hung malformed in the air above the others. Abruptly the tendrils disappeared and the drugged mice fell exhausted to the floor of their cage. In front of them, the broken body of the hwanan crashed with a soft splat.

"It works," Sam whispered and Brooke and Mi-Jung nodded vigorously. Had they not seen it, none of them would have believed it.

Together, they turned their attention to a cage marked *Batch Bravo.*

Felicima, Sam suddenly remembered, thinking of the rhesus monkey from their first lab in Cambridge. She had been cruelly treated by the other research animals, and David blamed her for starting the fire that burned his lab. It had been a preposterous accusation at the time but no longer seemed far-fetched. They were about to test that very possibility.

Sam's eyes turned toward a tiny Bunsen burner in the cage and his body shuddered. They had to be ready to immediately shut off the gas line feeding its flame. Brooke noticed his hand had moved to the valve and she nodded approval. They would have to be ready for anything from this batch.

Two hwanans were placed inside. Brooke's reasoning had been that, with fire, a stronger catalyst may be required. She placed the boxes and lifted the metal bars.

Sam counted silently, ticking off the seconds as they waited. Perhaps they needed motivation to leave their containers. He added a bit of food into the cage, placing it very near the resting experiments. Each of them ignored both his hand and the kibbles. Soon, pink noses emerged, sniffing the air and searching out the treat. Amazingly the hwanans tolerated each other's presence. More interesting, the drugged experiments had not flinched at their arrival.

"We may need to instigate," Brooke whispered.

Sam shook his head with disgust. There was a time when this sweet woman had been the peacekeeper, the pancake-maker when others had difficult times, when she had never spoken cruelness toward either human or animal. That was before she had betrayed Dr. Andalon, giving up his research and betraying his trust as a wife. To hear her speak of *instigating* an experiment made Sam think of her husband. That was the kind of desperate measure *he* would have resorted to.

"Let's leave them be," Sam insisted. "We can try again later."

One of the hwanans found some of the food laced with the serum and began to eat.

"Don't let him have that!" Brooke snapped.

"It won't harm him," Mi-Jung insisted. "He's not had the vaccine, so he won't be sensitive to the serum's effects, right?"

"I guess we're about to find out," Brooke said, settling down.

The hwanan abruptly dropped the food and began to heave, vomiting aggressively and falling to its side. As it fell it convulsed, kicking and writhing on the floor of the cage. The second hwanan fell upon it at once, savagely tearing flesh apart as if to devour him whole. Still, the others did not move.

"Pull him out," Brooke said, as disgusted by the display as Sam and Mi-Jung.

Without thinking or taking any precaution whatsoever, Sam reached instinctively to grab the hwanan. He caught it, holding it tightly with one hand while reaching in to grab one of the boxes with his other. It squealed against the sudden intrusion by a human, no longer angry but filled with fear.

Something caught his eyes. At some point the pilot light on the Bunsen burner had blinked out. All human eyes stared at where it had once burned, waiting and wondering when it had happened, each aware of the sweet smell of gas slowly filling the room.

Sam had frozen in place, his eyes slowly moving to check the mice once resting in the corner of the cage. Each of them had stood on hind legs, their eyes burning like golden orbs in their heads.

Surely that tiny flame wasn't enough for them to do me harm? Sam wondered, but his eyes flicked away to rest on the emergency cutoff. With both hands in the cage it seemed so very far away.

Brooked suddenly realized no one could reach the valve. "Back out of there slowly," she urged.

Sam nodded and slowly started to move, carefully watching the beady eyes staring up at him. As soon as he flinched he heard a whooshing sound, the kind made when a match hits a lit burner. Only, there had been a *lot* of gas flowing out of the cage, and the inferno that resulted blew him backward with arms flailing.

Brooke rushed forward as Sam toppled backward. She lunged, reaching for the emergency cutoff and turning it ninety degrees to stop the flow of gas fueling the flame. By then Mi-Jung had joined Sam's side, kneeling beside him smoking on the floor. The fireball had been concussive and the man's eyes were closed. Every hair on the front of his body had burned away, and she noticed his eyelashes curled and matted against his lids. She let out her breath when she heard him moan. He thankfully lived.

Her eyes moved to the cage, wide with shock at the display within. Four mice from Batch Bravo stood on hind legs over the dead body of the hwanan, staring down with golden eyes the color of fire. All at once, as if linked together by thought as well as action, they held up their forepaws and reached out as if to touch the bleeding rodent in their cage. Tiny wisps of flame poured forth from their palms, wrapping the body like bandages around a mummy, swirling and curling around its flesh. Within a matter of moments all that remained of the intruder was a burned husk.

One by one the experiments collapsed from exhaustion, their tiny fires puffing out as they dropped to the floor as ordinary mice.

This batch is dangerous, Brooke knew at once, finally understanding what David had witnessed from Felicima in the Mendel Lab. *But Michael will want this power most of all!* The scientist inside of her suddenly yearned to finish the tests, to find the extent of each new-found power.

Mi-Jung collected the dead rodents, at least one had perished in each experiment. Approaching the cage with Batch Charlie she paused, watching the living gather around the dead hwanan and seemingly mourned its loss of life. She stood mesmerized as, in a matter of moments, they had raised the fallen rodent, reanimating the husk to resume life beside them.

"Guys, come see this!" she called to the others.

"It's just as David healed and raised Ivan Petrov and Adam and Eve," Brooke remarked.

Sam had the idea to test the black bead further, by placing all those that had perished in the other cages in with Batch Charlie. The result had been extraordinary.

"They have compassion for life, *all* life," Brooke suggested.

"They're animals," Mi-Jung pointed out. "They lack the emotional reasoning of humans, how is this possible?"

Sam knew. "I saw the same with Felicima and the others back in Cambridge. What if this serum enhances emotional reasoning, even the flawed?"

"That would explain why David so eagerly raised Ivan Petrov on the battlefield," Brooke agreed.

Mi-Jung still watched the rodents with amazement. "It's like they're showing compassion for their fallen cousins." With a gasp she watched the living begin to sway and the dead rise.

"They're doing what David did!" Brooke exclaimed.

"There's hope for these experiments after all," Sam suggested, echoing the scientific curiosity in the room. As long as the results offered something other than destruction, the trio would eagerly pursue it.

CHAPTER TEN

Cathy Fletcher hurried to her hovel, eager to see her friends and to learn their fates, thinking foremost of Joshua. Despite the luxury in which she had rested while they were interrogated, no respite could come for a mother cut off from her only child. Max had prevented access to her son the entire time she was in custody, and her first order of business was to wrap her boy in a huge embrace. But she found him waiting inside with Mr. Starlings, his teacher, and skidded to a halt at her own door.

Josh never looked up when she arrived, focused fully on the toy trucks on the ground.

She stood there, looking down as the nearly five-year-old played with toys and spoke to his teacher. "How has he been?" she asked. Despite her boy appearing physically fine, his psychological condition would take decades to sort out. Starting with his Aunt Sarah, then his own father and finally Jenny and John Klingensmith, the boy had witnessed too much death in only a few months. He might *never* be the same.

Mr. Starlings offered her an empathetic smile. The teacher understood she had been kept away against her will, even if her son did not. "He's fine and has been working on his reading most of the week. He's already got the basic sight words down for his age. Don't you, Josh?"

The boy nodded, no longer speaking now that his mother had returned.

Most of the week. Cathy cringed at the timeframe. She really had been away from him that long, and he scarcely even bothered to care she was back.

Mr. Starlings stood to leave but paused and pulled out a tiny book. Without asking or offering, he placed it into her hand. "It's a devotional," he explained. "I'm not sure what your spiritual walk is, but I find these have been helpful when searching for answers in this strange new world.

I know you're busy running the hospital and being a mother, but taking the time to read scripture may help settle your heart."

"My heart is fine," she snapped, tossing the book on her cot without even a glance at the cover.

The teacher merely shrugged. "I can't force you to read it," he said, "but you *may* find it helpful."

"No you can't," she agreed. "And I won't have you forcing my son, either."

"I'm not forcing anyone," Mr. Starlings insisted. "He's receiving a secular education, I assure you. But it wouldn't hurt to look to God during times like these, and no harm would come if he sang a few hymns with the other children."

"I forbid it," she insisted. "Teach him reading and writing, but leave the morality lessons to me."

"Hmm," the man grunted with a smile, as if already judging all he knew about her life as both a woman and a mother.

What does he know about me? she asked herself. *Does he* think *I'm a killer, or just a bad mom?*

"If you won't take the time to pray with him," the teacher suggested, "at least talk to him about the things he's witnessed in the past few months. A child shouldn't have to bear that heavy a burden." With that he left the room, turning only once to offer a weak smile that betrayed pity for both mother and son.

Cathy knelt beside Josh. "I love you," she told him.

"I love you too, Mommy," he replied with a shrug, pulling away slightly without looking up.

She hugged him closely and talked to him despite his lack of response. She told him how proud she was, of how well he had been behaving, and how much he was learning in his school. He shrugged again, so she knew he listened.

Movement in the next hovel announced the arrival of Linda.

"I'll be right back," Cathy whispered to Josh, then moved next door to check on her friend.

"What do *you* want?" her friend demanded, staring with angry resentment. She held her belly like the baby would come at any moment.

"Just to check on you."

"More likely making sure no one implicated *you*," Linda insisted. Anger lined her voice.

"Me? I thought nothing of the sort. Max locked me up too, intent on speaking to you and James separately. Where *is* he? Have you seen James?"

Linda looked away. "He admitted to it," she said flatly.

Cathy's eyes grew large with shock. "He *didn't*!"

"He did. Sergeant Walters told me that James admitted to putting the ricin in the pot. He must have doubled back after I left to give you the crackers, but I don't know how he figured out where I hid the packet."

Cathy suddenly felt sick, dizzy and queasy enough to spew her insides. That sweet, young man, so loving and so kind, had killed thirty people and for what? Out of jealousy? *For me,* she realized. *He killed them for* me. Her knees buckled and she slumped beside her friend.

"He would have gotten away with it," Linda accused. "Why'd you tell them about the poison?"

"I felt I *had* to," was the honest response. "So many people died, but I didn't think Max would continue with the investigation."

"It was interrogation, not investigation!" Linda snapped. "You've *no* idea how they treated me for three days! They *tortured* me!" She touched her belly again, feeling for the child within. "What if it had been *me* who did it? You would've condemned me to death! Would've made my baby motherless!"

"I doubt..." Cathy was going to say she doubted Max would have done that to her, but she really had no way of knowing, did she?

Bells abruptly ringing near the front doors signaled newcomers had arrived, cutting off the rest of their talk. New arrivals meant the doctor's services would be required for several hours.

"Will you watch Josh while I greet the new refugees?" Cathy asked her friend.

Linda shrugged. "Like I have a *choice*?" She corrected herself, "Sorry, that was rude. Of course I'll watch him."

Cathy, so eager to spend time with Josh, walked away with a mixture of sadness and regret. *After three days apart, what's a few more hours?* she wondered. *He won't say much to me anyways.*

Her mind raced as she made her way to the entrance. She *had* to make a better effort as a mother, and things would have to change. Maybe she should cut back her hours in the infirmary? Regardless, she couldn't leave her boy all the time with Mr. Starlings—he'd have him giving baptisms and preaching on rooftops. That thought surprised Cathy. She never had a problem with religion and realized she just wanted to be the one who taught her son about it. Instead she was stuck working the hospital and the grueling hours therein. Until a real doctor came around, she was only one woman pulling extra duty.

She rounded the bend to find the front doors open wide. Soldiers and civilians milled about, some even standing on tiptoes to get a glimpse of those coming inside. Max and Shayde were also there, so she stood between them.

"Linda said James Parker admitted to the killings. Is that true?" She asked bluntly, not even hushing her voice.

Max nodded. "He did."

"Where is he now?"

"Exiled. I gave him a chance to leave and live with shame instead of being torn apart by the rest of the soldiers. Killing him would've been a waste of a decent man and wouldn't have done any good for morale. Besides, even if I had chosen imprisonment and kept him under lock and key, the men would have strung him up before next daybreak. At least exile gives him a chance to survive," Max insisted.

"How did you learn the truth?"

Max paused, his teeth grinding and dancing within his cheeks as he decided whether to tell her.

"Max? Did you torture him? Linda says…"

"Linda's one to talk. She caved after a single day in sensory deprivation. Don't put too much stock in her opinion."

"Max."

"Drop it, Cathy," the general snapped, no longer his usually calm self. "Don't push this no matter what, or you won't like what you learn!"

She stepped back, a mix of terrified and astounded by his cruelness. "Max..."

"Drop it," he growled.

Cathy did drop it, watching the newcomers with a bit of sadness. She would miss James Parker, maybe even more than she had expected. He had been sweet, a bit of fresh air in a stale world of leering eyes and dirty minds. Maybe one of these new arrivals would prove worthy of her friendship.

The first to enter the Shelter were a man and two women, one of whom held a newborn infant. It was perfect, at least from where Cathy stood, with a normal face and all eyes and toes. The news of it would prove promising for Linda. Cathy took another look at the trio. They were all about the same age, and the man closely resembled one of the women. They appeared like they could be related.

Brother and sister, maybe?

Next came a taller man, distinguished looking and carrying several canvas satchels. He clutched each as if filled with priceless gems and gold. Cathy noticed right away he wasn't bad looking, a few years older than her, but seemingly humble and a bit shy—a scholarly type, probably boring.

Cathy stared at the woman beside him, regal looking with long blonde hair tied into a sharp bun. She almost had a military look to her. She, too, was loaded down with canvas satchels and clutched them as if they were more precious than anything else they brought.

They're probably a couple, Cathy suddenly realized, discarding them as two uppity rich folks left penniless by the apocalypse.

The next to enter the Shelter were two children about ten years old. It was hard to exactly guess their ages, their eyes and somber faces making them appear older than they probably were.

Their children? she wondered. One of them, the girl, looked Cathy directly in the eye and sent a shudder up her spine.

Then another man entered, certainly a military man by the way he was dressed and equipped. He wore a rifle on his back and a large pistol on his belt. He had knives and hand grenades as well, with eyes that could blow up a room as easily as he graced it. Some of the soldiers seemed nervous around him, and Cathy realized none of them had even attempted to take his weapons, usually the first order of business with new arrivals.

"Military?" she asked Max and Shayde.

"United States *Chair Force*," Shayde explained, "but the good kind—TACP special forces. He'll be valuable. The other man and woman are doctors. They delivered that child just two days ago."

Cathy felt her heart leap. There was a chance now. She could spend more time with Josh with *two* doctors around. She could finally give over the stress of running the hospital. "Isn't it odd," she asked, "that they survived out there this long yet remained so healthy. Where were they before finding the Shelter?"

"Not sure," Shayde replied, "we still have to debrief them. All we know is what they reported to our scouts and we just told you."

The soldiers at the door moved and another man entered, loaded down with several more satchels. Behind him Regiment members pushed a handcart filled with secure plastic bins. Something about the newcomer seemed familiar—the way he walked and held his jaw, for one. Cathy knew right away she knew this man, but her eyes never recognized him until he turned, blinked, and grinned a broad smile at his ex-wife.

"Hey there, Kitty Kat!" Clint Fletcher said with a wink, clearly back from the dead.

Cathy drew the pistol from Shayde's holster and rushed forward with a scream. Everything moved in slow motion then, as she struggled to distinguish fact from dreamy bloodlust. In one version of reality she squeezed off several shots and struck Clint in the chest, dropping him to the ground like she had into the river.

The other reality was much different, as strong hands tackled her harmlessly to the floor before a single shot rang out. This one hurt much more than the other and resulted in a loss of breath from her lungs. But oh how she yearned for the former reality, a world wherein Clint Fletcher lay dead and bleeding out on the floor of the Shelter.

"What the *hell* are you doing?" Max Rankin growled into her ear while pinning her to the ground. It was his arms that had tackled her.

"That's my ex-husband," she gasped, "the one I told you about. The murderer!"

"You said you *killed* your ex-husband in self-defense," Shayde said, taking back his sidearm but not moving to help Max release her.

"He's obviously alive!" she realized, wishing he would have died and left her and her son alone. How had he made it here from Michigan, finding her this far south in Indiana?

"Take that man into custody," Max Rankin's voice commanded.

Finally, a man who speaks reason, she thought.

"And Ms. Fletcher too," the general added, his hands slipping flex cuffs around Cathy's wrists. "Make sure neither has contact with *anybody* until we sort this out!"

Max Rankin and Shayde Walters stood at the front of the office, each with crossed arms and staring down at Cathy Fletcher sitting in a chair. With her hands cuffed tightly behind her back, she sat propped upward and leaning forward. Her eyes stared angrily up at the leaders of the Regiment, daring them to proceed with their interrogation. So far, neither men had, each too shocked and confused by her actions.

Max finally broke the silence. "What the hell was that back there?" he demanded.

"I told you, he's my ex-husband."

"And that makes attempted *murder* okay?" Max uncrossed his arms, standing straighter. His body, no longer calm and relaxed, seemed as tightly wound as a panther ready to pounce its prey. His eyes drilled down into her soul, demanding answers.

"I was married to that man for three years," she explained, irritation brimming and desperate to be free of the flex cuffs. "I endured *everything* at his hand! He beat me, burned me, abused me, even *raped* me the entire time we were married!"

"That's no reason to break the law now!" Max snapped. "I won't *allow* it here!"

"He murdered my sister!" Cathy suddenly screamed. "He killed Sarah! He beat her head in with a pistol and pointed the same gun at me that very night! *He's* the murderer and *deserves* to die! I can't live in the same place as him! I *won't!*"

Max glanced at Shayde and the two men exchanged a look.

"What?" she demanded.

Shayde moved between her and Max and sat casually on the corner of the desk. "We meant to have this talk with you, but it just hasn't been the right time."

"What do you mean?" she asked. "How can *any* time be the *right* time? Take these cuffs off of me and say what you want to say!"

"Cathy," Shayde began again. "You're valuable to the Regiment, but we can't have your drama anymore. It *has* to stop. It's affecting others, and you're not even aware of it."

"Drama?" She grew so angry at the suggestion, that *she* would be the source of theatrics. After everything she had endured, first with Clint, then Hank and Steve, now again with Clint, she was sick and tired of being the victim. It was time to be done with Clint once and for all.

"I want him dead!" she demanded. "You exiled James Parker for killing thirty people, but just welcomed a real monster into the Shelter! James is one hundred times the man Clint Fletcher could *ever* be!"

Shayde and Max exchanged another look. Max nodded and Shayde continued. "Before you showed up there wasn't any infighting within the Regiment. We had strict discipline and no crimes to investigate. Since you arrived, though..."

Cathy sensed it, the brewing accusation and tried to stand up and face it head on. "I'm not responsible for *any* drama!" she protested.

Max slammed her back into the chair and held her down by the shoulders.

Shayde calmly explained, "You blinded a man, Cathy, for simply looking at your naked friend. Had you just reported it, the Colonel could have investigated Steve and fined or demoted his rank. That's how we do things in the military."

"He *deserved* it!" she protested.

Shayde shook his head. "No man deserves to be blinded, and you did so without a trial."

"One time!" she growled. "I lost my temper *one* time!"

"Then thirty people died, most of them innocent, and lost their lives to the weapon *you* brought in."

"I didn't kill them! You told me yourself, James admitted to it!"

"Now this," Shayde went on. "You told everyone your husband was dead, that you shot him in self-defense on the night of the missiles, but here he is walking among us and telling a different story about that night."

"He's a liar! His story doesn't matter, and you shouldn't believe him at all! He's a murderer!"

Max spoke up. "You're a great nurse, Cathy, and we trusted you to run the hospital. With that kind of trust, you can't be target to whispered murder accusations and can't be seen drawing guns and charging newcomers."

She settled down. He was right. She had overreacted both by gouging Steve's eyes and now when charging Clint. "I just want justice," she admitted.

"Justice is slow to arrive," Max told her, "and you're not giving it time to play out on its own. Stop being a vigilante, you've only created more messes and drama for us to clean up."

"I'm sorry," she said, finally understanding. But the problem with her ex-husband in the Shelter fueled her anger. "I want Clint gone. He's a murderer and it's a mistake to keep murderers alive and in our midst. But you'll probably just exile him like James! I want him *dead* for what he's done, the penalty should fit the crime!"

Shayde and Max exchanged that same look as before.

"What?" she demanded. "What *is* it you're not telling me!"

Max sighed audibly. "James admitted to the killings because we asked him to, Cathy, but he *didn't* do it. He could better serve the Regiment if he took credit for the killings, that's why we sent him away. So it's best you don't speak so passionately about punishment fitting crimes."

Cathy was shocked. If not James, then did they think it was *her*? "Who then? If not James, *who* killed the officers?"

Max reached down and cut her free of the flex cuffs, then sat on the table beside Shayde. "Only one other person besides James and Linda heard your plan, knew where the poison was kept and where Linda stashed it to use later."

Cathy gasped, full realization guilting her so deeply she felt her heart skip several beats.

"We separated all *four* of you for a reason. While you slept in a comfy, warm bed, Josh admitted to Mr. Starling that he put the poison in the stew. He claimed he did it to make his mother happy because, in his words, she stopped being happy after hers and his daddy's divorce. He said he did to those people what *Mommy did to Daddy*. Those were his exact words."

Cathy broke down in tears.

PART II
MIRACLE WORKER

CHAPTER ELEVEN

Miko Robinson stared out at the University of Southern Indiana campus, his eyes settling on a cone shaped building in the center of what had once been a green field of manicured lawns. The trees encircling that field hid their leaves from the shivering cold of nuclear winter, filled with hope they would emerge fresh and green after it ceased to fall on the land. Everything about this place had once stood for hope, but only for some—an empty promise from the colonizers for those European-looking enough to enjoy privilege.

Standing here felt strange to Miko. The closest he had previously come to walking this campus had been one summer spent swinging a weed whacker around the parking lots. Even then he was prevented from walking on the main grounds—he hadn't passed the background check to get a badge. No, this place wasn't for people like him.

Now he could own it free and clear. Max Rankin had offered it to him, a boon for doing as he's told. He lit a cigarette, a luxury only the wealthiest could own, and drew a deep breath.

Max Rankin... a man with a face like his, yet just another colonizer. To Miko he represented everything bad about America, having gone off to fight an unjust war that was never his own to fight. To Miko, soldiers followed orders given by those who wished to perpetuate the slavery of poverty—that entity called capitalism.

Miko let out his breath, allowing the smoke to slowly swirl from his nostrils. With resentment he shook his head, taking another look at that cone shaped building in the center of campus. To him it proved the existence of racism in America. Built as a place of union for students, they had meant it to pay homage to the indigenous from the area, hence the tipi shape. But Miko and his warriors knew better. Colonizers build homages to placate emotions while demonstrating power and dominance. All their statues and buildings served the same purpose. In this case, they made the statement that the tipi structure no longer belonged to the people who lived in them. Ever since it was built, euro-descended masters had been taking meals inside this place of borrowed culture.

It *would* make a good watchtower, though, a perfect overlook should he accept Rankin's terms and claim this campus for his settlement. Settlement? New World Order was a better term. Miko Robinson dreamed of redistribution, taking what once belonged to the slavers and claiming it for people like him—those on the losing side of capitalism.

He almost wanted to accept the Regiment's terms, to abandon the city to settle here. It was a good offer, one that surprised him even more than the fact the Colonel and all his officers were dead. That's why he wouldn't reject it completely. He was losing the battle for the city and needed to fall back and regroup. *But not for long,* he thought.

"Your old man sounds desperate," Miko said to Tom Rankin, "to offer us *this*." He had to admit it was in a good spot, one that offered protection and could sustain an entire community. What once were lawns could serve as farms, and the dorms would be perfect for housing. It could be a city of its own, an easily defensible one.

"He must be," Tom agreed. "But he never thinks of others, so this deal has to benefit *him* somehow."

Miko had already considered that. He knew the way of things, having served five years of a ten-year sentence in Branchville. Deal makers never brought their best offer to the first visit around the table. This was an issue of turf, and the Regiment wanted to hold the city around their precious Shelter. They also wanted to extend northward to hold the airport. The area around that would be perfect farmland once replanting could begin.

So why would he give me their western flank? He was no tactician but knew an attack from the south would make this spot crucial in defending Evansville. Football terms he understood, and this was the blind side.

"He wants us to block his right side while he fights the Nature Boys in the south," Miko explained to Tom. "But then he'll turn on us as soon as they're beat."

"Makes sense," Tom agreed.

"I like this place, though," Miko admitted. "He's right about offering it to us, and I think we'll take it."

Tom blanched, turning to protest.

"But we won't pay his price," the leader of the gangs added with a smile. "We'll get settled here then attack *his* flank as soon as he's tied up with the Nature Boys."

Tom grinned ear to ear at the thought of beating his father.

"Now go tell the others we're moving to this location. It's perfect, with only a few dozen families camped out at the dining hall and coliseum. They'll be our first prisoners, the ones we use to break ground in spring."

Tom paused. "We're taking slaves? My dad... Max said that's what the Nature Boys are doing."

"Then we better have bodies to trade for our *own* people, shouldn't we?"

Miko watched as the boy nodded then turned to relay his orders to the others. It would be a long night, but the New World Order would reign over this plot of land.

Tom made it back to his apartment later than he had hoped, eager for a hot meal and knowing none waited inside. He knocked four times, no more, no less, and waited for the de-cocking of a pistol on the other side of the door. A moment later he heard the lock click open. He hated they needed a secret code, but looters were everywhere. They could even be his own friends. He trusted nobody, at least not now when food and water was scarce.

He pushed the door open and smiled as if he had not spent the entire evening rounding up slaves for Miko. That had been the worst of it, watching faces filled with fright plead for their freedom only to be shackled and bound in servitude. It made him sick, and he almost wanted to flee Miko's New World Order. *But to where? Not my father.*

"Hi, Mom," he said to the woman waiting inside, smiling away his worry.

Betty Rankin holstered the gun and hugged him close. Every time he returned from doing jobs for Miko it was the same thing, her desperately happy to hug her son and checking him over for wounds. Stepping back, she frowned.

"You're covered in blood," she observed.

"Not mine," he replied, taking as seat at the table, ready to dig into the meager rations she had set out for him.

"Give thanks for that first," she demanded. "God provided, and we must be humble."

Miko provided it, he thought, but bowed his head while she prayed.

"Lord we thank you for this food and shelter, even while the world awaits your coming. Evil walks the earth, Lord, and it has many faces. We pray you bring my husband home safe from his travels, and that he'll take Tom and me to someplace safe and more abundant. Thank you for bringing my son home safe from his business today, and thank you for the many blessings you have yet to bestow."

Tom flinched during the prayer, closing his eyes tightly and holding down the many lies he had told. It was best Max didn't know she lived, but Tom dreaded her finding out that *he* did. "Amen," he said after she finished, then took a bite.

"Did you get into a gunfight?" she asked. "You smell like gunpowder and smoke again."

"Don't ask, Ma. I told you not to ask about that. It's a war out there."

"Just wait," she said. "When your father gets back to us, he's going to take us to a place with food, water, and opportunity. He'll be home soon, I'm certain..."

"He's not coming back, Ma," he said gently. *Why can't she see him for what he is? A traitor, a sellout, an Uncle Tom?*

"Yes, he is. I know your father. He loves us and will be back to take care of us..."

"He's *not* coming for us, Ma!" Tom snapped. "He's not, so shut up about him!"

Betty frowned, taken aback. "Tom, you *are* out looking for him, aren't you? For his truck? He'll return. He promised no matter what he'll always come back."

"He's not!" her son screamed. "He's dead! Almost everyone out there is! All that matters is surviving!"

Betty fell silent. Tom shouldn't have spoken to her that way, but she had to know her husband was never coming back to them. He had chosen his side and it wasn't *theirs*.

"Did you bring more rations?" she asked after a while.

Tom suddenly realized she had nothing on her own plate. He pointed to his bag. Inside was his allotment—three military style MREs and a jug of boiled water. It wasn't much, one ration was originally meant for a soldier to eat in a single day, but it was all they had to stretch between two people for a week. He watched her look at it and frown.

"It's food, Ma."

"It's not much." Something in her eyes betrayed a deep hunger and Tom paused.

"What did you eat today, Ma?" he demanded.

She shrugged.

"Ma? When was the last time you ate?"

"Me? Oh, it hasn't been that long," she replied.

Tom shoved his plate toward her. "Eat the rest of this," he told her.

"No, Son, that's for *you*. You need it because you're out there keeping us safe. I only lay around here, doing nothing, so I don't need it."

He looked at her closely, then, realizing how gaunt his mother had grown. She must have lost twenty or thirty pounds and never really had that much to lose in the first place. Pushing up from the table he said, "I'm going back out but will be right back." He grabbed his satchel and rifle and made for the door.

"Son?"

"Yes, Ma?"

"Your father will return to us, never lose faith in him, just like you shouldn't lose faith in the Lord. Our savior will return soon, we're in end times. Even if your father *has* died, we'll be with him soon, him *and* the Lord. Don't lose faith, son. Ever!"

Tom started to tell her the truth but held himself back. Instead he simply said, "I'll just be downstairs, Ma. I'll be right back."

The door closed firmly behind him, and he waited until he heard the lock set behind him. Six flights later he reached a door, knocking firmly then stepping back to wait. It opened with a shotgun muzzle sticking out.

"I need to see Miko," Tom said, ignoring the weapon.

"He's busy," a voice said from within.

"He needs to hear this."

The door slammed in his face, but Tom waited. After three or four minutes it opened fully and Mike Salwell stared back. "What do *you* want?" he demanded, then stepped aside. "Make it quick."

Tom entered the apartment to find Miko sitting on a couch with three women laying in his lap or against his shoulders, each as undressed as the next. All three were strung out, high from the white lines drawn on the table. Miko had a bit of the powder on his upper lip and stared at Tom with irritation.

"Why're you bothering me?" he demanded.

"I thought about something my Dad once said, about his time in the war." Tom lied. His father *never* spoke about the war. "He said they were pinned down in Baghdad and put their allies, the Iraqi forces, to their right flank. As soon as the enemy pushed their center, their own allies moved in behind them, cutting him off from his main supply line and trapping his unit against the Euphrates River."

Miko sat up, his cloudy eyes trying to focus while his mind realized. "Speak in football terms," he said.

Tom tried again. "They ran a sweep to the left, and the running back and tight end turned on the quarterback, pushing him into the line."

Miko stared blankly for a moment, then two, then three, finally erupting with riotous laughter. "You're saying don't waste any more time, and hit him the moment he's attacked from the south?"

Tom nodded. "The moment the Nature Boys reach the river, cut him off from the Shelter and take both the University *and* the airport. Make your deal with the invaders first though."

"You're good, kid! I like you!" Miko pointed at the drugged girls laying around. "Take one of them, any one you want," he offered.

But Tom's eyes looked toward the kitchen. On the table lay twenty or more open MREs. Someone had probably been tossing through them to find the Chili Mac. Next to those, someone had poured out several more to find the candy.

"Thanks," Tom said, "but can I have a few more rations? My mom and I share, and she's skipping eating to feed me."

Miko laughed, a long, deep laugh interrupted by a cough. Unable to speak he pointed at the pile and gave a thumbs up.

Tom walked to the table and loaded his bag with as many as he could carry. As he did, he noticed a dozen or so empty bags and boxes discarded on the kitchen floor. Miko had been consuming all the food he wanted while the men and woman in his care starved. Tom felt anger rise at this but kept his eyes down and left as quickly as he could.

On the way out, he thought about his father. *Maybe I* should *take Mom to him. We'd eat better, and live better.*

But he knew the truth. Tom would rather die in squalor or a firefight than to admit to his father, Max Rankin, he was wrong about the side *he* had chosen. His best bet was to help Miko win the fight ahead than to tell his mother the truth—that her husband had returned and was fighting for the other team.

CHAPTER TWELVE

Brooke Andalon held the final product, a tiny pill neatly compressed into a spherical form. Hard-packed with a glazed finish, the sheen off the white coating revealed a tiny bead so smooth it appeared nearly metallic. The object most closely resembled a pearl and would be just as sought after by those seeking wealth and power. Holding one up to the light she marveled at the potential it held, her emotions mixing as worry washed over scientific curiosity.

Is this it, then? she wondered. *Have we given Michael all he craves as David had hoped? Will this tiny pearl be enough to end his search for emotancy?*

Only human testing would answer her questions.

"I hope you were right about the coating," Mi-Jung said to Sam. She and Brooke had argued against it, insisting the spherical shape would cause problems, more easily bouncing or rolling away if dropped. But Sam insisted the pills needed an extended release coating, a process limited in shape options by the manufacturing tools on hand.

Mi-Jung had first discovered the absorption problem while testing the liquid form on rodents. Though the abilities manifested perfectly, the effect merely flashed and then was gone. At first she and Sam had raised the dosage, but that proved fatal and killed entire batches after suffering prolonged seizures. If this were to have military application, it would have to release slowly enough to endure an entire battle, and the coating was their best idea.

Now, holding a white bead in her hand, Brooke shuddered at the thought of success.

Across the table Sam Nakala smiled softly, a reassuring look that let her know he shared her worry.

"It's time," Mi-Jung announced and Brooke nodded, unable to find the words to protest. She placed the bead atop a pile of others in a jar, then added it to the tray with three more options.

Four in all, the scientists had chosen to divide each batch into colors: white, red, black, and blue—one for each of David's batches. With white they knew mostly what to expect from Alpha, sourced from the drones designed after Adam and Eve who crafted the air around them. The scientists had only a basic assumption how the other abilities would manifest in humans. The red bead represented Bravo, as dangerous as Felicima, the angry monkey who burned the Mendel Lab to ashes. Black, they learned by testing mice, was what David had given to himself and represented organic life. The blue bead's powers involved water and worked much in the same way emotancy affected air.

Brooke feared them all, but curiosity drew her attention to the black beads. *What else can you do, David? What is the extent of what you've done to yourself?* She wondered, turning her attention to the Batch Charlie cage. All the mice were there, even the hwanan, eating and drinking side by side without quarrel. Those resurrected by the serum lived alongside those who had raised them, virtually indistinguishable... except they no longer were.

Brooke set down her tray of beads and approached the cage, watching the mice inside as if entranced. "Ivan Petrov," she exclaimed suddenly.

"What about him?" Sam wondered, walking over. The Russian general was seldom mentioned by any except Michael and Jake.

"He was raised by David, just as the mice in Batch Charlie raised the others."

Mi-Jung frowned. "Didn't you tell us David said something on the battlefield at Waghäusel? When he reanimated Petrov, he said that *he* was in control of him, but would share that control with the chancellor."

"Yes..." Brooke had not understood that part, finding the suggestion both strange and foreign—unbelievable, and so she pushed the memory aside. "Michael *is* in control of the general, and that's how he easily conquered the Eastern Bloc nations. But I don't know now, if that's such a good thing."

"Why not?" Sam asked.

Brooke pointed at the mice in the cage. "Last time I checked this cage the occupants were indistinguishable. I couldn't tell the original batch from those they resurrected. That's not true now."

Both assistants peered in, appraising the rodents to see what Brooke did. Mi-Jung noticed it first. "The eyes of some, they're fogged over, dull as if lifeless."

"The fur," Sam realized at the same time, "is missing in patches from those same ones."

"What if the those who had died are decaying at the same rate as they would have if not reanimated?" Brooke suddenly worried.

"Then General Petrov would be as well," Mi-Jung suggested.

"But Jake hasn't mentioned any problems with him, only that no one in Russia has even noticed he's different."

"These all died either by the craft or using it," Sam reasoned, "but Petrov died by a bullet."

"So?" Mi-Jung asked.

"What if *how* something dies affects its decomposition once raised," Brooke considered. "If its death involves these beads will it deteriorate and decay at a natural rate, versus a natural death which might be cleaner and a more perfect resurrection?"

The Korean lab assistants both shuddered at the thought but said nothing at first. The question had been a good one. Finally, after several moments, Sam suggested, "It's possible and, if so, that could be a problem for Chancellor Esterling. Anything or anyone his army reanimates wouldn't actually be living, merely dying more slowly."

Mi-Jung frowned. "I don't like it, it's unnatural..."

Like David, Brooke agreed, thinking of how her ex-husband had raised both the children and General Petrov from the dead. But inside she hadn't meant it. Truly she wanted to love David, to find a way across the ocean and go to him—to find and forgive him then beg his forgiveness of her. But it was all too much to deal with, the supernatural feeling of it all.

"Let's go. We have work to do," she finally said with firm resolution in her voice that ended further discussion. Only further experimentation would reveal the extent of this problem, and thinking of her husband would only sidetrack her from her true mission.

Jake Braston walked with his friend, the Chancellor of Astia, eyeing him and marveling at his newfound confidence. During the Battle of Waghäusel, when they defeated the Russian army, Michael Esterling had nearly lost both his cool as well as the battle. Had Adam and Eve not arrived when they did, all would have been lost. He seemed so much stronger now, a true leader more convicted in the direction he led his people. Michael was a new man. He was harder, harsher even, as well as more focused. He had almost grown into the leader the new nation of Astia needed.

"Petrov came through," the chancellor said suddenly.

"Really? All the way? Is it done?"

Michael nodded. "It's done. With the Eastern Bloc nations already in line, Russia was willing to listen to what he... what *I* had to say through him. They're sending an envoy to make terms."

"I thought your terms were *no* terms at all."

Michael smiled, a rarity of late. "Only while we perfect the bead Brooke designed. My terms will be a high placement for Petrov in their government. Once Petrov takes full control, he'll join our coalition and then abdicate and dissolve their constitution in favor of annexation by Astia."

The bead... such a simple term, yet one that gave Jake another reason to worry. *Changed or not, these beads are too much power for Michael to wield.*

Himself in line to test Batch Alpha, the lure of that power terrified him. The great Jake Braston, who was never afraid of anything in his life, felt desire grip his soul and dangle before him the strength of the bead— whatever its powers held. He wanted to reject it, to refuse his friend, but would test the bead for his sister and claim its magic as his own if need be. He had no choice, but he still feared it.

With a deep breath he gathered his wits then asked about their next campaign. "So we look westward now? I can move our expeditionary forces immediately if you desire, moving north into England."

"No, I want you to focus on leading those who can wield the beads. I've sent for Herr General Richter to return from France and will send him north upon his return."

"I see," Jake said with disappointment. "That would mean figuring out how to cross the English Channel. Does he have a plan for that yet?"

"What matters is that *I've* got a plan for that. River cruises."

"You're going to take a cruise vacation?" Jake laughed, wondering at the meaning.

"No, we found river boats belonging to various cruise lines, some of which could make it across the sea. If we can somehow outfit those with sails, we can gain propulsion."

Jake considered the option. It made sense, but the engineering behind sail power was difficult, especially for boats that size. He nodded, then paused to stare at the door now between them and Brooke's first round of human trials. He took a deep breath to ready himself for what was on the other side. He pushed it open and held it for his friend and chancellor. No matter what happened next, Jake Braston would laugh it off like every other worry.

Inside they found five waiting airmen, each strapped into a chair. They had all agreed to this precaution when volunteering. An empty sixth chair sat next to them. That was for their general, proof he was committed to the experiment and believed in its safety. With no way to predict the outcome of this experiment, restraints were only a part of the safety protocol. In the next room, unbeknownst to the volunteers, waited an armed squad. Their orders, if things went wrong, were to protect Michael and put down the test subjects—Jake included, if necessary.

Across the room, Brooke smiled at her brother, a worried look he knew very well. He merely smiled back, laughed off her worry, then listened intently as she addressed the subjects.

"Thanks for volunteering," she said, hiding most of the anxiety from her voice and holding up a tiny white sphere resembling a pearl. "This is the bead you will consume. Despite its smooth exterior, it's a pill, just like any other, and your body will absorb it as such."

"What happens then?" one of the airmen asked. She was young, only about nineteen years old, and appeared terrified. Not eager like the others.

Brooke strode over with a warm smile. "Airman McLemore, right?"

The young woman nodded. "Yes, ma'am."

"That's the only part we aren't sure of, what happens next and the timeline in which it occurs. Powers may or may not materialize at all and, even if they do, we aren't sure what form will appear in each of you. This bead represents forms of telepathy and aerokinesis, so we expect you to be able to manipulate the air around you. There may be other psychic abilities as well, based on what we know about Adam and Eve, but they kept most of those hidden, so we need your feedback to complete our study."

The girl swallowed hard, obviously scared but eager to participate. *She's a brave girl,* Jake thought, wondering if she had been present when Adam and Eve decimated the Russian army. If so, the power would be tempting for anyone, but also should be daunting to a good-hearted person.

"How long will it last?" another airman asked.

"That depends on your individual metabolism," Brooke replied. "We estimate it to last about an hour or more but not too much longer."

The airman frowned, seemingly disappointed at the short duration.

Jake noticed the reaction. Despite his own rise to the rank of general, he had always shunned personal ambition. He led men because they looked up to him and because he genuinely cared about their welfare, not because he craved power.

He scanned the other faces, noticing how each appeared more eager to get on with the experiment than Airman McLemore. He strolled over to her, leaning in closely. "What's your *first* name?" he asked.

"Penelope... my friends call me Penny... sir," she stammered, confused as to why the general had addressed her so personally.

"Penny," he said reassuringly, choosing the less formal, "no matter *what* happens, I trust you'll be able to handle it."

"Thank you, sir!"

He noticed she sat taller after that, ready for the challenge. It seemed, at least to Jake, that a good-hearted person only needs reassuring and not the promise of power like Brooke had offered. He nodded to his sister to continue.

"Let's get this started, then!" he said, climbing into the waiting chair. Sam Nakala strapped him in like the others and their eyes briefly met. The lab assistant wasn't merely worried; he was downright horrified by the experiment. "It'll be fine," Jake promised him but knew there was a big chance it wouldn't.

"We'll begin with the white bead," Brooke said as her brother tested his bonds and approached her brother. Her eyes met his, pleading for him not to participate, and pointed at a different jar instead, mouthing the word *placebo*. He shook his head, and she reached out a bead. "You're right," he said aloud, "it looks like a pearl. Perhaps that should be the name for this one, the *Astian* Pearl!"

Across the room, Michael smiled at this affirmation of his dream.

Brooke reached forward and Jake felt her place the pearl on his tongue while Sam and Mi-Jung attended to the others. It was cool to the touch and smooth, sliding easily down his throat with a single swallow, without the need for a glass of water. He marveled at the simplicity of it all and waited for what felt like an eternity, but later learned was less than a minute.

Someone retched down the row, the airman once so excited and looking forward to longer effects. As his body rejected the pearl, Jake fought against his own nausea by distracting his mind. He watched Airman McLemore—Penny—as her eyes met his, glazing over as she stared, then rolled back into her head. She slumped into awakened slumber, her muscles mildly twitching throughout her body. Beyond her one of the other men coughed up his bead then frothed, choking on foam and vomit.

Jake watched as Brooke and her team raced to clear the soldier's breathing tube. Since no one had thought of this result, they lacked proper medical gear. Sam aspirated the soldier's airway with his fingers while Mi-Jung leaned him forward. Either no one thought to loosen his straps or were afraid to. Somehow, the man managed a loud gasp.

Then another soldier retched. The pearl he had swallowed fell on the floor with a splattering of half-digested MREs, barely missing Brooke's shoes. He stared up apologetically, but she barely noticed. She was fixated on the final test subject, a young sergeant from Jake's own guard. That man had entered a deep catatonic state and she monitored him for breathing.

At first he sat rigid and wide-eyed, staring off into the distance, but then he fell into a fit. Instead of sputtering and drowning in puke like the other soldiers, his mouth opened, drawing in a lungful of the air around him.

Instantly the room changed, a violent maelstrom of cyclones tossing around anything close. Thankfully, Brooke had cleared it of anything sharp, so only metal trays and tables joined the tornado of terror filling the room. Jake watched as the jars holding each color of bead slowly slid passed Brooke still focused on saving the airman's life. The white jar holding pearls was open, and these slowly levitated before joining the wisps of air circling the sergeant.

Just as the lids flew off the other containers, Jake opened his mouth to alert Brooke she was losing her beads. Instead of warning, a stream of projectile vomit lurched toward and all over his sister.

Penny McLemore appreciated the kind words from the general. Though he had never spoken directly to her, she had heard from many others that was his way—full of kindness and authentic concern for his soldiers. It helped that he was good looking, even if he was nearly as old as her own father. Her last thought before swallowing the bead was how calm he appeared strapped in his chair, such a contrast to her own mixture of fear, excitement, and anxiety. Her next thought after swallowing was how oddly fast the pearl took hold of her body, slowing her heart rate and the world around her.

The sensation was not unlike falling, but was more accurately described as floating. If she had not been strapped to the chair she would have recorded in the after action report she had lifted into the air. That air, now a sensation all around her, became the closest she had ever come to resting on a cloud, something Penny had often dreamed of and yearned to experience as a child. In this perfect state, her eyes briefly met the general's and she felt instantly embarrassed to find his blue orbs even lovelier than she had thought before. In this state, they seemed to swirl like the ocean.

That was right before the bottom fell out of the floating sensation, sending her plummeting several stories to what would surely result in death.

With a lurch she was suddenly in two places at once.

While strapped in the chair, Penny also found herself flying above Ramstein, watching the airbase drift farther downward as she flew upward. She had seen the landscape since nuclear winter had begun to fall, had been at Waghäusel during the battle, and wasn't surprised the ashy snow spread everywhere in all directions. As she climbed though, she was surprised to see the mountain tops far to the south were pure white and clean, a sign that parts of Earth had survived radiation. That vision lingered as hope for her world.

After flying upward without slowing, Penny finally managed to level off and chose a flight path.

West, she thought, *to home.*

Home was, of course, in the United States, and she knew going that direction was a mistake. Her family, the reports already confirmed, had died after at least six missiles landed in San Antonio. What no one had, or could have, prepared her for was how much the landscape had changed. As she rushed over the Atlantic, she scanned the coastline for that gentle curve from Mexico along Galveston Bay and eastward toward New Orleans and the peninsula of Florida. All of that proved unrecognizable, and she gasped at the chain of islands that once made up the sunshine state.

Oceans have already risen! she realized. The eruption of Yellowstone and seismic shifts had changed every aspect of the landscape but especially the gulf coast. The new coastline reached what she could only guess was once the hill country of Texas. Houston had clearly slipped into the sea, and nothing remained of either Austin or San Antonio.

Something curious drew her even further westward.

Just east of the Guadalupe Mountains, she realized a giant fault line had opened up. A gash opened up beneath the ashy desert, belching steam and billowing ashy clouds from molten magma below. The crack in the surface reached northward along the high plains toward the front range of the Rocky Mountains. Beyond those, the large California quake had slammed the North American tectonic plate eastward, driving the Rockies higher as the new fault line cleaved it in two and pushed out in both directions and forced them higher than the Alps she had just marveled over.

Curious, she tried to see more of North America, but South America too had changed. The Amazon basin had flooded, and the continents had separated completely from each other at Guatemala. South of there, Costa Rica and Panama had become a chain of islands in the same fashion as Florida. Penny McLemore wanted to cry over the devastation, the massive loss of life, and the uninhabitable landscape that screamed she would never again return home.

Something felt wrong. The sensation from the pearl, once calming and relaxing, suddenly wracked her muscles. Her mind and eyesight had fallen dark as she plummeted, seemingly falling into an abyss that abruptly replaced the geographic world she had viewed. She felt as though she would plummet forever into the darkness, screaming against the wind rushing by. The writhing of her muscles, once mild tremors but now full-fledged seizures, took over. The pain was the only indicator to her awareness that she still lived.

Abruptly, the pain stopped, replaced instead by euphoria. Sensational, the feeling was unlike any she had ever experienced. She shyly realized her eyes were open and staring once more at General Braston as her body quivered, shook, and climaxed. She cried out, but neither from pain nor pleasure. The words she emitted were not her own and Penny did not understand any of it. Still dizzy from the sensation, she merely hoped none of it was about the general.

Eventually, Penelope McLemore passed out completely.

CHAPTER THIRTEEN

Max Rankin and Shayde Walters stood over a calm and unfazed Clint Fletcher. He carefully remained consistent no matter how many times he retold his story. By now they would be confused, believing that either Cathy was lying or this man was a master of deception. No matter which was actually true, Clint had a certain charisma neither man could shake. Besides, he was a battle-hardened warrior and could prove useful to them in the coming battles.

That was what he had worked so hard to convince them. Deep down he knew he was a murderer, even if he wouldn't admit it openly, and that made this interrogation a game to him.

"Did you kill your wife's sister?" the general asked.

General? No more than a sergeant, no matter his role now, Clint thought. "Of course not," he lied easily. Cathy wasn't his wife when he killed Sarah—beaten her head in with his pistol, to be exact. He had enjoyed that. That bitch was an endless talker.

"Tell us about that night of the missiles. Where did you take Cathy and Josh?"

"Take? I didn't *take* anybody anywhere. They came willingly. It was Cathy's idea, actually, to go boating at my father's old fishing cabin." He tried to come across irritated, so as to throw them off with false sincerity. Of course he had intended to kill that bitch too.

"Her idea?"

"I'd show you her texts," he said a bit too angrily, just to lure them in, "but my phone won't turn on! I swear! She said she felt it would be good for him and I to reconnect the same way my father and I did."

"Cathy says your father killed your mother in that very spot and forced you to watch," Shayde revealed.

"Really?" Clint scoffed. "My father loved my mother very much, and Cathy knows it!" He had actually grown angry for real. How *dare* she suggest there was anything between Mum and Daddy but *love*, the same love she offered every other man in the county.

"So your mother didn't drown?"

He held his face like a seasoned actor. "Mother died of a stroke, not in the river." Another lie. Daddy had shot her right through the temple, but Clint reckoned the end result of brains blown out and major stroke were similar, even if one was self-contained. He took a deep breath, only for show of course, then added, "The fact of the matter, is that Cathy lies. She can't help it and is covering up that *she* insisted we go boating then cuffed a cinder block to my leg and shot me in the chest." He ripped open his shirt to show them the circular scars.

"How'd you survive?" Max asked suddenly. "If you had a cinder block handcuffed to your leg, how'd you get free and live?"

"You're both military veterans," he said to them, "don't tell me you don't have a key hidden on you somewhere." Clint flipped his belt buckle over and pushed his finger into a crease in the leather. A handcuff key emerged. "I held my breath as long as I could, nearly a minute fussing with this belt but got it free. Despite how hard she tried, she didn't take my life!" Sounding really angry now, he added, "*She* shot *me*, that's what's important. She thought she'd get away with it, but I *lived*!"

Max Rankin and Shayde Walters exchanged a look. They had bitten the bait. Clint didn't smile, nor did he gloat. He merely leaned back and waited while wearing his best poker face. When neither asked another question, he knew he had them.

His turn, he asked, "Do either of you even know what it's like to be married?" He watched for a reaction. Rankin flinched first. *Good. I've got him.* Without batting an eye, he continued. "Women are emotional; they *react* while we're the opposite. We're calculated and have contingencies. Everything us military men do *must* be planned. They throw us off course just to see if we panic, but men like us can't afford to. No, they're so full of emotion they don't even see the drama they cause. All we want is peace while they stir shit up."

Rankin reacted, but not like Clint had hoped. He leaned in, lowered his tone, and spoke deliberately. "Your son backs her story."

Clint almost flinched. Almost.

There was the lie, he thought, *the last ditch effort to trip me up.* "Impossible, unless she's brainwashed him with her bullshit. Joshie knows I'm the victim." He let his eyes water, choked on the last words even, then added, "It's always been like this! She whispers lies into his ears to make *me* out to be the monster!"

It was time for the grand finale, and he rested his head on his hands while letting the waterworks flow. *Cry it out, Clint,* he thought, *make them believe*!

It must have worked, because the Marines left him alone, shutting the door softly behind them.

They'll deliberate my fate by arguing over who they trust more—her or me. That thought gave him a bit of a chuckle he hid with a cough.

From somewhere in the room Dean Martin sang, *Ain't that a Kick to the Head?* And it really was, all just a kick to their heads.

"What do you think?" Max asked Shayde.

"I honestly don't know. Either he's a psychopath like she said, and able to fool us with an Oscar performance, or she's not at all what we believed."

"She's lost it twice now, and big, don't forget." Max pointed out. "Who the hell gouges someone's eyes out then pulls a gun on her ex-husband? What if she really *is* the crazy one? Hell, she *could* have been the one who poisoned the officers after all."

Shayde paused, nodding his agreement. "You're the boss, Max. What do we do?"

"I don't know." Max needed time to think. This was too much at once to process. "Did you hear the first part, that he has combat experience?"

"Yeah. Second Battle of Fallujah. Man! What a rush!"

"Phantom Fury..." That was the name of it, and Max knew it well. He was part of the Marine diversion force. "This guy could be an asset. He's seen what we have, all of it, and won't flinch in battle. Let's assume for a minute that Cathy *is* the crazy one. This guy would be just like any of our buddies who made it home to find either a Jody sleeping in his bed, or a wife who simply no longer wants him. A bad woman can ruin a man, Shayde, just as easily as a good one can save him."

"But if he's not good at all to *anyone* anymore? What if he's like some *Apocalypse Now* Marlon Brando type? That dude was whack, totally insane," Shayde offered.

Max remembered that movie and had seen that type of insanity in the service. Even the Colonel had suggested there were some in his ranks he should weed out. Only... little Josh had done it for him, taking down every single officer at once. *Or was it her? The sick mother who would let her son take the fall.* The thought of it hurt his heart and soul.

"What?" Shayde asked, concern heavy on his voice.

"It's best we keep this soldier on patrol for some time. Send him right into combat and watch him close. Do it yourself."

"What am I looking for?" Shayde asked.

"Watch him kill, and make up your own mind about him. Whatever you decide, I'll back you."

"You think he might be a psychopath?"

"That," Max agreed, "or a hero."

Cathy sat next to her son, seeing him much differently than she had before. Not even five years old, he had committed murder on a grand scale, killing thirty people with a single dose of ricin. Surely he hadn't understood what he had done.

But she had asked him and he had. He was fully aware of his actions and did it with intent to save his mother from the bad men. The idea to use the poison had been hers. She had openly talked about it in front of him to the others, and he saw himself as the only person who could carry through with the act.

She would never forgive herself.

"What do you feel, baby?" she asked him. "Do you feel bad about doing it?"

He shook his head. No, he did not.

She picked up a small book laying on her bunk. It was the devotional Mr. Starling had given to her when they last talked. At the time she had not realized he was sending her a message of support. *I understand your child is a killer, and it's your fault, but there's hope for both of you* he had said without saying. She understood now. That man already knew how bad a mother she was. He had given it to her as a path to repentance and a way to save her son as well as herself.

"Do you like Mr. Starlings?" she asked Josh.

He nodded and added, "He's nice."

That was good. Her son had bonded with his teacher. He did seem a nice man, and the other parents all agreed he was not only a good teacher but one they could trust with their children. He had actually been a real teacher before the missiles landed.

She turned the devotional over in her hands. *I've neglected his conscience,* she suddenly realized, *and he could turn out like Clint if I don't fix that.*

It was time, she knew, to completely change how she did things with her son, starting with reading the devotional. She would read it herself, then to him if she liked the message. If that went over well, she would even take Josh to Mr. Starlings' next bible class.

Linda's throat cleared at the entrance to her hovel and Cathy looked up.

"Max said to remind you that you're late for work."

"I'm not going in today."

Linda shrugged. "Actually, he said to tell you that you are. He wants you to examine the new doctors and get them up to speed so you can take time off later."

"Josh needs..."

"He said it's an order," Linda insisted, cutting her off.

She had meant to say that Josh needed his mother, that he had to learn right from wrong and how not to be like his father, but she suddenly realized the idea to kill the officers had been her own, not Clint's. Then she thought something no mother should ever have to learn about their child. *It may already be too late.*

She rose, resting a lingering hand on her son's shoulder, then nodded to Linda and left the hovel. Each footstep felt heavier than the other as she made her way to the stage. Passing the large doors leading outside, she saw Clint and Shayde geared up for a patrol. Heavy feet suddenly became anchors, preventing further walking. The leaders of the Regiment had trusted this murderer with a rifle.

Catching her watching, Clint seemed to read her mind, raising the firearm into the air with a wink the moment Shayde looked the other way. Then he blew his ex-wife a kiss, sending her feet very quickly moving toward the medical unit.

She found the doctors waiting patiently for her arrival and they were not alone. Max sat across from a man in his late thirties or early forties and more handsome up close than she had realized. She briefly wondered why she noticed that detail. He wasn't the usual rugged type she had always fallen for. He was the academic type, with smooth hands that had never done real work and a genteel nature. His smile as she arrived also seemed forced, but not in an overconfident way. This man seemed shy and introverted, as if wishing in private to quickly move on from pleasantries to business.

The woman and man waiting with him were different. The man was noticeably a soldier, one of the calculated types who did not brag nor boast. Sitting as close as he did to the woman, Cathy could tell they were the couple. The bump on her belly revealed they were more than even that.

"I'm Dr. Stephanie Yurik," the woman said to break the silence, "Captain, United States Air Force." She pointed to the male doctor. "This is Dr. David Andalon from Massachusetts Institute of Technology but, more recently, on loan to us as a DoD contractor."

The man nodded, his forced smile briefly returning. Something in Dr. Yurik's words troubled him. *A lie perhaps, or a stretched truth?*

The woman placed a hand on the soldier and made his introduction as her husband, Sergeant Benjamin Roark, then pointed across the room at the two children they had arrived with. "The children are Adam and Eve."

That's it? Cathy wondered. *Just Adam and Eve?* Yurik had carefully left out any details of who they belonged to or how they came to travel with military soldiers and contractors.

"The civilians we arrived with are Elijah and Emma Miller. Sally Miller, Elijah's sister, is the woman who recently gave birth."

"And you already know Clint," Max added cruelly, taking over. "Doctors, I'll leave you in the care of our top nurse, Cathy Fletcher. She'll give the lay of the infirmary and quarantine protocol."

"The protocol is very strict," Cathy explained. "You're to be under observation for ten days, more if you show signs of radiation poisoning." Turning to Max she added, "Which is why I'm confused you allowed *Clint* to gear up with Sergeant Rogers. We have to..."

Dr. Andalon cut her off. "We're all vaccinated against radiation. I'm certain you'll see no ill effects or residual side effects in any of us."

"That's impossible, there's no vaccine against radiation. It's not a virus."

"Perhaps *vaccine* isn't the right word for it. My mixture addresses the cellular response to ionizing radiation. The nucleus remembers its original structure, and my serum encourages the replacement of any electrons stripped away by the effects of fallout. Essentially, it tells the mutated cells to repair themselves."

Cathy couldn't believe her ears. If what this man was suggesting was true, then he was the answer to the prayers of all her severely damaged patients. "Come with me," she said, pointing to his bag, "and bring that."

Nurse Fletcher led David and the others to a woman, a mother of two teenage boys. She suffered from advanced stages of thyroid cancer, most certainly from radiation exposure. The goiters he felt on both sides of her throat were larger than any he had seen in medical books during college. Without alerting the others watching, he poured a bit of his essence into her body, poking the cancerous cells and finding they had also metastasized to her liver, lungs, and other organs. The goiters he could heal with the vaccine, the rest of the cells would require his newly discovered *healing* touch.

"Stephanie," he said to Yurik, "please draw two CCs of the vaccine and mix it with B-12."

The woman nodded and readied the syringe.

David caught Nurse Fletcher's eyes watching him closely as his hands hovered over the goiters. They watched with deep distrust, as if he were a holy man instead of a doctor.

"That's a strange technique for feeling goiters," she boldly accused.

"I find it easier to palpate the mass with the pads of my hands, especially when the nodule is this large," he lied.

His words seem to have made sense, though, and she settled. By then, Stephanie had arrived to administer the injection.

David stepped over to Nurse Fletcher, reaching out a hand to shake hers. She eyed it like a viper, unsure of the man and what he would do to her infirmary. She needed reassurance. "You've done a wonderful job here," he told her. "Your skill at medicine has no doubt saved most of the people you've treated. Please know I'm not here to replace you nor to force you to change your methods. I'm only here to help."

Very slowly the woman reached out to grasp his hand, and did so firmly, he noticed. Besides being both attractive and intelligent, Cathy Fletcher had an inner confidence that he admired. "Tell me about Clint. Why you were so riled by his arrival. Besides being your ex-husband, of course. General Rankin filled us in with that detail."

"Clint Fletcher is an awful man," she replied with a low voice. "He is a narcissist, a murderer, and a..." Her eyes lifted from their hands, still grasped in mutual respect, and added, "He is a rapist and a beater of women."

"I see," David said sadly, full of sympathy for her experiences with the man. "Had we known all that, we would never have travelled with him. Please know that with all my sincerity."

Cathy nodded, finally pulling her hand away from his.

Introduce her to us, Eve suggested. *I like her.*

"Would you like to meet Adam and Eve?" David suddenly asked. "I promise you will find them very special children."

Cathy nodded and looked toward them, both smiling and waving, doing their best to appear normal. They approached, smiling and talking about things normal children would.

Brooke has perfected the beads, Eve said into David's mind.

He tried not to appear surprised, keeping his face neutral in front of Nurse Fletcher. *Already?* he asked.

Yes, but they've only tested the pearl.

Pearl?

Batch Alpha.

"Ah," he said aloud.

"Hmm?" Nurse Fletcher asked, confused by his utterance.

"Oh, nothing, I just had a thought, is all."

There's more, Eve urged.

Can it wait?

No. Two of their test subjects reached Da'ash'mael and one of them reached a full state of Ka'ash'mael.

David could no longer fathom the conversation, especially with such strange words whispered into his mind. "I'm sorry," he explained to Nurse Fletcher, gently leading Eve by the arm. "I need to have a word in private with my daughter."

"Of course," the woman replied with a smile, a lovely one, he noticed. She really was quite striking.

You like her. Eve accused. *That's good, it fits the plan.*

Shut up! David snapped, careful to keep it in his and her minds. Once they were out of earshot he demanded, "What the hell were you talking about back there? Da and Ka, and Smeagol?"

Eve laughed at the Hobbit reference, a book she had read long ago, and the child she really should be leaked out from behind her usual stoic nature. "My preeeeciousss!" she snarled and laughed once more.

"Stop that at once! Explain why all that you said was so important!"

Eve fell abruptly calm, once more her usual self. "The word *ash* is rooted in several languages and refers to the leavings after fire. When a modified human consumes a bead, they digest it in the same way calories are burned only the leavings are the ash absorbed into first their bloodstream and then their nervous system. The term mael refers to the storm—a maelstrom, if you will. Thus, the Da'ash'mael is the storm that rages in the mind when the bead is first absorbed into the mind."

David stood flabbergasted. He had never considered such technical absorption, much less the practical levels of higher thinking related to the gift. "What about the other, the Ka, as you called it?"

"Ka is like a soul, but more akin to the part of it that humans attribute as connected to their gods. The ancient Egyptians had it more closely identified and gave it this name. In the case of the bead, it is when the soul reaches full consciousness, freed from the mind itself and separate of the body. When one reaches Ka'ash'mael they attain the same level as Adam and I reach while *Dreaming*. Their soul is unbound, capable of prophecy and so much more."

"It sounds dangerous," David gasped.

"It is and will result in the death of more latents than Astia will right away appreciate."

David frowned at her words, pondering their deeper meaning. He was about to open his mouth to ask when Nurse Fletcher called his name.

"Doctor Andalon!" she shouted, urging him to rush over. She stooped over the woman he had just healed, marveling at her goiter.

He frowned as he arrived, shocked to see the mass had already fully subsided. He had hoped the process would have taken at least a day or two.

"You did it! Your vaccine," she gushed, "it works!"

"Yes," he agreed, *and quite quickly.* "I'd like to administer it to everyone in quarantine, and to the soldiers, as well."

"I'll give General Rankin my full endorsement," she promised with a smile, "and would like to sign up my son, Josh, and myself as your first inoculated."

She's falling for you, Eve whispered in his mind.

Shut up. he nearly said aloud, but the thought of what the girl suggested calmed him if not excited the newly single man. He had not been this interested in a woman since first meeting Brooke so many years before, and it was nice to have feelings beyond those for his lab and experiments.

Doctor David Andalon smiled back at Nurse Fletcher. "Of course," he promised, "I'd be happy to."

CHAPTER FOURTEEN

James Parker dismounted outside the gate, unsteady but bearing himself with false confidence. This visit to the Donelson Compound felt tenser, with suspicious eyes glaring down from the wall while palms rested on buttstocks or pistol grips. At least none of those weapons pointed at him... not yet. Surprise remained on his side. They viewed him as an oddity, a lone rider daring to approach, one either lacking sense or loyalty.

The gates did not open on his arrival.

Mike Donelson finally appeared above, staring down with a pair of challenging eyes. "What do you want?" he demanded. "We already paid tribute this month."

"I'm here to talk," James insisted, his empty hands held away from his body with palms facing skyward.

"We're not interested in talking to you or any more lackeys. Go back to the Regiment and tell your Colonel to come in person next time!"

James grimaced. He had dreaded this moment. "The defector you met before, who told you the Colonel was dead, he was right. There *is* no more Colonel. He's dead and so are all his officers."

A sly smile crossed Donelson's face, but it quickly disappeared into a thoughtful frown. "Who killed them?"

Parker froze. Though he had rehearsed his speech the entire way from the Shelter, it now felt oddly fake and insincere. He answered simply, "I did."

"All of them?" Donelson demanded without losing his frown.

"All of them."

The leader of the compound, Crazy Mike as Cathy had called him, stole a look toward the south. Toward the Nature Boys, maybe? Chad Pescari had suggested this man may be cozying up to both militias. "Who really runs the Regiment, then?" Donelson finally asked.

"A pair of Marine sergeants."

"Actual Marines, eh? So, Shayde Walters is one."

"He is."

"Figured as much. And this other one I was told about, he's not really the armorer, is he? He's in charge, not Walters?"

"Sergeant Max Rankin *is* in charge. They now call him *General*."

"Did this *general* order you to kill the Colonel?"

"No, sir. I did that on my own, over a woman. One of the Colonel's men had his way with her, and I didn't like it."

"Go figure, a righteous man…" Donelson laughed, then stopped abruptly and signaled his men to open the gates.

They moved slowly, too slowly for James' liking, and he led his horse forward. As soon as he was inside, the heavy gates closed more quickly than they had parted.

"Seize him!" Crazy Mike commanded, and all at once ten rifles pointed at Parker's chest.

"I'm a defector!" James shouted, raising his hands into the air. "I have information for the Nature Boys! That's why I'm here, to make a trade!"

Mike was already moving down the ladder. As soon as his feet hit ground, he was flanked by two large men. One of them held a long rope, the end of which was tied in a noose. "We promised we'd *hang* any more of your defectors! Besides, if I take care of General Rankin's problems, he'll be keener on dealing with me later if the Nature Boys fail. Besides, he owes me primers. Our continued arrangement benefits *both* of us, at least until they've won."

"So, you *are* dealing with them? The Nature Boys?"

"I'm dealing with whoever appears to be winning," Max replied, then signaled. He watched as his henchmen tossed the rope over a makeshift gallows and tied it off.

James stared up and shuddered. The rope would hold his weight for sure.

Strong arms grabbed James from behind and two more shoved the noose over his head. Panic overtook him as the knot tightened against the right side of his neck—just off-center to ensure the vertebrae snapped cleanly. These men were well practiced in their art and forced him up onto a stool. In all his life he never dreamed twenty-four inches would be such a terrifying height.

He found it difficult to think, his mind clouded by the need to survive. His next words could be his last and they had to be well chosen to prove lifesaving. "You want primers? I know where they are, along with the rest of the armory! They have everything you need to..."

The stool suddenly disappeared beneath him, kicked away without warning and sending his feet flying forward in front of his body. He felt himself falling, the sensation feeling much too long for the actual height and expecting his neck to break at any moment. He was ready to die, sick of this apocalyptic world and heartbroken by Cathy's refusal of his affections.

The small of his back hit the ground first, followed by the back of his head. The jarring sensation caused spots to dance before his eyes, a sign he had also forgotten to breathe. He stared upward at the sky as Mike Donelson's men laughed, realizing for the first time in months a glimmer of sunshine had broken through the thick clouds of nuclear winter. It would have been beautiful had a heavy boot not struck his chest. It pressed hard against him, pushing out every bit of air from his lungs.

"There, I kept my promise," Crazy Mike told him. "It's a shame to waste a strong back like yours, and I know just how to put you to work."

Around his neck the noose tightened, cutting off any attempt to refill his lungs. The black spots and stars dancing in his eyes merged together until he fully blacked out.

James Parker awoke with a gasp, then rolled over trying to breath deeper against the pain in his ribs and around his throat. The effort took more energy than he had, and he struggled to open his eyes. Both throbbed for some unknown reason, swollen and shut. He touched his face and pulled away a sticky, wet hand, warm from what he assumed was blood. A sudden coughing fit came over him, revealing new aches across his belly. His entire abdominal wall was bruised, as were his thighs and all muscles along his back. He had taken a beating, it seemed, after passing out.

"Relax," a soothing male voice urged. It was low, the kind of baritone that would have carried a jazz song back in the fifties, and sounded sincerely concerned for James' health. "You've been beaten bad, man, but not the worse that I've ever seen. Our count is six bruised ribs, four on the right and two on the left. You're lucky they didn't crack and pierce a lung, though, and that's why you gonna heal up."

"Who...?" James was going to ask who the owner of the voice was, but a stabbing pain shot through his right his side.

"I said relax, man! Your nose was broke and so was a finger or two, but Alice took care of those."

"Alice?" Another painful wave rippled through his ribs and James cut off abruptly.

"Alice," the voice agreed. "She's the Angel of Life in this place. Keeps us alive and able to work. You gotta get healthy, too, or they'll kill you just because you can't."

"Can't?"

"Can't work," the voice replied. "That's what *slaves* do, brother. We work and stay alive."

"Who?" James tried to ask, but the words disappeared in another wave of pain.

"Shh," the man urged. "Don't talk now, but when you can, call me Curtis."

Curtis, James repeated in his mind, hoping to live through the pain to look upon this person's face. The pain. He had never felt anything like it, but it was worth it, to save the boy by taking his blame. He felt himself drift off into sleep but wondered as he did how little Josh was getting on.

CHAPTER FIFTEEN

Vincent Starlings paused from reading aloud, rudely interrupted by a clearing of throat. The interruption was untimely, just at the most interesting part of the story. The teacher did not slam the book closed, nor did his voice falter, he merely finished the last sentence of the paragraph he was on. As he lifted his eyes, he found the irritation on the children's faces matched his own, each eager to hear the rest. But the arrival of two more students quickly changed his demeanor. The more students in his classroom the better, and all were welcome. For what was a teacher for, if not his students?

"Hello!" he greeting them pleasantly, the newly arrived boy and girl. He had expected them to remain in quarantine longer, at least two more weeks.

They appeared to be around ten years old, but their eyes held a sort of wisdom that sent a shudder of uneasiness through his mind. Vince had worked as a teacher for two decades and had seen this look before. Usually it meant some dark trauma resided deep in the child's mind, lurking and threatening to interfere with his or her chances for higher education. That look was everywhere since the missiles landed in North America.

Both new arrivals stared curiously at their new teacher, seemingly forgetting to respond to or choosing to outright ignore his greeting.

Vince tried again. "Welcome to my classroom. I'm Mr. Starlings. What grade level did you both last leave off on?" he asked pleasantly, his warm smile hoping to ease their anxiety.

"Grade level?" the boy asked quizzically, cocking his head slightly and furrowing his brow in confusion.

"We've never actually been in school," the girl explained, taking charge and stepping in front of her brother. "We are... self-taught."

"Ah, home-schooled!" Vince reasoned. He would have to test them both, of course, to determine their reading level and knowledge of mathematic reasoning. Hopefully they each had a good grasp of science and the arts. "No matter! I can quickly determine where we should pick up..."

"No," the boy replied curtly, almost corrective of the adult. "We are not *home-schooled,* we are self-taught."

Vince paused. There was certainly something else, an oddness lurking behind the emotionless eyes of these two children. "How old are you?"

"We are ten," the girl responded, "just barely... I think."

The children all snickered at this.

"Who doesn't know how *old* they are?" Josh Fletcher accused, garnering hoots of laughter from the others. The boy had been increasingly moody of late and no wonder with all the trauma in his tumultuous life.

"What are your names?" Vincent asked, ignoring the outburst.

"I'm Eve, and this is Adam."

"Ah, Adam and Eve like in the story of Genesis!" he said with a smile. A devout and faithful Christian, Vincent studied the word voraciously and found the names comforting in these dark times.

The two children exchanged another look of confusion. "What... is *Genesis*?" Adam asked. His question instantly sent the other children into riotous laughter.

"Are you stupid?" Josh Fletcher blurted out rudely. The boy seldom spoke anymore, and never harshly, so this second outburst shocked both the teacher and other students. "It's from the Bible, idiot!"

"Josh!" Vince cautioned.

But the boy only shrugged and added, "I bet you're from the *Garden of Eden* too!"

"Yes!" Eve's eyes lit up, missing the sarcasm and seemingly pleased at his mention of the place. "That's *exactly* right! We were raised in the Garden and only left after Father arrived."

There was no managing the children at this point, not with Josh acting so cruelly toward the newcomers, and Vince found himself doing something he seldom did as a teacher—he sent the boy from the classroom.

"Josh!" he snapped, pointing to the door. "That's enough of you for today! Leave and come back tomorrow!"

The child stood, but stared defiantly at Adam and Eve. He walked slowly by them, purposely bumping his shoulder into the boy's chest as he passed. Vince expected a shoving match or battle of words to ensue, but Adam and his sister merely watched the younger boy's back with curiosity. As soon as he cleared the doorway, Eve leaned forward and shut the door behind him. Adam's eyes fixated on the wall as if watching Josh through it.

"Please have a seat up here," Vince urged, hoping to regain control of his class, but a loud crash in the hallway interrupted his next words. He darted past the children, pulling open the door and skidding to a halt. Josh lay in a heap against the far wall, moaning and holding his arm. "Are you okay?" the teacher asked, rushing to his side. "Did you trip?"

"I was pushed!" the child insisted, with angry eyes staring over Vince's shoulder.

Starlings turned his head to find Adam watching from the doorway, smiling broadly at the injured boy.

"You and your sister find a seat!" Vince commanded. "Find a picture book and I'll be right back!" Scooping Josh into his arms, he rushed him to the infirmary and to the child's mother.

Eve frowned at her brother. *You shouldn't have done that,* she said into his mind.

Adam shrugged. *He deserved it. Besides, I didn't hurt him badly, only a broken arm.*

You'll ruin everything we've planned if you're not careful! She did as the teacher had told them, choosing a book from the shelf and finding a seat. Only, a picture book would not do. Though suitable for their age, she and her brother were far beyond those. *Who was King James I, again?* she asked her brother, staring down at the thick, black book with leather bindings.

King of England via Scotland, he followed Mary Tudor.

That's right, I didn't pay close attention to the succession of monarchs following the War of the Roses.

There had been gaps in the reading material they had available in the garden but, reading the spine, she found the king's name above the word *Bible* and vaguely remembered reading he had made a translation of the book. Why it was so important, she never knew. Now, holding the tome in her hand, she remembered asking Dr. Yurik about it. But Stephanie had told the children not to worry, that the Bible had no bearing on their studies. Now curious, Eve found a seat and began to read.

Adam chose a book of his own, no doubt to prove a point to the teacher when he returned. On its cover was the title, *War and Peace,* something they had both read years before. *Don't be childish,* she warned him, *Mr. Starlings won't believe you can even remotely understand that one.*

No more than you reading that one? Besides, I'm tired of hiding our abilities. We're more intelligent than all these adults combined, even Father.

Be patient, Eve urged her brother, *we will reveal ourselves soon.* Her mind returned to the words on the page, reading them with wonder and anticipation. *In the beginning,* she read, *God created the heaven and the earth.*

CHAPTER SIXTEEN

Michael Esterling and Jake Braston stood in the lab. Neither spoke, both overwhelmed by the strange occurrence and needing time to process the fiasco. His first thought, the rational one, was to pull the plug on the entire experiment. The easiest option now, it seemed, was to build a fleet of sailing ships and go to North America and track down David Andalon and the two projects he escaped with. But that too felt impossible. Besides, he knew these experiments would work... Adam and Eve promised him control over emotancy.

"You think they're finished cleaning up?" Jake asked, breaking the silence.

"Your puke or the smashed equipment?" Michael, so stressed and overwhelmed for so long, let out a chuckle. After a brief moment, so did his friend.

"Funny." Jake had meant the beads that had scattered, four colors flung in every direction.

There *had* been a lot of puke in the room. Soon they were laughing like the old days when they and David shared a dorm room in the Kappa Sigma house. "Geez, man! I haven't seen you blow chunks like that since that keg stand went wrong after pledge week!"

Jake groaned, then let out another laugh. "Don't remind me! Stacey Gallagher was so pissed I ruined her sweater!"

The humor was long needed and Michael felt himself relax a bit at the memory, but he pushed the urge to laugh the night away behind him. No longer a frat boy, the chancellor had a nation to build.

"Four of you puked up the pearl," he pointed out, "those aren't good odds."

Jake shrugged. "Then we test another group of subjects and get a better sampling size."

Michael thought about how the girl had nearly died, her blood pressure first skyrocketing and then plummeting to barely life sustaining levels. He had been the first to notice her falling into seizures and contortions. *And those words she uttered, what had those been?*

"The airman, she said something, Jake, it was profound."

"I only caught part of it," the general admitted. "What did she say?"

"Something about the rise of Astia depending on the fall of Andalon, but there was more, so much more. She mentioned both the beads and the powers and something about death."

"Not death, I remember that part." Jake corrected. "She said, 'the *dead* must rise to channel the craft,' or something like that."

"That sergeant in there channeled it."

"He also nearly died. His heart stopped, and Brooke had to use the AED to revive him."

"There's so much to unpack about that entire round of testing," the chancellor admitted.

"Then what do we do now? I'm only a soldier, Mike, the tactical knife you use to settle disputes or prevent them. This science stuff isn't my bag, hasn't been since college."

"I wish I knew." But Esterling *did* know, he just didn't have the manpower for it. He needed his army of emotants, and the only way to build that was to test every man and woman in his service. His only worry was the casualty rate of such an endeavor. "Two out of six nearly died," he pointed out. "Where do I draw the line? When is too many? When do we decide David played us like fools, stealing away Adam and Eve and leaving us only with false hope and lies? We could kill my entire army, attempting to recreate his promise, and we can't afford losses. I want to *build,* not *destroy!*"

"You can look at it that way, or you can say two out of six succeeded," Brooke's voice answered from the doorway. "I think I know what happened. Come with me, gentlemen, and I'll fill you in."

Jake and Michael followed willingly.

The chancellor was tired of the mystery and eager for simpler solutions to his problems, but mostly he was just worn out. He found a chair and collapsed, weariness settling in as exhaustion as soon as he found comfort. "Enlighten us, *please*!" he commanded.

Jake took a seat next to Brooke.

"Well, for one, we know David was telling the truth. He *did* leave us a pathway to emotancy, he just didn't make it easy for us," Brooke explained.

"Elaborate."

"Airman McLemore."

"What about her?" Jake asked, lifting his eyes to watch the young woman enter the lab with Mi-Jung.

"Tell them what you experienced, Airman," Brooke urged.

The young woman fidgeted nervously, but found her voice. "After swallowing the pill, I travelled."

"Where?" Michael demanded.

"To North America. I flew above it."

The chancellor had his doubts, but this claim would be easy to prove or disprove, since Adam and Eve had described flying over it and gave clear details to Stephanie Yurik who logged every description. Only he and Jake had ever read her notes, so this would not be something easily fed to the airman. "Describe the landscape," he commanded.

"Much like here, but covered more deeply in snow and ash. The major cities have been leveled, turned to rubble, and the coastlines have changed. The Gulf of Mexico reaches the Texas Hill Country."

"Hmm," Michael nodded. *Easily guessed,* he thought.

"Also, a new fault line opened up east of the Rocky Mountains. It's a crack belching ash and cinders into the sky, running north and south the entire length of the continent, reaching all the way north into the Yellowstone Crater."

Well now, that is *something,* Michael decided. She described what Adam and Eve had first called *Cinder's Crack*. "Okay, Brooke, you've proven your point, but what was the last part?" Addressing McLemore, he asked, "What happened at the end when you started speaking strangely? What did all that mean?"

"I don't know, sir. I blacked out and don't even remember what I said. I was…" She stole a shy glance at Jake. "I was somewhere *else* when I talked, the words didn't come from me."

"Thank you, Airman, you can leave us," Michael said, dismissing the young woman.

"I need her to stay in observation for a while," Brooke interrupted.

"Fine, but we need the room," he snapped. This had to be discussed immediately. Brooke read his face and tone, shooing the airman out to rejoin Mi-Jung and Sam Nakala. As soon as she shut the door, Michael spoke freely. "None of us wrote down what she said, Brooke. If that was a prophecy, or bullshit, we needed it recorded!"

"I had my iPad filming," Brooke replied flatly.

Michael sat up. Electricity was scarce in the world, only existing in the lab and a few bunkers like it across Europe—mainly where electronics were shielded from the electromagnetic pulse. He hadn't realized a simple item like an iPad had survived end-times. "Play it back to us."

Brooke complied, replaying the entire event from the beginning, right up until the point that Jake blew chunks on his sister.

That was when the girl began to speak, writhing in her straps as if possessed by spirits and flinching from either euphoria or pain—or both. "Rise, Astia, from the rubble, dependent upon Andalon's pearls. The key to controlling unlocked power is death, control over death is the pearl. Only sight belongs to the living, until the son of Andalon returns. Hear now! Heed the Ka'ash'mael and fear its words, welcoming the gift the most powerful provide. Harken the destroyer, sever his line before it roots!"

Brooke replayed the recording three times until Jake finally stopped her, turning to face Michael. "That certainly *sounds* like a prophecy, and certainly the kind Adam and Eve already boasted about knowing. I think it's real, Mike. I think the Astian Pearl worked."

"Yeah," Esterling agreed, "funny you called it that right before she spouted all that."

"You think she made it up?" Jake asked with a bit of concern. "In her defense, she said *Andalon's pearls.*"

"Possibly... maybe. I don't know. We need further testing." Michael turned to Jake's sister. "How do we do that? How can we continue testing on a larger scale without killing or sickening our entire army? What do *you* think? You were *married* to David. How does his mind work these days?"

Brooke wiped sweaty palms on her lab coat, a fresh one she had changed into after Jake's MRE explosion. After a brief moment collecting her thoughts, she spoke her mind. "I think Airman McLemore is proof David's inoculations worked. He resequenced many of the soldiers, and maybe even us, to hold latency for the craft but not full emotancy."

"I agree," Jake added.

"But we don't know the method he used to divide up the four types. All six subjects we tested came from the same vaccination group, thinking he would have used the same serum on each group, but it was more randomized than that. Either subtle differences in their DNA determines which pearl it will accept, or David had a rotation or method to divide batches throughout the serums."

"Or," Jake suddenly realized, "he gave specific people access to certain batches."

"What do you mean?" Michael demanded.

"What did he say on that hill at Waghäusel? Something about Sam and Mi-Jung's child, and something about your own, Mike? He planned this all the way, and it wasn't by chance."

The chancellor winced at the threat David had made on the hill while bargaining his release. "He said my son is an emotant and will challenge my rule, but an Esterling will always sit on the throne." Brooke placed her hands on her belly while he spoke, wincing at the words and deeply troubled by the state of her unborn child. "He also said Sam and Mi-Jung's child would be able to harness *all* powers, meaning Jake is right, David doled out the serums very carefully and with forethought."

Brooke nodded her understanding and added, "So we need to figure out who he gave what."

"Right. Test *everyone* on the pearl, then each batch thereafter."

"Wait," cautioned Jake, "the bead nearly killed two men in the first test, and David himself gave a warning."

"What warning?" Brooke asked.

"Only the Nakala line can consume all four beads, meaning it could be death for *everyone* we test if we don't space out the dosages. I don't think we should mix beads. Ever."

Brooke agreed. "I had the same thought just now. This will take time. We don't know how long each bead will remain in each subject."

"Figure it out," Michael commanded. "Test everyone. I want each soldier catalogued and sorted by latency."

Brooke, with her hands still on her belly, left the room to prepare. Once he and Jake were alone again, the chancellor addressed his general. "I think I know what the prophecy means. David gave us weaker versions of the emotants, meaning we're going to be farming with a lesser quality seed. The warning... what did she call it, a Ka'ash'mael? It was a warning against using the clones. It's a good start, but eventually we'll need to harvest the *real* power, the pearl provided by Andalon's creations."

"Michael..." Jake warned. "Don't go there. We should let them be, to live in peace."

"No. They will always be a threat to Astia, a *much* more powerful race of beings. If we can't destroy them, we'll need to find a way to control them. In all of history, energy has been the strongest resource—whether wood, charcoal, coal, oil, or nuclear, energy dominance reigns supreme. I *will* have to claim that dominance, and that prophecy told us exactly what to do. I'll use what he gave us to learn *how* to eventually harvest David's abominations."

Michael watched his friend process the idea. He could tell he didn't like it. That was the way of Jake's peaceful demeanor, but inside the general lurked a cold-hearted killer. He was a weapon, after all, just as he had said.

"Okay, Mike. When we get to that point you have my word I'll make it happen."

CHAPTER SEVENTEEN

James Parker blinked open two bruised and sore eyelids, finally seeing and taking in the world around him. He could move, but not without stiff difficulty. Crazy Mike's men had done a number on his rib cage, leaving the skin neatly lined with black and blue streaks. He stared at the rows of empty cots lining every wall. This had to be an army barracks of sorts or, even worse, the slave quarters Max had expected him to find.

This plan had better work, Max! he thought, thinking of their last conversation.

"Josh Fletcher killed the officers," Max had revealed with Shayde Walters nodding along. "The kid had already witnessed so much violence he didn't hesitate when left alone with the cookpot. He saw Linda hide the ricin and didn't flinch when pouring it into the stew."

"His only thought was to save his mother," Shayde had added, but that did little to lift the guilt James felt for not doing the job himself.

James' thoughts had immediately gone to the child's mother. She rejected his love, claiming she needed time to clear her thoughts, stating she wasn't ready for a relationship despite he had fallen hard for her. The problem Max had brought to him, that Josh was a killer, became an easy decision for James. The idea that he should leave the Regiment had been his own idea, a selfless plan to shield the child from consequences while also giving Cathy the space she had needed.

"We can't tell the people of the Regiment that Josh killed them, General Rankin," he had urged. "They won't understand, nor will they see a chance to help him now—to change him before it's too late. He's still young and has a chance for life. He doesn't have to remain a killer."

"We know," Rankin had agreed, "and that's what I'd hoped you'd conclude as well. So you don't mind shouldering the blame for a bit?"

"I'll do it," James had offered, "as long as it takes."

"This is an opportunity," Shayde added, "to shift focus off the murders and give us time to unify the Regiment and maybe even add to our numbers. We need *you* to admit to the crime, then disappear as if you ran."

"Go undercover as a defector," Max suggested "and get into Mike Donelson's camp. Find out who's building those fortifications, get a solid troop count, and learn all you can about his connection to the Nature Boys. Then, after you escape and return to us, we can convince everyone that you weren't the killer after all. Time would have worked on everyone's memories by then, and no one will care what happened to the Colonel and his officers."

"Maybe Cathy will have changed her mind as well," James had hoped.

"Perhaps she might," Max nodded along. "A mother might see a man differently once he's sacrificed everything for her son."

That had proven the deciding factor—the hope to win Cathy's heart with his sacrifice, and now here he lay, beaten and broken on an army cot.

Movement outside a small door turned his head, and James watched it open wide. Men and women entered one by one, each wearing a dismal expression of physical exhaustion and emotional defeat.

A man, tall and muscular with dark skin and stained clothing, smiled down at him. "Ah, I see you're awake!"

A name found its way to James' lips. "Curtis?"

The man nodded. "That's me, Curtis Mathews. Now that you know me, what's your name, friend?"

"I'm James, James Parker." He looked around, scanning the other faces. Staring back, they were a blend of diversity. Mike Donelson had taken slaves from all backgrounds without regard to race, gender, or creed. James' eyes landed on the chains around each person's ankles—a harsh equalizer that ignored all previous privilege. Pulling back his blanket, he found similar shackles around his own. "How did you all get here?" he asked.

"That Mike Donelson is a liar and an evil man," Curtis explained. "Most of us stumbled upon this place looking for a haven, but some, like me, he bought from a militia near the Tennessee border."

"Bought from the Nature Boys?"

Curtis' features darkened by some not so distant memory. "What do you know of *them*?" he demanded, suddenly guarded.

"I've been scouting them for weeks, tracking their movements and hearing rumors of their strength in the south."

"Strength?" Curtis scoffed. "They got strength alright. They're the new government in what was Tennessee. It's all theirs now. They even hold Fort Campbell."

James tried to sit up, sending a flash of pain through his side that quickly subsided. He would be sore but able to work and maybe even fight.

"Easy," the tall man cautioned, moving to wad an extra blanket behind his new friend. "You won't be worth a damn to Donelson if you don't heal up. He said you have three days to be on the line, and you already slept through one."

Line? A working chain gang, more like it. "What are we building?" Parker asked.

"Walls, shoring them up mostly. But we're also digging a lot."

"Digging? What for?"

Curtis shrugged. "Don't know. Donelson said we'd know when we found it. Feels like we're mining, though, when we dig."

"Mining? The only thing around here is coal."

Curtis nodded. "Some of the others said that as well, so it's probably right."

Coal. So that's Donelson's play? He would bargain with the Nature Boys, keeping his compound as long as he provides them with coal. It made sense. For the near future it would become the world's primary fuel source.

James leaned back against the blanket, suddenly wishing for a mattress, a hot meal, and Cathy to help nurse him back to health. He was grateful, though, for Curtis.

"How many?" he asked his new friend.

"How many what?" the man demanded, frowning deeply but with laughing eyes.

"How many of us are there, and how many guards?"

"You ain't crazy enough to be planning an escape as soon as you're captured, are you, James Parker?" The dark man roared with laughter, waving for a few of the others to come join them.

"Damn right I am. I'm with the Regiment out of Evansville."

"They said you defected after killing a bunch of officers," one of the newcomers accused. "I don't think we can trust him, Curtis."

"It was a lie. I'm here to gather intel, to figure out why the Nature Boys are pushing so far north, and free any slaves I find," James insisted.

"Well then," Curtis said with another laugh, "you can start with yourself, because you're the *only* slave crazy enough to fight the Nature Boys."

"I'll find a way. If I do, are you in?" James whispered.

Curtis never stopped smiling but his eyes betrayed deep worry. "You're too late, friend."

"What do you mean?"

"We already got a plan to get *ourselves* outta here," the black man said with a grin.

"Yeah," one of the others added, "we don't need no *white* savior to free us."

"What's your plan?" James asked. Things would be easier if they had already planned things out.

"We'll tell you later, once we decide we can trust you," Curtis promised. "Besides, we gotta wait. The Nature Boys arrived while you were sleeping. They're camped right outside the walls, hundreds of them."

James sat up, ignoring the pain in his chest as he did. "What kind of weapons? How many, exactly?"

"Slow down, and keep your voice down," Curtis warned. "Hundreds, with machine guns and those tube things. I also heard one of the guards say they've got boats stashed upriver. Lots of them, with motors that work."

"Tube things?"

"Yeah, those things you drop a big firecracker into and it shoots off."

"Mortars," James blanched. Hundreds of Nature Boys with artillery and boats could overrun Max and the Regiment. He had to get out. "Help me," he pleaded. "Help me escape so I can warn the Regiment."

Curtis only shook his head. "Crazy fool," he muttered. "Only just woke up and he's ready to get killed." After a bit of thinking and more frowning, he added, "I've not made up my mind about you, James

Parker, but I think you're telling the truth. When we break out, we'll take you along."

CHAPTER EIGHTEEN

Tom Rankin walked with purpose, his shoulders back and his body sauntering to a rhythm that exuded confidence. Miko had trusted him to deliver a message to the Regiment, an answer to his father's offer. His father... Max was no longer that, not since choosing the wrong side.

Tom and his four friends, barely teens only a few months ago, chattered all the way along Lloyd Expressway. They bragged about the action they had seen, but none of their boasting amounted to much. Other than a few brawls and target practice, none of them had actual combat time. Jacks had come close, claiming to have fought against Max on the night he killed a half dozen of their friends.

Just another reason for me to hate you, Dad. No, not Dad, not any longer. Max Rankin was a selfish loner, a sellout, good for nothing and no one misses him... *except Mom. He's the only man she ever loved, and now she's a heartbroken mess.* But was Mom a good enough reason to forgive the man, the *Marine* who abandoned his family for a life on the road, coming home only when it suited him and rolling off again whenever the lure of the white lines called? *He chose to live on the road, not with us,* was all Tom needed to silence those thoughts.

By the time they reached the end of the bridge Jacks had frozen in place. "What is it?" he asked.

"Do those look like machine guns?" Jacks squinted at the far side of the park, staring at a dark shadow beneath a line of trees.

"Probably, they've put a few of them up," Chris replied with a shrug.

TeKay and Jeb both looked to Tom. Neither had a clue what to do.

"We can bum-rush it," Jacks suggested, but no one liked that idea.

"Let me think!" Tom insisted, scanning the open space between the guns and them, fully vulnerable standing in plain sight on the bridge.

"We're here with a message, not to fight. We just need to figure out a way to let them know."

Jacks pointed south at two soldiers slowly walking toward them. Everything about these men screamed confidence, even the way they held their rifles in a casual but ready position.

Shayde Rogers watched the new guy closely. Clint Fletcher was either going to be an asset or a problem, and he and Chad Pescari had little time to figure him out. When he first arrived, Max had suggested they take him on patrol, a sure-fire way to judge a man's salt, and Shayde completed half a dozen outings with the man since. His final evaluation, watching him now as the checked fortifications, concluded this soldier was seasoned—the real deal, fighting-type the Regiment needed against the Nature Boys.

Of course, his continued presence would strain the situation involving Cathy Fletcher. Choosing one over the other had become an even tougher decision for him and Max, but they *would* have to choose. There was no way Clint and Cathy could coexist, not with her lightning quick anger and capacity for violence. Shayde had witnessed the same from Clint on occasion. Though he had so far controlled his inner demon by maintaining bearing and following orders, a killer waited beneath the surface.

Skilled and merciless, this soldier was good—*too* good at keeping that demon in the shadows. Though Shayde had not *seen* him commit any crimes, the man was capable of anything. Clint enjoyed violence, laughing at the wrong times and the sickest of jokes, and his stare always seemed to savor a gory sight instead of being repulsed away. Cathy's case against her ex-husband was strong, but the evidence and her own son's murky version of the story locked the pair in perpetual tug of war over truth. At least the choice to force one of them to leave would involve Max and not be Shayde's alone.

On this patrol they walked the southern defenses, appraising the hasty fortifications. A line of cars, debris, furniture, and whatever else they could grab snaked from the southeast edge of downtown, along the swollen banks of the Ohio River, and up Mulberry Street. Then it turned northward toward the expressway, forming a triangle that reached west-ward toward the old retail yard. The entire barrier had taken weeks to set up and, looking at it now, Shayde realized their meager attempt would do nothing to keep out a determined foe. The city was too widespread and cluttered with buildings to defend.

With a nervous glance Shayde worried about their vulnerability to the west and northwest. There, Miko Robinson and his gangs still ranged. The leader had failed to give answer either way regarding Max's proposal. Though no patrols had been harassed in over a week, there had also not been any reply.

"It'll hold up against small arms," Clint offered while examining the barrier, "but not shelling."

"Max doubts they have artillery," Shayde agreed, offering hope. He knew all too well the damage heavy munitions would rain down.

"He doubts but isn't certain," Clint pointed out. "This line also stretches our supply lines and, if they cut off one section, we lose the east."

"But it's really only about holding the Shelter at this point."

Clint shrugged then pointed at a small squadron manning a line of cars. Thirteen men stared across the Ohio River with no idea whether Max's truce would protect their backs when the Nature Boys arrived. Similar squads dotted the entire length of the barrier.

"You jarheads and your fireteams," he spat. "Three groups of four under a squad leader holding off how many? Three or four dozen at a time may cross here."

"It's worked fine so far," Shayde pointed out. The criticism did not bother him; it was actually healthy. He and Max seemed to agree on every-thing, so fresh eyes may prove helpful.

"How do the western defenses look?" the former Army sergeant asked as they cut to the northwest.

"Pretty much the same, but better protected. That's the old retail yard, mostly flat with few buildings. It's also the widest part of the river, and our machine gun nests have two hundred and seventy degrees of coverage. It makes a perfect kill zone."

"So it's doubtful they'll cross there." Clint agreed. He glanced eastward toward the tall buildings around the Shelter and, with a frown, pointed out, "You really need to clear those extra buildings and improve the kill zone around the colosseum. I'm surprised snipers haven't been a problem."

"We've been lucky, so far. Thankfully these are street soldiers, not marksmen."

"Those Nature Boys will have shooters, damned good ones if they're a true militia." Clint suggested as they approached the skate park. It was a nice clearing, with more machine gun nests aiming out over Pigeon Creek and watching over two bridges crossing from the west. The larger of the two remained intact. "I'm guessing that's the gangs' only access this far south?"

Shayde nodded again. This position forced their roamers on a long walk to get around to the north and had worked well to thin their activity in the south. He abruptly paused, spying movement on the bridge. A team of five armed men stood in the open, blocking the road westward but not yet crossing over to this side.

"They're waiting for something," Clint pointed out. "Maybe your answer to the truce?"

"Maybe."

Shayde repositioned his rifle, adjusting the sling slightly in case he had to raise it quickly. He noticed Clint Fletcher hadn't shifted his at all. That man, with nerves of steely ice, had never relaxed his even once since leaving the Shelter, holding it properly as if it were a part of his body, a tool he needed to breathe as much as it was a weapon to stop another man from doing so.

One of the Regiment machine gunners fanned their approach and Shayde held up his hand, cursing under his breath. "Point that somewhere else," he growled at the panicked rookie. "How long have they been standing there?" he demanded.

"Only a few minutes," the gunner replied. "What do they want?"

"Probably just to talk," Shayde replied, looking over Clint and wishing for an entire fireteam instead of one partner. In the end he decided the two of them would have to do. "Come on, let's go meet new friends."

Stern faces watched the pair approach, but not one of the five gangsters raised their weapons. Shayde scanned their eyes for fear and found none, so he knew it was either respect or orders that kept them from firing as he and Clint approached.

"Good evening," he said casually, careful not to smile or come across anything but neutral.

A young man stepped forward, barely eighteen but clearly in charge of the squad. "I've got an answer for Rankin."

Understanding washed over Shayde. "You're his son, Tom, aren't you?"

Uneasiness passed between the other four men watching their young leader. Perhaps this was a touchy topic to avoid.

"My father's dead to me, a sellout to his people."

"I won't debate you," Shayde replied dryly. "What's your message?"

Tom paused or hesitated, difficult to read through his anger. He finally answered. "Tell Rankin he's got a cease fire. We accept the University and all the western territory in exchange for a truce..."

"Until?" Shayde demanded.

"Until the Nature Boys are pushed back."

"We were hoping for longer. Your father..."

"*Not* my father!" Tom snapped so loudly the watching machine gunners rattled belts and trained muzzles. Sensing the tension, the teen took a breath and calmed his voice adding, "Your general will have to bring better terms if the peace is to last. Miko wants the year of food he was promised but also weapons and ammo."

Max would never go for the demands, but he was desperate for peace so Shayde nodded. "I'll pass that bit on to him. In the meantime, tell Miko we'll send over the first of the food. There's been a lot of activity to the south, and Nature Boys could arrive at any time."

As if to prove his point, gunfire erupted directly to the south, turning all seven heads that direction.

"The retail yard?" Clint guessed.

"Yeah," Shayde replied, eyeing the gangsters accusingly. "This isn't y'all, is it? A ploy to catch us looking the other way?"

"No," Tom insisted, but his and the others' eyes seemed uncertain.

Clint moved where he could get a better shot, flanking the five men while they watched Shayde. "Start walking south," he commanded softly, his calm voice eerily full of death. "You're coming with us to check it out and, if it *is* the Nature Boys, helping us fight them off."

Shayde almost laughed, watching fear grow large and round in the eyes of the boys. Clint Fletcher was full of surprises.

Clint jogged behind the gangsters as Shayde led the group south toward the retail yard. Up ahead small arms fire lit up the shoreline and soon machine guns joined in, flashing muzzles and sending occasional tracers across the broad waters of the swollen river. Several small boats were trying to cross, buzzing around and spraying bullets of their own. The Nature Boys had decided to announce their presence.

"Is this it?" Tom Rankin sputtered, his voice trembling with fear. "Is this the invasion?"

"No," Shayde replied, "they're testing our flanks." As if on cue, flashing lights downriver revealed a second attack.

"They're taking census, getting an idea how heavily we're manning the shoreline." Clint grumbled, wishing the attackers weren't so organized.

"What's that mean?" the boy demanded.

"Counting us," Shayde explained. "Analyzing our rate of responding fire and getting a sense of our strength."

"Like I said," Clint growled with irritation, "taking census."

Tom and the other gangsters fell quiet after this, silently calculating the meaning of his words. They knew it wasn't a good thing but still had no idea how serious this matter was.

Clint stared at the back of the boy's head as they jogged. It would be so easy to put a bullet in him and the others. All five were expendable. The soldier wondered why he had forced them to come along instead of dropping them all on the bridge.

Dean Martin's voice suddenly filled Clint's head. *Ain't that a Kick to the Head?* The crooner asked, and Clint hefted his rifle, imagining taking the shot and putting a hole right between the kid's ears. In his mind the others whirled around, soaking up shots to their chests before falling. He licked his lips at the thought of the blood trickling down their faces and bellies, but eased his finger off the trigger.

Shut up, he told Dino... *this isn't the time.*

The retail yard was a flurry of activity by the time they arrived, an amphibious landing as busy as D-Day but on a smaller scale and with fewer boats. The invasion force was well armed, systematically coming ashore but not too deeply. They wanted a foothold, but not at the price of their troop strength.

This isn't the main attack, Clint knew, *so why are they coming ashore?*

Shayde chose a row of machinery to duck behind and the group followed, giving them all a view of the enemy's left flank. Ten men were making their way onshore, leaving their boat where it had run aground. He turned toward Clint and nodded.

He means to capture a boat, the soldier realized.

Walters then stared directly into Tom's eyes, treating him as the leader of this small group of gangsters. "Spare your ammo," he said, "and aim for center mass. Don't waste anything over their heads."

The boy and his four partners nodded with eyes widened by fear.

"We'll wait until they move in ten more yards, then slip behind them. Do *not* fire until I do. Once we clear this team, you three move to flip the boat. We'll use that for cover and move to the next team."

Clint nodded along with the gangsters. It was a good plan, a great way to get behind the invaders.

"Focus on me," Shayde said, then took a deep breath and stared Max's son in the eye. The kid and his friends weren't soldiers like him and Clint and would probably die on this shoreline.

So what if they do? Clint mused, salivating at the thought of their spilled blood.

But Shayde wouldn't allow that to happen. Max would never forgive him if he lost his only son, and the gangs would break the peace over it.

Clint shrugged. If he couldn't kill them, then it was time to make these boys into soldiers.

CHAPTER NINETEEN

No one appreciates a good night's sleep until they go without. Nurses know this especially well, also single parents. It's always worse when they're both, and Cathy had hardly slept in the days since learning her son's awful secret. Her mind interfered, riddled with thoughts, fears, and remorse.

If only I'd been a better mother, she thought, *been home every night instead of taking my clothes off for spare cash.*

The arrival of Clint had also played its part. Who could sleep at all with that monster around? Though he had kept his word and not come anywhere near her or Josh, the threat of running into him loomed. When she *did* sleep, it was with one eye opened, expecting him to pop through the tarp wall like Jack Nicholson in *The Shining* saying, "Here's Johnny!"

Despite all that, there was a new problem... the dreamy doctor who brought Clint into the Shelter. This *Doctor Andalon* everyone talked about. He was, to everyone he met, nothing less than a rainmaker miracle man healing everyone he touched. Don't misunderstand, Cathy was glad to have a real doctor on board, much less two with him and Doctor Yurik around, but her pride kept reminding that she was once again only a nurse.

No, it wasn't that.

What bothered her the most was how every time he healed someone, he first laid his hands upon them like some faith healer. It was being noticed, a part of his stigma, and why all the patients loved him. They were captivated by his touch, almost seeming to believe that act of touching alone healed their ailments.

But Cathy was being unkind and irrational. He was, after all, a real doctor and truly had put everyone he treated on a path to recovery. She just wished he wasn't so charming, calm, and good looking as well as wickedly smart.

She eyed the crowded stage, bursting at the seams with new arrivals, and wished once more for a bigger clinic. The Regiment needed the space or it would succumb to pandemic or worse. Max would have to find it soon. There was no other way to improve the conditions here. A coughing fit nearby made her jump, then caused shivers to run down her arms.

Scanning the sea of sick and wretched for a single family, she spotted a woman sitting up with her two teenage boys. The young men laughed, telling stories while their mother grinned ear to ear, her jaw no longer hurting from the pressure underneath. Cathy paused. There was no pressure at all on this woman's neck, her goiters seemed completely gone. Driven by a need for certainty, she navigated the sea of sickness and moved toward them.

"Nurse Fletcher!" The woman lit up as soon as she arrived, able to speak which was a miracle of its own. "Thank you so much for all you've done for us."

Cathy feigned a smile, a flimsy cover for the stress inside. "No problem at all. How do you feel?" She reached forward and the woman tilted her chin upward, a motion that should have been painful had Dr. Andalon not treated her. *Laid hands upon her goiters,* she thought, then briefly imagined him laying hands on *her.* She quickly pushed that thought aside.

"Honestly, I've never felt better. Even my arthritis seems to have let up."

"Hmm." Cathy pressed firmly where the goiters had been, finding everything as normal as could be. "Any bleeding of gums? Muscle fatigue?"

"No, none of that."

"Well then," Cathy announced, stepping back with another fake smile, this time covering up her own fatigue, "I declare you fit as a fiddle. You three may leave quarantine just as soon as you've found housing."

The boys cheered at this, running and leaping off the stage to begin their search.

The mother was moved to tears and hugged the nurse closely. Cathy allowed it, too tired to protest but also genuinely happy for the family.

"When can I thank Dr. Andalon?" the woman asked.

Dr. Andalon... the mysterious savior who emerged unharmed from a radioactive wilderness. That this woman could speak and swallow was his first miracle, and he *did* deserve thanks. "He's expected in later, but Dr. Yurik is here. Or I can send for him, if you'd like."

"No, don't bother them. I'll find him once he's arrived," the woman decided, her smile returning as she let go of the nurse. "I'm just so thankful for that vaccine."

Oh yes, that. By now there was no arguing it worked, especially in healing radiation damage as much as preventing it. Everyone he had treated had already grown stronger, even Josh. Her boy had more energy, even if his melancholy had not improved. So far, Cathy had refused it, prioritizing patients.

Normally she would treat herself so that she could treat others, but she had so far escaped any effects of radiation and didn't see the point. She owed most of her health to the kind and loving attention of John and Jenny Klingensmith who first fished her out of the Ohio River. She missed that couple so much. She pushed that thought aside as well, both of their deaths and her kidnapping by Mike Donelson shortly after.

Crazy Mike. Now here was a thought she couldn't just simply slide out of the way. He had tricked her, sold her to the Regiment, and taken everything she had of value. That thought hit her in the stomach so hard she wavered, suddenly feeling ill. She quickly said goodbye to the woman then hurried to find a quiet place away from the crowd.

Backstage she nearly collapsed against the wall, trying hard to breathe against the tightness now in her chest. When she had last seen Clint on the night she shot him, she had all his bags in the boat, even the jewels he had stolen earlier that night. Crazy Mike had those now. Abruptly she understood why Clint had been on his best behavior, why he was acting so strangely. He was buying his time until he could find where she hid his wealth.

What happens when he figures out I don't have it? But she knew the answer. Clint Fletcher was a killer, and there was only one thing left in this world to stop him from killing *her*—he wanted his wealth.

A kind voice interrupted her thoughts. "Are you okay?" Cathy opened her eyes to find Dr. Yurik.

"Yes... I... No." She thought quickly. "I just had an emotional moment with a patient, is all. I wanted to be alone, didn't mean to break down."

Stephanie smiled, sliding down the wall to sit next to her.

"Trust me, I understand. Sometimes I feel like the Air Force expected me to be a robot, emotionless while chaos existed all around me, constantly hiding my true self." She touched her belly. "I guess that's why I let my personal life break down *behind* the scenes. I had become an uncontrolled mess and fell into a relationship with a very important man whom I grew to fear. He *pushed* me into a relationship when I wasn't ready for one."

"You mean Sergeant Roark? But you two seem happy together."

"No, he came into my life later, toward the end after the other romance had burned out."

"So, your child isn't... you cheated on the other man with Roark?"

"Yes and no. I *did* cheat with Ben, but only after I knew I was already pregnant."

Cathy stared at the woman, so proper, so orderly, yet so candidly as broken as her. "Oh my god! Does he *know* the child belongs to the other man?"

"Yes. Ben knows my entire story and so does David. Other than you and them, I've only trusted one other with the truth. Though that relationship started off okay, full of affection and dreams of the perfect life with him, I watched Michael descend into a darker version of himself. Things we learned from ... *classified* things we learned on the job changed him, and he gradually replaced his original convictions and ambitions of helping others with something far more self-serving. He changed his approach and used his influence to help bring about changes I didn't agree with."

"How high up in the military was he?"

"He was a civilian—one of the highest ranking in the government."

"Would I know of him?"

"Possibly, but please let me keep *some* of my personal secrets, okay?" Stephanie said with a smile.

"Did you consider getting rid of the baby?" Cathy asked slowly, afraid to venture too far out on the ice with this woman who had already risked much by revealing the origin of her child.

Another nod, this time sadder and with a bit of regret. "I *was* looking to terminate the pregnancy, but then I met Ben... that's *how* I met him, actually. I was on the train to Frankfurt, on my way to a clinic, when he recognized me on the train. He, too, had business in the city."

Stephanie continued, "I quickly realized Ben was the opposite of what Michael had become, polite, not forward, very kind, and well-tuned in to reading my emotions. He could tell right away how stressed I was at the time. Officers and enlisted aren't supposed to be friends on any deep level, especially not to form relationships, but I found a friend on that train. I told him everything in that couple of hours and he listened. He cancelled his plans and I cancelled my appointment, then we spent the day together as Stephanie and Benjamin instead of captain and sergeant. We first became intimate that very night in the city."

"And you're a couple now?"

"We are. We fell in love and both realized neither wanted to be in the Air Force if it meant being apart. David Andalon gave us a way out and now we're here."

Suddenly, Cathy felt less alone. "Thank you for sharing, but why did you tell me all this? You barely know me, much less trust me."

"I have a sense about you, Nurse Fletcher. I saw your eyes when you lunged at your ex-husband and recognized the fear behind them. I know that feeling, have been there before, and understand you've been through hell with that man."

"He's a monster."

"A lot of men are," Stephanie agreed. "That's why I wasn't ready for a relationship when I met Michael. I was reeling from an awful divorce, one with a man who filled me with the same type of fear I saw in you. He would beat me on a whim or force himself on me when he fancied. He was the worst kind of man and I barely got away. When my bid for orders came up, I requested remote oversees duty but never even told him I was leaving. The movers came, packed up the entire house, and I shipped out that same day after stopping by the divorce lawyer on my way out of the country."

"But now you have Ben. I wish I could find one, a good man, but I'm afraid to trust any of them. I doubt any really exist, anymore—not what *I'm* looking for, anyways."

"There are a few left. Ben made me realize that."

"Can I ask you something?"

"Sure."

"What's the deal with Dr. Andalon. Is *he* for real? Why isn't *he* married. He seems so perfect. Kind, caring, and smart. Josh even loves him. He's been really quiet lately, but the doctor treated his arm and now he won't shut up about him. Mr. Starlings told me it looked broken before, but now it's barely a bruise. Josh didn't even feel him set it if it was."

"David is a good man, and he *was* married, but not anymore. He gave her a final chance to come with him when we left, but Brooke had already chosen a different path."

"What do you mean? She didn't fight him for the children?"

"Adam and Eve aren't his biological children... I guess you could say he adopted them. David can't have children of his own. He's sterile."

"Is that why his wife left him? She wanted to bear children?"

"Sort of... She had discovered another way to get pregnant with *Michael's* baby, let's leave it at that."

Cathy felt her eyes grow wide with wonder. "*Your* Michael?"

Stephanie nodded.

So Doctor Andalon... that man... that *gentle* man was hurting inside, yet he healed others without making a big deal over his own painful loss. She suddenly viewed the doctor in a different light. He was compassionate, kind, and caring of other people, even while devastated on the inside.

"I still considered ending my pregnancy after that, mostly out of fear of Michael," Stephanie suddenly admitted, "but Doctor Andalon talked me out of it. He convinced me there was a difference between not wanting a child and not wanting *this* child because of who is father is. In the end, he convinced me to see it differently, and now I view my child as Ben's. It isn't Michael's because I won't let it be. My child will be loved by who raised it, not who conceived it. That simple outlook makes carrying it to term so much easier."

"And David's wife chose the opposite? To see her child as Michael's instead of David's?"

"Yes, because she fears Michael and knows he's a vicious man who would never allow it to be anyone else's but his. She'll be stuck with him if she carries that child to term."

Laughter and cheers erupted on the stage, and the women turned their heads to take a look. David Andalon had arrived with fanfare. He grinned shyly at the applause, shaking hands or hugging his patients as each one thanked him for their treatment. So many of them felt stronger, full of vigor, since his arrival, and attributed it to him. He saw the women come around the corner and made his way toward them.

"Well now, I certainly did not expect *that*!" he said, blushing at the attention.

"You deserve it," Cathy heard herself say. "You're a welcome addition here."

"Thank you," he replied shyly, as if he weren't accustomed to praise.

"I've got to make rounds," Stephanie suddenly said with a smile and hidden wink toward Cathy, then left the two alone.

"I like her," Cathy said after she departed.

"She certainly is a special kind of woman," David agreed.

"How are Adam and Eve?"

"Settling in. They seem to be enjoying school and spend most of their time with Mr. Starlings. They are trying to drag me to an evening study he's putting on tonight."

"Oh, that." Cathy remembered the devotional he had tossed on her bed. "He's a bible thumper, but at least he keeps it outside of the school."

"I don't mind. I grew up with strong faith, raised Catholic even, but fell away in college like many people do. Perhaps it wouldn't hurt to get more involved. Will you be going tonight?"

"No... I've been under a lot of stress and want an evening to myself."

"Oh," David appeared disappointed, deeply so. "I was going to ask you to go with me if I ended up going, but maybe a quiet dinner would be nicer."

Cathy laughed. *Did he just ask me on a date?* she thought, filled with excitement she hadn't felt since before Clint ruined her idea of romance. "Dinner between the two of us? Do you know of some fancy restaurant that stayed open after the apocalypse?"

David grinned. "As a matter of fact, I do. How about I pick you up around six? Do you like Italian?"

Cathy's stomach growled. It was her favorite and a part of her old life she missed. "It's a date," she agreed, then ran off to do her own rounds, eager to tell Stephanie what transpired. "See you at six!" she said over her shoulder, hiding her huge smile then mouthed, *Oh my god!* Nurse Fletcher had a date with a doctor.

CHAPTER TWENTY

The retail yard erupted in gunfire as several small boats ran ashore. The machine gunners of the Regiment responded, ringing welcome to their invaders by spraying hot lead over a snowy beach. The Nature Boys had come, just as Max had warned, and Tom watched with wide-eyed wonder as his father's soldiers fought them off with disciplined precision. A total of six vessels formed a perfect row behind which the invaders sought cover.

Tom and the others crouched behind the hulking container, one of many in the yard, watching the boats race aground the swollen river. There were soldiers loaded into each, buzzing around and spraying their fire toward the shore defenders.

How are their engines running? Tom wondered.

"Focus on me," the white man said, and Tom met his eyes. This man was like Max, a military type and probably a Marine as well.

Shayde, the other soldier had called him.

"This is only a diversion, not the real invasion. They're probably sending snipers and fireteams ashore somewhere else, but we have to push them off the beach or they'll pull us into something bigger. When I give the word, we'll flank that line behind the boats and force them back into the river. Clint, lay down cover fire to keep them focused ahead. I want to catch *them* off guard, not the other way around."

"Got it." The second man grinned, humming a jazzy tune under his breath as he moved into position.

"When I give the word, run along this tree line and set our attack angle," Shayde told Tom and the others. "Put your rifles on fully automatic now, so you don't forget later. When you do fire, do it in small bursts to save ammo."

"Fully automatic?" TeKay asked from beside Tom. "What's that? I've only got fire and safe."

"You guys haven't converted your rifles from semi?" the man named Clint snickered. "Jeez, it's a wonder you're still alive."

"Never mind that, semi will work for now. We'll show you how to change them later. Get ready," Shayde commanded. After watching the line of invaders shift to the east he nodded. "Let's go!" he said as he took off down the tree line.

Tom took a breath and followed, thankfully TeKay, Jeb, and Chris did as well. Jacks took up position next to Clint, following the man's lead and firing at those closest attackers who could turn around. Without looking back, Tom followed Shayde to a position behind the line of men.

"This is a good angle," Shayde announced. "When we charge, form a line about three paces apart and stretched out to the right. Shoot whoever is in front of you, prioritize those who turn around to face us."

Tom felt woozy. He had taken part in looting and raiding, even practiced shooting the rifle, but he hadn't yet had any real combat time. TeKay had, so had Jeb and Chris, but they all looked like rookies compared to this true soldier.

Was Dad right? he wondered. *Are we fighting for the wrong cause? Am I on the losing side?*

"On my mark," Shayde prepped with a whisper. "Move out!"

Tom followed the man at a full sprint, his boots softly crunching the snow alongside the others as they raced toward the enemy's left flank. Up ahead, twenty-five soldiers crouched behind their boats, four men to each, with eyes locked on their targets ahead. Amazingly, they seemed unconcerned with moving forward, content only on returning fire at Clint and Jacks.

Shayde was right, Tom realized, *this is only a diversion.*

He flinched as the Marine beside him fired off several shots that hit their mark, dropping two men from behind. The man directly next to them turned, training his rifle at the sound of gunfire. Tom lifted his, realizing how impossible it was to fire while running, and slowed his pace. The fixed iron sight bobbed and swung violently, so much so that lining up a shot proved impossible. He stopped running and dropped to a knee before pulling the trigger, hoping more than aiming as he fired.

The man fell backward, pressed hard into the side of the boat. The bullet had killed him instantly. Tom stared appalled by what he had done, but instinct commanded him to live. He turned slightly to the right and fired two more shots at the next invader, wounding the man's shoulder. Tom tried to align another shot, moving sluggish and slow as if in a dream, his eyes locked on the wounded soldier's weapon now trained right at him. A bullet whizzed by, disrupting the air with a sickening pop. The next shot from either man would be a killing one.

By now Shayde had reached the boats, squeezing off two shots and dropping the man. Looking back, he spied Tom frozen in place and staring forward. With a curse he sprinted back and grabbed the boy's vest, heaving him upward pulling him forward. "Keep moving," he growled, "and stay out of the open!"

Up ahead, TeKay and Jeb had already reached the boat, unloading their rifles into the three remaining men. Chris knelt beside them, training his rifle at the next boat thirty yards away.

The line of invaders, now twenty in all, knew they'd been flanked. Either unwilling to or not wanting a fight, they broke and ran toward the water, diving in and swimming hard as waiting boats quickly swung around to pick them up. The suppressing fire forced Tom and the others to dive low on the ground.

"Aim at the machine gunners, I'll hit the engines," Shayde suggested, then carefully fired three short bursts.

Tom flinched with every pull of the trigger but fixed his eyes on the boats as men dropped into the water. A few more were hit while climbing aboard to join their rescuers. He tried to lift his rifle, to help his friends and this Marine drive off the enemy, but it felt oddly heavy. Firing bullets into men was nothing like target practice, and his hands suddenly trembled at the thought of the man he had killed.

In a matter of minutes, the firefight had ended, and the Nature Boys had been driven across the river.

"Woooo!" the man named Clint exclaimed in celebration. "Ain't that a rush?" he asked, jogging over with Jacks. The younger man's face wore the same grin as the soldier, unable to hide the euphoria each felt inside.

The others were just as excited, celebrating life by recounting how they had killed the men they faced. Shayde gave each a clap on their backs. "Great job, men. You all did well. With a bit more training you'll all make great allies in this war."

Tom flinched away as the man's hand grabbed his shoulder, moving toward the body of the man he had killed. Lifeless eyes stared upward, unseeing for a mind that no longer thought—no longer felt. Wishing he could drop his rifle and run as far away as he could, the boy suddenly understood his father's need for solitude, and why he had so often chosen to spend nights on the road instead of at home.

He went to war, a real *war, and he lives with this every day and night, doesn't he?*

"I know it's hard," Shayde whispered low enough the others would not overhear, "and it's okay you feel this way. It's normal."

"Are you trying to tell me that I'll get used to it?"

"No, I'm trying to tell you that it's best that you don't."

The sound of celebration had not stopped, with Clint congratulating each of the others on their bravery. He dipped two fingers into the bullet holes of each of their kills and blooded the boy's faces, marking them as warriors. Tom watched their eyes, basking in the praise from this man, no longer different than him except by the number of kills.

"I don't like it," Tom admitted to Shayde.

"Neither does your father, but he's cursed with being good at it."

"That's why he drove a truck, isn't it? I always thought he was avoiding Mom and me, but now I think he was avoiding himself."

Shayde nodded. "The road is a good place for veterans who can't work a nine to five. It demands your full focus and attention and customer service is never needed."

"So my father drove to forget?"

"From what I know about him, yeah, I think so."

Tom was thankful this man stood beside him, but a part of him wished it was his father instead.

"What are the chances," Shayde asked, "that this Miko will honor our peace and we'll become allies?"

"I don't know," Tom admitted. Looking down at the weapon in his hands, the boy silently prayed, asking his mother's God to spare him from the need to ever kill another man.

The rest of the night was less eventful, a walk westward in the dark. Jacks, TeKay, Jeb, and Chris had changed, walking taller with heads on swivels, more tuned to potential dangers surrounding them. Even their hands had changed, carrying their rifles like Shayde and Clint—at the ready and with purpose. They weren't soldiers, not like the men they had fought alongside on this night, but they were all finally killers. Even their boyish chatter had disappeared, replaced by quiet communication about potential threats along the road.

By the time they returned to the university all that changed, the battle-hardened men all at once became boys eager to brag about their kills to any and all who would listen. Their bravado caught the attention of Miko, who called them for a debriefing. They found him in what used to be the student union.

The entire space had been transformed since the last time Tom had seen it, an unrecognizable display of plundered wealth. The walls had been draped with silk curtains and tapestries, and spoils of plunder were displayed proudly. Everything Tom and the others had gathered since the missiles fell had become Miko's, and the room felt more like a king's banquet hall than a place for unity. The entire setting made the feeling surreal, as if Tom and the others were actually being brought before a king. On a raised dais, Miko even sat upon what could easily pass as a throne.

The next thing Tom noticed was the "king's court". Armed guards surrounded their leader, ready to protect him no matter the threat. Attendants, some of whom Tom recognized as once living in the dormitories they had cleared out, knelt nearby to satisfy his every whim. Miko himself, after all his talk about oppression, had taken slaves of his own. The young women among them had been dressed according to their new station—as scantily as possible—and forced into his ever growing harem of addiction. Tom avoided their drugged eyes as he entered, repulsed by the hopelessness.

TeKay, Jacks, Chris, and Jeb whooped with excitement at their surroundings, basking in the glory of their leader. To them this great hall stood for power, the new society their leader had begun to build. It only sickened Tom, and he did his best not to betray his disgust. As they approached Miko in his chair, the boys poured out the details of the night. All except Tom bragged about their kills, gloating over the rush it had given each of them and told how they were eager to get out and do it again.

Miko's eyes turned steely as he listened, bothered or concerned by something only a king would notice. After they had finished, they waited, staring at their leader expectantly. Concluding they had done a good job, Miko rewarded them proudly, handing each a hand rolled joint. Shocked by the gift they all stared at the rare piece of wealth, a boon none had expected. This new world only offered ways to die instead of getting high, and the boys licked their lips with anticipation.

"Go smoke," he said, "enjoy this moment, because we're going back out tomorrow night."

"Out?" Jacks asked.

"While you were delivering *my* message, another was delivered here. The Nature Boys have promised me the city—all of it, including the Shelter, in return for flanking the Regiment. All we gotta do is repeat what you did tonight by killing our true enemies."

Wide grins filled their faces, boys eager for more kills and to savor their rewards. All except Tom immediately put the joints to their lips, lighting the tip and taking a joyful puff before heading off to their dorm rooms.

"Ain't my shit good enough for *you*," Miko asked Tom as he walked away, locking him down with a dangerous look. "You were quiet, just now, while the others debriefed. Didn't you help? What happened, did you freeze?"

"Not at all, I... I just don't like bragging," the young man replied, averting his eyes and staring down at the rolled paper in his hand. The thought of it repulsed him, a reward he neither wanted nor deserved. Before the bombs, he realized, he had smoked to enjoy his time with his friends, to

calm his mind and ease the pain of living with a father who never loved
him. It had helped him deal with the stress of being the man of the house
whenever Max was on the road. Now, it seemed foolish, a way to deaden
his mind and to hide from the world.

"Did you kill anyone?" Miko demanded.

"I killed one and wounded another."

Miko nodded, noticeably relaxing. "Good," he said. "But we're no
longer shooting Nature Boys. The deal I made is against your father." His
eyes narrowed. "You gonna be okay with that?"

"Of course. I want him dead," Tom lied. He had wanted that once,
but no longer.

"Good. Go rest up," Miko ordered with finality.

Tom moved casually, leaving the hall with his head held high, but
inside fought the urge to run. He maintained that calm all the way to
his dorm. Reaching the door, he knocked four times and waited for the
locks to turn. As soon as the door opened he stepped in and hugged his
mother tight.

"What's wrong, baby?"

"I've been lying to you, Mother," he admitted, the words twisting his
gut as they came out.

"What do you mean?" Betty asked, holding her son tighter.

"Dad's not dead. He's here, in Evansville, and leading the Regiment."

She stepped back, a look of confusion on her face. "I don't understand."

Tom pointed to the gun she still held in her hand, slowly taking it
away and setting it on the counter. "This is his. I was on patrol on the day
he arrived. I came across his rig in Kleymeyer Park and broke in. I found
this in the glovebox and brought it home."

"But you gave that to me months ago," she reasoned, foggily thinking
back to that day. "You've known he was back all this time?"

"Yes, Ma."

Betty's hand suddenly flew through the air, striking him across the
cheek with a stinging ring that burned his ears and cheek.

Tom did not step back. He merely stood there and waited.

"Your father has been home for *months*, and you let me believe he was dead?" she demanded, a rage brimming beneath her words. "You've known this entire time, but let me believe... *urged* me to accept he had died?" She slapped him again. "What kind of son *are* you?" she demanded, slapping his ear over and over again.

Tom never raised his hand, neither to fend her off nor to fight back. Tears rolled down his cheeks as he stood there, deserving every blow she gave.

Finally, in either exhaustion or distress, she collapsed and hugged her son tightly, bawling out six months of worry against his chest. "Take me to him," she finally demanded, still clutching him tightly. "Fix this!"

"Yes, Mama."

CHAPTER TWENTY-ONE

Brooke pushed open the door with a heavy sigh, departing the testing lab but unable to leave her work behind. It now plagued her day and night, a burden no one else could carry but herself.

This had been their final cycle of the pearl and now every soldier not stationed elsewhere in Europe... *no, Astia,* had been tested. Michael and Jake would be happy with the results, blind to just how tedious the testing processes had been on both her and the medical team. Three soldiers had died out of one hundred tested, but that was three too many for her conscience.

Once again, Michael waited in the main laboratory, no longer hanging around for any prophecies. There had only been two besides McLemore, and he had decided it was better to watch the footage than waste his time smelling the puke of failed attempts. He and Jake were speaking in low voices when Brooke arrived. They broke off immediately and all eyes locked on hers.

"What are the final numbers?" the chancellor demanded as soon as she crossed the threshold.

"You'll get them when I'm ready!" Brooke snapped, her feet swollen, her belly heavy with child, and her temper hanging by a thread.

"Out of one hundred tested," Sam Nakala's calm voice replied, entering the room after Brooke. "Ten are Oracles and five are Conductors." Oracles were the name they gave those with the ability to astral project. They dubbed that ability *Da'ash'mael,* since it seemed to precede the prophetic *Ka'ash'mael.* In his native language, *da* meant good, or better, and that was how he viewed this less dangerous state.

Michael frowned. "So only five percent can fight?"

"Five percent of your fighting force is enough, at least till the rest of your soldiers return from the east," Jake reminded. "We've got five thousand more to test, which could give you two hundred and fifty Conductors."

"Even more," Brooke added, "you could get five hundred more Oracles."

"Oracles," Michael sneered. "What do I do with Oracles?" Jake started to reply, but the chancellor cut him off. "I know, I know... gather intelligence, but that only goes so far! I need warriors. A fighting force!"

"You've got one," Jake reassured, "just a mostly *conventional* one. Be patient, we still have to test the rest of the beads, and the first round of those is coming up." He looked to his sister as soon as he spoke, silently asking when she'd be ready for that ordeal.

She sighed again, this time heavier than the first. What she needed was rest, a good night's sleep and to get off her feet. Pre-eclampsia was dangerous, and she was certain she was showing signs of it. Thankfully there had been no protein showing up in her urine, and her blood pressure remained mostly elevated instead of high. *No rest for the wicked,* she thought, then cursed David and his selfishness. Had he remained, none of this would have fallen on her in the first place.

"As soon as the room's prepared, we're moving to the next bead."

"Batch Bravo?" Michael asked, just a bit too excited for Brooke's liking.

"No, Charlie," she corrected. "Bravo's still too dangerous to consider. All five of your Conductors had zero control over their first manifestation. I need to figure out safeguards before we play with fire."

"I agree, Mike," Jake offered, giving his sister a knowing look. She appreciated the gesture but wasn't afraid to stand up the chancellor on her own. "Plants are *much* safer. What's the worst thing that can happen, allergy attacks? Brooke, I'm in this next group, right?"

She nodded, too exhausted to speak the words. Jake was up next.

Jake entered the testing lab wearing a broad smile, a rain slicker, and rubber overshoes, breaking the tension for all inside. There were nineteen seated soldiers and one empty seat waiting for him. Everyone erupted with laughter when he opened an umbrella.

"This puke shield is for Doctor Andalon," he explained, handing it over to Brooke. He winked and she smiled weakly. The poor thing was exhausted. "You okay?" he whispered.

"I will be, as soon as we finish this testing," she whispered back.

"Sis, I hate to break it to you, but I don't think it ever *will* be over." He resisted the urge to give her a hug and strode toward his waiting chair, grinning at the shy airman staring up from the next seat over.

"Airman McLemore? Are you ready for another round of vomit?"

She laughed. "Yes, General! I figure it's my turn since I flew last time."

He took his seat and Sam Nakala strapped him in. "So, what's next? I doubt anyone will be flying without air this time. This is Batch Charlie, so we may be swinging from vines. Not sure *what* to expect!"

"Perhaps it's simpler than that," she suggested. "Doctor Andalon became a healer, didn't he? After he administered this batch on himself?"

Jake almost lost his smile, but decades of practice held it in place like a well-fitting mask. "After a fashion," he replied, but his mind was replaying the events on Waghäusel hill when his college buddy knelt over two dead children and one dead Russian general. David was more zombie-maker now than healer.

Four soldiers entered the room pushing handcarts. On each were various houseplants, mostly ivies, they must have dug up from the Eden Lab. One of them parked in front of McLemore, and the other three were spaced out evenly in a line before the test subjects.

"You may be right, General," the young woman teased. "It looks like some vine swinging is planned."

Jake chuckled, feeling the shy stares coming from the pretty young airman, but resisted returning even a glance. He was an officer and she enlisted, and protocol remained one thing General Braston would never break. Besides, he couldn't divert his eyes from his sister. She looked awful, beyond fatigued and with dark melancholy lurking beneath her exhaustion. *The unborn child, maybe? Or simply missing David?* he wondered.

As Sam and Mi-Jung administered onyx-black beads to the soldiers, Jake wondered about something Michael had suggested. Once they understood the nature of the beads and the powers they unlocked, Astia would need to gain control over the free-ranging emotants in Andalon. *What did he mean by that? Does he mean to round them up?*

He pushed the thought aside as a worry for later then opened his mouth and took the bead, swallowing it right away before turning to watch the room. Nearly everyone had already vomited, including McLemore. Her eyes watered as she dry-heaved, asking for water between gasps for air. But two men and a woman stared intently at the potted plants. They, like Jake, had somehow retained the beads, holding them in their bellies. Jake followed their gaze and switched his attention to the plants, focusing his mind and trying to become one with their stalks and leaves.

He felt silly, like when he was a child after first watching Star Wars. He had run around the house and neighborhood trying to move objects with his mind for weeks, intent on becoming the next Jedi. Even now he stretched his hands against his bindings, reaching fingers toward the plants. If he could only become one with their essence, he felt he could almost move them.

His stomach rumbled. Fearing he was about to puke he relaxed, disappointed he would fail at this too.

Brooke had been watching Jake reach out toward the plants like a fool, grasping and yearning for them to respond to his futile attempt. At first, she nearly expected him to succeed but, as he relaxed, the disappointment on his face mixed with confusion. He was one of only four who had not yet vomited up the bead.

Her attention turned to the others, one woman and two men, all sergeants but from different outfits. The woman she recognized as working in the cafeteria, and one of the men she recognized as a soldier originally brought in by Herr General Richter. The German swayed, a rhythmic chant uttering under his breath, with his eyes locked on one of the plants. It was an ivy, with broad leaves on thin stalks.

Brooke blinked, unexpected movement had caught her eye. The ivy had trembled, shivered, even, if that was possible. Her eyes flicked between the German sergeant and the plant. All at once she realized the rhythm between the pair were connected, their bodies swaying to some unheard music. Then the cafeteria sergeant matched tempo with the German, swaying and humming along with music only they could hear. Soon the third sergeant joined in as well, a tall fellow, one of Jake's strike team. She wasn't sure but thought he might have been the man who replaced Benjamin Roark.

Three humans and one plant danced the same eerie sway, humming along with perfect harmony and seemingly united as one.

Brooke watched with awe as the ivy reached out toward the test subjects on the front row, stretching and growing before her eyes. Like snakes, the many branches coiled around ankles, twisting and tightening as if to cocoon their victims and devour them whole. She turned to Jake for help. Would these three mistakenly harm the other test subjects? She considered calling upon the armed guard hiding in the next room.

But Jake was also frozen, locked in a rhythmic sway and chanting under his breath. Whatever the bead had done, it affected all four as a unit.

"Jake!" she shouted, rushing forward and shaking him violently. Unseeing and unfeeling, he ignored her desperate plea. By now the vines had worked their way up the legs of the subjects.

The baby inside her womb moved.

It wasn't the first time she had felt him shift weight or flip over, but she had never felt a movement so violent or sudden. Grasping her belly, Brooke fell to her knees and cried out.

$$\bowtie\!\text{I\!I\!I}\!\bowtie$$

Jake welcomed the effects of the bead, unexpectedly comforting like a siren beckoning ships toward a rocky shoal. Unable to resist, he first listened to, then felt the rhythmic pulse. His body kept time. The experience felt euphoric, as if he were two places at once—both aware in his mind and also experiencing the ecstasy of a dream. All discipline had fled the general, replaced instead by an insatiable desire to be one with the rhythm.

No longer seeing with his eyes, he was aware of the lifeforces pulsing around him. The three soldiers, those also locked on the plant, matched the row of foliage in front of the subjects. All others were out of phase, pulsing their own beats and ignoring the perfection of those locked with his. One of these, standing where he last remembered Brooke had been, fell to the floor. He recognized another lifeform then, a child forming within her womb.

Tiny and not fully formed, its consciousness found its way to his.

Without words, the fetus conveyed a need to be free of its surroundings. Terrified, it fought against the walls keeping it captive, urging Jake to help it find release into the waiting world.

Not yet, he begged his nephew, *it's not time.*

"Not time!" three voices echoed from across the room.

Stay where you are, and be calm, Jake urged.

"Be calm!" the three sergeants echoed.

A scream from Brooke echoed the anger of the fetus, now insistent upon its release.

Jake fought against the draw of the rhythmic pattern and sought his reason. *Is this child like David? A product of Batch Charlie?*

But then he felt another tone, a different pulse beating out of sync with the connection he shared with the sergeants. The fluid surrounding the fetus rippled with this lifeforce, a mixture of mother and child, and Jake abruptly realized that same tone resonated also within him. Unlike that shared with the plants, this tone was disruptive, powerful and crashing as if to pound away everything in its way.

He realized his nephew had reached out through the amniotic fluid. *But how?* he wondered, brought to full awareness by another scream. All at once the rhythmic pulsing ceased its draw, and his connection to the plants and three sergeants abruptly severed. Seeing again with his own eyes, he focused on his sister, now staggering to regain her footing.

"Brooke!" he called out.

"I'm fine," she lied, but rushed to release his leather straps. "That scream came from one of the other three!"

Other three? He mused as he turned, looking past a terrified Penny McLemore, her eyes pleading with his for comfort. But there, several rows back, were the three sergeants he had briefly connected with. One of them, a woman he recognized from the dining hall, had slumped in her chair after losing consciousness. Sam and Mi-Jung Nakala stood above her, desperately searching for a pulse. With sadness in his kind eyes, Sam turned to Brooke and shook his head. The woman had passed.

No, Jake realized, still fueled by the bead, *not fully dead.* The woman's lifeforce faintly pulsed inside her brain, rippling down her spine. Suddenly filled with power, the same wielded by David Andalon, the general understood he held control over life itself. Rushing forward he removed the woman's leather bonds and laid her on the floor.

At first Jake reached out like he had toward the plants, forcing his mind to try to bond with her lifeforce. Just as before, he failed.

Gentler, he thought, remembering the plant's hypnotic rhythm and finding hers. *We have to share the same beat.*

He tried once more, breathing slowly and humming along with the beating pulse of the dying sergeant. It briefly surged within her, causing him to jump. It almost felt as if a piece of himself had jumped into her.

I can't do it by myself, he realized, *the draw upon me is too great, and I can't control how much she takes.*

He lifted his eyes and, while still swaying to the dying woman's tempo, locked eyes with the sergeants looking on. Each had recognized what he had done and seemed eager to help.

"Release those two!" he barked at Sam, who complied without hesitation. The pair knelt beside their general, terrified and looking to him for guidance. "Just as before," Braston commanded, "find *her* rhythm!"

The trio connected right away, finding it easier to match a second time. With Jake in control, the other pair tempered his finesse and gave him strength to reach out his vibrating lifeforce. He touched it to the young woman's and four lives briefly converged into one. *And one other,* he realized, sensing a foreign lifeforce from somewhere else in the room.

The young woman's eyes snapped open, but she made no move to rise up.

Jake and the others pulled back, no longer swaying in tempo. Though disconnected, he still felt a strange kinship to the woman, staring blankly upward but lacking cognizance.

"Can you stand?" he asked.

"Yes," the woman replied without emotion, her voice echoing in his mind as she had spoken the words.

The other sergeants flinched, somehow sensing the same strangeness of her voice in their minds.

Jake tried again. "Can you stand? If so, rise up."

"Yes," she said, her voice once again echoing through Jake's awareness. As she stood, he grabbed her hand to help steady her gait, flinching to find it as cold as a corpse. Instead of returning to her chair or asking for instructions, she stood with blank eyes that never blinked.

"Have a seat," Jake insisted, and the woman—*no, no longer a woman,* he realized, *barely even living except by the simplest of definition*—complied at once.

A throat cleared, and Jake became aware of Michael standing behind him. "Can we control her now?" he asked. "Is she like Petrov?"

"No..." Braston replied slowly, then corrected himself. "Yes, it seems I can, but not like Petrov. She's different, not at all alive..."

"Animated," one of the sergeants now standing beside Jake suggested. Both Braston and Esterling looked expectantly for him to continue. "She's alive, but not with her own lifeforce. We somehow combined our own and put it into her. When she talks, I hear her voice, but it's also in my mind."

Jake considered that description, it was better and more accurate than he could have put into words. He turned to the reanimated sergeant and said, "Speak only into my mind," he said, "and tell me the general orders you learned in boot camp." The resounding echo recited every word of each of the eleven. After she had finished, she stood silently awaiting more commands. "Protect me," he said.

She neither nodded nor answered, only stood motionless.

Jake quickly released the bonds of the nearest airman, the one he now recognized as replacing Benjamin Roark on his team. The young man was an accomplished martial artist.

"Attack me," the general commanded.

"What?"

"I said attack me, swing a punch, or a kick, or..."

Before he finished talking, a punch hurled toward his chin, stopping in midair—caught by the female sergeant's hand.

"Again," Jake ordered, and the young man stepped back, this time kicking with a roundhouse toward his chest.

The reanimated sergeant stepped into the way, catching his foot with both hands and pushing him backward. As he toppled to the ground, the vines from the experiment, now long and fully-leafed, twisted and grabbed his arms and legs, binding and holding him spread eagle on the floor. Several more branches slowly coiled around his neck but Jake intervened.

"Stop!" he shouted, and the vines held tight but no longer moved. *Release him,* he thought toward the reanimated sergeant, and the ropelike stems uncoiled immediately.

"Well now," Michael said with an approving nod, "this is *finally* something useful."

CHAPTER TWENTY-TWO

Max Rankin listened intently, focused on every detail of Shayde's report. His and Clint's encounter had been brief, but the same event occurred elsewhere along the defensive barrier. The reports there were all similar. The Nature Boys had arrived, tested their defenses, and landed soldiers on the beach before retreating. The battle for Evansville had begun.

"How many boats did they leave behind?" he asked.

"Six each in two different spots," Shayde replied, "all pull starts."

"That's how they survived the EMP," Max realized.

"We recovered them and brought them up close in case *we* need them."

It was odd, to leave behind that many without a care, not in a scarcity time like this—especially with running engines and seaworthy hulls. "And total? How many more did you see them using on the river?"

"Two dozen or more," Clint suggested.

Shayde nodded his head in agreement. Such a fleet. "They landed here and here," he said, pointing at a map. Yellow highlighter had marked their reinforcements to the makeshift wall. Both points were strongly defended, and with one glance Max could pick two or three better landing zones their enemy could have chosen.

"It was a distraction," Clint added, saying what they all knew out loud.

Max stared at the circles he had just drawn, trying to figure out their importance. "The retail yard is wide open space, a true kill zone. Four Freedoms Park is the same, with the brewery parking lot just beyond the road." Another thought struck him. "Did you search the boats for explosives, hidden compartments?"

Shayde shook his head. "We did, but found nothing. They were normal boats, not Trojan horses."

Trojan horse... Max chewed on that phrase in his mind and moved toward the window. Gazing out he stared once more at concrete and brick, walls and windows too close for comfort and looming over him, teasing sniper fire.

"At least we don't have to worry about the gangs hitting us from those windows," Shayde said with a chuckle. "Miko sent your son with a promise of cease fire. They won't attack till the Nature Boys' threat is settled."

Tom. The thought of his son stung. "How'd he do?" Max asked quietly. "During the firefight, how'd Tom do?"

"He couldn't handle killing a man," Clint said with a devious grin, as if judging the boy's cowardice.

Shayde cut in. "He actually did pretty well, followed orders and showed good instincts. He'd make a good Marine." Shayde replied. "He did feel remorse for his kill. It bothered him so much I was worried about him at first, but..."

Movement beside the desk caused Max to turn just in time to see Clint diving for him. It was odd, to attack him here in the office, and the general moved sluggishly, not expecting the tackle. His wind escaped his chest as they slammed into the floor, and Max lost precious seconds in which he could have fought back. In Jiu Jitsu he always did well on his back, but couldn't get his hands up quick enough this time.

Almost the moment they landed, the window above them shattered.

"Stay down," Clint growled to Shayde. "Sniper!"

Then it all made sense as Max's thoughts came into focus. The Nature Boys had landed swimmers while the boats had drawn all eyes to the open spaces.

Shayde knelt behind the desk, grabbing his own rifle and scanning buildings. He searched for a glint of sun off a scope or any movement to betray the shooter's position. "Bell tower!" he suddenly announced. "City Church!" He ducked immediately, just as another shot blew plaster from the wall above his head.

All three men scrambled out of sight of the shooter. Max still moved as in a dream, his thoughts elsewhere, working out the enigma of the attacks.

Shayde's eyes examined the hole in the wall. "That's a fifty caliber, probably a Barrett."

"Then it ain't no street gang," Clint pointed out.

"No, it's a Nature Boy," Max agreed, looking down at the map now laying on the floor beside them. He took his finger and pointed at a spot along the river, just east of the retail yard.

"What's that?" Clint asked.

"A piece of irony, I'm guessing," Shayde said with a frown.

"LST-325," Max explained. "A landing ship from the second world war, built in Evansville. It's now a museum. They distracted us from the real target, a swim team or teams who boarded and hid out inside the ship until we stopped looking for them."

Clint laughed, finding sheer joy at the joke. "So, while we fought off the fake landing party, they boarded a landing ship *actually* used to storm beaches during WWII?"

"Sums it up," Max agreed.

"Cheeky bastards," Clint said with a smile. "I love it."

"That sniper's moved on by now, Max," Shayde guessed, but kept his head down.

"Possibly," the general muttered. *I need those buildings knocked down!* he screamed in his head. "Clint, go take a shower and get some sleep. I need to talk to Shayde, and then he'll do the same. I need those snipers shaken out along with any patrols they hid all around us."

"Got it," the soldier said with a salute, then eased up the wall and made for the door, careful not to cross in view of the window.

As the door shut behind him, Max turned to Shayde. "How'd *he* do?"

"Clint? He did *damned* well. He's the real deal, like I said before. He's experienced and performed without a single hitch over six patrols."

"That's both good and bad," Max said, closing his eyes.

"Yeah, been thinking about that. We can't keep both of 'em."

"No, we can't keep both of 'em." Max agreed.

David led Cathy upstairs toward Officer's Row and past General Rankin's office. Though excited for their date, she paused at the door with chills running down her arms. *Will I ever get over this feeling?* she wondered, thinking of her final meeting with the Colonel in that room.

"What's wrong?" the doctor asked, and Cathy forced a smile, hurrying to catch up.

"Nothing," she lied.

I'm being silly, she thought, *to be nervous around this man.* But the nerves persisted. They were butterflies, really, a mixture of excitement and worry just being alone with him. The excitement came easily, enjoying both his company and conversation as much as his physical presence. Despite the nerves, she couldn't quell the desire to get closer. It was the worry that was the problem, reminding her she didn't need any relationship, neither physical nor emotional.

"It's right up here," David could barely contain his own excitement.

Their destination, it turned out, was the last door on the left. Dread suddenly rushed in as Cathy recognized the door as the same Max's soldiers had pushed her inside once before. That was when *he* wined and dined her for a much different reason than David.

No! I won't let that night ruin this one! She thought, intent on having fun no matter what. She tried some humor to lighten both their moods. "It doesn't look like a door to a fancy restaurant, sir!" she said in a flirtatious tone. "I'll have you know a girl doesn't take fondly to bait and switch tactics."

David laughed, the most beautiful sound she needed right then, and she grabbed his arm without thinking, hugging it close. She hadn't meant to, it was an instinct, like an old habit from the last time she had a really good date. It caught them both off guard.

"Here we go!" he blurted out a little awkwardly as they reached the door. He turned the handle and led her inside.

Her stomach recognized the smells at once, even before her eyes noticed the tablecloth, flickering candles, and bowls of garlic bread— *buttered* garlic bread.

"Nope," she said a little over a whisper, "no bait and switch at *all* here!" She rushed forward and grabbed a piece of bread, shoving it into her mouth. She ate it nearly whole, laughing as crumbs dribbled down her chin.

David laughed along and joined her feast. After several bites he remembered to check the oven. "I almost forgot the main course!" he said, spitting crumbs as he talked. "I hope you like lasagna!"

"Lasagna? How did you find the makings?"

"There was a frozen one downstairs in long storage hiding behind a box of tilapia. I snagged it just as it was thawing out."

"I would have taken the tilapia," Cathy jested, laughing while licking the garlic butter off her fingers.

"I can go get it for you."

"No!"

"Just kidding," he grinned triumphantly.

"Where did you find the bread?" she asked.

"Same place, a frozen remnant of a world gone by sitting high upon a shelf where no one would find it but me."

"You rescued it for the damsel in distress?"

"Exactly. I wanted to see you lick your fingers instead of using the napkins on the table," he teased.

Looking down she found what he mentioned, laughing louder and feeling like Julia Roberts eating escargot in *Pretty Woman*. Just like that character, Cathy suddenly felt she didn't deserve the expense and attention. But she was along for, and enjoying, the ride.

"I haven't had this much fun since *Pirates of Penzance,*" she joked.

David didn't get the meaning. "What?" he asked as he pulled the meal from the oven.

It was steaming hot and the smell of it savory. She yearned to run up to it and dig in like she had the bread but held back only because she did not want to burn her fingers. "Oh, nothing, just a movie line."

"I never had time to watch many movies, work always took my spare... well, spare *anything*. My work took most of my time."

"Of course, doctors rarely have any time at all. What *was* your specialty?"

David frowned as if considering how to answer. "I'm a doctor," he finally said, "but haven't practiced in a while."

Cathy couldn't believe her ears. "You aren't practicing? I'm shocked! You're so good at it! I figured you had your own practice."

"I don't have a practice because I've recently been working in a research laboratory."

"Stephanie accidently mentioned a lab without going into detail. Did she work with you?"

"Only recently. My ex-wife was my research partner but was giving my trade secrets away to a competitor. That was how I met Stephanie. She worked for that competitor."

Cathy quickly pieced two and two together, that Stephanie worked for a military or defense laboratory headed by that Michael guy. *High ranking civilian?* she wondered. *A politician, then?*

"Cathy, I've got a lot of baggage. I was betrayed by my wife and my best friends. She provided my research while they secretly funded my project at MIT through senate slush funds, only to forcibly cut off funding to force me to join their military projects."

Senator? Oh damn.

"Did you know what Stephanie told me on the journey here? She said Michael even funded the terrorist who hacked our missile defense system and started this whole damn thing. The attack came from my own campus. Can you believe that?"

He was growing angry, or maybe just passionate, she couldn't tell. Either way it was a red flag, but Cathy ignored it... she loved her men adorned with flags, it seemed. She groaned in her mind then changed the subject. "This lasagna is the best thing I've eaten since the apocalypse."

David had taken a mouthful and nodded his agreement, trying not to laugh without burning his tongue. After he swallowed, he picked up on the conversational shift. "I'm sorry, I don't mean to ruin our date. It's all just so fresh, only happened a few months ago, and I haven't talked about it with anyone."

"It's okay, I have ex-husband baggage, and mine's closer to home."

"I'm sorry. I forgot about Clint entirely. I swear I wouldn't have brought him along if I knew. He had a river boat and we desperately needed both boat and pilot."

"Probably stolen," she grumbled, then added, "but we *do* need to change this conversation. So far it's only been about exes and doomsday."

"Agreed. How 'bout them Cowboys?"

"Oh, jeez. You're not from Texas, are you?"

"Born and bred in Round Rock right up until college. Drove a pickup truck and wore boots right up until a few years ago."

"I really do have to pay attention to these red flags," she said, then laughed it off. She had no intention of reading *any* of them with this guy. "Favorite color?" she asked, turning it into a speed date.

"Mauve."

"Wait? What? Really?"

"No. I was trying to make another joke. It's blue. Cliché, I know. What's yours?"

"Yeah, don't make jokes. You're funny enough when you don't try. I like blue also, hate pink. Were your parents divorced or together?"

"Dead. Happened when I was an infant and I only ever knew my adopted parents. They were together until dying in a car accident while I was in college—happened during finals of my senior year if you can believe it. Yours?"

"Divorced. That's why I have daddy issues. Speaking of, what do you think about sex on a first date?"

David blanched, turning ghost white and caught completely off guard. "Wait, what?"

"Just kidding," she said without even a blush.

"Oh," he laughed. "In that case I'm one hundred percent on board."

"So am I, actually," she replied with a shrug. "The hell with it." Cathy stood up and reached across the table, surprising David with a kiss. He responded wet and awkwardly, hopefully to be blamed on the lasagna and not on him being a bad kisser. *We'll work on this,* she thought, and climbed up on the table. "There's a bed in the next room," she panted.

"How do you know?" he asked.

"Just trust me." She slid off the edge of the table and onto his lap, kissing him and letting him touch her. Unlike every lap dance she had ever given, where the man pawed at her incessantly to the point she had to fight

174

them off, David was a gentleman. She had to place his hands on the spots she wanted, but that was all the encouragement he needed. His passion sprang to life and he stood, picking her up and carrying her into the bedroom.

"A reading from John, chapter eleven. The rising." Mr. Starlings began, telling the story about a man who had died and his family sent for Jesus. "Though it had been four days, Jesus said, 'this sickness will not end in death.' Lazarus is only sleeping."

Eve loved this story. She had read it five times in the past week, having consumed the entire bible in only a few days. Adam had not understood why, at first, questioning her fascination with the book.

She had simply explained at the time, "We'll find it useful." He had shrugged, and she went on memorizing the bits they would need. This passage had been one of them.

Meanwhile, Mr. Starlings had moved on to another reading, this one from the letters of Paul, talking about darkness and light. He, of course, was speaking to the Ephesians as Eve knew. She mouthed along the words as the teacher read. She knew them all.

It was nearly time for her to kick off her plan, but she had to time it perfectly. David was currently having sex with Cathy and she couldn't interrupt him just yet. Though she didn't know how much time he would need, she understood the mechanics. In her vision, though, the one she had many months before, it wouldn't take very long.

Finally, just as Mr. Starlings was finishing up his sermon, she sent off a tiny wisp of air. It moved so fast no one saw it form right in front of his mouth and nose, trapping it open as he was about to breathe and not letting any air inside. Thankfully his hands moved instinctively, one to cover it while trying to claw at whatever was invisibly there, and the other to his chest where Adam would be hitting him repeatedly with a tiny concussive blast. Timed perfectly, the man and everyone in the room would swear he was suffering a heart attack. Two minutes later he passed out and fell to the floor. Eve kept the invisible wadding in place to ensure he wouldn't accidently breathe again.

She and Adam rushed to his side, pretending to give CPR while all the children and adults watched with shock. Eve took special care to hide the wadded air with her cheek as she faked listening for breathing. "Go get our father!" she screamed. "And Doctor Yurik!"

Several of the adults rushed out and Eve counted to twenty, deciding it was time enough to call him herself.

David held Cathy close against his chest, both panting for air after their passion was dually spent. This woman had proven amazing and brought out an eagerness in him for more. He doubted he would ever make love like this again.

Father, come to the schoolroom, there's been an emergency, Eve's voice echoed in his head.

What? What happened?

Mr. Starlings stopped breathing and clutched his chest. It looked like a heart attack. Please hurry!

He sat up in bed, startling Cathy with his urgency. "I can't explain, but there's been an emergency in the schoolroom. We have to go *now*!"

"What? David, how do you know this?"

"I said I can't explain!"

"David, after what we just shared you *damn* well better try!"

He paused, reading her face and measuring how much he could share. "My research project involved telepathy and telekinesis. Eve just told me that Mr. Starlings had a heart attack and we had better hurry."

"What the hell? Wait, *we*? How does she know *we're* together?" She shuddered with revulsion. "Ew!"

"No, *me*! She meant *I* had to hurry, but you're with me so I said *we*!" He *hoped* that was the case, and the thought that she may actually know what he was doing suddenly bothered him on so many levels. He pulled on his pants and grabbed his shirt. He would put it on in the hallway. "Come on," he urged and she followed, buttoning her blouse as she followed him into the hallway.

Clint stepped out of Max's office and leaned against the wall to savor the meeting they just ended. It was about to be wartime, and that's when he knew himself best. Clint Fletcher was born to kill, and war offered so much opportunity. He could almost taste the metallic tinge of blood in his mouth as if he had bitten his own lip with excitement.

He was about to turn and go take that shower, but the door at the end of the hall abruptly flew open. A man, Dr. Andalon, rushed out while sliding his shirt over his head. As he did, Clint noticed his belt was unfastened and his zipper fly down. He was about to giggle and crack a joke at the man rushing by, but then the woman followed, hot on his heels and buttoning her blouse. As she passed their eyes met. Clint stared disbelieving at the horrified expression on her face.

All at once the murderous sound of Dean Martin leapt into his mind and a song played. *Who is that lady?* it begged.

His mind furiously worked through what he had just seen, rewinding it and imagining David and Cathy behind that door. Their sweaty bodies writhed in his head, full of sin and betrayal against her marriage vows.

"That was no lady," he spat the words of the son at Cathy's back as she turned the corner. "You're *my* wife!"

Clint's shower would wait, no sense in taking two, he would need one later. He would soon be covered in blood. The blood of a rival. David Andalon would die that very night.

CHAPTER TWENTY-THREE

The staff meeting filled the conference room, reminding General Braston how much he hated the burden of command and missed racing across the skies.

"What do we do about Sergeant Mason?" the chief master sergeant asked the room. "When can I return her to the cafeteria roster?"

Jake interrupted the captain before he could go into detail. "Jeanne Mason's been reassigned, put in a special cadre," he lied. Right at that very moment she was sitting in a cell and staring blankly at the wall. She hadn't eaten nor had anything to drink for several days and seemed not to need it. The last thing she had ingested was on a command by him. "There are more names coming that will be added to the cadre, just as soon as Brooke... Dr. Andalon is done with her testing."

He felt bad for his sister, who looked more haggard each day. This pregnancy was a difficult one, and he had never seen any expectant mother endure so much. He had urged her to get off her feet, to take a week off to rest, but she refused. Even after that episode in the lab, when the pain had brought her to her knees, she insisted on working through it.

He had asked her about that episode, but she dismissed it. *I swear that child talked to me,* he thought with a shudder. Though it had not formed words, the fetus clearly communicated its needs in the same way Sergeant Mason did after he had consumed the bead—he felt more than heard her communications like they were locked in a collective hive mind with sergeants Baxter and Price.

Baxter, it turns out, was the man he ordered to fight him. A Tactical Air Control Party (TACP) specialist, a recent addition after losing Benjamin Roark. Tough as nails, those TACP guys, the kind Jake liked having around. He would find a good use for him in his new cadre—if Brooke could figure out how the powers of the bead could be controlled.

"General? Sir?" The chief master sergeant had asked a question.

Jake had not heard. His mind was everywhere but on the meeting. "Sorry, Chief. Can you repeat that? My mind wandered."

"I said we need to consider when we can move into the other parts of the base, and which buildings we'll use now that the cleanup is done."

Cleanup. Chief meant, of course, the disposal of bodies. That had begun as soon as radiation levels lifted enough so the vaccinated teams could search the rest of Ramstein. He had never realized just how big the base was until that project began—nor how many people had perished outside of Michael's bunker.

"I'll talk to the chancellor," Jake muttered, "but let's wrap up for now. I have another meeting after this one." He stood to leave, and the room snapped to attention. That was another part of the job he had tired of, all the pomp and circumstance.

He left the room, making his way to the lab. Hopefully he would find time to chat with Brooke, to check up and gauge her need for a break. He would order her take one, if he had to.

On the way, he collided with Airman McLemore.

"I'm sorry, sir," she said shyly, blushing and stepping back. She had been walking with her head down, paying as little attention to her surroundings as he was.

"No need, part of the fault is mine. I just can't seem to focus on anything that matters today. I'm sorry, Airman, please forgive *me.*"

He stepped away, intent on getting to his next meeting and having no idea at all what it was about. Brooke had called for it, that was all he remembered. As he moved down the hall, he realized Airman McLemore had matched steps beside him. "Where are *you* headed?" he asked, breaking the awkward silence between them.

"Dr. Andalon called me to the lab, said she had questions for me," the airman replied in a little over a whisper. She seemed as eager to get away as Jake felt.

Of course, Jake remembered the reason for the meeting. Brooke was debriefing all those who manifested powers, going over their surveys with hope she could learn more about the powers. Another thought struck the general, and it related directly to the airman.

"McLemore," he asked once they stood outside the door, "after you consumed the pearl, what did you experience?"

She abruptly turned scarlet, as if he had demanded something personal from her, so he rephrased the question.

"I mean, at first, when it started working, what did you feel? Did you hear voices or feel like someone... some *thing* was trying to communicate with you?"

She relaxed a bit and thought. "No, sir, nothing like that at all. I felt calm, relaxed even, like I had taken a benzo." Jake had raised an eyebrow, so she explained, "When I was in high school I tried some, most of *my* generation has..."

Ouch, he thought, suddenly feeling much older than he was. But he was still twice her age, and it was better she thought of them being from separate generations. He relaxed a little and so did she. "So nothing like a hive mind," he asked, "or a collective? You never connected with anyone else in the room?"

"No, sir."

Jake wasn't sure if this information helped or worsened his worries. That he swore his nephew had communicated made him feel out of sorts, as if he had hallucinated after taking the bead.

"But I did see things. I *flew,* General, in the clouds over home."

Well then, at least I'm not alone with my hallucinations. "Flew? Like in a plane?"

"I soared as if *I* had really flown. Real-time, too, as if I were really there up in the sky. I saw it all, the clouds, the ashy snow, even a big crack in North America."

Jake paused, suddenly a little sick. Adam and Eve had described the same sensation, even the crack. *Cinder's Crack,* they had called it, though no one understood why. It was a secret they had all kept, and only Michael, Brooke, Stephanie, and he knew that detail. It was one they even kept from

David. That Penny McLemore mentioned it meant she was the real deal, a true seer like those raised in the Andalon Project.

She had flown, the words finally struck him, and Jake couldn't help but feel a bit jealous. He yearned to soar above the clouds once more. The sky had always been his playground. Since the EMP, his F-22 was buried beneath several feet of ash and snow leaving him to pilot a desk. That was the only reason he had looked forward to Brooke's experiments. Despite he lacked affinity for the Astian Pearl, the process was a thrilling reminder he was once free to push the envelope instead of paper.

"Tell all that to Dr. Andalon inside," he told the girl. Then he reached down and turned the knob, pulling the door open and holding it while she walked through. She smiled shyly, and he flashed one back, full of confidence until she passed by. Then he frowned deeply, still troubled by Brooke's exhaustion, his hallucination, and the fact he was perpetually grounded while others flew the skies.

Penny McLemore walked past the general, eyes locked ahead and very aware of the fact her cheeks burned red hot. That he was handsome for an older man did not bother her, it was his confidence that drove her crazy. But, she would never break protocol, even if the world had ended, which it had. Even though he was one of the only men left in the world, General Braston was still her superior officer and off limits. Thankfully, he was not like the rest of her superior officers and NCO's, none of whom any longer respected either the rules of the UCMJ nor her boundaries. But the general was a silver fox, and that made her blush.

Careful not to brush him with her shoulder as she entered the lab, she quickly found Dr. Brooke Andalon waiting inside.

"I'm here for debriefing, ma'am," she said without the shyness she had for the general.

"Right this way," the scientist greeted her, then nodded over her shoulder toward the waiting general. "I'll be with you in a moment, Jake."

Jake. The informal sound of his name felt odd on Penny's ears, but she remembered the pair were brother and sister. Dr. Andalon led her through another door and into a private room. Inside were two lab assistants, the Korean husband and wife brought to Ramstein from MIT. The woman's belly was as round as Dr. Andalon's.

Brooke offered her a seat, then sat down and went straight to business.

"Tell me about the effects of the bead. Your experience from the moment it began to work, and how you knew it..." The scientist doubled over, grabbing the corner of the table with her hand and dropping her clipboard to do so. It landed with a clatter and the whoosh of papers flew across the floor.

Penny immediately jumped to her feet, helping the woman into the chair she had just emptied. Whatever was happening, it resembled the time she fell to her knees during testing.

The Korean woman appeared worried but took over from there. "Are these contractions, Brooke?"

"I think... no. No, they're not, Mi-Jung." Brooke replied.

"Have you had any spotting? Bleeding?"

"No, nothing like that. Just pain, and I've been tired... dehydrated, maybe."

"Then you're probably anemic too."

Dr. Andalon nodded, too busy breathing against more pain to agree.

"We have iron pills," the Korean male offered.

"Thank you, Sam," the doctor panted, "but I'm already taking them. The baby seems to consume whatever I swallow as soon as it enters my body. I can't take any more without worrying about toxicity for both him and me."

"We at least need to get an IV in you," Mi-Jung insisted.

"I will, but first let's finish these interviews." The doctor's face abruptly changed, then added, "and no matter *what*, none of you tell Jake or Michael about this!" Her eyes met Penny's, who vigorously nodded agreement. "Tell us how you first knew the bead was working."

Airman McLemore could not help but respect the woman's dedication to her science but agreed with the others. Brooke needed to slow down and take liquids. After a deep breath, she answered the question. "It was odd at first, like I had popped a Xanax or another benzo. A calmness came over me after only a few minutes, so I guess it worked fast. Before I knew it, I felt euphoric, like all my pleasure senses were on overload while my nerves relaxed and took a break."

"How long did that last?" Brooke asked, her pain subsiding enough to breathe regularly.

"A few more minutes, then my mind did something I hadn't expected."

"What was that?"

"It left my body."

The trio of scientists exchanged a look and then all three jotted notes.

"Was that wrong?" Penny asked. "I swear that's what happened."

"Not wrong, just unexpected. What next, after your mind left your body?"

"I surged upward, literally through the ceiling of the bunker and over the base. I hovered for a moment, then flew up into the clouds. I couldn't control it at first, not till I was really high up. I... It was like those pictures from high altitude when astronauts enter low orbit. I saw the curvature of the earth."

"And then?"

"I picked a direction and headed that way."

"I see that, yes. It was in your report. You flew over North America?"

"I did, yes."

"And you saw a crack?"

"Yes, ma'am. From what was Yellowstone all the way south into what was Mexico. It was long and wide."

"I won't get into all the specifics of your previous report. I'm mostly interested in the transition into what we're calling the Ka'ash'mael. What did *that* feel like, and how did you know you reached it?"

"I didn't know, not exactly... well, not at first. It was like a dream..." Penny eyed Sam uncomfortably. This next part was private, not something she wanted on record, but knew she had to tell—only wished it wasn't in front of a man. "I had an orgasm, or that's what it felt like. It pulsed through my entire body, like none I'd ever experienced." She knew she was blushing again, felt her cheeks betray her, but kept going. "It was like every nerve ending that was previously resting suddenly awakened with life filled with pleasure. That's when everything faded and I was no longer in control—not of my breathing, nor my body, but especially not my mind or the words I spoke. It was like someone else was talking, and I was a bystander hearing them for the first time." Penny paused. This was the troubling part. "Then the pain started. Everything that had once filled with pleasure suddenly and abruptly felt only pain—excruciating pain like my body would be torn apart."

"How long did that last?" Brooke asked.

"Until a few breaths after the final words were spoken, and then it suddenly stopped... not gradual like turning the wheel of a spigot, but immediate."

Brooke Andalon seemed for a moment to be fighting against her own pain and curtly asked, "Anything else you'd like to add before we finish?"

"Ma'am, earlier you said you found it *unexpected* that I left my body. Why?"

The trio of scientists exchanged one more look, then Brooke shrugged off the question dismissively. "That's classified."

"With all due respect, ma'am, I'm part of the experiment. I want to understand what I experienced. How was it different than others?"

Brooke sighed, perhaps too exhausted to argue. "Of all those who reached Ka'ash'mael, you all first reported flying, but only you felt your mind completely leave your body."

"But you weren't surprised, only found it unexpected? Was that what the children experienced when they prophesied? Did they leave their bodies too?"

"Yes," Brooke replied truthfully, "but I don't yet know what that means for you *or* for us."

Brooke listened intently as her brother gave his own debriefing, glad to spend time with him even though Sam and Mi-Jung were also present. The pain in her uterus persisted, lingering but less intense. Though she would never admit this to the others, she was terrified she was losing the baby and considered letting an experienced obstetrician check her out. They had one on the medical staff, but she wasn't ready for the answers he may give. Besides, whatever she told him would be relayed to Michael, and she feared how he would react if his child were not delivered to term after Adam's prophecy.

This baby's not normal, not after what David did to him. But what *had* he done? There was no way to know for sure. Before he abandoned her and chose instead to take Adam and Eve to North America, her husband revealed that he had changed the fetal DNA, ensuring she would give birth to an emotant. But which kind? So far, none of the four options consoled her fear.

Jake was finishing up, talking about how he had raised Sergeant Mason from the dead. "Brooke," he asked gently, "can we ask Mi-Jung and Sam to step out for a moment? I have some things to tell only you."

"You can trust them, Jake."

"This is private, personal, even."

Brooke shrugged, then nodded. The pair left immediately, respecting the sibling's privacy if not obeying orders from the ranking officer and lead scientist. As soon as they left she asked, "What's this about? What's got you worried?"

"At the exact moment you collapsed during the testing, I swear your child spoke to me."

"That's impossible," she protested, shaking her head. "A fetus has no understanding of complex speech, much less an ability to communicate. You were confused, maybe even by the connection you felt with the three sergeants."

Jake shook his head. "No. Those three spoke in unison, remember? When I didn't?"

Brooke frowned then checked her notes. "Yes, I do. They both said something about *Not yet* and *Be calm*. Do you know what that was about?"

"I do. That's what I was urging *him*," he said, pointing at her belly. I felt a connection with all three, Mason, Baxter, and Price, but felt a stronger, different, bond at the same time. I think he was reaching out to me through the amniotic fluid. He was begging to leave your womb. I felt this urge, an *overwhelming* urge, to get free and enter the world. Are you okay in this pregnancy, Brooke? Are you losing the baby? I know it's too early for him to come."

Brooke considered his words, finally too exhausted to continue and ready for a nap. "I think I might be, but I'm not sure. This pain, it isn't anything I've found in OB/GYN journals, and it certainly isn't simple contractions. But the baby's heartbeat is strong. It's never wavered or even fallen weak, not like early labor. I'm anemic, badly so, and can't consume enough fluids. I drink enough water to drown a camel, but hardly ever pee it out. It's like my body's using *all* of it—or *he* is." Then a thought struck Brooke. "Jake, the next test is Batch Delta."

"So? Water? What about it?"

"I think I just realized what the problem is."

"Tell me," Jake pleaded.

"I will, *after* the experiment. I don't want to taint your results beforehand, but I think I understand what David did."

CHAPTER TWENTY-FOUR

David pushed his way into the schoolroom, not so gently shoving onlookers aside as he ran up to kneel beside Mr. Starlings' lifeless body on the floor. Eve, seeing her father had arrived, moved to the top of the man's head, her eyes filled with frantic tears.

"Is he dead, Daddy?"

She seemed odd. Something was off, but David could not tell what it was. Usually wise and emotionally calm for her years, this was the most human he had ever seen her. Even Adam seemed shaken up, both visibly and mentally. This was *not* the first time they had witnessed death; they had dealt it by thousands on a battlefield just a few months ago.

Then the truth hit David like a hammer. This was all an act. *What did you do?* he demanded.

Go along with it, Eve begged in his mind. Her voice so calmly disassociated from her outward frenzy. *It's important that you do.*

Go along with what? Raise him from the dead? Did you kill him?

He had a heart attack, Father.

But David looked him over and knew at once that wasn't true. The man died from suffocation and his lips were already turning blue. *No, he most certainly did not! What game are you playing?* he demanded, trying hard to appear calm and not angry while looking over the body.

We need him, please raise him.

No!

"David," Cathy whispered, kneeling beside him next to the body. She pointed at the blueish lips. "Asphyxiation? How?"

"I don't know, choked maybe?" He shot Eve an angry glance then regained his composure.

"He clutched his heart," one of the bible class members shouted out. "Was it a heart attack?"

"Maybe," David mumbled, shooting another glance at his daughter's pleading eyes. "Cyanotic Heart Failure *could* look like this," he explained to Cathy.

Before he could stop her, she reached down for a pulse. She looked up and shook her head. "He's gone." The crowd murmured in response to the news.

"I..." He stole another glance at Eve. *Why did she do this?* How *did she do this? There was no need for it!* But to leave this man dead would hurt the community, and Eve must have had a reason. He locked eyes with her. *You* do *have a good reason for this, right?*

I promise we do, Father.

Ok.

Repeat after me, she commanded. *He's not dead, he's merely sleeping.*

"He's not dead, he's merely sleeping," David repeated, finding the word choice very odd, especially from Eve. *You'd* better *have a good explanation!*

Now rise up, Vincent Starling, it isn't your time. Rise up and get back to work!

"Rise up, Vincent Starling," David repeated. "It isn't your time. Rise up and get back to work!"

The people behind him began to murmur louder, muttering words and phrases he could not make out. But one phrase was clear. "Miracle," someone whispered.

David went to work using his craft to peer into the body, finding its lifeforce. Very little remained. *I can't restore him with his own. It's not like when I raised you, when it was stored in the eagles!*

Use some of ours and yours, Adam suggested. *Equal parts of all three if you can, more of us if you need to. We can spare it more easily.*

David nodded and did just that, pouring theirs into the body with his own just like he merged Michael Esterling's into Ivan Petrov.

David finished weaving life into the man, working it into his body and healing the damaged organs. Once he was certain he would revive, he bent over and breathed air into his lungs, hoping that effort would make this appear less mystical and more closely resembling CPR.

Vince Starlings' eyes shot open at once and bellowed out the breath. "I saw the light!" he screamed into the room. "I saw heaven and the savior is coming!" he added, then calmed and looked around the room. "He told me he will reveal himself soon."

David felt his stomach drop, suddenly realizing what the children had tricked him into doing. *You're making him say that now, aren't you?* he demanded.

I am, Eve admitted.

This gave you the ability to control his mind and words. Is that what you wanted? To control your teacher?

Yes, but for a good reason, Eve insisted. *We need him.* You *need him!*

Don't you dare *bring me into this!* David nearly screamed aloud at Eve.

It's too late, Father, Adam said into his mind. *There's no turning back now.*

David swallowed his anger and stood, taking the teacher's hand and pulling him up off the ground. "Go about your evening, Mr. Starlings. Finish your work." Then he turned his back, ignoring the hushed murmurings from those gathered around. There were nearly thirty witnesses present, and that was thirty too many for Dr. Andalon's liking. Full of anger and a need to be alone, he felt all eyes on his back as he rushed from the room.

"David!" Cathy hurried after him, grabbing his arm. "What just happened?"

"I'm sorry, Cathy, I haven't been truthful to you. I have certain... abilities."

"I think I know," she replied. "When you healed Josh, all those people on the stage, you *actually* healed them, didn't you? It wasn't medicine?"

"Most of it was, but yes, some of it was healing. And yes, Josh's arm was fractured, only a greenstick, so it was easy to heal."

"You... healed a greenstick fracture on your own without splinting or casting?" She narrowed her eyes. This would all be too much for her to understand or accept. "How?" she demanded. "Tell me now! Are you a healer or a doctor?"

David sighed. Their brief love encounter would come to a crashing halt now, and she may even out him and the children to Max Rankin. "I'm not really a medical doctor, Cathy. I had enough medical school to know the basics, but I was never board certified to practice. I told you I mostly worked in research, but the truth is I finished med school at MIT, then jumped into genetic sciences. That's where I stayed after graduation and taught MRNA resequencing until just before the big day."

"What's that? Like the old COVID vaccines?"

"Sort of. I figured out ways to resequence the body to repair itself at the cellular level. Remember what I told you about my experiments? That the children and I share a telepathic connection?"

"Yes, just now, after we... Oh please, no. What *did* we do?"

David recognized the look of regret flash across Cathy's face. In an attempt to console her, he said, "We enjoyed each other's company, Brooke."

"I'm Cathy," she corrected. Before he could respond Cathy added, "Enjoyed each other's company? Oh, wow. That makes it sound even worse. What were your experiments, David? What *can* you do?"

"I discovered a way to alter DNA, to adapt and untap our potential for different abilities. The way Eve communicated to me earlier was one." He thought he would stop there, to avoid giving her any idea about their ability to manipulate air. If she knew that, she would know they killed Vince Starling, and it would all come crashing to a head. "But also my ability to heal."

"You practiced your experiments on yourself and your two children? That's disgusting. It's so unethical and *wrong* on yourself, but on children? Who *are* you? We should never have..."

"Brooke, I..."

"I'm *Cathy!*" she abruptly snapped.

"Cathy, I didn't make Adam and Eve what they are. I rescued them. Stephanie helped me. Michael Esterling used *my* research, what *Brooke* sent him, to create lab-grown humans with telepathic abilities. They were prisoners, and I helped them escape."

She stared at him, disbelieving. "You're not telling me everything. Where was this lab? Germany? How the hell did you get across the Atlantic in less than six months, much less find your way *here*?" she demanded.

"We sailed."

"Where's your boat, then? If you had a boat, why did you need Clint's help?"

"I can't tell you that!" David nearly exploded with anger. He had not meant to scream, but he could no longer keep his cool under her rapid fire interrogation. She was too close to the truth about Adam and Eve—knew too much about the Andalon Project. *If I tell her more, Eve won't be happy!* he realized, thinking of how she manipulated him into raising a man she killed because 'we need him,' as she had stated. *If I tell Cathy about all her abilities, Eve will kill her too, because we* don't *need her either.* He paused. *But I need her,* he realized.

"How did you bring Mr. Starlings back to life?"

"That's part of what I can do. I can heal the body and raise the dead."

"Only people, or animals too?"

"I don't know. I'm still figuring it out. I've no idea what else I can do."

Cathy had heard enough and turned to leave.

"Where are you going?" David pleaded. "Don't go."

"I need time to process this... *all* of it. It's sick, demented, twisted, and just plain *weird*!"

"Cathy," he begged. "Please don't throw away what we have."

She whirled. "And what *do* we have, David? A mutual enjoyment of each other's company?" After that, she was gone, leaving him alone and rejected, standing in the hallway watching her leave.

David stared into the darkness, gripped by worry and unable to find sleep amid swirling thoughts of doubt. Earlier, the night had been consumed by his fight with Cathy, but most recently was lost over Adam and Eve. After the incident in the schoolroom his fears had multiplied, filling his night with crippling anxiety over their true agenda.

They're controlling everything, he realized.

Each time he managed to close his eyes amidst the lull of fatigue, they would shoot open with some other realization, something forgotten or left out during their upbringing. Neither child seemed bothered by what they had done, and the doctor realized no moral compass guided them. They completely lacked empathy for others.

Michael had ordered them raised in a lab, a controlled environment without proper structure. That was the root of the problem—as experiments facing certain destruction since birth, no one had bothered teaching them right from wrong.

As late as the hour was, he would have to talk to Stephanie about all this in the morning. Perhaps she would have some idea of how to fill in the gaps and give insight into what may be driving their agenda. Of course, context was everything, and these children lacked any motivation outside of self-preservation of their species.

They killed without remorse, lacking conscience as well as empathy. That was the biggest problem for the doctor and why it kept him awake. Conscience and empathy were the most important components of humanity. That separating factor divided humans from animals. *Without either of those, they're merely sociopathic.*

He mulled over each of their conversations over the past few months and came to a startling realization. *They've manipulated my every move. Even inside the Andalon Lab. They had set up this outcome!*

They had wanted out... no, *needed* out of that prison and used him to do it. But why?

Because they... and now me... are a different species altogether, the scientist concluded, *and will stop at nothing short of survival of that species.*

Worse, David had contributed to that survival as well, spreading his vaccines to so many refugees. He had inoculated hundreds in the Shelter, using the original batches—much like the one he had used on himself.

They tricked me into spreading their species onto this continent. And now there was no telling how much damage he had already done.

The signs had been there all along, if only David had known to pay attention. The first clue had been when Adam and Eve destroyed the Russian army at Waghäusel. They had chosen the precise moment, arriving on the battlefield in the nick of time, to rescue Michael's army from certain death. But their arrival had also been timed for the widest of audiences, with all eyes watching the children float in upon a ship constructed entirely of air and accompanied by a massive flock of eagles. There had been no need for a spectacle, unless marking the event a public demonstration on the grandest of scales.

It was all a show of power, David mused. *A mere demonstration of what only an ounce of what their power could do to them all if Esterling follows us to North America.*

Or worse, he suddenly realized, they were daring Michael to do so.

What are their true plans for this continent? he wondered. *They keep calling it Andalon, enticing me along and leading my actions toward their goals... they even chose* this *place to settle, sparing no effort in making us believe it was our only chance at survival.*

Somehow, after tossing and turning for several hours, David managed to fall asleep.

He had only slept for a short while when a fist struck his nose, waking him violently. That protruding piece of cartilage exploded with a crimson splash of pain, sending shockwaves throughout his head and jolting him upright from the bed. A second blow followed the first, then another and another. Just as David was about to cry out, strong fingers gripped his throat, cutting off his plea for help.

With blood dripping into his eyes, he could barely see his attacker through the crimson haze. He recognized him at once as Clint Fletcher. The man was atop him, staring into his victim's soul as if savoring the kill. In a flash Clint moved, bringing his forehead downward into David's already broken nose. Everything after that occurred in total darkness, and the doctor was barely aware he was being murdered in his bed.

Strong hands again gripped his windpipe, pressing hard as if the man were trying to not only cut off his air supply, but to crush the entire apparatus it relied upon.

He had seen us, David had forgotten till now, *coming out of the Officer's Mess in various stages of undress.* It would have been obvious to anyone what they had done, and now he would die over a woman. Clint's blind rage was a killing of passion, fueled by knowledge David had lain with his ex-wife.

David tried to struggle, desperate to fight the soldier off, but every attempt proved useless. Each movement grew more sluggish with every punch or kick he tried. As he struggled to breathe, the doctor thought of Vincent Starlings. Clint wasn't a pair of ten-year-olds with telekinesis, but David would die the same way as the teacher—starved of oxygen until the brain no longer controlled his body. Only, unlike Starlings, no foolish pawn of a doctor would come rushing in to resurrect him.

Resurrect. That word seemed so odd. The teacher was gone, and in its place lived a remnant of thoughts that only believed itself alive.

Suddenly, a thought occurred to the doctor.

Eve, he cried out in his mind, *Adam! Help!*

That desperate plea was all he could manage, coming out weak. With each attempt he found it more difficult to forge contact or hold onto a connection.

One more time he tried. *Help me!*

The pressure on his throat grew heavier as his nerves quickly faded. His brain would follow, and David understood this is what dying felt like. Once the ringing in his ears began, he knew his blood pressure had either risen or fallen—and did so quite suddenly.

He tried to form another bond with Adam and Eve but failed, resulting only in a single thought within his own mind... *Help.*

David's fading hearing detected a mild grunt.

The hold abruptly released at the same moment he heard the sound and, no longer pressed into the cot, his body lurched upward. For a brief moment the fingers released then squeezed down once more. The doctor gasped in just enough life-giving air. It filled his lungs and granted another two minutes of life.

During that long countdown toward death David heard another grunt, this time more audible as his senses recovered. He either opened his eyes or they finally focused on the face of his attacker, and found Clint sitting with full weight atop him. The killer's face burned red with rage, completely ignoring the man standing behind him.

The newcomer's arm moved in and out against Fletcher's ribs.

Clint finally realized what he felt upon his back were not punches but stabs piercing his body. He finally turned and growled into the face of Vince Starlings. The teacher bore a somber expression, with uncaring eyes that seemed unaware of the actions of his hands. In each he held a pocket knife, plunging over and over into Fletcher's ribs. Each strike was calculated, the precise spots to fill a man's lungs with blood and drown him from within.

Clint's eyes suddenly grew less wild and more worried, releasing David completely. He shifted his weight, reaching to grab ahold of the teacher but fell to the ground face first. Reaching out he crawled, pulling up onto his knees, trying to lunge with an adrenaline-filled final rage.

David kicked, sending the man crashing hard onto his own belly.

Adam and Eve suddenly appeared in the doorway, waving their arms like conductors of a silent orchestra, the instruments of which intending to bind Clint to his doom. Their wisps of air curled like boas around his arms, legs, and neck, holding him and twisting, turning the would-be assassin over for their teacher.

Starlings knelt and finished the job, his lifeless eyes unseeing the evil work of his once godly hands.

"No!" David pleaded, as both blades plunged deep into the chest of Clint Fletcher. The monster, as Cathy called him, died instantly the moment his heart stopped even if the lifeforce in his mind lingered.

Now that he has died, Eve commanded, *raise him as ours.*

"No," David begged, wishing he had not the ability.

A single wisp of air rose around his body, twisting and turning as if she would strangle *him* for noncompliance. His body shuddered, then forced sobs from his chest. But the coil, unconcerned about his neck which had suffered enough on this night, caressed his face instead.

Father, Eve said into his mind, *do not be afraid. All of this is necessary, and soon you will see. Michael Esterling is building an army of Sensitives, those who can mimic our powers. They will eventually come, and your children, us and those you have seeded, will be targets of his greedy wrath. He intends to farm us, stealing our craft to create his sick abominations and fuel his lustful drive for power... unless we prepare our* own *army now!*

"I cannot," David pleaded hoarsely, his throat aching from the damage by Clint's hands. "None of this should be happening. None of it is right! If I steal control over another human's life, then I'm no better than Michael. Each life we take control over steals away our own humanity."

Clint Fletcher is not a human. He is a monster. And you and we are not humans either.

"What are we, then?" David demanded, unable to scream the words or he would have. "Do you think we are *gods*?"

Yes, Father.

"How? How can you believe that, knowing the truth? We are products of science. Of man."

The girl did not answer, gently pushing him forward with her coiled wisp and guiding his trembling hands toward the body.

It is time, Adam suggested. *Combine him with all of us just as you did before. Join ours and your lifeforce into his, but this time also add a bit of Mr. Starlings.*

Yes, Eve agreed. *It is time for our collective mind to grow and, with it, our freedom from Michael Esterling.*

David felt a wash of guilt overwhelm him—a gulley of shame that scrubbed away the last of his hope and desire to make the world right. The children were correct. The war between emotants and humans had begun, and he must aid them in the fight for survival. With a defeated nod David Andalon did as his children commanded, bringing forth the worst monster imaginable.

CHAPTER TWENTY-FIVE

Jake had more than tired of the testing, he was downright sick of it. Despite his success with Batch Charlie, no other subject had yet shown affinity for more than one bead. He grumbled at this, silently wishing for another chance at the coveted pearl and one more attempt at flight. He sighed as Sam strapped him into the chair.

"Batch Delta, then?" Jake muttered, though he knew perfectly well it was. At the front of the room stood two large aquariums each filled with more than one hundred gallons of water.

"Good luck, General," the lab assistant said with a smile, but the weariness of all this testing had worn thin on his face as well as Brooke's.

Jake turned to Airman McLemore. Penny seemed just as sick of the testing as he, staring intently at the jar of beads as Brooke approached. "What do you think happens here?" Jake asked her with a grin. "We have a water fight, only without balloons?"

The girl managed a laugh. "Why not? It would be more interesting since we're strapped in. Being tied up is always more fun." Then she turned scarlet and tried to back track. "Not that I like bondage," she quipped. "I mean... Oh god."

Jake turned away to hide his own cheeks from blushing at the suggestion. He had a comeback but saved her from further embarrassment and himself from saying something inappropriate to a subordinate.

Brooke saved them both from having to speak further by popping a blue bead in each of their mouths.

Jake swallowed his at once and caught glimpse of McLemore doing the same. Almost as soon as his eyes returned forward, intense pain, unlike any he had ever felt, wracked his stomach. He doubled over in his chair, his bowels and esophagus spasming along with the quivering organ. His body convulsed, then vomited the bead. But his pain did not end there, his body continued to convulse, pushing out every trace of the bead as if it had been poison.

Next to him, Airman McLemore vomited her own bead but, unlike the man beside her, immediately settled into her chair relieved to be rid of hers.

Something was terribly wrong with Jake. He lifted his head, intent on finding Brooke to let her know he was in trouble and found her curled up in a heap on the floor. Some unseen force inside her mirrored his own pain, seemingly ripping her insides apart. He found her eyes locked on his, pleading for help amidst her screams.

The room abruptly fell ice cold around him.

But his agony had not ended and he gasped against the pain, his breath then puffing out as a fog. His mind raced with anxiety, the need to be free screaming wordless warning into his body. As if tied to Brooke's pain, each desperate plea coincided with another spasm in her womb and her guttural scream pleaded for mercy. Then Jake understood, her fetus was attacking both of them from within her womb.

But why me? he wondered, just as both aquariums burst, spilling their contents onto the floor. Water and shards of glass cascaded over the side, surrounding Brooke and pooling just beyond Jake's feet.

Then Braston was aware of another feeling, a raging tantrum that meant to tear itself from its surroundings. The child inside her womb violently seized Jake's consciousness, melding it with its own, and forcing him to see from its perspective. The darkness was chilling, frightening and full of unseen dangers. The general suddenly yearned to flee, to rip apart the walls of his prison and emerge to safety. Only the water provided comfort, not that near his feet, but the fluid surrounding Brooke's child. Cool and inviting, it starkly contrasted the heated fear within her womb.

Then the water on the floor began to move. Jake could not see it, locked in this prison of flesh, but he felt every molecule as it pressed against Brooke's skin. The need to escape now drove both the water and his mind, an orchestra of movement conducted by the terrified fetus. The fear pushed the water into a frenzy, whipping it into a maelstrom.

"General Braston!" a voice yelled nearby, but Jake could barely hear it over the screams of the child. "Wake up!" the external voice tried again, as something struck his leg again and again.

Jarred from the trance, Jake opened his eyes to find Airman McLemore kicking him into consciousness. She brought the heel of her boot down hard into his thigh and struck a nerve.

"I'm awake!" he roared, with eyes still locked on his sister.

Unable to stand, Brooke watched as the current of water pooled around her, spinning and carrying the shards of glass with its current. The edge of one caught her cheek, adding a tinge of pink into the water. Faster it spun, until a frothy mixture began to foam.

Jake pulled at his straps, realizing the fetus meant to cut itself free from its mother. He bellowed for Sam to help, but a shard of glass suddenly flew at the lab assistant, narrowly missing his throat. The man ducked uselessly behind a table.

Most of the water now spun several feet high, a cyclone of liquid and glass closing in slowly around Brooke. Jake had to reach it, to feel and control it like the child was doing. *But how?* he wondered. He had already vomited up the bead.

I didn't need the bead, he suddenly realized. *Just like that time before, when the child reached out through the amnio fluid.* Jake considered that for a moment, the irony of what David had done, to take someone so happy in the sky and force them to live a live bonded with another element... with *water* instead of air. That was David's revenge upon his brother in law.

Just beyond his left foot Jake saw the water creeping closer, and spied within the puddle a single shard of glass. Swinging his body that direction, he inched closer with both feet and kicked off his boots. *I have to touch the fluid,* he realized, *like he is in the womb.* Pressing one heel at a time against the other socked toe, he wrenched off the cloth, exposing bare feet. It was close but almost not near enough, and he had to stretch out completely to merely make contact with the moisture.

His eyes returned to his sister, watching as she screamed in terror at the glass now circling close to her body. The water felt cold beneath his toes, but not nearly as chilled as the air around him. That gave him hope, that *something* could happen if he could just wrench control away from the fetus.

I can't force it, he knew from the past two experiments, and knew he could not force the water to comply. Still focused on Brooke he felt desperation overcome him, strapped in the chair and useless to defend her.

I couldn't save anyone! he realized. *I left Mom and Dad to perish so close to Yellowstone, doing nothing to warn them or move them away. The people of this base could have been warned as well, told to go underground before the attack. But instead I listened to Michael, saving only David and his team, bringing Brooke here, only for her to die while I watch.*

The air around him was now like ice, so cold he almost failed to notice the water had moved onto his foot and up his leg, carrying the shard of glass upward. It made its way up his chest, then down his arm and into his hand.

All of it had moved, and not a single bit of moisture showed on his uniform where it had touched, wicking toward his outstretched hand. There, it pooled and swirled like the cyclone about to rip his sister to shreds. In his palm he held the piece of glass. The pool of water moved to the leather strap around his wrist and soaked deeply into its pores.

Little time remained, but thankfully the leather cut more easily when wet. After what felt an eternity of sawing, he succeeded in ripping his arm free. He quickly unbuckled his left and bent over, going to work on his legs. Now completely free he rushed forward, sprinting to his sister and stopping at the wall of water surrounding her. Several pieces of glass had broken her skin, but only faint lines scored her body and face. They were both running out of time as those swirled deeper with each passing.

Jake plunged his right hand into the cyclone, uncaring if the glass cut him as well. Somehow, it moved away from his skin, avoiding him while hell-bent on slicing open Brooke. He closed his eyes and focused on forcing the water over his hand. Again he failed, just as he had before with the vines.

With the connection still strong in his memory, he matched the child's determination with sheer will and met his tantrum with calm. If Jake Braston was anything besides a tremendous pilot, he was a leader of men, and that required patience and control over emotions. But the need to protect his sister won and emotion leaked out.

No! he pleaded with the child with his mind. *You will kill her!*

He was answered not by words, but what he now recognized as a childish tantrum and desire to escape the womb.

You will die if you persist, and so will she!

The tantrum intensified, and the wall of water and glass moved closer, making deeper cuts.

He doesn't understand words, Jake realized, and changed his tactic.

If a child is doing something unsafe, or holding an unsafe object, the first step was to remove the danger. At this moment, that was the toy in the child's control—the water and glass. Jake closed his eyes and let the water wash over his hand, thinking soothing thoughts and sending them through. In the end, he did the last thing he ever thought he would.

He sang a lullaby to his nephew.

He had not thought of nor hummed this song in decades, much less sang it, but did so now, in front of the entire room. His voice, a deep baritone, came out soothing and melodically filled with emotion. "Hush sweet child, don't you cry, I'm gonna put you down to lie. Danger is gone, and I'm close by, you are safe and so am I."

As he sang he felt the water slow. Soon shards of glass began dropping to the floor. And so he continued, singing the only verse he knew several more times. Eventually, something in the feel of the cyclone changed— no, it was in the water itself. The anger, the fear, and the insane desire to escape had left it. Jake's soothing calmness had replaced all those. He lowered the water gradually to the floor, nothing more than a large pool surrounding Brooke.

Jake knelt and took his sister up into his arms, then whispered to Sam. "Open the door. We need her far away from any sources of water."

The lab assistant nodded, then hurried to comply.

Brooke awoke several hours later, her hands reaching immediately to her face. Panicked, she scanned her arms for cuts. Puzzled at finding she had none, she placed her hands on her belly to feel the child within. He rested calmly. For the first time in several weeks, she felt no pain in her womb. Whatever had happened, it was over now.

Jake smiled at her from a chair in the corner. "Welcome to the land of the living," he said happily, as if nothing had happened.

"I didn't actually *die*, did I?" Brooke asked, aghast.

"No, but you've been asleep for quite a while. Mi-Jung gave you a sedative so you both would rest."

"My cuts are gone. How?"

"I made Sam give me a bead from Batch Charlie and, well it turns out I can heal people. I'm not medically trained like David, but I know a bit about first aid." He winked. "You shouldn't have any scars."

"I'm not worried about scars, I'm worried about bringing this baby to term." She paused, frowned, then asked, "It was *him*, wasn't it?"

"It was, and I'm sure he'll do it again. Like I told you before, my nephew doesn't like dark, cramped spaces and yearns to be out in the world."

"Well he has to wait a bit longer," she said with a huff. They sat silent for a moment, considering the events.

"He did it again, Brooke. He communicated with me. I don't know how, but I was aware of him the entire time, even after puking up the bead. How did I do that, without any beads in my system?

"So, you hadn't kept it down?"

"No," Jake frowned. "I threw that thing up right away. It made me sicker than the pearl, actually. I've no idea how I communicated with him or..." He paused.

Should I tell her about the water? he wondered, deciding he should.

"I moved the water, Sis. It carried a piece of glass up my leg and into my hand. How the hell did I do *that* after rejecting the bead?"

"I'm shocked you can do this and also work Batch Delta." Brooke marveled. "I wonder how many others can work two crafts..."

"It *does* change things," he agreed. "It also gives merit to what we're doing."

"How many others could work water?"

Jake frowned. "None in my group."

"Well then, we need to try again with the other test groups."

"Mi-Jung and Sam already did. Michael *insisted* they continue the tests, even with you out of commission. I'll check with them in a bit and get a count."

Brooke felt anger rise above her wooziness but quickly pushed it down. "Of course, Michael insisted the experiments continue," she complained. "He's scaring me. Before Stephanie left, she told me some things about him, things we never saw in college."

"Like what?" Jake asked, a look of genuine concern on his face.

"That he's obsessed for one thing, hell-bent on creating Astia no matter the cost. She said he wasn't violent but had a pushiness that ignored boundaries. I think she worried he would lose all moral compass when building his new society."

"I saw a bit of that at Waghäusel," Jake admitted, "when he started to doubt Adam's prophecy. Once that doubt crept in, he lost control and wasn't the same Michael I've always known."

"Jake," Brooke said quietly, "I'm worried."

"You'll be fine. Just keep away from large bodies of water and the little guy will stay settled. Soothe the little fella and sing to him, he likes that a lot, and I found it helps when he's scared."

"I don't mean the pregnancy, but thank you. No, I mean I'm worried about Michael. After what I just went through, I'm terrified. What will my son be able to do when fully grown? Will Michael take him from me and force my child to be a weapon? To show this much power in the womb means whatever he does will be tremendous. Bigger, even, than Adam and Eve."

"That's a big fear and very much valid. I felt his strength." Jake agreed.

"That's not what worries me... I'm afraid to give this power to Michael. I think he'll abuse it and make my son into a weapon."

Jake frowned. "I'll talk to him."

"No. I don't think he'll listen. Just promise if something ever happens to me, that you'll take him away to David. As mad at him as I am, I think he's the only one who can handle this child if I'm not around. The boy will need a father and David will need a son, even if it's Michael's."

"I can't promise that, Sis. Michael's the chancellor *and* my friend. I've sworn loyalty."

"He'll use you too," Brooke snapped. He still didn't understand.

"How? By denying me the beads?" Jake laughed. "Trust me, I can do without this power."

"That's just it, Jake. Your affinity for Batch Charlie is one thing, but Delta is another. I think it's a gift from David?" Brooke felt a rush of emotion when saying her husband's name. *Why couldn't he have just stayed here with me?* But she knew the answer and touched her belly. The baby inside was her biggest mistake and she ruined her marriage for him.

"A gift? I don't understand."

"Damn it, Jake, read between the lines! You have two powers but only held down one bead! David screwed with you, made you an emotant!"

"I..." He still didn't get it.

"You're an emotant, Jake! David gave you the same power over water as my baby, that's why he can communicate with you and how you can move water!"

Jake frowned, putting together the pieces in his mind. "I have to tell Michael."

"No, don't you dare!" Brooke insisted. "At least wait and see what his plan is for my child. Please, Jake. For me."

She watched his eyes struggle with inner conflict, duty for family over his sworn allegiance, and realized she had no way to predict her brother's choice.

PART III
GODS AND MEN

CHAPTER TWENTY-SIX

Curtis had not understated the grueling amount of work he and the captives endured. It was back-breaking and tedious, nonstop on a level of exhausting James Parker had never experienced. In one morning they moved three more trucks into place, finishing the last portion of wall, and framed it in for the catwalk extension.

James sat atop this structure, hammering nails the old fashioned way while his friend handed up boards. He cursed, missing the iron head and striking his thumb.

"Easy, champ. Don't stress those ribs," cautioned Curtis. He watched James hit his thumb a second time and offered, "I can take over if you want."

"No, I like the vantage point here," James replied, wincing. It wasn't a lie, he had a clear view of the entire compound. As he shook feeling back into this hand, he thoroughly scanned his surroundings and the tents outside the walls. So far he counted two hundred, with three men sharing each. *Six hundred men,* he reasoned, knowing more would be camped elsewhere, closer to the river. Inside the compound he also counted Crazy Mike Donelson, his group of twenty, and fifteen Nature Boys officers.

Curtis had also been right about the Nature Boys and his fear of them was real. These fighters were seasoned, *actual,* soldiers. Their uniforms matched their bearing, with insignia, caps, and well-stocked ammo belts. They were ready for war and looked like they could dole it out easily enough.

James eyed the makeshift stables and frowned. They even had horses, about fifty in total, a much bigger cavalry than Pescari's Outriders.

"What do you think our chances are?" Curtis asked.

"Not good at all, and our odds are worse. Are any of your guys veterans?"

"Got a handful. Seth served a bit but only pushed paper around. Frank and Wylie served some time in the pen for gang violence, so that counts, right?"

"It'll do, I guess. Wait, no. I guess it depends on how and why they got caught."

"Wylie was drunk and shot Frank in the leg."

"Nope, doesn't count."

Curtis laughed. "Alice was a combat medic, did some time in Iraq with the Army."

"That'll work."

"Yeah, figured you'd like that."

"Quit your yappin'!" one of the guards called up from below. "It's not your place to talk!"

"Yessir, masta'," Curtis called back down sarcastically, giving James a wink. Then he frowned, chewed on a bit of anger, then added, "Who would have thought that after nearly two hundred years we're back to this? A black man bowing and scraping just to avoid offending his *betters*?" he said with a spat.

"No one here is *anyone's* better," James pointed out, "and I don't think this has to do with skin color."

"No, you're right. They're just assholes with power and greed. Regardless, my great granddaddy must be rollin' over in his grave. After all he worked for, all my daddy earned, and all I've attained, we're back to this."

"Yeah," James agreed, "take away societal rules and the system crumbles fast. What about you, Curtis? What did you do for a living, before all this?"

"I owned my own roofing company. Made a ton of money fixing homes after storms. I had a gorgeous home near Fort Campbell, a boat, and everything I could ever want. I kept a promise I made to my father and made something of myself without taking handouts."

"I said pipe down!" the guard yelled up.

"Let's hurry up and get the hell outta here," Curtis whispered with a smile.

James caught himself smiling too but felt guilty about it. After what felt like a suitable amount of time, he restarted the hushed conversation.

"I think we can do it. There's thirty of us, and we can hit 'em as soon as these visitors leave. I figure they're gonna attack the Regiment soon. Saw them hauling some more boats up the creek."

"We've seen that too. They're staging here, planning an attack on your friends. For their sakes, I hope they *can* fight 'em off," Curtis said with a bit of doubt. "This is a true army they're up against."

James looked down at his chains, locked in place with padlocks. "As soon as the army breaks camp and moves, we'll need to strike fast. What we need first is a way to get these leg bracelets off."

"That's part of the plan. A good swing with a pickaxe would do the trick," Curtis offered, "and we got plenty of those in the mine."

"Well, hopefully we get in there soon." Then James frowned, thinking of Cathy, Josh, and his friends up north.

"You're in luck," Curtis whispered. "We always work the mines after lunch so I'll be showing you around soon. Only, when it comes to breaking chains... I've seen you hammer, so best I handle that part."

The mine wasn't far from Crazy Mike's compound, dug into the side of a ridge just south of the structure. The opening was small, nothing like mines he had seen on television, probably a natural cave Donelson had discovered on his property. It was low to the ground, about four feet high, and only one man could enter at a time.

The guards unchained them one by one from the others, leaving only their leg irons before sending them into the hole. They ordered Curtis in first, followed by James.

Parker crouched onto his hands and knees, breathing shallow against his sore ribs which tightened as his body entered the confined space. As he crawled he felt his previous work of the day, from moving the vehicles into place to building the catwalk and parapet. It had been exhausting, but a slave's day doesn't end when the work is done. There's always another project.

Holding a kerosene lamp with an outstretched arm, James followed Curtis down a steep ramp. As he emerged into a larger chamber, he let out the air he held with a sigh, wondering if this day would be the one in which he dies. The entire cavern had an ominous feel.

"What did I tell you?" Curtis asked? "They got us diggin' a mine!"

"Yeah," James agreed, "and not a very stable one at that." Bits of dirt tumbled from overhead as his eyes scanned the walls and ceiling of the cavern. Curtis had told him earlier that the guards never followed the slaves underground, and it was no wonder. The entire thing could collapse without any notice. He ran his fingers along the dirt walls and pulled them away. Each tip was smeared black. "Definitely coal," he said.

"What good is coal gonna be?"

"Heating, cooking, and making steel," Curtis explained. "Donelson's setting himself up for America 2.0."

Six other men entered the mine dragging railroad ties left over from the parapet. They dropped rather than placed them in a pile, sending more scatterings of dirt to fall like rain.

"I've got no idea what I'm doing here," James admitted.

"We'll start by shoring up these walls so the damned thing doesn't collapse and kill us all," Curtis decided.

Parker looked around, holding the lantern high enough to see the ceiling and walls. Most was rock, but not the good, solid kind. Hammering would be out of the question and could cause the very cave-in they were trying to avoid.

"How?"

"Ain't you never watched a western movie?" Curtis asked with a laugh. Gripping his pickaxe near the head, he slowly trenched out a groove in the ceiling the exact size of a timber. While two men lifted it over their heads and pushed it into place, he and Curtis each grabbed a tie and braced the board on the sides. It wasn't much, but it would hold at least a few feet of the ceiling. It took several hours, but they eventually got enough timbers in place to prop up the main shaft.

James hoped it would be enough, eyeing the ceiling every time a bit of dirt fell. He noticed the others did as well.

Next came the hard work, sinking the first shaft. Like Parker, none of these miners had any idea what they were doing and aimlessly dug into the darkest, softest of the dirt. After several more hours a piece of the wall broke away, sending the crew running beneath the braces for safety.

The wall had actually cleaved instead of crumbled, and James realized what they thought at first was dirt turned out to be thicker and smooth. Holding the lantern close to the wall, James confirmed they had hit a seam. The coal was shiny, with a layered feel like soft sandstone.

Crazy Mike Donelson was about to become a very rich man.

A shout from the entrance warned it was time to go. Nightfall neared, and the guards wanted their dinner. "Hurry up!" one of them shouted. "Leave your tools and come out one at a time."

Curtis signaled one the others to head up the ramp. "They have to chain us together like when we came," he explained. "It's almost dark by now, and they're afraid of us." As he talked he peered through the lantern light as it flickered off the shiny surface of the coal. A plan formed in his head, and a large smile crept from ear to ear at the wealthy pile laying before their feet.

"What're you smilin' at?" James asked.

"Coal burns, doesn't it?"

"Yeah, so?"

"And this seam runs right underneath the compound."

James' eyes grew wide, bulging brightly in the kerosene light. Eventually the same plan formed in his own head.

"We're not getting out of here, after all," Curtis said with a wink. "We're gonna kill Crazy Mike and his men, then take all this for ourselves!"

CHAPTER TWENTY-SEVEN

"I hate ships," Shayde muttered, angling his shotgun around the bulkhead and peering into the confined space. It was their final check, a bilge room off the starboard shaft. Thankfully it, like all the spaces before, was free of hostiles. Only a few empty MRE casings had been any indication the Nature Boys had hid out here. "Clear," he added, giving a nod to Max standing just behind him.

"Let's get topside then," the general suggested, as eager as his partner to see daylight. Without power, the ship felt more of a tomb than a vessel.

"Gladly," Shayde muttered.

Clearing LST-325 had been a grueling process, moving through the ship from fore to aft and then topside down, methodically checking every space within. Two security teams had moved downward, one level at a time, securing each while another team ensured no one else entered from above. In all, the sweep took more than two hours and only proved the Nature Boys had hid out there while waiting until the Regiment let their guard down. As Max feared, they had already moved out into the city.

Max dreaded the rest of his day and the massive job of clearing every building within his picket lines. But in truth, he was also thankful for the ability to get out of the Shelter. It had been weeks since he went on patrol, mostly at Shayde's insistence that keeping their leader alive outweighed his need to avoid boredom. But there was no stopping him this time. Every spare hand was needed, especially those with experience breaching and securing the urban buildings.

Inside, he still worried. God knew how many snipers and fireteams lurked in the dark shadows of the abandoned structures, and it would take all day and night to flush out the enemy.

Once topside, he and Shayde rejoined the rest of their squad made up of three fireteams and thirteen fighters in all. Max, as the battalion commander, guided Shayde as the squad leader and decision maker of the first fireteam. That included Clint, Benjamin Roark, and Chad Pescari. Thankful for the experienced group as his escort, the general let out a held breath.

As he led them across the brow to the pier, however, he eyed the city's buildings with new worry. The snipers could be anywhere.

"Once this is done," he told Shayde, "we *have* to knock down some of those buildings."

"And do what with the rubble?" the sergeant asked.

"Build a tall wall around downtown."

The other men nodded along but said nothing. This was a time to remained focused and alert, with a head on a swivel as the old drill instructors used to say. Max could almost hear their ghostly voices critiquing every move as the squads fanned out. They would sweep east to west in four squads, each moving building to building down First Street, Second Street, Ohio, and West John.

In position to move in, Rankin gave Shayde the signal and the sergeant breached the first door. It was going to be a long, dangerous day.

Max had underestimated the toll this day had taken on him and his squads. Clearing the city had been worse than grueling, it had worn their patience and worsened their moods as well as worked to exhaust their bodies. With the sun beginning to set outside, he leaned against the wall, catching his breath and looking down at the dead bodies on the floor. Shayde's flashbang still rang in his ears, along with the ghostly tat-a-tat-tat from Roark's automatic fire.

The room they cleared was on the second floor atop the YMCA, where they found a sniper and her spotter. The gunman was a pretty girl wearing pigtails, but her corpse wore the same combat uniform of every member of the Nature Boys. The crimson trails on the breast of her navy blue uniform matched her red hair.

Shayde stepped up beside Max, angling his body so the others in the squad wouldn't see his hand motions. With eyes locked on Clint he signaled *danger*, then shot Max a worried look that seemed to say, *we need to talk.*

The kills had been clean, but there were more buildings to clear. Max only shrugged and pointed at his watch as if to say, *now isn't the time.*

He glanced out the wide window facing the old gymnasium. It was a red brick building with no windows across the top. There, another fireteam breached the main door and entered. Max sent them a silent prayer for safety. This clearing of buildings was taking too long and the sun dipped way down. It was already dusk, and their job was becoming increasingly dangerous.

But Shayde insisted they communicate, shoving a sharp elbow in his upper arm. His hands flashed again, signaling *danger* once more. His thumb quickly pointed at Clint.

Max was about to respond when, off in the south, a trail of smoke arched across the sky. "Shayde," he said, pointing toward it. He knew what it meant, but disbelief demanded confirmation from the former artillery Marine.

"Mortars," the sergeant said, "but nothing too large, by the looks of it." His hands flashed *danger* three more times in rapid succession.

Max sighed. "Clint, you, Chad, and Ben go wait by the front entrance. Shayde and I need to talk privately."

All three moved from the room.

Off in the distance, probably near the retail yard, an explosion rang out. Two more trails could be seen in the air, both closer to the center of downtown.

The general knew he was running out of time. The sun was nearly down and the enemy had artillery. Now that shelling had started, the real fight would soon follow. He and every squad would be needed on the defensive walls. He glanced out the window once more, again wishing he could do something to level the buildings surrounding the Shelter.

"What is it that can't wait?" Max asked with irritation, desperate to get a move on.

"Something's different about Clint," Shayde explained, "and I don't trust him anymore. He's changed."

"How so? I think he's doing great, following orders without saying a word against." He leaned forward for a better view of the river. The glass against his cheek felt cold, but it was still warmer than the fear pulsing his veins. If the enemy had mortars they would also be better armed than expected.

"Yeah, that's the problem. Normally he would have cracked a joke about that sniper being a chick, or something more vulgar about poking holes in her. He hasn't said more than *yes sir, yes sarge,* or *on it,* since we started clearing. Usually he gets more obnoxious as we go on, but he's been locked in all day."

"Everyone has an off day," Max argued. "I'm sure he's fine."

"Something's different, that's all. It's like as if he's suddenly a different person altogether."

Several more explosions rocked the city, and Max felt the glass rattle against his ear. "We can't finish this job," he said leaning back, "not with shelling. I can't see their approach from here and need to check on the main line to see how it's holding up. Someone also needs to get to the Shelter to warn them of a pending invasion."

"Max, you need to listen to me about Clint. He's acting strangely."

"Clint won't matter once we're overrun. We can barely man the primary defenses as it is. They won't last long and we need to form a second perimeter."

A voice at the door made both men raise their rifles. "I'm fine, Walters, whatever you're thinking is wrong," Clint said casually.

"I told you to man the entrance with the others," Max said with authority, "and this conversation doesn't concern you."

"No, but I heard enough to know it's *about* me. Look, trust me or not, we have to defend against this attack," Clint argued. "The enemy has artillery and knows how to use it. From what we just saw at the door, they're hitting our best defended points along the barrier."

"Give me your rifle, soldier," Shayde ordered abruptly, reaching out his hand.

"Please. Wait," Clint begged. Something in the man's voice, his confidence maybe, had earned Max's attention. "I have an idea."

Stepping between the two men, Rankin asked, "What's your idea, Clint?"

"We can barely hold the picket line with the main force. Their artillery will soften that, killing way too many of our defenders. Also, we don't have a secondary line established and no way of stopping the flood once they breach the barrier. But there's still time to establish one."

"Go on," Max commanded. So far the man was right.

"First, we have to move as much debris as we can around the Shelter. Cars, dumpsters, and the like. Then, we should open the armory up to anyone and everyone who can fire a gun. We've already cleared those buildings right around it, so we can move our best shooters atop the taller buildings like the church and courthouse."

Shayde disagreed. "Max, you're not thinking of arming the civilians, are you?"

Max shrugged. The idea made sense when facing overwhelming odds. "I don't see any other option, do you?"

"You're just going to get them all killed," the sergeant warned.

But Max's mind was made up. "He's right. We're talking about the difference of defending thirty city blocks or three. Roark!" he shouted down the hall. The man came running right away, as if he too had been listening nearby. "You and Clint return to the Shelter. Arm every civilian there. Get them started forming secondary pickets from Vine to Ingle. Also, put sharpshooters on the church and town hall."

Shayde wasn't convinced. "This is wrong, Max..."

"It's our only option." Leaning into the hallway he shouted to Pescari, asking, "Chad, what are the chances your Outriders could get out of the city?"

"They're easily mobilized. I could have them riding out within twenty minutes."

"You might not have that much time. Scramble out the north, then circle wide of the attackers. Flank but don't engage. They're most likely hitting us head on, so see if you can get behind them and destroy or capture their artillery once they push in."

The man nodded and hurried away with the others.

Max turned to Shayde. "Now let's go check the main picket. I need to see what the enemy's doing."

"You shouldn't have sent Clint. I tried to tell you I don't trust him!" Walters said one more time. "There's something off, and I don't like his idea at all!"

"Good thing I'm in charge then!" Max snapped.

Inside he knew Shayde was right to worry about the plan, that arming civilians was a gamble. But Clint was right too. With artillery, the odds of the Nature Boys breaking that first line doubled or tripled. "Once our barricade falls, tactics will no longer matter. This battle is now about freedom, and the Shelter's our last stand to hold it."

Shayde frowned at his friend and commander. "Clint's not himself and I'm worried, Max. What if he's working for someone else's interest? We don't know much at all about him, only what Cathy warned—that he's a murdering psychopath. What if he only wants to burn it all down? What if his plan is to set up innocent noncombatants to die while he slips off into the shadows to spread chaos elsewhere?"

Rankin placed a hand on his friend's shoulder. "Right now his plan is all we have. Now let's go see how bad things really are."

CHAPTER TWENTY-EIGHT

Jake Braston pushed open the laboratory door, heavy with dread facing the final experiment. He found the other side as quiet as a tomb. The rows of chairs sat empty in the lab, new safety precautions to ensure no one burned the entire place down. With a bit of sadness, he stole a glance at the empty seat where Airman McLemore usually sat. There would be no witty jokes about the experiment and no blushing laughter from the girl.

What a shame, he thought, missing his young comrade and her jests. *That part was the only fun.*

Brooke, Sam, and Mi-Jung waited inside, standing beside a single chair set before a table holding two candles. One was lit, the other was not. The smell of recent smoke lingered on the air, and the general scanned the walls, spotting three chairs pushed out of the way, each with charred leather where the straps had once been securely fastened. He raised an eyebrow toward Brooke.

She shrugged. "Only three positives so far, and you're the last subject."

"Wow," he replied. "About the same results as Batch Delta."

"Yes, and Michael's angry about it," she added, exchanging a knowing glance with Mi-Jung. The two obviously shared some thoughts regarding the chancellor. She continued, explaining, "It's evident David intentionally limited those batches, keeping the most dangerous powers out of Michael's hands."

"I noticed he's not around today. Did he get tired of watching?"

"He had too many affairs of state that couldn't wait while we performed one test at a time. So, yeah, he's in his office."

Jake took his seat, letting Sam strap him in one final time. "These experiments remind me of that time when we were kids and you tried to cook dinner so Mom wouldn't have to."

"How's that?" Brooke asked.

"I really hope I puke them up."

Ignoring her brother's joke, his sister strapped him in. This close he realized her face had grown noticeably gaunter than he last realized. Worse than exhausted, his sister ran on fumes.

Mi-Jung hurriedly placed a trash can in Jake's lap. "Just in case," she said with a wink followed by a smile toward her boss.

Jake smiled too. At least *someone* still had a sense of humor.

Brooke approached, stoically pushed a red bead into his mouth then stepped back, watching with eyes locked onto her brother's. They didn't have to wait long, and ten seconds later he filled the trashcan.

"Well, that's that," he said with a grin, a trail of vomit running down his chin.

"Not really, now we have to take this data to Michael." Brooke said, freeing his arms and handing him a towel. The weariness on her face betrayed deep reluctance as she traded another glance with Mi-Jung.

Michael looked up from his papers as soon as the door pushed open. Very few people were still bold enough to enter his office without knocking, and he wasn't surprised when he saw Jake and Brooke walk in. They were the last of his friends, really. His closest allies in this foreign land. He greeted them with a smile but did not stand. He *was* the chancellor, after all.

"How'd it go?" he asked.

"The final tally is twenty-five Sensitives. Four can work the black bead, fifteen the white, three the blue, and three the red," Brooke reported, avoiding eye contact as she spoke. She must have realized he would be unhappy with the results, and he was.

Trying not to betray his seething anger, he calmly admitted, "That's way lower than I had hoped." He locked eyes with Jake who wore a somber expression, reflecting the mood of the experiment. "At least it's not a total failure. How many are Conductors, those who can use the power to fight?"

"Not many at all," Jake said with disappointment, "but the Oracles will also prove vital. Don't forget, gathering intelligence is just as, or more important even, than fighting."

"Bullshit!" Michael yelled, bringing his fist down hard and surprising even himself. He hadn't meant to be so angry, but the stress of the chancellorship weighed heavy. Taking a breath to calm his voice, he continued. "I expected more... I *needed* more, Jake. We've got a war to win and, after we secure Europe and Asia, we're going after Andalon."

"What's David got to do with this?" Brooke demanded. "Can't you just leave him and the children alone?"

Michael watched the doctor carefully. She hid so much from him now. Having been friends for so long he thought he should be able to read her better, but those angry eyes held secrets. Betrayal, maybe? *I expected her to become a liability after my son's birth, but it seems she may have become so sooner*, he realized.

"Keep your promise to them," she urged.

Esterling noticed she held her stomach while talking. Hopefully he would not have to wait long for the delivery. "I didn't mean David," he said quietly.

"Then what, Michael?" She pushed. "What do you mean by *going after Andalon?*"

"I'm renaming the continents as we take them over, it's part of my Great Reset."

"Great Reset? Is that what you're calling it now? This new world? What happened to *Astia?*" Jake asked, his face matching his sisters. "Isn't Astia enough?"

Michael frowned. Braston, too, could become a liability. *The army is fiercely loyal to him so he poses the greatest threat to my reign.* Half the fighting men and women would throw themselves on a grenade for their favorite general, when they *should* be doing so for their chancellor.

With a sigh he explained. "The Great Reset is exactly what it sounds like, and Astia is only a part of the bigger change. In it, North America will be called Andalon, because that's where we'll farm David's emotants."

"Farm?" Brooke's eyes narrowed, turning toward Jake and watching for his reaction. The fact he looked away betrayed his knowledge of Michael's plan.

"Yes, *farm*. We'll need more of those beads once we get the Oracles up and running, and the lab drones won't keep up with demand. I've designed four missions, one for each sensitivity and element the Oracles represents. Wind, fire, earth, and water will be represented by the seasons: Spring, Summer, Autumn, and Winter. You're right, Jake, that intelligence is important, and I plan to make use of it. But, it doesn't come close to the ability to conduct the elements. Out of those I will find the Conductors for my army."

Jake nodded, his military mind making the connection. "You'll make these Oracles into training grounds, to develop more fighters?"

Michael smiled, ready to reveal his surprise. "No. They'll be *hatcheries*. Sergeant Mason was the key to unlocking the real fighters, Jake."

The door behind them opened, and the sergeant stood in the hallway, staring straight ahead with two lifeless orbs where there were once eyes.

"How?" Jake asked. "I raised her up and control her. Why didn't I know she had left her cell?"

"David did something to me, too, when he raised Ivan Petrov, though I don't think he meant to." the chancellor explained. This was his real secret, the part of the Great Reset he had never revealed to anyone, even these closest of friends. "I may lack sensitivities, but he accidently gave something to me far stronger when he shared my control over the general. He unknowingly altered my mind when gifting the ability, and I figured out how to take majority control over my collective."

"Collective?"

Two more figures stepped into the doorway, the other two sergeants who aided Jake in raising Mason. Both Baxter and Price wore blank expressions like their comrade.

"Yes, *my* collective. With Mason's help, I have full control over all three now, in addition to Petrov. With them, I will expand Astia's influence over every continent."

"You murdered these people and raised them up?" Brooke was appalled.

Next to her, Jake's look of shock matched hers. "Why did you kill my soldiers, Michael?" he demanded.

"You mean *my* soldiers!" Michael shouted angrily. "I most certainly did *not* kill anyone. I simply did further testing, gave them a few more of those beads to test their capabilities. The fact they died in Ka'ash'mael was a beneficial bonus which granted many more opportunities than I had when they were alive."

"Just these other two, or more?" Jake demanded, his anger now matching his sisters.

Tsk-tsk, Michael thought. *Too bad they don't understand. They have* both *become liabilities, it seems.*

"What did you do, Michael?" Brooke's angry voice broke as she spoke, interrupted by a labor contraction. She doubled over as soon as she asked the question.

The chancellor shrugged. "Only some experiments of my own. I tested a select few from each batch of Sensitives, all except this latest round. In doing so, I discovered quite a bit about the process. It turns out the Ka'ash'mael can be deadly but does something to the host of the prophecy. It unlocks a greater potential for conductivity of the craft—after death, of course."

Another figure joined the others in the doorway.

"Ah, Airman McLemore!" Michael greeted her blank expression with a wide grin. "She was one of the first I tested, and the first to die after Ka'ash'mael. The most powerful Oracle yet produced! I used Mason, Baxter, and Price to raise her." He had to do the same to them, of course, once they gained knowledge of his private experiments. Thankfully they produced several more Ka'ash'mael visions before their bodies finally wore out and died. These visions he would keep to himself.

"You killed her?" Jake appeared so angry he may rage.

"No, she died naturally, and now she's part of *my* collective." And it really was his alone. These and others, like Ivan Petrov, belonged fully to Michael now, their bond with Jake completely severed.

The chancellor watched his friend and waited for the anger to pour out. That part of Jake had always been kept locked down, a secret the man kept hidden by his jovial demeanor. But Michael had seen it plenty of times in college, the ability of the man to berserk and explode with blind fury when pushed to anger. When he raged he did so dangerously.

The general stepped forward, clenching a fist and raising it in front of Michael. The chancellor merely watched the show with unfeigned amusement. He had just said *no* to Jake Braston. Abruptly, wisps of air coalesced around the general's arm, pulling and spinning him to face McLemore. Jake's eyes grew wide as he realized what was happening, and more wisps tied his arms to his sides before spinning him round and round like a spider weaving a cocoon around its victim.

"Relax, Jake," Chancellor Esterling said with authority. "Your anger won't serve you here, not when aimed at me. You're lucky we're like brothers, or I'd have taken a star for that, or worse."

"Let him go," Brooke demanded, doubling over once more. Her contractions had worsened, and a puddle of water formed at her feet. She *had* begun labor, it seemed. This softened the mood of the room, changing it from anger to concern.

Michael nodded to McLemore, and the wisps of air dissipated rapidly allowing Jake to run to his sister's side.

"I'll get you to sick bay," he told her. To the others in the room, he barked, "Call the medical team to meet us there."

"Mi-Jung," Brooke corrected, gasping hard between contractions and words. "Call only for Mi-Jung! She's my midwife, and I *need* her there!"

Michael smiled as Jake rushed her from the room. His son was about to be born, but not to a midwife. He had already instructed his own doctor what to do.

CHAPTER TWENTY-NINE

James Parker spent most of his day indoors, chained to a long table with nine other captives. There were several tables in the room Crazy Mike called the *factory* which was nothing more than a pole barn. James cringed at the thought of how much residual radiation emanated from those metal walls, slowly killing every person in the room. That thought chilled him worse than the freezing temperatures inside. With only his parka to warm him—a military surplus special that reeked of mothballs—James could barely feel his own fingers.

They currently fumbled with brass casings fresh out of the tumbler. His job at the table was to reach down, pull the casings out of the bin, and inspect them for defects. Finding none he would pass them to his left for one of his fellow prisoners to load with a primer. They, in turn, would pass them to someone with a scale and bucket of black powder. The next person in line would align the lead bullet and crimp it to perfection. James had never done any of this before, and that's why he was only the brass checker. The bad casings he tossed in another barrel for another team to trim and size.

He eyed Curtis across the room, sitting at another table. Having been in the compound the longest, the man worked deft fingers that ignored the cold while measuring out black powder. While James reloaded .223, his friend had some sort of pistol caliber on his table, frowning over each measurement as if perfection meant his life. James watched the shrewd appraisal by one of Donelson's men. Only then did he realize his friend's life really did rely on perfection.

"Less powder," the soldier overseer snapped.

"That's not what you want here!" Curtis argued without raising his eyes. "We're using a heavier bullet, so it's already slower."

"Boss said he wanted these perfect!"

"And I'm *making* them perfect!" the prisoner argued without raising his voice. "I know what I'm doing, and you just have to trust me to do it..."

James cringed as a rifle butt crashed into Curtis' jaw. The force of the blow spun his head, spattering blood on the person to his right.

"Less yapping and more measuring! Pour exactly how much I said!"

Curtis lifted his head, a bruise already forming above the split lip. Through bloody lips he agreed, "Yes, boss. I'm sorry." After that he kept his eyes glued to the scale, but he and James shared a brief glance—momentary eye contact that seemed to scream, *soon we kill these bastards!*

The prisoners loaded ammo all day, and the only positive James could think about the grueling ordeal was, that despite that radiation filled room, it was indoors and not out in the snow. The breakout would happen soon, and he and Curtis needed their backs rested for their plan. A few hours later, the mining team was selected from the others and one by one attached to the longer chain.

Led from the factory, there was no time for talking, only walking with head down against the crisp afternoon. The compound was quiet, with no activity except the work party making its way toward the main gates.

"Where is everyone?" James took a chance and asked one of the guards.

"Shut up," was the response. The man appeared more than irritated by drawing the late afternoon duty and spat before shaking a cigarette loose from a pack.

James, though not a smoker, eyed the man's wealth and how easily he burned it away. In another age that pack of rolled paper and crushed leaves would have only been worth a few dollars in a gas station, a symbol of cheap thrills and addiction in a box of twenty. To smoke one now bragged of abundant wealth and this man's disregard for scarcity.

An idea struck James. "Can I get one of those?" He watched the man hurriedly slip it into his pocket. *He's left handed,* Parker observed as the guard ignored his request. Quick eye contact with Curtis urged him to go on. "Seriously man," he tried again, "how much for a smoke?"

The guard turned slowly, saying nothing. After a moment of dangerous silence, blew a steady stream of smoke into James' face.

Grimacing against the foul stench, James stood defiantly and regained his composure. "Thanks, but I'd rather get it first hand?" he remarked with a smile, then reached with his left hand for the cigarette.

As he had hoped, the guard took advantage of the opening and brought up his own left hook, crashing hard against the side of James' head. Collapsing in a heap against the man's chest, he hugged him tightly, burrowing his face to avoid blows.

"I'm sorry!" James cried. "It was a joke, I'm sorry!"

But by now two other guards had joined the first and peeled James Parker off their friend. After tossing him to the ground they kicked and stomped while he curled into a ball.

"Not too much!" Curtis begged with a shout. "We need him in the mine!"

After three or four more kicks, the guards relented. "Help him up," one commanded Curtis, "and let's get going."

James waited till they were all facing forward and had fully exited the compound before opening his hand behind him, carefully showing his friend the cigarette lighter he had stolen. With a glance backward, he winked a bloodied and half-closed eye to Curtis.

They were getting out that very night.

Tom moved as swiftly as he could, slowed only by his mother's weakness. Her leg muscles, malnourished and frail from atrophy, could barely hold her upright yet somehow managed. He knew it was dogged determination that pushed her onward, with skinny arms clutching an overnight bag. Inside that she owned only a change of clothes and some MREs. Atop those she had packed her husband's gun. She had nothing else in the world and carried only that bag and disappointment in her son.

Tom stole another glance, making the mistake of meeting her angry eyes with his own, watching as she slipped in the frozen ash. She careened but found balance by grabbing ahold of a roof carrier atop the remnants of a vehicle. There were several atop the bridge, mostly buried and useless, hulking reminders of an extinct world. He moved to help, but she refused with eyes filled with heartbreak and anger toward her son.

Why should *she trust me now after my deception?* he wondered. *I swore her husband, my* father, *was dead. I kept her locked in a prison of cruel ignorance.* Tom wondered if she ever *could* trust him again. *Would I even deserve it, if she did?* Turning shamefully away from her drilling stare, he led her onward toward the other side and, hopefully, the Shelter.

The pair slowed as they approached the end of the bridge. *This was where I met Shayde and Clint two nights ago,* he remembered. Then he stopped and pulled a white cloth from his pocket, giving it a wave toward the machine gun turrets. Once he was certain they had seen him, he placed an arm around his mother. Hopefully his father's men would see them for what they were, refugees fleeing the wrong side.

Tom held his breath.

A soldier, one he had never met, stood and gave an exhausted and weary wave of his own, reluctantly indicating they could advance.

Tom released his breath slowly, letting it pass through his lips. He felt some relief, but not completely. This stressful evening was all but over. Mother and son had missed role call and Miko may have patrols looking for them. *But will he?* he wondered. *Are we that important?* Perhaps not but, as the wife and son of his enemy, maybe so.

The Regiment soldier greeted the pair curtly, as if wishing they had arrived on someone else's watch. "I'm sorry," he said, "we can't let anyone into the city tonight. It's on full lockdown. No refugees allowed."

"But we're more than that," Tom explained. "I'm Tom Rankin and this is my mother, Betty. We're Sergeant Max Rankin's wife and son."

"You mean *General* Rankin?" the soldier laughed. "Now I *know* you're lying! Everyone in the Shelter knows his wife's dead."

"Isn't his son the graffiti artist spray painting *sellout* all over the city?" one of the machine gunners asked with a laugh of his own.

"I swear," Tom protested, "I'm his son, this is his wife, and we're defecting."

"Look, kid, I can't check your driver's license and, even if I could, it wouldn't matter. No one gets in per orders of the General. You'll have to come back tomorrow if the Nature Boys haven't stormed across the river by then."

Tom was about to step forward to protest when his mother spoke.

"Sir, I understand you have orders, but we aren't a threat. Search us, take my son's weapons if you must, and send us through unarmed. I promise we're no danger. I haven't seen my husband since the night of the bombs and just want to see him."

"Orders are orders, ma'am," the soldier said again. "If you come back tomorrow, I'm sure the lockdown will be..." Whatever else the man was about to say was cut off by the sound of a single gunshot.

Tom's head turned as if on a swivel, his eyes scanning the bridge they had just crossed. There, about four hundred yards away, he spotted several figures kneeling behind the same SUV his mother had stumbled and grabbed onto. Desperate to be out of their line of fire, he turned to face the guard blocking their way. A tiny trail of blood now dripped down his forehead, slowly crawling from a small circle.

As the man's legs buckled, but before he slumped into the ashy snow, machine guns opened fire on the bridge.

"This way!" Tom grabbed his mother's arm, pulling her toward a grove of trees just east of their position.

Her feet refused to move, locked in place by eyes staring upward. Tom followed them, only just noticing a shrill whistling of a firecracker racing across the sky, its smoky trail descending toward them. *No,* he realized, *not a firecracker... artillery!* "Move!" he shouted and this time she obeyed, finding strength to run with her son for cover. Just as they dove, the gun turret exploded.

As the pair cowered in the trees, Tom's eyes focused on the sky and spied several more trails of smoke making their descent upon the city. Someone in the south, he assumed the Nature Boys, had begun their attack. Nearby, the machine gun turret was gone, blown apart along with the men who stood between them and the bridge. Several dark figures raced as fast as they could toward the east side, heading straight for mother and son.

Desperate to get away and indoors, Tom scrambled to his feet and pulled Betty to hers. "Hurry," he urged, half dragging her out of the trees.

Together they sprinted past Gateway Plaza toward Seventh Avenue. To the south several more explosions rang out, no doubt the retail yard and the Regiment's defenses there. The Nature Boys' invasion across the river was imminent.

Maybe Miko won't follow, he wished inside his head, but shouts from behind revealed Miko had every intention of hunting them down. Tom heard the gang leader cry out his name, and a furtive glance over his shoulder revealed a dozen or so men, all his friends until this evening, were in hot pursuit. After that he made another wish, that the deep snow wasn't slowing them down as much as it was.

He looked at his mother, now muttering madly under her breath. *No, not madness,* he realized. Betty Rankin was praying as she fled. *Wasted breath,* Tom knew, because no god existed to listen.

They *had* to make it to the Shelter. Only his father could save them.

As shells whizzed overhead and snow crunched beneath feet, Max sprinted southward toward the defensive line. He prayed to God it held. A strange thought abruptly occurred to him. *Since when do I pray?* Betty had always been the spiritual leader of their home, a steadfast rock of faith the size of a mustard seed, the constant reminder to his conscience there was a higher power. *No, not a mustard seed, her faith was much bigger.* He pushed the thought aside as he and Shayde approached the picket along the water's edge.

The former Marines skidded to a halt, each pulling out a set of binoculars. The general marveled at the enemy numbers across the river, crossing with determined speed.

"There's too many of them, Max. They outnumber us three or four to one."

"How big is a mustard seed, Shayde?"

"What?"

"A mustard seed. How big is one?"

"I don't friggin know! Maybe one or two millimeters, why?"

Betty had the faith of a million, *maybe?*

"Seriously, why that question now?"

Max shrugged. "No reason. Just doing some math." He chuckled at the thought of a million mustard seeds filling a Smart car.

He trained his binoculars on his defensive line. His men were spread out all along the makeshift wall, holding the perimeter with more hope than ammunition. Three explosions in rapid succession rocked the center of it, sending men and their cries flying in all directions. The blast cleared a gap large enough for ten men to run through abreast. "That proves it, then," he admitted. "Clint was right. Until we knew they had artillery, this wall was a good idea. Now it's suicide. They'll pick as much of it apart as they want, dwindling our numbers as they do."

"I hate to admit it, but yeah, he was right," Shayde agreed. "What do you want to do?"

"The hardest campaign to win is the urban scenario." Max said, looking around. Suddenly, the tall buildings looming overhead were a godsend, and he sent Betty's god a quick prayer of thanks. "We fall back, not to the Shelter but into the city."

Shayde paused, soaking in his meaning. "That's a great plan, actually," the sergeant agreed.

"Then let's split up. I'll inform the troops downriver and you go up. Tell them a tactical retreat is in order, incremental until we meet at the Shelter. I'll need you there during the final assault."

Shayde nodded, fighting a big grin trying to creep up his cheeks. Max knew exactly what his friend was thinking. *Why hadn't they thought of this plan before?*

CHAPTER THIRTY

Jake waited for Mi-Jung to open the door. So far, Brooke had insisted only she attend, and the medical team waited in the hallway with the general. Everyone shifted their weight back and forth nervously, waiting as the clocked ticked away time. Even the general worried.

The door abruptly opened and Mi-Jung stepped out, her face stern with a different kind of worry, one that Jake had never seen the girl wear.

"Come with me," she said, commanding the general without any of the timidity or subservience she had always shown her superiors.

He nodded and complied, following her from the waiting room and toward the Eden Labs.

"Is she okay?" he asked.

"She will be."

"And the baby?"

"Is coming..."

That was all she said as they made their way into the primary research hub, the object of David's full attention during his entire stay in the bunker. This was one room Jake had not stepped into since his friend's abrupt departure, and stepping inside now felt odd. He half-expected to find him basking in the holographic glow of the computer and analyzing a DNA strand.

Mi-Jung activated the computer and stepped inside, loading a sample. Jake watched inquisitively and waited, trying to figure out what was so important instead of tending to Brooke. Whatever it was, both women had thought it vital, and intended for him to watch. Two DNA strands suddenly appeared in the hologram between them, and Jake realized at once they were very similar, almost matches.

"Who's is that?" he asked, pointing to one.

"Michael's," she replied, scrutinizing each for comparison.

"And the other?"

"His son," Mi-Jung explained, bringing up a third. It was identical to the second.

"And that one?"

"His other son."

Jake pondered for a moment, then his eyes grew wide. "Dr. Yurik lied to him? When she said it was Roark's?"

Mi-Jung nodded and a fourth sample appeared next to the others, a perfect match for Michael's. Jake gasped when he recognized two matched pairs. "What's the difference? It's only slight."

The lab assistant did not answer. She moved to open a panel on the wall and pushed a button to raise it, revealing the experimental fetuses floating in the tank. Kept in stasis, these waited to become hosts for mass production of the beads.

Michael's farm, Jake realized, swallowing down a bit of anger. He hadn't seen the signs, ignored the warnings and protests of Stephanie Yurik, David and, most recently, Brooke. His best friend since college had left the rails, riding on a crazy train fueled by ambitious power. *I have to stop him,* he thought, *lead a coup d'état, if necessary. He's no longer listening to reason.*

"What are we doing with those?" he asked the lab assistant. They could destroy them here, right now, ending Michael's army of Conductors and Oracles before it gained him true power. Part of him yearned to do so.

"We're doing nothing with these because there's no time. Saving Brooke's baby is more important," Mi-Jung said, punching in a coded sequence then shutting the panel. Another door opened, this one leading to the Eden Labs. "Come on," she urged, "I'll explain once you've seen Brooke's plan, not before." She led him out across the gallery, the raised platform over four identical *Gardens of Eden* separated by thick walls. This was where Adam and Eve had lived and were raised.

They descended a spiral staircase that led to a circular vestibule with four doors. Mi-Jung led him through a different door than that which once locked away the twins and guided him into a mirror image of their garden. Once the door shut behind them, the lab assistant began to explain.

"This is where we've been keeping the drones, those producing the beads for the experiment." She waved her hand, indicating several rows of neonatal bassinets. Each contained a sleeping infant, locked forever in a dream world and producing serum harnessed by spiraling tubes and catheters.

David pointed at a camera overhead and then to his ear.

Mi-Jung shook her head. The camera did not matter. "Disabled and showing security footage from an hour ago, just like the lab we were just in. Brooke set that up a few weeks ago when she realized what Michael was really planning. From what she just told me, he confirmed all her suspicions to the two of you. We can speak freely now. Assume I know everything because I do. Brooke clued me in on day one, when she found out about her pregnancy."

Jake couldn't believe his ears. "She suspected what Michael was doing even then?"

The young woman nodded. "She did and feared he would kill Adam and Eve, eventually. Stephanie Yurik had the same concern, so they set all this up. I was caught up after Stephanie left Europe."

"Is this why she refused to go with David to North America?"

Mi-Jung nodded. "She wanted to, and it broke her own heart to turn him down, but she had to be certain about Michael's plans for these children."

"She knew, even then, he would reanimate those who perish in Ka'ash'mael?"

"It was one of Adam's prophecies, actually. He divulged it only to Dr. Yurik before she left. That was why she went with David so easily."

"I had wondered about that. So, Stephanie's child?"

"*Is* Michael's, not Sergeant Roark's."

"And Brooke's?"

"Also Michael's, but we're about to change that," she said with a grin.

Jake followed her to a small orchard, then through a row of dense honeysuckle. It parted easily, as if a secret door had been intentionally placed in that spot. On the other side he found a small tank holding about ten gallons of artificial amniotic fluid. Inside a slightly premature fetus kicked and wriggled while sucking its thumb.

"Not a drone?" he asked.

"Nope," Mi-Jung answered with a grin. "It's fully sentient and human, a perfect copy of Michael's child, only without emotancy. Brooke stripped that from its DNA when she cloned it."

"That's what you were checking just now in the lab? This is the fourth strand that matches his own?"

"Yes, last minute verification ensured we had a near perfect match, distinguishable only by lack of emotancy."

"And we do, so what do we do with it?"

"Birth this one, then switch the babies out," she replied with a grin, as if it were normal—just another day in the Andalon Project.

Brooke breathed through her contractions, hoping she could hold off labor till Mi-Jung returned. The small dose of terbutaline was wearing off by now, and the girl needed to hurry.

"You're doing fine," the medical doctor said. "Just relax and don't fight the contractions." He readied a spinal catheter as he talked.

"No," Brooke told him.

"No, what?" he asked matter of fact.

"No epidural. I won't have pain medication."

"It was ordered, so you will" he replied.

"Ordered by whom?"

"Chancellor Esterling demanded you be sedated. He insisted this delivery be made easier on both mother and child."

"Well," Brooke said through clenched teeth, "I'm the mother and I insist there won't be any pain meds!" She flinched as an attendant stuck a needle in her IV, quickly injecting something, an opioid maybe, or fentanyl. The effects were almost instant, dizzying and clouding her mind. "No, I said!" She tried to get up, but two more attendants sat her upright, turning her feet to the side and holding her firmly so the doctor could perform the spinal tap. He didn't bother to numb the area first, and she cried out with intense pain that kicked off another angry set of contractions.

"Brooke's in trouble," Jake suddenly said to Mi-Jung, his link to his nephew sending up alarms. He swayed as if something had entered his bloodstream, a brief but powerful wooziness that blurred all senses. "They're injecting her with pain meds, lots of them," he explained.

The lab assistant's face dropped, overcome with concern. "That was part of the prophecy! We have to hurry!" She finished drying the child and placed it into the secret compartment of the bassinet. After lowering the lid, it appeared empty, a comfy spot to place the other child once born. She pushed it across the lab, hurrying to a waiting dumbwaiter in the wall. Originally designed to send food down to the subjects and to retrieve their waste, it usually had a sensor to detect lifeforms trying to escape. Apparently that had also been disabled by Brooke. Mi-Jung closed and sent it upward.

"This way," she urged, and led Jake back the way they had entered the gardens. Once they were back in the lab, she opened the dumbwaiter and retrieved the bassinet pushing it ahead of her.

Jake opened and held the door to the hallway, and the pair nearly ran to the medical bay. He opened the final door with more shoulder than necessary and swung it open wide for effect. Every eye in the room looked up with shock, just as the doctor was standing over a drowsy Brooke with a bloody scalpel.

"What were you going to do with that?" Jake demanded.

"General Braston, you can't be in here," one of the medical staff warned.

"Get out!" Jake roared, sending shockwaves of fear into everyone. Even Mi-Jung flinched beside him as he strode forward and grabbed the largest male, flinging him from the room and into the waiting area.

"Call security," the doctor hollered to the remaining attendant, who nodded vigorously and sprinted away.

Jake reared on the man, demanding, "I asked what you're doing with that blade? Tell me, now!" he screamed, the full extent of his rage let loose. All at once, both sinks on the wall began pouring hot water at full pressure.

It steamed above the counter, sending a shimmer into the room that made the general appear more hellish.

"I'm performing a C-section," the doctor replied with a tremble in his voice. He pointed down at Brooke who, despite being awake, was lying with an exposed womb. Jake's nephew wriggled inside.

"On whose orders?"

"The chancellor's!"

"Stop at once, and put down the knife," the hulking general warned.

"No," the doctor said. "The chancellor outranks you, and I won't disobey orders. Besides, she's already open, and the procedure is nearly complete."

"I'm sure you, just like everyone else in this bunker, have heard the expression, *nobody says* no *to me*?"

"Well, yes. Yes, I have, and I just did."

Jake smiled, an eerie sight that clashed with his rage. "Well, there's a reason for that saying." His huge fist blurred in the air, meeting the doctor's cheek and spinning him around. The scalpel flew across the room. The man crashed to the floor and Jake bent down, grabbed his leg, and dragged the unconscious doctor into the waiting area. The sound of footsteps met his ears, warning that security would arrive soon.

He rounded on the remaining attendants, sending them scurrying away with another roar. He sounded beastly then, more dangerous than a lion and as strong as a dozen, and slammed and locked the door behind them.

"Don't take it out," Brooke slurred. "He must come... natural."

Mi-Jung rushed to Brooke's side. "We have to take it out, Brooke, you're already opened up." The girl went to work finishing the work of the doctor. Her hands trembled as she chose a clean scalpel and cut the final membrane. "I wish you had let *him* finish," she scolded the general.

"I didn't trust him," he retorted.

"Jake," Brooke whispered, "I'm dying."

"No, you're not," he said, scooping up her hand in his. "We'll get the baby free and make sure someone stitches you up right. We..."

"Listen to me," Brooke interrupted. "It's part of Adam's prophecy. He warned me against letting them give me anything for the pain, insisting the childbirth must be natural. He said Michael wanted me out of the way once my child was born." She was so out of it, her eyes nearly closing as she spoke. It took so much effort to speak.

"What did they give you?" he demanded.

"A mixture, no way to tell."

"Fentanyl, probably," Mi-Jung retorted as she pulled the baby into the world, placenta and all, then went right to work to suction its mouth and nose. It cried out at once. She quickly measured and cut the exact length of umbilical cord.

"Clean it off, quickly," Brooke commanded from her bed. "Then smear the other child with the blood and dip it in the amnio fluid."

Without hesitating, Mi-Jung complied, switching out the babies and slamming the false bottom of the bassinet shut. Just as she dipped the clone in blood and fluid, the door burst open. Security and Michael Esterling had arrived. She turned to hand the child to Brooke, but it was too late.

The spirit of life had departed the mother.

Jake roared with anger, both at his sister's death and the arrival of four emotants.

The three Spring Emotants stepped backward, allowing room for Penny McLemore to advance.

CHAPTER THIRTY-ONE

"Wake up," the kind voice commanded, a gentle hand shaking James Parker awake. "It's time."

James opened his eyes, resting them on Alice. In the flickering light from candles she somehow appeared more lovely than in daylight.

Everyone else in the bunkhouse was already awake, dressed as if ready to begin the work day. The mood of some reflected fear and uncertainty while others, especially Curtis, Seth, Frank, and Wylie, appeared ready to sow chaos during the night. James couldn't blame them, his eagerness to be free rivaled their own.

Curtis had chosen a nighttime uprising for several reasons. First, the captives were separated in the bunkhouse, only wearing leg irons, not linked together as during the day. Second, there would only be a few pairs of eyes watching the compound. The rest, including Mike Donelson, were resting peacefully in their beds.

"Have you explained the plan?" James asked Curtis.

"I was just getting to that," the leader replied, standing to address the others. "We're bustin' free tonight," he said quietly enough the guards outside would not overhear.

"Says who?" demanded one of the captives. He was a farmer before Donelson took him, his spread just a few miles down the road. "What if some of us don't want to."

"Why wouldn't you want free?" James asked the man.

"Of course I want free, I'm sure we all do. But I'd rather not have my ribs busted in for *your* failed escape."

"No one's getting their ribs busted in tonight," Curtis promised.

"How can you be so sure?"

"Because we planned it carefully," James tossed in. "It's a good plan, and it's already in motion. We... did something today, and now there's no turning back."

"What did you do?" a woman demanded. She was plump when she arrived at the compound, one of the first slaves taken by Donelson and his sons. Now her face, like the rest of her, had grown gaunt and haggard. Her skin full of sores and peeling scabs from the radiation.

"You'll know soon enough," Curtis replied.

"I want to know now," the woman insisted.

"I thought you'd want to be free more than the rest of us," Alice said kindly. "What difference does it make what these men did?"

"Because I want to know if it's punishment enough for what those men outside have done to *me!*"

Curtis approached her tenderly, placing his hand on her shoulder and looking the woman directly in her eyes. "I promise you will enjoy vengeance tonight," he said just above a whisper. "What we're about to do will change everything."

"What if it works? What will we do after? The Nature Boys will eventually return, and they won't deal with *us* like they did Donelson," the man complained. "They'll kill us all and take it for themselves."

"The Nature Boys are attacking the Regiment in Evansville," James explained. "After we take the compound we'll ally with the leaders there."

"You're assuming they'll win," the man argued, "but how can they? You've seen this army for yourself. There's no way the Regiment survives."

"Either way," Curtis interrupted, "I'd rather die fighting as a free man than live as a slave."

"Damn right!" Frank tossed in, standing and moving beside Curtis. Wylie joined them as well.

Seth also stood, moving to face the man and woman and hoping to calm their doubts. "This is already in motion, like they said. We have one shot at it now, when it's only Donelson, his sons, and their hired guns. They have a plan, so we should let Curtis tell us what that is."

Both dissenters quieted, though it was obvious they still shared doubts.

"Alice is the only one allowed to move around at night, because she does the cooking for the compound. It's almost time for her to go to the kitchens, and there will be three men at the door when it opens—one escort and two guards."

"They've been lax lately," Alice explained, "because there's never been any trouble when they've come for me. All of you are always asleep, and I'm always up and ready when they come."

"What difference does that make?" the man asked. "We're all wearing leg chains, anyways. How will you fight them?"

Curtis smiled broadly. "That's all part of the plan. Now, when they come for Alice, we'll only have a minute or two to overwhelm the guards. They'll have keys for the padlocks, so I'll toss those to you after the miner team breaks free."

"Why the miner team?" the woman demanded. "Why not some of us?"

"Because," James replied, standing and taking his place beside Curtis, "we're already loose." All five men on the mining team squatted down, grabbing their leg irons with both hands. On the count of three they stood, pulling the chains and snapping them free without any trouble. The others in the room marveled at the spectacle.

"How?" the farmer demanded.

James reached down and grabbed two damaged links from his chain, holding them up so the others could see. "We broke these off in the mine with our pickaxes, then bent them just enough into place the guards only *thought* we were hobbled. Like Alice said, they're getting lax in their duties."

"But you've got no weapons," the woman protested. "How will you fight them off?"

Curtis lifted his chain up into the air, gripping one end while swinging the rest of it in a wild circle. "Chains are the only weapon a slave needs... Let the masters die under the very bonds they used against us."

"It's almost time," Alice warned. "You should all get into your places."

"Parker and I will position by the door," Curtis explained, "while Seth, Frank, and Wylie take these bunks close by. The rest of you get under your covers and act like you're sleeping. As soon as we strike, be ready to get free and join us outside."

James moved into position, crouching low in the shadows and watching as the others did as Curtis commanded. In a matter of moments, the bunkhouse appeared as it did any on any other night.

Alice stood in full view of the door and waited. After a few minutes, a key rattled in the lock. Moonlight soon flooded the building, deepening shadows in all but the center of the room.

An armed man, meant to be Alice's escort, poked his head in and scanned the room. Satisfied the slaves still slept, he motioned for his kitchen slave to follow. "Let's go," he ordered, and she followed him out into the night.

Curtis moved quickly, leaving the shadows to slide a wooden board against the base of the door jam.

"What the hell?" one of the guards cursed into the night as the door refused to shut properly. He slammed it three times before kneeling to examine the problem.

"It's a trap!" the captive farmer cried out, meaning to warn the guard of danger lurking in the shadows.

But James was ready and looped his chain around the slaver's neck and twisted as tightly as he could. Curtis grabbed the man's rifle, wrenching it away and tossing it to Seth now sitting up in his rack. They were committed now to the plan, having the crossed the Rubicon and committed to the plan.

Sounds of a scuffle somewhere in the bunkroom suggested the betrayer was dealt with.

As soon as Curtis tossed the rifle he slammed the door open wide, hitting the second guard in the face and chest. Reaching around he grabbed the man, pulling him inside and letting the door close once more against the board. James held the man's arms, keeping his hands from the trigger as Curtis slowly choked out his life.

Seth had moved to the doorway, peering out to watch the compound. "Hurry up," he urged. "Alice's escort didn't hear anything, and they'll reach the kitchen in about another minute."

"If she was right that leaves us two lookouts to deal with," Curtis explained. "We don't have much time!" He quickly looted the pockets of both guards until he found the key, tossing it to Wylie. "Free the others, and chain that loudmouth up good. And gag his mouth so he can't cry out again!"

"I have a more permanent solution," James muttered to his friend and moved to where several of the others held the man.

"Please don't," the farmer begged.

His chain swung down hard, striking the loudmouth across his temple. Once, twice, three times he struck him, until only dazed eyes stared at the chain in his hand. "Next time you endanger *any* one of us, you're a dead man," James promised. Turning, he jogged to join the Curtis at the door.

"Was that necessary?" his friend demanded.

"This world has changed," Parker told him, "and the only mistakes we can make are the once we leave to bite us later."

"Get going," Seth urged, handing his rifle over to James.

Curtis held up the other rifle and nodded. "Seth, keep everyone here until we drop the first lookout. Then take everyone to the kitchen, kill her escort, and get Alice free of her chains. After that, don't move until they've noticed the distraction."

Only one of the lookouts had a clear view of the bunkhouse. He was easy to spot in the moonlight. They waited until his back was turned before the pair crept out, moving in the shadows along the wall. From here they watched the second night watchman. His back was also turned staring off toward the mine.

"I hope it worked," Curtis whispered, following Parker as he ducked beneath the raised platform.

James shrugged, placed a finger to his lips, and urged quiet before pointing upward. The lookout was right above them. The goal was to take the man out before he could sound the alarm or get a shot off. Either one would bring every man out of the compound, armed and ready to kill. They had to time it perfectly, but the problem was they didn't know which lookout would see the distraction first.

The ground abruptly rumbled, a small earthquake shaking the compound.

That's not good, James thought. *That'll wake them before the lookouts see the smoke or fire!* He knew they had to move, couldn't wait for the distraction now burning in the mine. The night suddenly filled with a screeching hiss as the ground rumbled once more. There was no more time to wait, and James had to take out the guard. Leaning his rifle against the wall he hefted his chains, praying they wouldn't give off the slightest rattle.

Creeping slowly up the stairs he approached the lookout peering into the darkness, staring off in the direction of the mine. *We should have seen smoke or flame by now! What if the fire went out on its own?* he worried. As he moved into position behind the night watchman another rumble violently shook the platform. Beyond the lookout the darkness seemed to fall in upon itself, the ground belching an inferno into the night sky.

James paused, not expecting the coal seam to burn so wildly and stared at their handiwork with disbelief.

The lookout turned, calling out, "Fire! The mine is on fire!"

James and the guard locked eyes, mere inches away from each other and equally as shocked as the other. Parker did the only thing he could do, no longer possessing the element of surprise. He grabbed the watchman and hugged him close, turning his body just enough to push with his foot. With a grunt the two men toppled from the open side of the parapet, falling twenty feet to the ground. They landed with a thud.

Dizziness quickly took over as James lay atop the fallen lookout, his mind barely hearing the commotion as men ran out of their living quarters into the compound. As he rolled over, he could barely focus on Donelson and his men racing up the rampart, each vying for a better view of the inferno that was once a coal mine.

"Now!" Curtis shouted to the kitchens, his rifle exploding into the night.

As James' eyes swam back into focus, he realized there was no missing the targets. Illuminated by fiery moonlight, Donelson, his sons, and his men never saw who was shooting up at them. One by one they fell over the wall and, by the time Seth and the others stormed from the kitchen, there was no one left to kill.

Together, James and Curtis pushed open the door to Crazy Mike's home. It was neater and more orderly than Parker expected. It wasn't piled high with beer bottles and strewn food wrappers. Donelson, it seemed, ran his entire compound with strict military discipline. The search and inventory of resources proved far easier than first feared.

"My friend Cathy told me he stole from her," James said to the freed man beside him. "Her husband had robbed a jewelry store, and she had a bag full of cash and gems."

"You know she ain't gettin' them back, right? It's due all of us who earned it."

James frowned, but that *was* a fair offer, after all.

Each room in the house was set up more like officer's quarters than the barracks they expected to find, a place for each of Crazy Mike's sons to enjoy their own space and privacy. His master bedroom was no exception, the heart of the man's dubious dealings with both the Regiment and the Nature Boys. The maps on his walls were accurate, both to the changes in geography and the political lines both sides had drawn.

James let out a whistle.

"What is it?" Curtis asked, moving beside him.

"He knows the strength of both sides, meaning he's got spies in each. Look here, how he drew the Regiment's defenses. Max and Shayde just built those in the last month. He even marked how many men are in each defensive position and where the machine guns are set up."

"That's not good for your friends."

"Not good for them at all," James agreed. "I've got to get word to them."

"No way. You ain't gettin' through the Nature Boys in time." Curtis picked up a notepad, reading the scribble. "Besides, according to this they hit them tonight."

Worry filled James' heart, both for his friends but especially for Cathy and Josh.

CHAPTER THIRTY-TWO

David looked first on the stage, stepping through the masses awaiting their release to join the rest of the Shelter. Cathy had been correct. Not only was the area bursting at the seams with refugees, it was a dungeon of darkness that had outgrown its usefulness. Thankfully Dr. Andalon had treated nearly all of the people here.

Stephanie welcomed his approach with a warm greeting. "Good afternoon, David," she said from behind worried eyes.

"Have you heard any word? The rumors I'm hearing are bad," he admitted, hopeful for details of the fighting outside.

She shook her head. "Ben's out in it, said he'd be clearing structures for possible snipers." There it was the source of her worry.

"I'm sure he's fine," David offered, hoping he had spoken truth.

Stephanie shrugged. "This is the danger of loving a soldier. We get stuck living with all the worry, stress, and emotion they've cut themselves off from. They suppress it, thinking it's no longer their problem, but it manifests here, in the hearts of their loved ones."

David paused and considered her words. He had never thought of it that way. Clearing his throat, he asked about Cathy. "Have you seen her?"

"She said she isn't coming in today. Wanted to spend time with her son."

Disappointment washed over David, betraying his eagerness to spend time with her, himself. *But you ruined that, didn't you?* He knew it was true. Cathy was an easy woman to fall in love with but difficult to hold on to with her slowness to trust. *I frightened her away.*

"Well then," he said with stiff resolve, "I'll let her be. What's needing done around here?" He looked around after asking, mentally taking inventory. It was quiet, with most of the patients feeling better after their vaccination.

"It's been quiet, so far," Stephanie pointed out. "We haven't taken in a single new refugee in days."

Stuck in his own head lately, he hadn't realized they had stopped taking any in. *Of course,* he realized. That explained the lack of more urgent medical cases. "I'll go tidy up the pending lab results," he offered.

"I finished all blood tests this morning, as well as the urine samples." Stephanie smiled, hoping to offer consoling, but there was a lack of work to be done between the two doctors. There just simply wasn't anything left to distract him. "Maybe you should go spend time with Adam and Eve," she suggested, "they've been asking for you."

Yes, David thought, *and I've been avoiding them as fiercely as Cathy's been avoiding* me. The three had not spoken for a full day, not since Clint attacked him in his room. He shuddered, the freshness of the memory still lingering, and briefly relived that moment in his mind. All of it haunted him, the metallic taste and smell of blood, his own at first then that of Clint's, the pressure against his throat and the heaviness on his body, but mostly the dying—the fear of it bothering him less than his reluctant acceptance of Clint's.

Had the children not sent Mr. Starlings when they had, he... he what? They still might have saved him themselves.

It all suddenly felt like another of Eve's tricks to David. The simplicity of it, as if it were a plan conceived by a person so full of intelligence but clouded by arrogance, made him wonder if he should worry over the details or fear she and Adam had bigger plans. Who could he tell? Certainly not Cathy. She scurried away the moment she learned they shared telepathy. Surely not Stephanie. Though as close if not closer to the children than he, Dr. Yurik had never witnessed Eve's darker nature. Would she even listen to him, now, if he found the courage to express his concerns?

"David!" Cathy's voice called across the gymnasium.

His head lifted, full of hope. *Had I been wrong?* he wondered. *Does she want to spend time with me after all?* His heart beat rapidly as his eyes found her moving slowly toward the stage. She wasn't alone. Linda Johnson clung to her shoulder with one hand while the other clutched her pregnant belly.

"David!" Cathy called again. "Help me with her! She's in labor!"

"I'll prepare a bed," Stephanie said understanding right away, "and gather what we need."

Of course, the doctor thought, shaking his mind free of distracting hope. He rushed forward, taking Linda's free arm and placing it across his shoulders. "How far apart?" he asked Cathy, happy for any conversation with her at all.

"Two minutes, but something feels wrong."

"Because it's a monster," Linda exclaimed between breaths. "He's ripping me apart from the inside out."

"Nonsense," Cathy snapped. To David she explained, "She's at term, but her body's acting like it isn't ready. She hasn't dilated at all."

"What else?" he demanded as they climbed the steps toward the infirmary.

"Her water broke," Cathy explained, "and she saw something dark floating in it."

They found the bed Stephanie had prepared and laid Linda gently down. Cathy went to work raising a portable shower curtain for privacy, the best they could do with all tents occupied.

David knelt beside the mother-to-be. "What was it?" he asked. "What did you see in the fluid?"

"It was black, like tar. It wasn't clear like my other..." the woman choked back tearful memories of her other children, lost from the world just before Yellowstone erupted. "Not like my *normal* children," she finally said.

David wasted no time, not even caring if they had finished raising the curtain, and pulled her pants free. The streaks he found were dark as mud but not tarry, as Linda had described. He found it jelly-like, instead.

"It's dead, isn't it, Doctor?" she demanded.

He placed his hand over her stomach, feeling for the lifeforce and finding it pulsed strong. "No, your child is alive, Linda."

"Promise me, if it's a monster you will kill it and spare me from seeing it!"

Cathy appeared by David's side inside the ring of curtains. She carried a tray with basic surgical tools and a speculum. She frowned and demanded, "what *else* do we need, Doctor?"

"I don't..." He paused, realizing he didn't know how to even use what she had brought. Then his eyes met hers, fiercely appraising his every move as he prepared to help her friend through childbirth. That he held his hands over Linda's stomach like a faith healer became hotly obvious, and he removed them quickly as if struck by a viper. "I've... I've done this before," he said. It wasn't a lie. He had delivered Sally's child.

"Without using your powers, or *whatever* you call them, can you tell me what's wrong with her?" Cathy demanded. "*I* know, do *you*?"

His hands reached out instinctively to finish appraising Linda's condition, but Cathy stopped him, grabbing his hands within her own.

"I said *without* using your powers," she hissed angrily.

"I can't," David admitted, defeated by the truth. "I'm not that kind of doctor."

"Then move out of my way, charlatan!" Cathy said angrily, pushing his hands away with disgust. "If you want to hang around, then do so, but as *my* nurse! She has meconium in the womb, a condition when the child passes its first stool while inside. Get me a suction bulb and saline, that's what *else* we need!"

Shocked, David stumbled from the birthing tent, his eyes meeting Stephanie's as he did.

"What happened?" she asked.

"She knows... I told her about my craft a few days ago after I helped Starlings. She guessed I'm not a medical doctor, and I just proved it to her."

"Go," Yurik suggested. "Find Adam and Eve and spend time with them. I'll make things right between you and Cathy."

David nodded, too speechless to agree or argue. He turned, meaning to step off the stage to the gymnasium floor below, when he saw Benjamin Roark approaching. "Stephanie," David called and the woman paused, reading the same seriousness written on Ben's face.

"What is it?" she asked as the sergeant approached.

"They have artillery and are shelling the main line. They'll break through tonight, and General Rankin has ordered every able-bodied man and woman be armed and form a second barrier.

"That's it?" David asked. "That's Rankin's plan? Everyone who can is to grab a rifle and be ready?"

Roark shook his head, turning to face David. His eyes, angry at lies unspoken, accused. "How long have you been controlling Clint Fletcher?" he demanded.

Deny him, Father. Deny his accusation.

"David?" Stephanie stepped down, joining the two men on the gymnasium floor. She had heard her lover's accusation. "What have you done?"

"I haven't done *anything*," David insisted.

Good, Eve praised him. *Make them even more angry once they figure out you've lied,* she laughed in his head. *Or, you can tell them the truth, and they will hate you even more than this.*

David looked back and forth between the two faces, each watching him, waiting with a mixture of mistrust and scorn, ready to disdain him for making their imaginations real. He stood taller, emboldened or empowered by their judgement, he wasn't sure, and stated plainly, "I did nothing of the sort. I *don't* control Clint Fletcher."

It wasn't a lie.

Max held the line, shouting supportive orders to his brave men facing an onslaught. All around them the makeshift wall had blown apart, leaving only fragments of cover behind which to hide. The artillery had been the backbreaking blow, but not for long. The enemy held the beach, enough having landed they would soon press forward. The time to retreat had come.

"Let's go!" he shouted, "Fall back!"

Like a single machine they moved, one fireteam after another as he had instructed, peeling away under cover fire from their right and left. Soon those squads would follow, and others would too all along the defensive line. Max and Shayde's plan was simple, pick off as many as they could while the enemy dug in on the beach, then fall back before they push again. They would bend the line before breaking, by drawing the enemy deeper into the city. Their hope was to weaken the Nature Boys by striking and running away, keeping them busy until sunup and diminishing their numbers the nearer they came to the Shelter.

It was Max's squad's turn to sprint away, flee and regroup. They did so as a unit on his command, racing down Main Street. Two blocks later, having reached Second Street, he gave the signal and they slowed.

"Fireteam One," he commanded, "on me! The rest of you spread out, find cover, and await the next retreat."

He looked around, they were just outside a bar called *The Peephole.* Max led his team inside, then watched as the other fireteams disappeared into similar shops on both sides of the street. Once inside he found cover and knelt, watching both directions from which the enemy could advance. "Have the back door ready," he told a corporal. "Watch it and be ready to leave on our signal."

All that remained to do was to wait.

After about ten minutes he noticed the shelling on the beach had stopped. Enough teams had fallen back that the Nature Boys may have finally pressed forward. They would be cautious, though, and that's why Max and his fireteam had to be patient. Footsteps outside finally crunched the snow. These were the scouts, the recon teams he would let through. *Better to let them feel safe than to form a defensive line where we don't want it,* Max knew. Thankfully the other fireteams knew as well, and no one fired.

A few minutes later, the regular troops arrived, more confident than the scouts and wrongly thinking the area was safe. Two by two they emerged. *Army formation,* Max noticed. They walked with heads held high, looking side to side while crossing the street, unseeing the key positions where the Regiment soldiers waited.

Max gave the hand signal and Fireteam One relayed the command. All along the street soldiers rose from their cover, firing bursts into the sitting ducks crossing the road. Two by two the Nature Boys fell, heaps of matching uniforms and superior weapons falling in the ashy snow. Elsewhere in the city the scene was the same, as a line of hidden partisans stripped the attackers of life.

Shouts closer to the shoreline relayed the danger, and survivors quickly ducked for cover before regrouping out of range of Max's hell storm. As soon as he was able, he gave the signal to fall back, and fireteam after fireteam peeled away as before. This time, however, they had recon troops waiting.

The enemy scouts had taken cover, but not very well. They didn't know the city, not like Max and his Regiment. They had also been caught off guard, unsuspecting the brief firefight that opened up behind them and then ended just as abruptly. Many of the scouts made a crucial mistake, running right into Max's alert and ready forces. Their poor choice ended in a second hail of gunfire.

"Move out," Max ordered the moment they reached Fourth Street, turning his team northwest toward Sycamore. He eyed the taller buildings looming overhead, cringing at the thought of snipers they had missed. But for the ground battle it was a good spot, and Max Rankin watched the final line of defense form around him—just two blocks away from the Shelter.

This might actually work, he thought. They had already killed more than he had hoped.

CHAPTER THIRTY-THREE

Michael stepped up from behind the husk of Penny McLemore, his eyes locked on his son in the Korean woman's arms. With Brooke dead and out of the way, the child was all his.

When he spoke, it was to Jake. "One of the prophecies this young woman spoke in Ka'ash'mael came right before her passing. She said:

'Natural born and passed through woman, the destroyer is the son of Andalon. Dually wielding both Autumn and Winter, bringing forth darkness and rain, the storm brings down pain upon all of Astia. His coming harkens total destruction, the end of modern times.'

So, as you can tell, I can't let *any* of that come to pass, so we pumped Brooke full of drugs and took the infant by C-section. Unfortunately, though, he bears the stain of being born to an Andalon, so I'll have to raise him myself and steer his actions to ensure the destroyer never springs from my own line."

"You've lost all reason," Jake growled from across the room. His face was grotesquely twisted in anger, his cheeks dancing with fury.

Michael had seen this before, in college, right before he took on an entire room of frat boys for taking advantage of several sorority girls. Jake's anger had been just at the time, and may even be so here, but Michael knew what he was doing was best for everyone, though it also meant losing both Brooke and Jake by ridding them from this world.

Michael stepped forward and took his child from a quivering Mi-Jung, then moved to leave the room. As he passed by the husk of McLemore, he said simply, "Kill him, but leave the lab assistant alive. I need her and her husband to complete the bitch's work."

The wisps of air came more quickly than the last time, materializing less like boa constrictors and more like whips. They lashed out around

Jake's neck, arms, and legs with a single flash, binding him with arms outstretched like the Philistines lashed Samson to the great pillars. And it was a good thing, too because, like Samson would have, Jake Braston was about to rip Penny McLemore to pieces right before she bound him.

With each struggle his anger grew, eroding his mental clarity and turning everything crimson before his eyes. The berserker rage had fully gripped him now, forcing the beast out into the light when it preferred the calming darkness. The wisps of air were strong, braided like ropes and, despite his efforts, would not break.

The ringing in his ears took over, drowning out the sound of running water behind him. The steam of it was already searing his back, but he did not feel the heat, only the wash of cold all around. Everything around him misted like winter, even his breath.

The helplessness of it all mixed in his mind, amplifying the hatred for Michael and fueling it with grief over Brooke. He felt it all in that moment, all the souls that were lost in the apocalyptic event he could not stop, including his own parents. He finally grieved for them, once living so close to Yellowstone they would have vaporized without pain. That small comfort no longer held away the pain, and it grew too much for the man who had so casually set it all aside. He had pushed it away so he wouldn't feel, and now the feeling of it poured out of his very soul.

The temperature in the room dropped suddenly, frigid except over the steam rising above the sink. From over Jake's shoulders, tendrils of an invisible Kraken reached out from the sinks, scalding hot and thicker than the cool air holding him, thrashing about the room and shoving the animated husk of McLemore against the far wall.

The violence chased a terrified Mi-Jung from the room, pushing the bassinet beside the security detail. Jake noticed that, unlike them, she refused to watch the carnage as watery tentacles beat and thrashed Airman McLemore about. Jake felt her wisps of air suddenly vaporize, the sound of their sizzle eclipsed by the sudden shattering of the bones in Penny's back.

Looking down and flexing his arms and hands, he took a mental image of the awkward way her head twisted, looking up at him from under her raised arm—unseeing eyes marveling at the Kraken rising from the sink. He felt sorrow then, for the girl who once looked at *him* through those orbs. They were once so beautiful and, like her, so full of life... but no longer. He strode into the next room, his watery tentacles trailing behind him on the floor.

His eyes briefly met those of the security officers, each trembling so badly with fear the upturned muzzles of their rifles shook.

"Leave, and I'll do the same," he said. "I just want to get away from Ramstein."

One of the soldiers opened fire.

His tentacles lurched without warning, slapping aside the bullet, then striking the man, a private, across the face. His nose twisted all the way around to face his squad leader standing behind him. The entire team watched as his legs gave out, then collapsed. But it was too late. The onslaught of the tidal wave washed over them all, forcing a heap of twisted limbs and torsos hard into the far wall. Not all of them died, but the sound of shattering bones let Jake know that none would be fighting back.

A different movement caught his attention in the hallway, a swaying and humming he recognized at once.

They're raising her!

The general whirled, turning around just in time to see Penny standing behind him with arms outstretched. As she once again conducted an invisible orchestra, the air around Jake formed into a life sucking bubble. As the oxygen around him slowly leached out, he fought dizziness and to stay on his feet.

He became oddly aware of a split occurring in his mind. That part which controlled the water pooled it together on the floor, forming a massive ball that nearly filled the room. Like a splitting cell it formed into four parts, three snaking off into the hallway, while one surrounded Penny. It was a race now, to find out which of them would die first.

He saw the bubble of oxygen form around her mouth just as the water arrived, but it was too little and too late to help. As she gasped the final bit of it, her lungs filled with scalding water and drowned her thrice dead lungs. In the hallway, three more emotants suffered the same fate and Jake ended Michael Esterling's chances to raise more abominations.

Jake turned to help Mi-Jung off the floor. "Grab the child and let's go," he commanded.

"I can't. I have to stay behind and finish what Brooke began." She lifted the false bottom of the bassinet and pulled out the child, handing him to Jake. Then she pulled out a backpack and strapped it over his shoulders. "In here you've got Brooke's instructions, some gear to help with the baby, and a map. She's been planning your escape a long time and thought of everything. On it there's the serial number of one of the trucks you took off the Russians, and it's packed with enough supplies to keep you and the baby alive for years—there's even baby formula."

Jake fought back tears, then wrapped the sweet, compassionate young woman into an embrace. "Take care of Sam. I like that man."

"You take care of *you*," she told him with a smile, "and this little guy." Then she added something in Korean."

Jake laughed, "What does that mean?"

"'A successful man is one who can lay a firm foundation with the bricks others have thrown at him.' It means, go make something good in this world, General Braston. Stop destroying and start building, and use as your inspiration all the pain and anger you have suppressed for too long. Now, go!"

Jake gave the young woman a brotherly kiss on the cheek and then hurried out, stepping over three drowned bodies now lying atop a large puddle. As he passed by, the water coalesced behind him, reforming the tentacles and trailing behind while keeping pace. Mi-Jung was right. He had work to do, and escaping Ramstein was only part of his mission. With that, General Jake Braston, the pilot who would never again fly, took flight.

CHAPTER THIRTY-FOUR

David reached out his hand. The doctor and bringer-of-life whose entire existence had revolved around enhancing the living, accepted an instrument of death from the armorer. It was a simple weapon as the soldier explained, with a spot underneath to insert a magazine, a bolt to chamber the first round, and a safety selector. The armorer instructed him to keep it on semiautomatic when firing to save ammunition. Then he handed him three 30-round magazines and sent him on his way.

From there, Doctor Andalon followed the line of noncombatants outside. There, outside the Shelter, they were divided up by Clint Fletcher and Benjamin Roark. Some, those with experience shooting any type of weapon at all, were directed to find spots on rooftops or high windows overlooking the southern defenses. When the Nature Boys pressed the center of Evansville, they would be met by stiff resistance and bullets would rain down, according to Fletcher.

Only, it wasn't really Clint Fletcher, as David knew all too well. The look Roark gave him when stepping outside told him he had figured it out as well, despite his lie.

Though Fletcher acted normal, he was too precise, overly calm, and less psychopathic than before. Though his mouth opened, and his own voice spoke, David couldn't help hearing the words of Eve instruct the newly armed refugees.

Relax, Father. We have a plan. The side of right will win tonight, she also whispered in his mind.

David, having no experience with any weapon of any kind, was directed by Roark to a line of trucks and dumpsters hastily pushed into a row along the corner of Court and Market Streets. Here, a makeshift aid station stood behind a line of defenders. From what David could tell, these were a mixture of experienced fighters and those civilians who had never fired a weapon. *Bullet sponges,* David heard one of the veteran's joke, and hoped it wouldn't come to that. But he knew better.

Off in the distance the artillery shelling had stopped, replaced by intermittent bursts of gunfire that seemed to be making its way closer with each engagement. As Roark had briefed, Max Rankin and Shayde Walters were slowly leading the enemy toward the center, hitting and running with alternated strikes and controlled retreats. He hoped the shouts and wails leading to the waterfront were from the enemy and not the Regiment.

He put the rifle down, knowing he would never pick it back up no matter what. His eyes fell on the entrance to the Shelter, on the bronze statue on the steps and the inscribed words above it. *Soldiers and Sailors Memorial Coliseum MCMXVI.* He had read them when he first entered the building but barely noticed. This building, standing since 1916—just one year before the United States entered World War One, was a prayer for peace. That war, the war to *end* all wars as the people then called it, was meant to be the last evil thing mankind did in the world.

Because sometimes, Father, you must contribute to what others see as evil if you are to have lasting peace, Eve explained.

Is that what you're doing? Are you the benevolent benefactor to mankind? You killed Starlings and Fletcher, but for what? One final battle against evil?

Exactly...

It won't stop here, David explained. *After this army is defeated, there will be others.*

Until there is nothing left but peace, Father.

Peace? Michael Esterling will never *give us peace!*

No? Then eventually we will have to bring it to him *as well.*

"It's a girl." Cathy said, abruptly joining David in the aid station.

He jumped at her sudden arrival. "What?"

"Linda's child. It's a girl, a healthy baby born into a world full of monsters."

"So there were no defects, no ill effects of the radiation?"

"None at all. All of Linda's worry had been over nothing."

David nodded. That, at least, was some good news. "Cathy, I'm sorry I've lied to you, but these secrets aren't the kind people would understand."

"I know," she replied, "and I'm sorry I pushed you aside back there. I wanted Linda to know her child was born naturally, not using magical powers or hocus pocus."

"So you accept what I can do is real?" David asked, finally making eye contact with his lover for the first time since raising Mr. Starlings.

"It's real, even if I don't understand it."

"But you're okay with it? With me? Please tell me it won't come between us."

"I don't know," Cathy admitted, looking around at the ragtag assemblage of armed noncombatants. "Ask me again after all this is over."

"What about it is so bad, Cathy? What about my abilities scares you the most?"

"At least you got my name right," she muttered, then sighed deeply before answering. "I'm afraid to believe, David. I wasted my entire life believing in men, the system, my country, even God. Clint changed that, stripping away my trust and faith in anything. Then the end of the world changed what little faith I had left."

"I won't hurt you, not like he did."

"No, not like he did," she agreed, "but you're more like Clint than you know. In the short time I've known you, secrets and lies have already crept between us. I'm scared, not by what you've told me but by what you haven't. Stephanie says I should trust you, but you have to convince me I can. Prove to me you don't have a secret agenda, that you're not planning to use your gifts to do things the way you think is best for everyone else— no matter what *we* want."

"I'm sorry, Cathy. I'd like to begin fresh with you if you'll let me. I'll tell you everything about my projects, how the craft works and how it was created, just know I have *no* motives. I don't want power and certainly don't need prestige. All I want is to help others and help Adam and Eve become adults."

"That's all?"

David nodded, reaching out to take her hand. "That's all, I promise. If I do otherwise, I'll understand if you never want to see or speak to me."

Cathy pulled back her hand and narrowed her eyes. "If you do otherwise, I'll leave you as fast as I can, running as far away from you as I can, just as I always have with Clint. I'm a runner, David. That's how I cope."

She stepped forward, placing her hands on his chest and looking left then right. Her eyes briefly settled on Clint busy organizing the line of ragtag fighters, and David could almost hear her thoughts as she weighed the risk. In the end she must have decided she no longer feared her ex-husband and leaned in to kiss David openly in front of everyone.

"If we die tonight," she whispered after pulling away, "at least know I loved the *idea* of being with you."

David closed his eyes and kissed her again.

We no longer need her, Father. Eve's voice said into his mind.

The doctor's eyes shot open with alarm. Cathy was right. He had a long history of selfishly refusing help from others. *I even got in the way of my own experiments,* he realized. *I should have listened to Brooke and asked Jake and Michael for help.* Had he done so early on, the entire Andalon Project would have been different. Adam and Eve would have been raised with morals and ethics instead of with disdain for the outside world.

Ethics.

What have I done? he asked himself, suddenly aware of how wrong his own actions had been.

He looked around at the civilians and soldiers lined up to protect the Shelter, so eager to preserve their way of life they were willing to die. *They have no idea what I've done to them!* His thoughts shifted to Felicima and how the monkey had torched the lab to defend against... to *protect* her and the others against... *Against* me. *I'm the problem. I pushed my experiments no matter the consequence.*

I doomed these people, he said to Eve.

No, you made them into something better.

Better... that ambiguous word, so subjective, the bearer of false hope. *I made them like you!*

No, Father, you made them like us!

Tom led his mother down Carpenter Street, the last stretch of road before reaching the Shelter. Though exhausted and weak, she fought through the tears and found enough energy to keep up with her son.

"We're almost there," he encouraged. "We'll be with Dad soon."

They passed the tire store, the word *sellout* emblazoned on the bricks. Tom cringed as his mother halted in the street, reading the words and frowning.

"Did you... did you do this for your father to see?" she demanded.

"Yes, Mother. It was a childish response to anger over things I didn't understand, but I do now." If he could take it all back, he would.

A nervous glance behind him revealed darkly clad figures closing in. Miko seemed willing to chase them all the way to the Shelter. It was so close now, fifty yards away and crawling with people. They had formed a defensive line, their backs to him and all eyes scanning the south. Tom could hear gunfire echoing from that direction they stared, a battle raging and these men and women ready to defend.

"Come on," he urged his mother. "We're almost there!"

They tried to run, but the effort proved too much for Betty, and exhaustion folded her legs. Abruptly, his arm tugged in its socket, muscles popping against the strain of his mother's fall. He turned, shifting his weight in an awkward way that sent shockwaves through his left knee. It buckled, sending blinding pain that came with an audible pop.

As he tumbled, landing beside his mother in the ashy snow, Tom realized they would never make it to the Shelter. Their pursuers had caught them.

Miko had been joined by his entire army, at least eighty men, women, and teens in all. Each carried a rifle or handgun, but a few also gripped bats and swords and whatever else they could find to cause pain or bring death. Before Tom and Betty could stand, they found themselves surrounded.

"I knew you'd run to him sooner or later," Miko said with a laugh.

"Then why'd you keep me on if you knew? Why'd you trust me?"

"Trust you? I never came *close* to trusting you, I *used* you."

"For what? What am *I* worth to you?" Tom demanded.

"You're *his* son and she's *his* wife. You're my bargaining chip, that's what you're worth."

"Bargain? He won't deal with you, that's part of his mantra as a Marine, *never make deals with terrorists.*"

Miko stepped forward, a Louisville Slugger hanging from his left hand. "I'm *not* bargaining with *him,* dumbass." With an upward swing it met Tom's chin, spinning him around and plunging his mind into darkness.

Max and his team were the last to provide cover fire. He looked around at his men. Though ammunition was low, morale was high. They had easily killed or wounded two hundred Nature Boys throughout the night, and it was nearing time to peel off and head for the Shelter. He waited until the last fireteam reached Vine Street then gave the word.

"Fall back," he said for the final time, following his soldiers down Fourth. After this there would be nowhere else to retreat to.

He felt so vulnerable, sprinting past Sycamore and Vine, but breathed a sigh of relief when Court Street and the Shelter appeared ahead. The first thing Max noticed were the vehicles pushed or pulled into place around the building. Behind that makeshift wall rifle muzzles pointed beyond his squad and terrified civilian faces watched him approach with wide eyes.

Two shots rang out from above, their targets the enemies hot on his heels and gaining.

Several more shots followed as his team leapt and dove over the vehicles, the people of the Shelter cheering their arrival.

On the safe side of the barrier, he looked around. All of the teams he had commanded had joined the civilians with rifles. Suppressive fire began the moment the last member of his squad reached safety. Rolling over, he watched several Nature Boys fall dead in the street. The rest, realizing they'd been led to a defensive line, ducked behind buildings for cover.

Those damned buildings again! After only a few minutes, the attack stalled to a standstill with neither side firing at the other.

"They're digging in," Shayde Walters said from behind. So focused on the Nature Boys' approach, Max hadn't seen or heard his friend's arrival. "How many did you guys get?"

"Easily a hundred, maybe twice that," the general replied.

"Us too. They still outnumber us, but we've got them locked down for now. If we can hold through the night, we can try a flanking offensive tomorrow."

Max looked around. He found Benjamin Roark standing with Doctors Andalon and Yurik in a makeshift aid station. Cathy Fletcher was with them, kneeling beside a wounded soldier. "Where's Clint Fletcher?" Rankin asked his sergeant.

Shayde shrugged. "He helped organize the civilians, but I haven't seen him since I arrived. Maybe he found a rooftop?"

More gunfire erupted from the south, followed by the sound of whistling mortars in the sky. Max followed their trails, watching them cut glowing lines across the darkness. He held his breath.

"Incoming!" Shayde yelled to the line of defenders and everyone took cover behind the barrier.

But Max never took his eyes off the sky, watching as the artillery shells arced then began their descent several streets south of the Shelter. The explosions, close enough to shake the ground with their angry arrival, brought a wide grin to the general's face.

"Pescari deserves a promotion!" he yelled to Shayde over the cacophony of violence. "He's firing at *them*!"

If they could now just hold the line, the Regiment had a chance to survive the night.

CHAPTER THIRTY-FIVE

Clint Fletcher stood alone, away from the defensive line and out of sight of everyone. His mind, which had so recently been enjoyably his, now raced with new, terrible thoughts. They intruded upon his own, struggling to process and remember what had happened the night he and Shayde fought the Nature Boys off the beach.

We saved Max Rankin's son, I think...

That memory dangled just out of his reach of clarity and, after that, he vaguely remembered debriefing the general upon their return. The Nature Boys were attacking, he knew that much, but everything since that meeting hung in a fog as if it had occurred many years before. Muffled singing also taunted him, a sweet voice he missed but could not remember whose it was. Like a whisper behind a closed door he yearned to hear the music with clarity.

Worst of all, the *girl* haunted him. Her voice boomed in his head, unwanted and unwelcome despite he had grown to crave her visits. Her voice was drug like, euphoric almost, and welcomed. When she spoke Clint could escape to the music, letting her take over his mind while he retreated to enjoy full melodic tones. When the girl took control he was no longer burdened by the nagging feeling of loss and shame, of the memories of pain under his father's hand. He had lived his entire life with those, remnants of a time long ago before his mother had gone away.

No, he thought, *she didn't* go *away.* They had all been out on the boat, fishing for supper when the argument broke out. She called his father a drunk, said he was no good to anyone, especially her, and that she would take Clint far away. But where would they go, the boy wondered. To drown out the argument he had turned on his Walkman cassette player, listening to the same worn out tape he had found in his father's truck.

The gunshot had echoed over the sound of crooners, cracking jokes between songs in true Rat Pack fashion. Dean Martin had been Clint's favorite, even more than Frank Sinatra. His drunken act painted a picture of what his old man could be, if mother hadn't made him so angry when he drank. That was the night the old man had killed her, forcing the young child to watch his mother slip beneath the waters of the lake. He had never questioned or protested that night as he grew, merely accepting his mother was finally free of his father's heavy knuckles.

Dead, his father's voice suddenly interrupted. *Gone away because she was unfaithful to me. She* chose *to leave us, boy!* his father's voice explained, now a fading reality Clint hoped would stay.

Why are you clinging to that awful memory? Eve abruptly demanded, her voice like a chorus of trumpets so much louder than the other.

No reason, Clint lied. He *needed* the memory as much as his body demanded food and water. It had marked the last time his father had laid a hand on both mother and child.

We've talked about this, Clint, Eve warned. *If you fight us, you will die.*

"I *want* to die!" Clint screamed suddenly, his voice drowned out by sounds of artillery dropping on the Nature Boys. "Get out of my head!" he demanded, pleading to Eve and not his father.

Do not resist us Clint, the voice of Adam demanded. *We will cause you pain if you do.*

Don't you want your wife back? Eve asked. The question would have been delivered in a friendly tone had it not boomed so loudly, so much louder than her brother's.

My wife? Clint was confused. He suddenly found himself back in the Iraq war, holding a letter.

I gave birth to our child, the note read, *a healthy boy. I named him Joshua after your father, Joshua Fletcher. I hope this fuels you to come home to us. Please return soon and in one piece. I love you ..."* The signature was blurred in Clint's mind, and he strained his eyes to read the name.

My wife... he wondered again.

Focus on the battle, Eve's voice boomed again. *It's not over, despite the Regiment is winning. Find your way back to it, and be there when Doctor Andalon uses his craft!*

Doctor... Andalon... He sounded the name in his mind, a collection of syllables barely making sense. Abruptly, the letter was once more in his hands and he read the name. *Cathy!*

Remembrance crashed into Clint's head with blunt force, sending him reeling.

Clint, Eve's voice inquired, now barely a ghostly whisper, *don't think about that!*

It was too late.

Cathy, he recalled. *That bitch slept with Doctor Andalon!*

You're nobody, Dean Martin sang as the music in the background of his mind grew louder, *until somebody loves you!* That was it, Clint Fletcher was a nobody, worthless to the world... *until somebody cares...*

He cocked his head and waited, the voices of Adam and Eve now inaudible whispers drowned out by Dino. He remembered it all.

We're losing him, Sister, Adam said to Eve, his voice fading into a whisper.

That's not possible. He cannot escape the collective once joined...

Clint fumed, recalling how first David Andalon and then Cathy emerged from that room—buttoning blouses, zipping jeans, and tucking in shirts. *The whore gave herself over to him,* Clint realized, as full remembrance brought the image of him strangling the doctor in his bed.

Slowly, Clint peered around the corner and saw Cathy and David sitting together behind the makeshift barrier of cars and dumpsters. They sat hunched close together as if talking, whispering conspiring secrets—celebrating how they had made a fool of her husband. His eyes were drawn to their hands and how they held each other's.

Clint Fletcher roared his anger into the night.

David held Cathy's hand firmly, leaning against a dumpster and flinching against her tight squeezes. She couldn't help it and jumped each time a mortar landed on the city. She was terrified, but so was he.

Father! Eve suddenly warned. *You're in danger!*

What's wrong? he tried to ask, but an explosion ricocheted off the dumpster, a flash of light and searing heat that split the couple apart and sent them tumbling to the ground. David rolled, looking up to see Clint Fletcher striding toward him with searing hatred in his eyes. There was something oddly familiar in them, the way they had turned golden. Seemingly burning with internal fire, they threatened rage and fury.

Then David remembered, he *had* seen those eyes before but not in Clint. *Felicima*, the angry rhesus monkey from his Mendel Lab, had looked upon him with those same eyes.

Clint lifted his hands, pointing them at David, and a stream of fireballs raced out like roman candles. They seared his body as they crashed into the doctor, singeing clothing and hair while burning away any flesh they contacted. With each blast the monster stepped forward, screaming into the night and relentlessly bringing hell upon the doctor.

Max heard the commotion even before he saw the look of horror take over Shayde's face. He turned quickly, watching as Clint Fletcher cast endless balls of fire toward the aid station. Everyone except David Andalon and Cathy Fletcher had fled that medical area. She stood with feet locked into place, frozen by fear. Clint's angry, glowing eyes were fixed on Andalon, and Rankin heard him shout above the roar of fire.

"She's my wife!" Fletcher screamed. "She wasn't yours to screw!"

Without hesitating the general raised his rifle, pointing the muzzle at the crazed man and pulled the trigger. Beside him, Shayde did as well, followed by several more soldiers along the line.

Without taking his eyes from Andalon, Clint raised a hand, forming a wall of blue flame between him and the projectiles. As each piece of lead crossed through, they sparked with hues of orange and red, then splattered as molten pieces of metal against the man's combat fatigues.

"Cathy!" Max yelled, breaking the nurse from her daze. "Get away from him!"

Her feet moved at once but did not flee. Instead she raced toward her ex-husband, drawing a knife from somewhere in her jacket. She lunged, but Clint stepped aside, hitting her ribs with a fireball and knocking her to the ground.

Max raised his rifle, pointing it once more at the distracted mad man. But before he could pull the trigger the entire gun began to smoke, turning red with heat. He dropped it, staring down at scorched palms and watching the entire weapon melt away near his feet. Next to him, Shayde and the other soldiers stared down at theirs turning into pools of molten metal.

Shouts of alarm turned his head once more, this time drawing his attention to the south. The Nature Boys had begun their final assault, pushing forward while their enemy was distracted. Rankin drew his pistol and called for his soldiers to do the same, but Shayde's words turned his eyes northward.

"We've been betrayed," the sergeant said and pointed as Miko Robinson and eighty gangsters gunned down the Shelter's right flank.

Max trained his pistol, taking aim to fire, but quickly pointed it toward the ground. Next to Miko, pulled along by a rope, were two bound and gagged figures. Rankin recognized them at once. The Marine faltered, consumed by a host of emotions. The foremost gripping his body were fear and doubt.

"Hold your fire!" he commanded his men. To Shayde he whispered, "They have my wife and son!"

Unabated, the first wave of Nature Boys poured over the barricade.

Max Rankin fell to his knees and placed his hands behind his head. To the troops under his command, he pleaded, "Surrender! We surrender! Surrender and live!"

Tears streamed down his face as he locked eyes with Betty.

David felt the searing heat melting the skin from his body, shivering against a ghostly cold. *I'm going into shock,* his rational mind told the emotional, now a weeping heap begging to die. He stared through flame and tears at the eerie specter bringing his pain. Clint Fletcher loomed above him, the doctor's biggest mistake.

"Batch Bravo," he muttered though no one was close enough to hear, then chuckled aloud.

Don't let him kill you, Father, Eve urged. *Stand up and fight!*

"Fight?" he laughed again. How could he stand much less fight against a fire wielding madman.

Heal yourself... take him on.

For a brief moment the fireballs ceased raining down. Clint's attention had turned elsewhere and the sound of gunfire suggested someone had engaged. That aid, as futile as it was, abruptly stopped as soon as it started but not before the air around Fletcher erupted with a wall of blue fire.

Thoughts of Brooke and all he had left behind for Adam and Eve flashed before David's eyes. He could have forgiven her betrayal, and should have. They could have started over in Michael's Astia, and they could have even adopted or found other ways to get pregnant and raise children. *I was selfish,* he realized.

Stand up, Father! Heal yourself!

"Finish me," David begged, ignoring Eve's voice.

No! the girl screamed into his mind. *Heal yourself and stand up!*

Something inside David clicked. She had controlled Clint before, was she doing so now? Was this part of her broader plan? Filled with anger, he would no longer be a puppet to her games. *No!* he declared. *I won't let you win.*

We no longer control him, Father, Adam's voice joined his sister's. *His instability somehow broke his mind free, something we hadn't expected.*

Take back control, David begged.

We cannot, Eve explained. *We realize now we can only control a sound mind, one not already fragmented. Heal yourself, stand and fight him and we will help!*

David could not fight if he wanted to. His life was already fading. Pain no longer hurt, and only the draw of nothingness waited.

For another brief moment the night was filled with gunfire from every direction. As quickly as it began it ceased, replaced by shouting. Max Rankin's voice rang the loudest. "Surrender!" he commanded, and David yearned to comply, ready to surrender to death.

His vision had begun to fade, but the doctor willed himself to stare up at his attacker. Clint had been replaced by a demon from hell, Felicima in a man's form who turned his attention to a wounded Cathy.

"No!" David cried out, hoping to draw attention from the woman. This was *his* fault, not hers.

Save her by healing yourself, Eve urged, *but hurry!*

The doctor had no idea where to start. Should he heal the skin, forming it anew around the charred muscle and bone beneath? Or start on the inside and work his way outward? How could he do either? He barely had held enough of his own lifeforce to draw upon.

Use ours, Adam explained.

The heavy doors to the Shelter swung open with a blast of air and two tiny figures stepped out. Adam and Eve waved their arms, swirling and catching the fire Clint meant for Cathy. The fiery whirlwind they now controlled danced off, crashing harmlessly into the side of the coliseum.

⫘⫯⫘

Max knelt with the barrel of a gun pressed against his head. All along the line his soldiers did the same, staring forward while Nature Boys, shocked by the spectacle before them, flooded the barricade and froze in place to watch. Even the gangs had paused, with all eyes watching Clint Fletcher's fiery duel. All, that is, except Max Rankin. He stared beyond the elemental battle, fixated on his wife and son.

Betty's alive, he realized. His son had lied.

Blinking away tears Rankin refocused, trying to make sense of the chaos around him. His Shelter had fallen and the battlefield stood frozen in time. All three factions had become spectators to clashing gods.

Clint Fletcher burned like a demon, his eyes glowing embers in the night. Those orbs followed every move the children made, tracing their hand motions and anticipating their movements. Adam and Eve in turn controlled the air, sending braided ropes to bind his arms and legs. These only fueled his raging fires, adding oxygen that surged his flames hotter.

Behind the crazed killer, lying on the ground, Max recognized Cathy kneeling beside the burned husk of Dr. David Andalon. Mostly charred and steaming, the man lay dying over... over what? Anger? Jealousy?

Max scanned the line of gangsters to once again find his wife.

A collective gasp snapped his attention to Andalon. The man, assumed dead by all watching, had stirred. Slowly he pulled his knees to his stomach and rolled, pushing into a kneeling position. It was now clear a transformation worked to heal his body, with flesh reforming where there had recently only been charred remains. The new skin was clean, pure and free of soot and ash where it regrew on his arms, chest, and legs. The crowd murmured as his face slowly reconstructed, reforming into the handsome doctor.

Once again whole, David placed both palms on the ground. The earth began to rumble. Slowly at first it trembled, then grew into a thunderous roar as tiny cracks formed beneath his fingertips. Each branched outward, breaking apart the ground between him and Clint Fletcher. With a mighty crash, a deep schism formed, a pit from which the mad man had no escape.

As the ground disappeared beneath him, Clint stumbled backward, waving his arms as if hoping to fly. Just before he tumbled into the chasm, a wisp of air formed between the children, a braided rope in the shape of a noose, that grasped the falling man's throat like a boa. He fell but not far, dangling from their ghostly gallows and kicking his feet for traction. The children, small and once thought innocent, snapped his neck with a mighty tug before dropping him down into the chasm.

But Doctor Andalon, now standing tall and ominous over the chasm, was not satisfied with the death of Clint Fletcher. With a thunderous clap he commanded the ground around him, collapsing the walls of the chasm with a violent shake. That tremor grew as it caved in over the madman, rippling unabated outward—shaking and twisting the buildings all around the Shelter.

One by one glass rattled into tiny shards. Bricks broke way, falling several stories into heaps upon the snow and ash. Throughout his rage, a single crack formed in the solid granite of the Shelter, splitting the steps and cracking the facade nearly in half.

From his knees Max watched the crumbling buildings, laughing at the irony he had finally received what he had desired for so long. His laughter continued, joined in by Shayde's own, as every building for two miles collapsed. After David had finished, and all the rumbling had stopped, only City Church, the courthouse, the YMCA, and the Shelter itself stood above the rubble.

-What happened next caused Max and all those watching to marvel with a collective gasp. The children, shimmering like angels, lunged off the top step and flew up into the air. On their backs tiny wisps formed into angelic wings. Upward they flew, hovering above all watching, as the clouds above them parted. Every eye stared with wonder or filled with tears of joy as the stars and moon were revealed to the people for the first time since the night society had ended.

"Hark!" Eve cried out, "I herald the coming of your savior, the vanquisher of evil!"

Upon her words the renewed and shimmering body of David Andalon rose into the sky with arms outstretched. Slowly he turned above the gathered assemblage, dangling from an invisible cross. On the ground everyone knelt in his presence, no matter if they served the Regiment, the gangs, or the Nature Boys. Everyone in attendance laid down their arms and prayed for peace.

David felt the children bear him upward. *No*, he pleaded, exhausted by the ordeal, *not like this! Don't make them think I'm him!*

Eve responded. *Look around, Father, at all the death these people have created. The result of their warfare reaches the river and beyond and will spread if you do not unify them now. Raise up the dead, restore life into the bodies littering the streets and gutters of this world!*

David did see the death but also scattered bits of lifeforce strewn all across the city. Feeling each vibration as they worked their way into his body, he drew from Adam and Eve and tossed in what of himself he had not already spent.

"Rise," he commanded, his mouth speaking the words Eve now put into his mouth, "and walk this earth as proof the killing in this world is done."

One by one, the bricks slid aside as human forms rose from the rubble. In the streets, they stood up from the snow, slowly walking forward to rejoin the living. Every face gazing upon this glory that was once David Andalon did so with reverence as a resurrected army gathered around.

All faces that is, except one.

That part of David the children did not control gazed down upon Cathy, recognizing the revulsion in her eyes.

She'll leave me now after what you've made me do, he told the children, weeping at the sight of his lover running into the Shelter to gather her son.

We don't need her, Father. We have plenty kneeling at your feet, Adam told him.

I don't want them to kneel, he pleaded. *I don't want this at all.*

No, Eve agreed, *but it's not up to you, is it? You drew upon our lifeforce to heal yourself and all those standing among the living. You are part of us now. A god among men.*

Unable to resist the power of his children, David bowed his head upon his invisible floating cross. With tears streaming down his face, he shouted the words Eve spoke through his lips, "Father forgive them, they know not what they have done!"

Upon speaking this blasphemy, the world around him fell dark, and Doctor David Andalon retreated his consciousness into the one place the children would never find him. They may control his body, but the rest of him had joined the earth.

CHAPTER THIRTY-SIX

Jake Braston followed his sister's instructions exactly. As Mi-Jung had promised, Brooke planned his escape down to every detail. He found everything exactly how she described, sparing no detail. All the fleeing general had to do was follow instructions. He first sought out the motor pool, finding a truck fully loaded with several years supply of food, water, diapers, and baby formula just as promised.

He smiled down at his nephew as they drove off the base. "Your mother was a genius, he said to the infant. I wish you could have met her."

The child was too young to coo. It only made a face that was either a smile or gas. The smell emanating not long after confirmed the latter.

"You need a name," Jake said to the boy. "My father, *your* grandfather, was of strong Welsh descent. His name was Braen and was defiant and, like you, full of determination. He bossed me around like you do too. How would you like that name? Do you want to be called Braen?"

The child stared up at him, unable to protest.

"Good, that's settled, then. You are now Braen Braston, the continuance of our headstrong lineage!"

Little Braen scrunched his face and added to his diaper.

"So here's the deal, little Braen. Your mother, my sister, left me this list of how to get out of here. The Rhine River is due north, and she wants me to go to a town called Bingen. She said there's a boat there, and we'll know it when we see it. How does a road trip sound?"

The infant gurgled.

The route Brooke had planned twisted and wound through back roads that were densely covered by snow and ash, but Jake found Bingen easy enough. As he drove over the hill and looked over, he found the town nestled in a swollen river valley. Right away he realized why she had chosen that spot. On the riverbank, run aground, was a river cruise ship. The name *Fjorik* was emblazoned on the hull, and the boat itself was a large yacht capable of carrying two hundred passengers.

Jake vaguely remembered Benjamin Roark mentioning they had run across this boat and others like it during their early scouting, and he smiled at his sister's flawless memory and cunning planning.

He missed her, and sad thoughts of loneliness tried to crack his military shell. *Best to push those out for later,* he told himself, then frowned. There was no way to sail the ship without electricity. Pulling out the note, he checked to see if she had considered that problem too.

Use your craft, she had hastily scribbled in the margin.

At first glance, he thought she meant the boat itself, much larger than a small craft, but then remembered hearing David and Stephanie use that term in debriefings.

He spoke to the infant. "We've got no sails and no electricity, so we can't start the engines. If we're going to get this thing up the Rhine and out to open sea, we'll need some magic." Jake paused and considered.

That's what the children, Adam and Eve, called their gifts. They called it their craft. *Well I have a craft,* he realized. *I can move water.* "I'll be damned," he said then quickly apologized to his nephew for the language. "I mean, I'll be darned, she knew I'd be able to sail it."

The rest of the day was spent loading supplies for both the trip and after. It took longer than he expected, being one man, but the process went quickly considering. Jake had just carried little Braen aboard when several trucks pulled up. The former general set his nephew's carrier in the ship's pilot house and glanced out the window. Ten soldiers in German uniforms stood beside their jeeps, watching as if waiting for Jake to come to them. One of them was Herr General Richter.

If Michael had sent them there would be a fight. They hadn't shown aggression yet, so he decided to find out if they were friend or foe. If it came to a fight, he had plenty of water around him, much more than he used to fight his way out of Ramstein. As long as he could tap into that, he would be fine. He paused on the deck and waved to the man on shore.

"What can I do for you, Herr General?"

"General Braston?" The man appeared more amused than shocked to see his friend aboard the boat. "We were returning south when I saw your truck, but I'm surprised to have found *you*. Where are you going, Braston?" the German general asked. His tone was calm, as if inquisitive instead of commanding he comply. "Do you even have a way to sail this thing?"

"Yes, I've got a way to move it. I'm going away from here, ready to retire."

Richter smiled. "You ran afoul of our chancellor then?"

"I did."

"Where is your sister?"

"Died in childbirth, along with her baby."

"You mean the chancellor's baby."

"The same. Can I go now, Richter?"

The German shrugged. "I've no orders to detain you, so why not? Even if they await my arrival, I don't have them now. Where will you go?"

Jake looked west, downriver, as if seeing across an ocean and two continents. "That way. My home is there, somewhere, and I aim to return."

"Good luck, Braston, I hope we never see each other again."

"Why is that, Richter?"

"Because I will probably have orders to kill you on sight."

"Yeah, you probably will. Drive slow back to Ramstein, will you? Give me a head start?"

"Certainly, my friend," Richter said as he turned to leave. "Always follow the evening star at night, and you'll find what you seek. Put it astern in the morning. Other than that, use the sun."

Jake smiled big. He hadn't thought about navigation.

As soon as the general's jeeps turned onto the road, Braston rushed to the pilot house. He was surprised to find little Braen awake and not fussy.

"Let's see how this works, shall we?" he asked his nephew.

The last time he had worked the craft he had been angry, fueled by a rage that frothed and forced the water into compliance. That wouldn't work now, he was exhausted after the fight and long drive. Closing his eyes, he reached out with his mind, sensing the water surrounding the boat. With a gentle tug *Fjorik* lurched then floated out onto the river. After that it was much easier, as the river flowed northwest toward the Netherlands.

Jake soon found himself making good nautical time and smiled down at his nephew. "This is it, little Braen. Just you and me about to do something very foolish." He shrugged. "I guess that runs in our family genes."

The infant said nothing, but Jake could sense him on the river, just as he had while in the womb. Trust is what he felt, a comforting trust that told his uncle to get on with it. Jake gripped the helm and steered, following the river to the sea and, after that, hopefully to home. Once they were far enough out on the water that he had completely lost sight of land, Jake Braston let himself rest. Mentally and physically spent, that rest turned into sleep.

Jake and little Braen sailed for an entire week, floating along their makeshift current without incident. The first thing Jake noticed was that the sky had darkened, deepening and growing more ominous the further west they cruised. It wasn't long before a storm erupted, with fierce lightning that lit the pilot house, leaving dark shadows in the former general's eyes.

He struggled to hold the current and keep *Fjorik* steady, and discovered a different kind of battle—man against the sea. Dense rain obscured the waves which battered the hull and tossed the ship about. Having no idea how to sail, and not knowing he should keep veering starboard, aiming for the right side of the storm, he lost control and the ship dropped hard over the crested waves. After a while, he found that by ignoring his desired path and moving horizontal instead, he could lessen the impact. Soon, Jake no longer piloted the vessel, choosing instead to ride out the massive waves, *Fjorik* becoming nothing more than a large cork at sea.

After an hour or so both man and baby calmed, even if the storm had not. They huddled close, with Jake singing and trying his best to entertain his nephew. He succeeded but also found he had calmed the storm. As the ship slowly settled he walked to the window, looking out to find he had calmed only the area around *Fjorik*. Beyond that, the storm still raged, daring not to enter his aura of tranquility. They continued like this for three more days, no longer steering, only riding the current.

By the eleventh day the storm had passed and Jake looked out, amazed to find a large body of land on their port side. He steered *Fjorik* around steep cliffs and mountainsides, each speckled with dense forest covered by an ashy gray blanket of snow.

"I've no idea where we are," the uncle admitted to the infant. "We may have sailed north though. This doesn't look like any American coastline I've seen."

Desperate for a harbor, any haven that could offer a break from the angry seas, Jake pressed onward until he found a tranquil bay near the mouth of a river. With relief he ran them aground. After a feeding and a change for Braen, the pair of castaways allowed themselves a nap, earning the deepest sleep either had ever experienced.

ᗛᔕ

Jake awoke hungry. Braen awoke fussy. After another feeding and change of both diaper and clothing, it was decided a nice walk in the outdoors would do them well. Jake bundled up his nephew and placed him in a soft carrier Brooke had included in his pack. Having no idea where they were, Jake also brought along a rifle and extra rounds, just in case they ran into trouble. After a second thought, he also brought some earplugs along for the child. Finally, with little Braen strapped snugly across his chest, they stepped off the ship to explore their new surroundings.

It was quiet, cold, and snowy, and the first thing Jake noticed was how much cleaner the snow appeared. It was almost pure. The second thing he noticed was a large polar bear looking for fish along the icy shore not a hundred meters away.

"I think I know where we are," Jake said to little Braen, "and it isn't anywhere close to home." His suspicions were soon confirmed as five men approached, each dressed in thick fur coats. He clutched his rifle and felt his hip, ensuring the pistol was easy to grab if these men meant harm.

One of them said something that sounded French and asked it pleasantly enough. He was slender though well-fed, and held his rifle in a neutral posture.

Jake reminded himself he was encroaching on *their* territory, not the other way around. "I'm sorry," he said, "I don't speak French."

"Ah! You're American then, eh?" The man exchanged a look with the others and they all noticeably relaxed. "We've been starving for news around here. How are things down south in *your* country?"

Jake took it all in... the use of both French and English, the polar bear now ambling off into the distance, the way the man pronounced the word *south* like *sooth*. It all caused him to relax as well. *Canada then?* It was close enough, for a while. "I'm afraid there's not much left in the south. I myself just came over from Europe."

The man looked over Jake's shoulder, eyeing the hulking vessel behind him. "You had propulsion, then?"

"No, just floated along the current."

"That must have taken months," the man said with a frown.

"Almost," Braston lied, "but we got lucky when a storm pushed us along."

The man pointed at little Braen. "You have baby formula?" he asked. "What about medicine?"

Jake considered his options. He could lie, hoarding everything for himself, or he could make friends by offering over everything he had. Of course, they could still take it and leave him dead on this frozen shoreline. In the end he decided to trust. "I've got a cruise ship that's fully stocked. I've got food, shelter, and medicine enough to share. Do you have wounded or ill among you?"

"Aye," The man's eyes grew sad. "Food's scarce with all the refugees we're taking in, and many of them have radiation sickness."

"Where are they out of?" Jake asked.

"The south, mostly Toronto and Ottawa, and villages between us and them. They moved north because we had less fallout and ash the further they wandered. Unfortunately, we can barely feed and take care of them. Things are scarce as it is."

Jake paused, considering. "How many?" he finally asked.

"About two hundred in all, mostly families."

He reached out his hand. "I'm Jake Braston. Who's your mayor or governor, or whatever provincial leader is in charge?"

The men exchanged a look and the man held out *his* hand to shake. "I'm Edouard Boucher, and I'm the mayor of Moose Factory, Ontario."

"Well, Edouard, come aboard and show me where to park my boat. We'll bring your refugees onboard *Fjorik* and house them there. I can accommodate two hundred, and I've food and medicine enough to sustain all of us for a year."

"I don't know if we can impose," the man said doubtfully.

"Nonsense," Jake said with a smile. "It's only me and the boy, and we're already tired of being alone. Besides, I never take *no* for an answer!"

CHAPTER THIRTY-SEVEN

Cathy Fletcher departed Evansville with only the essentials. On her back she carried a rifle, and over her shoulder she slung a satchel made lighter by its exposed secrets. In that single bag she fit a change of clothing for her and Josh, extra ammunition, food, and water. They walked northwest, hoping to find another pocket of survivors to disappear into.

She had not made it far before riders caught up along the way. She recognized the leader as Chad Pescari. "I'm not going back," she stated with an air of finality.

"It's okay," Chad admitted, patting his swollen saddle bags, "neither are we."

She stopped, curiously looking up at the rider. "Why not?" she asked. "I thought you were loyal to the Regiment."

"There's something wrong about it... him, especially, the doctor that is. It's obvious Max and Shayde aren't in control of anything anymore. Those weird children and the doctor make the rules now."

"You don't believe they're gods?" Cathy asked, watching the riders close when they answered.

"While most are convinced he's is the second coming, many of us still have our doubts."

"Are Rankin and Walters convinced?"

"Not completely, but Max's wife is, and that means he's on board. Either way, god or man, the war's over. The gangs fell apart, the Nature Boys surrendered, and... you won't believe this... the Donelson compound is under the control of James Parker and some new friends he made. The Regiment now holds what used to be two states."

"Yet, you're still leaving?" she eyed him questioningly.

"Absolutely. I've nothing against religion but, like I said, there's something wrong about all this. I wasn't there to see it, but I really have a hard time believing angels fought demons in Evansville, Indiana. How about you? Why are *you* leaving?"

"I can't be around David, not knowing the truth."

"What truth is that?" Chad asked.

"For starters, he's not a real doctor. He's a genetic scientist who engineered those powers, cloned them into those children, and experimented on himself. He's no god, he's a man playing at one and, to me, that's more dangerous."

"That explanation's good enough for me," Pescari decided.

"Where will you go?"

"West. I've looked at some maps and figure there's gotta be another safe zone along the Mississippi River. I'm thinking it's probably near Independence, Missouri." He pointed at his Outriders. "We're gonna find 'em and blend in."

"Max may reach you, even there." Cathy warned.

"Perhaps, but we left in good standing. He knows our leaving had nothing to do with him, so we'll be fine. What about you? Where are *you* headed?"

"Anywhere... Northwest, probably. I've got some family in Minnesota if they survived. I doubt they dropped a lot of nukes on Duluth, and I'm not worried about radiation anymore."

"At least he gave us that vaccine."

"I'm worried that *vaccine* was part of the problem. He gave it to Clint before all of you. What if you develop those powers like he did?"

Pescari chewed his lip. He had obviously worried about the same. "Let's pray we don't. How about you? You took it too, didn't you?"

"No, I never got around to it."

Chad's eyes settled on Josh.

Cathy pulled her son closer and decided it was time to end the conversation and be on her way. "Good luck to you," she told him.

"Ms. Fletcher, wait..."

"Please don't call me that. I'm no longer a Fletcher."

280

"What will you go by then?"

"My maiden name was Thorinson, and so I'll go by that." She looked up at him, waiting for the soldier to say his final piece.

He cleared his throat. "You need to know that James Parker didn't kill the officers. He went undercover in the Donelson compound and that's how it fell. He worked it from the inside."

"That's good to know, but I already knew he was innocent."

"Yeah? How's that?"

She looked at her son, finally free of his father's influence. At least David had granted her *that* boon. "Because *I* did it," she lied. "Maybe not directly, but it was all my fault. I brought the poison and planned to use it, so the consequences of it being used falls on me." She hugged her child closer. "I'll do what I can to undo my mistakes."

Chad Pescari nodded, watching the way she gripped her son.

He already knew, she realized, *and spared me further shame. He might be one of the only good men left in the world.*

"Just be safe, ma'am," he urged. "There's a lot of bad people out there."

"Yes," she agreed, "I'm sure there are." Thinking of Jenny and John Klingensmith and James Parker she added, "but I know there's a lot of *good* as well. In fact, I think the *best* of people are still out there waiting to be found."

Pescari tipped his hat and smiled wide. "Good luck, ma'am," he said before spurring off westward.

Cathy Thorinson started moving as well, venturing out into the wilderness carrying only the essentials: things to ensure that she survived along with her son and unborn child—the offspring of either a god or man.

EPILOGUE

Things in and around the Shelter had changed by the time David woke up, and he ventured out to find Max Rankin. He found him standing in broad daylight without fear of snipers or invaders. The fact daylight shone down upon Evansville was a pleasant surprise as well, meaning the nuclear winter had either ended or lifted, and a new era would begin. The General of the Regiment smiled as the doctor approached.

"Three days?" Max asked. "You really had to sleep for three days? You've really planned all this out, haven't you?"

David cringed at the thought of another biblical prophecy fulfilled, and protested immediately. "I swear I didn't plan for *any* of this!"

"Well it worked, so I'm not complaining. The war's over and everyone's ready to replant and rebuild."

"Do you even want to know what it really is, what our craft really is?"

"Cathy Fletcher told me enough before she left, and Stephanie Yurik and Benjamin Roark filled in the rest. I really don't understand the genetic resequencing part, but I get it. You and the children share telepathy and can move stuff around with your minds."

"There's a bit more to it than that, but yes. The children work air. I'm connected to living organisms and their residuals in the earth."

Max shrugged. "Why the second coming bullshit? I know you're not a god."

"That was Adam and Eve's idea, and they set it up without my permission."

"And that bit about Clint?"

"Total coincidence. I haven't figured that part out yet."

"I see."

David could see Max still had his doubts. Clint *had* arrived with them, and it was a matter of time before others he inoculated exhibited powers too. "So are we free to stay, or will you run us off?"

"Some people, like my wife, are convinced you're the actual second coming. They've got a shrine built for you already."

"And others?"

"Everyone who witnessed your battle swore to the Regiment, even Miko Robinson. They're terrified of you and in awe of me for having you on my side, so I guess I'm stuck with you for now."

"So you're Caesar now?"

"I guess so..."

"And you have a plan? How do the children and I fit into it?"

"Yeah, I do, actually. I want you to do what you can for the settlements, then move on. Go somewhere else and fade into legend. Your presence here isn't good for long-term leadership, and the idea of you is better than actually having you here."

"You could make me a martyr, kill me and let the legend grow."

"I won't, because that's not how I work," Max promised and David believed him. "Get us on our feet, organized, and sustainable, then go."

"I will."

"Good. Now that that's settled, I need a few more of these buildings knocked down. The ground, too, is full of radiation. Is that something you could remove? So we can plant sooner?"

David thought long and hard about that, and concluded it was worth a try. "You'll need greenhouses, though. I can't do anything about sunlight and ambient temperature."

"I have a plan for that, as well. I just need the soil cleaned."

"I'll get right on that after I've eaten. I'm still a bit weak."

"No problem. We'll mark the buildings I want knocked down. Most are brick, like those you toppled the other night, so save as much of that in the rubble as you can. I plan to build a wall around this city, a tall, thick wall that's easier to defend."

David nodded. "Things have changed, haven't they?"

"Yes, Doctor Andalon. I believe they have. This world is no longer the one we knew."

"It's a paradox," David said.

"What do you mean?"

"This new world is a paradox. None of you should have survived, not here how you did, yet here you are. And us, our kind shouldn't even exist but we do."

"What are you saying," Max asked, suddenly wary of the doctor.

"I'm saying this world has become a paradox, full of contradictions that will either coexist or die. You don't want us here, but we *have* to take over. This continent is no longer yours and will never be a new American nation. So you see, I guess what I'm saying is I'll stay," Eve said through David's mouth, speaking as if she were him, "and do the things you asked, but we won't be moving on afterward."

"Oh?" Max asked. "Why is that?"

"Because," Eve said for David. "I may not be the second coming, but make no mistake we *are* gods."

Max abruptly reached for his throat, gasping for air against the bubble now covering his lips. Eve, in full control of her father, waited for Max Rankin's brain to mostly die before commanding her father to raise him up.

You've gone too far, Daughter, David warned.

We haven't *gone far enough,* she corrected. *As you'll find out very soon.*

Andalon
Awakens

Dreamers of Andalon - Book 1

PROLOGUE

A small man stood on the deck of a creaking frigate. Unable to sleep, he kept first watch listening to the nighttime waves lapping the hull. The ship stood on the open sea, stranded and thirsting for air that had remained strangely still for an entire day and night. He watched as the lack of wind seemingly laughed at the impotent sails hanging on their masts.

Complete lack of movement is rare at sea and the eerie calm had already worked on the imaginations of the crew. Fear had slowly built within each man, and the abrupt appearance of eighteen sails sent panic through every topside sailor. The little man pushed back his spectacles and sounded the alarm. Then he dropped through a hatch to wake the captain.

Inside the main quarters, a large man opened his eyes and groaned. The noise grew louder at his door, a rhythmic thumping that wrenched him from his dream. He fought back a euphoric shudder as the memory of his lover's embrace faded into the pounding of reality.

He only held her briefly in his youth and would only ever do so in this recurring fantasy.

Her warm scent of spring lilac lingered momentarily, as did the soft caress of her lips. Braen Braston groaned as he awakened, fighting against the urge to draw his knife against the neck of whoever pounded on his door. Tears squeezed from his eyelids as he tightly closed them against the waking world.

If only he could return to the world where sweet Hester waited. He yearned to rejoin her warm bed and to feel her silky skin against his rough hands. Having once been a nightly occurrence, Braen had languished without the dream for more than a span. His wish every evening was that slumber would transport him to her realm. Now that she had again visited, he worried he would not remember her touch after he fully awakened.

Faded love and death are the only promises time gives to mortal men, and Braen secretly hoped for the second. *Does death include dreams?* He was almost willing to find out when the waking world shook him violently.

The heavy door to his cabin nearly splintered, keeping time with the pain between his temples. Panicked fists beat upon its planks as he briefly considered death once more. His eyes shot open with alarm. Somewhere nearby men shouted, and a feeling of urgency rocked the ship. The pounding that drew him back to reality had nearly broken the oak from its iron hinges. The shouting that accompanied the beating came from topside as men ran to battle stations.

He furiously threw the wool blanket from his body, sweating from the adrenaline of either passion or terror, whichever his faded dream had held. Wincing, he realized her face had completely gone from his mind. Awakening had also robbed him of her scent. *Wasn't it lilac?* He could not remember. Reality and rational thought drew him out of bed. He would face the unknown foe who had attacked his ship while he dreamed of impossible fancies.

His boots slipped on easily enough and Braen did not bother replacing his shirt. Running bare-chested he emerged from his cabin and collided with Sippen Yurik, his engineer and first mate, lifelong friend, and makeshift cabin steward. The small man stopped beating down Braen's door when it suddenly opened inward.

"What is it?" Braen shouted over the sounds from above.

"Lady E-e-e-sterling's main fleet has found us." Sippen stuttered as he spat out the words.

The captain ran past the impish smithy and raced topside. As he emerged from the hatch, the icy wind met his muscled chest. The blast nearly took away his voice. His long blonde beard kept most of the gust from off his face and he turned to see that Sippen had followed. The small man held out a thick coat. *Thoughtful Sippen*, he thought and surveyed the scene.

Across the choppy, greyish water he spotted the faint white of sails against the dawn. He quickly counted the masts while Gunnery Sergeant Krill relayed a signal to ready the guns. While the cannons were loaded and range elevated, Braen looked for a target. Four large galleons loomed between him and a large fleet of eight cargo ships accompanied by six smaller escorts. Two fleets closed on his with vengeance. He stroked his chest-long beard. *How do they have wind and we don't?* He glanced at his now raised battle sails, dangling limp and useless.

Braen had expected to cross the trade convoy in the night before. When he had lost the wind, he assumed that they would suffer the same hindrance as *Wench's Daughter*. He had not expected the main fleet to be so close. But it *had* appeared, oddly timing the arrival with the cargo ships. How had they coordinated pursuit in open waters?

"Get us some wind!" He shouted at the helmsman. "Hard to port! Drop those battle sails and put up the mains! We need speed!" Braen had not yet fought atop *Wench's Daughter* and wished for his own *Ice Prince*. Suddenly, Braen remembered that *Wench's Daughter* promised bigger fire power. "Belay my last! Keep the battle sails," he ordered, "hard to starboard and all guns to port!"

With or without wind, his heavy ship would not outrun the swift imperial galleons. The large captain cursed as he remembered how he had been talked into leaving his own sleek-lined vessel at Pirate's Cove. Worse, the belly of *Wench's Daughter* brimmed with heavy stores stolen from Esterling's winter warehouses.

Wench's Daughter drifted where the larger warships preferred. He would have to fight on their waters with reef shoals directly south. He carefully chose and called out his first target, hoping a hit below waterline would drag the lead galleon in front of the other vessels. However, such a first volley would be a marvel of the gods if it actually found wood to splinter. For that task, Braen Braston trusted his loyal friend Sippen.

The little weaponsmith was not much to look at. Small framed, he was slightly larger than a ten-year-old boy. His head was too large for his body and his arms were twigs. Sippen Yurik was useless in a fist fight, and deathly afraid of sharp blades. He preferred mathematical equations over human interaction. Other than remembering small things like coats during a cold morning battle, the man appeared worthless on a war-going vessel. That is, until you witnessed him sighting weapons.

He had been the royal engineer at Fjorik and designed and oversaw the building of *Ice Prince*. Even earlier than that, a close friendship bonded the two men from boyhood. When Braen fled the city two years earlier, Sippen had been waiting on the docks with his tools and the ship, refusing to allow his friend to flee into exile without him. For all of this, Braen was eternally grateful.

From the corner of his eye Braen saw the unassuming man help the gunners make final adjustments for windage, furiously scribbling with chalk on a slate. Sergeant Krill called out distances, bearings and speed while Sippen calculated. "Guns readied," bellowed Krill, after Sippen had nodded to the one-eyed man. Braen briefly considered how a one-eyed gunner judged distance with such accuracy, but, as always, he did not openly question Krill's knack for timing and range.

"Stand by to fire!" The captain gave the preparatory. "Make your mark. Now, batteries release!" On Braen's command the cannons exploded toward the largest of the galleons. Perhaps a lucky shot, Braen halfway smiled as most of the projectiles struck below the waterline. The large foe listed as a sudden rush of seawater entered its hold. It semi-capsized as he had hoped, and it listed before drifting with the current toward the trailing fleet. As he had hoped, the sinking vessel briefly blocked the passage of the other warships. Braen finally enjoyed time to think the battle over.

Oddly, he noticed a sudden coldness pass through his body. Most likely the retreat of adrenaline after the initial chaos, he tried to dismiss the chill until it had grown into a storm on a mountain summit. Braen felt his skin raise into bumps such as you would find on a freshly plucked fowl. Chicken-skin, his mother had called the sensation when he was young. It radiated from within, almost as if his blood had cooled several degrees during the time to aim the guns and fire upon the other vessel. Braen pulled the collar of the heavy coat up against his neck.

While he pondered his next movement, three massive dark shapes rushed beneath his keel toward the wounded galley. At precisely the moment the shapes passed underneath, Braen saw sails flutter. *Gods be praised*, the pirate captain thought as the breeze caught. "Full to port. Ready the guns at starboard and prepare to take wind!" The dark shapes continued to speed toward the other vessels, and he briefly glimpsed long, trailing tentacles on the water.

Braen blinked as his eyes played tricks. *They're only mythological creatures*, he assured himself, but Artema Horn's prophetic words resounded through his memory. He grew colder. Everything was colder. Even the wood of the railing had grown icy.

Through the smoke and early morning haze, Braen spotted more sails on the horizon. Hurried calculations revealed at least twenty more of Esterling's fleet, at least five of them flagships. Those, along with the six escorts, would make for overwhelming odds.

He signaled for Krill to lob the next volley over the wounded ship. Just as he called for the second attack, three large monsters emerged from the water.

"Kraken!"

Braen did not know who screamed the word. His only assurance was that it might not have been him. He watched helplessly as large tentacles reached out of the water and grabbed all three of the enemy galleons. Huge suction cups curled around the warships as desperate cries for mercy reached his ears. Then, the hardwood splintered as all three ships shattered like glass ornaments against stone. Stunned, the pirate captain prayed to the gods for the first time in two years.

As if timed with the sinking of the third galleon, the sails on *Wench's Daughter's* again fluttered, then fully caught the wind. The ship lurched with a sudden jolt as the wind favored their escape. The captain smiled and gave the command to turn hard into the blessed current. Braen barked at his crew, "Square away these sails and get us away from this cinder cursed place!" Using the creatures and the wrecked galleons as cover, he silently hoped that the pursuers would remain distracted. He smiled and his crew let out a whoop as the now westerly blowing wind carried all of his vessels out to the safety of open sea.

———————

Ashima Nakala, the lead sister of the winter oracle in Astia, broke from her dream with a scream. Initiates clustered around her and helped to ease her onto the dais. She writhed in pain from the bead, feeling it loosen the grip on her muscles as it left her blood.

The worse part of the Da'ash'mael was the intensity of the release. In fact, most dreamers feared the deadly rush of endorphins that ended the dream state, brought on by large quantities of the oracle bead as the muscles absorbed its potency. Dreaming was a dangerous art that promised no result but always offered pain and the risk of death.

She arched her back and her white robe slipped, exposing her breast. The curve of the ribs beneath her bosom drew in an exaggerated collapse as she gasped for oxygen against a sea of air. Her muscles instantly knotted along her spine and she finally caught her breath. Her next came rapid and beat out a tempo with her racing heart.

Ashima was the most accurate oracle produced by the coven in generations. She had predicted twenty years of changing weather patterns, including two significant blizzards and three gripping winters that lasted into the late moon of planting. But aside from weather phenomena, she had never dreamed anything that compared to the vivid cold she felt inside the bearded captain.

Although the oracles were called dreamers, the Ash'mael was more than a sequence of patterns from the subconscious. The Da'ash'mael provided knowing that delved into the very existence of the dream state, often seeing current or future events from the perspective of another.

Indeed, Ashima had shared the pain of the sea captain as he had lain in his bed, smelling lilac, wishing for death, and remembering his lost love. Likewise, she had empathically enjoyed his surge of adrenaline as he raced topside to fight the imperial fleet. But the terror of watching the sea monsters rise from the depths had made her cry out in agony as a resurgence of the bead coursed through her blood. She convulsed as she watched the creatures tear apart the ships. Tears made pink trails as they mixed with the blood trickling from her cheek, bitten through by her contracting mouth.

The initiates fought to hold her on the raised platform as she entered the Ka'ash'mael, the dreaded second phase in the telling of Ash'mael. This stage rarely occurred, but when it did the oracle prophesied the connection of the Da'ash'mael and how the viewed events affected the future of her Astian people. The accuracy of the dream depended on the true strength of the oracle, and only occurred after the drug had finally released its hold on their body. Since this particular Ash'mael was so strongly woven into the future of mankind, the transition from Da' to Ka' was amplified beyond any she had ever known.

The change gripped her body and she shuddered in orgasm as the bead released her muscles. She drew in a deep breath as the pain turned into a physical pleasure that simultaneously stimulated every nerve stem. Ashima knew, as did all dreamers, that the euphoria was a chemical response to the drug. But she welcomed the change as an awakening of her mind as it freed itself from her body.

Her eyes flitted in euphoric rushes as the sensation grew inside her body. Slowly, almost rhythmically, the knowing occurred. Feeling as if she were floating above her body, she began to recite her experience in the language of the oracle. The initiates relaxed and loosened their grips on her body. Each leaned in to listen and record her revelations as Ashima began to speak with slow and deliberate speech.

Fatwana Nakala watched quietly as her sister breathed her final words. The tall raven- haired woman did not betray any expression as the initiates carefully transcribed the Ash'mael. In stunned silence she took every word to heart and was not surprised when she saw the attending priest draw the shroud over Ashima's head. Her body surged up from the table and convulsed before settling onto the stone altar with a shudder, her final words spoken.

Ashima Nakala spoke her Ka'Ash'mael prophecy, proclaiming truth that transcended the physical plane. This particular Ash'mael held importance to all oracles and would shake the very core of their existence. Knowledge of the awakening threatened change that would challenge the existence of the Astian lifestyle. After she had collected the transcriptions, Fatwana walked to the altar and placed her hand on the husk that had once held her sister's soul. She spoke softly, "Rest sister and join our brother. I shall carry this warning to all, so that they must heed." Turning, she strode from the temple, ignoring the warm tears that slowly fell from her eyes.

CHAPTER ONE

The sun rose over a green valley in Loganshire, casting shadows on the rich farmland as it peeked around the clouds. Rivers and streams rabid with white froth raced between the hills, anxious to be free of the mountains to the north. Winter was arriving late, explaining why the grasses clung to their green hue. Despite the unseasonable warmth, the trees had completely let go of their leaves. Their shed foliage danced in the brisk wind that rolled down the mountain into the valley.

Loganshire was a quaint farming region nestled between the kingdoms of Fjorik in the north, and Eston which lay to the south and west. Once, long enough in the memory of the old-timers, the valley was the focus of countless raids from the northern men. Those fierce raids signified the end of fall and the start of winter to the anxious people of the valley. For the past ten years, under the stability of the Esterling Empire, the raids had stopped completely, and the people enjoyed peace and prosperity.

One farmhouse had enjoyed a tremendous comfort, and Mauri hummed and danced as she washed the family laundry, hanging it on lines to dry in the breeze. That same wind tossed her red hair gently, nipping at her rosy cheeks as she spun and hummed. Her husband, Thom, baled hay with his brothers Franque and Jean on this day, and she had a stew warming on the hearth for their return from the labor.

Mauri and Thom had two children. Anne was three years old, and she resembled her mother with red hair and freckles from a life spent mostly outdoors. Anne played in the grass with a doll her father had fashioned out of straw and burlap. Occasionally she would lean over and talk to her baby brother, Clauvis, as he cooed in his basket. He was a perfect baby, hardly cried, never fussed, and brought so much hope to the family for the future of the farm. Boy babies were lucky, at least that's what Mauri's grandmother had told her.

A hawk flew overhead, circling the field. Mauri took a moment to watch as it glided against the clouds and then as it dove. With grace it swooped toward a group of men riding horseback up the lane. It rested on the gloved hand of a tall man riding in the middle of the formation and Mauri froze. Wearing a hood with a feathered collar he sat high in the saddle, glancing sideways around him and darting glances like the oversized falcon perched on his arm. Abruptly, the hawk squawked a shrill, high piercing sound and the man focused his eyes directly at the farmwife. Her load of laundry fell onto the grass and she screamed a blood curdling sound that brought Thom running from the field.

He reached his wife just as the riders halted their beasts in front of Mauri and the children. His brothers, still wielding scythes from the harvest, dropped the blades in the grass as Constable Wembley, local magistrate and leader of the group, spoke, "Thom and Mauri Thorinson. The Falconer claims you delivered a living child sometime after the fifth day of the month of fall planting."

Wembley should have been a military man. He was prim and proper, and, unlike other constables and their deputies, he wore his uniform clean and pressed, with his black beard and hair closely cropped. His harsh eyes narrowed on the family as he asked, "Why did you fail to report the birth to a midwife or a constable?"

"We ... We were afraid, Shon. You know we lost our second child after the beast examined her."

"Nonsense and superstition!" The Falconer behind the constable bellowed. The man was a hideous specter, one whose eyes seem to pierce through the hood and into another's soul. "The examination is a blessing, and infant mortality is a natural occurrence, not to be blamed on our ministrations."

The constable tried to keep everyone calm. "Thom, all you have to do is allow him to look your child over. Don't make this harder than it needs to be."

Thom's face was scarlet with anger. "Shon, you of all people should understand!"

"Let him work, Thom. Otherwise I'll have to hang the both of you." Wembley rode his horse between Mauri and the baby, forcing her and her husband to step backward. "I'm sorry about this. Really, I am. Just do as he says, and all will be fine."

Dismounting, the Falconer approached Clauvis in the basket lying on the grass. Anne, still clutching her little doll, scurried away from her brother's side. Terrified, she hid behind the legs of her father. The Falconer paid her no mind and knelt beside the younger child. The bird of prey on his shoulder stared intently at the baby, switching his head back and forth to view him with each eye. Mauri watched as her child made no sound while staring intently at both the man and the bird.

With a squawk, the bird spread its wings and flew up into the air to resume circling. The hooded man pulled out a small jar of oil and removed the blue lid. He rubbed two fingers into the mixture, and placed it under the tongue of the child before standing to address the family. "I find your baby healthy and free of defect. Enjoy a long life with the child." Turning, he added an admonishment. "In the future, report your offspring to the authorities." The man strode back to his mount and swung into the saddle.

The constable looked intently at Thom, who was grinding his teeth and seething with anger. "Your penalty will be an extra percentage of taxed goods when payment is due." To Mauri he added, "Be happy your child's healthy. Some of your neighbors weren't so lucky." He tipped his hat to the couple, and the group rode back down the lane the way they had come.

As soon as the riders had turned their horses, Mauri rushed to the basket and swept her child into her arms. Holding him tightly, she ran back into the house with Anne chasing behind, her doll swinging wildly in her hand as she sprinted up the walk. Thom turned to his brothers, who picked up their scythes. He shook his head and cursed the hooded man, rejoining his brothers as they walked slowly back to the field to finish their duties. The laundry lay in a heap upon the grass where his wife had dropped it, but that task was long forgotten after the tense meeting.

After Thom and his brothers had finished in the field, they washed in the stream before making their way back to the cottage. Dodging chickens on the ground, they walked and talked about the earlier event. Thom, although relieved that his baby was healthy, still worried over the incident. Their other child, Grace, had been two weeks old when another

Falconer had come. Like today, he had blessed their child and proclaimed her healthy and whole. The young parents had considered themselves luckier than most, as other families had had their sickly or mal-formed babies taken from them.

They both felt she was a special infant. Like Clauvis, she never cried nor fussed. They felt generally happier and more connected around their little Gracie and also thought of her as a lucky child. Thom remembered vividly awakening to the sobs of Mauri on the night of the last visit. Grace had died in her sleep. Crib death, the old-timers had called it, but he and his wife had distrusted their visitor and attributed the sudden death to his blessing.

A scream from within the cottage sent Thom and his siblings running the final steps toward the door. Thrusting it open, they halted at the display within. Mauri knelt over the crib, clutching the infant close to her breast. She wailed in grief as little Anne stood in the corner, also crying and squeezing her little doll in fright as she watched her inconsolable mother.

Thom broke free from the invisible grip that had held him, and stepped forward, placing a hand on his wife's shoulder. As Mauri turned to look up at her husband, he saw that Clauvis was lifeless and completely blue. The farmer's brothers took in the scene, then headed outside with grief. But this time the job was to dig a deep little hole.

A few days later, in the city of Logan, Constable Wembley sat in the corner of the *Mangy Dog* tavern. The tavern was noticeably empty on this day, despite that the city was bustling with activity. The constable was not alone. Across from him sat the reason the tavern was empty, in the form of the cursed Falconer.

Shon Wembley loved his job as constable, and it had been his desired career since childhood. As a young man he served as a deputy to his brother in Brentway where they had fought against northern marauders during the most recent raids. He loved his duties and served them well, but his two least favorite tasks included tax collection and overseeing the child blessings. Those blessings were the reason he had been stuck escorting this Falconer for an entire week.

Shon frowned at his mug of ale, unusually bitter for the season. "Are you sure that you don't want a mug?" When the beast-like man did not respond, he answered himself, "No, of course not." Then, under his breath he muttered, "You never do. You don't drink spirits; you don't eat rich foods or sweets and you don't look at the tavern wenches." After he had said his piece, the two men again sat in silence, the Falconer staring straight ahead, the constable's hard green eyes focused on his mug.

Shon found solace in the thought that he was nearly finished with his current duties. They had three more children to inspect in the city and had planned to begin at first light. So far, the blessings had gone smoothly. Only two farmhouses had produced children with defects, and those had been removed to the Rookery with little resistance and with only the expected grief by the parents. Since the Empire had gained a foothold in Loganshire, the tradition of culling the lame had become more widely accepted, possibly since more families were birthing healthier children with their newfound prosperity.

Only a few had tried to hide births, one of those being the Thorinson farm. How the Falconer had discovered the child was strange. It was almost as if he could communicate with his bird, or worse, see through its eyes. The thought unnerved Shon, almost as if the creatures shared foresight. But that theory was impossible, since all religions, regardless of belief, strictly prohibited telling the future or working magic. Both crimes were rewarded with the penalty of death in the Esterling Empire. Of course, magic did not exist, so that part of the edict never made sense to Constable Wembley. He chalked it up to superstitious nonsense.

Still, something about the Thorinson exchange did not sit well with the constable. So far, fifty children were inspected during the week, but Shon had noticed the blessings had included two jars of oil. Every other child had been anointed with the jar with the red lid, but that baby had received the substance from a jar with a blue lid. When he had asked the administrator why he had used a different jar, the beast-like man had lied and stated that he only has one jar.

Abruptly, the Falconer cocked his head to one side, suddenly alert. "Post men by the door. Trouble is coming."

Shon looked up from his ale, incredulous and feeling somewhat suspicious given his recent thoughts. He motioned his deputies, who stood from the table and moved into position like bookends on the inside of the oak frame. After posting the guards, the constable asked, "Did you hear something?"

Just then, the door burst open from the force of a large man kicking it in. Thom Thorinson charged through, wielding an axe and rushing directly for the Falconer. When he reached the chair, the hooded figure, who had never turned around, leaped from his seat and sidestepped a blow from the hatchet. The head of the tool sank deep into the table, spilling the plate of food and mug of ale that Shon had been working on.

Suddenly, with a screech a dark winged blur swept through the opening, sinking its talons in the back of the raging farmer. With its strong beak it tore at the man's flesh, ripping out chunks as it tried to peck out his eyes. Thom screamed and the bird squawked until the constable intervened. "For Cinder's sake restrain the man!" Only once they controlled his arms and pinned him face down on the floor did the raptor release its grip and return to perch on the arm of its master.

Thom Thorinson bled onto the floorboards, weeping and sobbing in pain of both body and spirit. The deputies stood him up and fastened manacles on his wrists. Shon approached and demanded explanation. "What the hell are you about, Thorinson? Explain yourself!"

Thom sputtered, "That abomination killed my wife and child!"

"Nonsense! Both of them were very much alive when we left your spread, and he's been with me the entire time! You know damned well that he had no hand in their death!"

"Clauvis died mere hours after his blessing and Mauri slit her wrists in grief that very night!"

"A coincidence, I assure you!" Shon was very disturbed by this exchange. *The blue jar*, he thought and silently wondered if Thom was correct in his accusation. He stared up at the ghoul with an expecting glare, watching for any change in demeanor but none came.

The Falconer spoke from where he now stood in the corner of the tavern, bird roosting on his arm. "Attacking an agent of the Queen Regent is a hanging offense. This was attempted murder."

Shon shook his head. Turning to look at the hooded man, he said, "Thom is grieving. I've known him and his entire family since their births. He's no murderer." He leaned in close to the farmer, and grimaced. "Smell him, he's drunk and acting out of grief."

"Death by hanging." Turning to look at the constable, the beast-like man added, "Certainly you will not disobey an administrator in his duties? Men have hanged for that as well."

Shon muttered under his breath, "Well, shit." After pondering for a moment, he shook his head and faced the others. "Take Thorinson to the jail. I'll speak to the magistrate and turn him over to the city officials for a trial." He placed emphasis on the final word as if willing it would ensure justice.

The next day, Shon wrapped up his duties, finally able to part ways with the eerie hooded beast. None too soon, he packed his saddle bags, mounted his mare, and spurred her flanks to a fast trot. As he rode out of the city, he tipped his hat to the swinging corpse of Thom Thorinson, the ripped-out portions of his face hidden within a hood of his own. The once stalwart lawman unpinned his badge and tossed it in the river as he crossed the bridge out of town.

Thank you for enjoying Andalon Paradox and a sneak peak of
Andalon Awakens!

Please help the author by leaving a review, then click or visit the site
below to learn what happens next in the Andalon Saga!
www.tbphillips.com

Books by T.B. Phillips are found in online bookstores.
Signed copies can be purchased by visiting:
andalonstudios.com

Chilling Tales
Ferryman (October 2022)

Corrupted Realms
Wailing Tempest (April 2021)
Howling Shadow (September 2021)

Andalon Saga

Andalon Origins
Andalon Project (May 2022)
Andalon Paradox (April 2023)
Andalon Prophecies (expected Fall 2023)

Dreamers of Andalon
Andalon Awakens (June 2019)
Andalon Arises (July 2020)
Andalon Attacks (December 2020)

Children of Andalon
Andalon Legacy (September 2022)

Made in the USA
Middletown, DE
10 June 2023

32352422R00175